COLOMA PUBLIC LIBRARY

W9-ASA-588

3015100000100.

DATE DUE

DE 29 '06		
JA 23 '07		
FE 10 '07		
MR 09 '07		
MR 28 '07		
JE 13 '07		
N 13 '07		
SE 28 '07		
JE 09 '08		
SE 17		
MR 10		
NO 17 '10		

Demco, Inc. 38-294

COLOMA PUBLIC LIBRARY
COLOMA, MICHIGAN 49038

The Fourth Bear

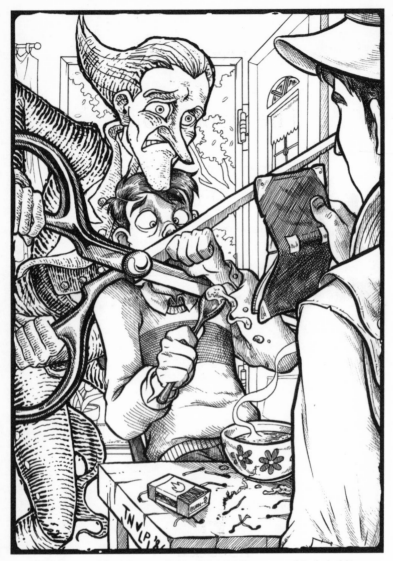

'DCI Spratt of the Nursery Crime Division,' announced Jack, holding up his ID. 'Put down the scissors and STEP AWAY FROM THE THUMB.'

Jasper Fforde

The Fourth Bear

An investigation with the
Nursery Crime Division

**HODDER &
STOUGHTON**

Copyright © 2006 by Jasper Fforde

First published in Great Britain in 2006 by Hodder & Stoughton
A division of Hodder Headline

The right of Jasper Fforde to be identified as the Author
of the Work has been asserted by him in accordance with the
Copyright, Designs and Patents Act 1988.

A Hodder & Stoughton Book

1

All rights reserved. No part of this publication may be
reproduced, stored in a retrieval system, or transmitted, in any form
or by any means without the prior written permission of the publisher,
nor be otherwise circulated in any form of binding or cover other
than that in which it is published and without a similar condition
being imposed on the subsequent purchaser.

All characters in this publication are fictitious and any resemblance
to real persons, living or dead, is purely coincidental.

A CIP catalogue record for this title is
available from the British Library

ISBN 978-0-340-83571-5
ISBN 0-340-83571-0

Typeset in Bembo by Palimpsest Book Production,
Polmont, Stirlingshire

Printed and bound by
Clays Ltd, St Ives plc

Hodder Headline's policy is to use papers that are natural, renewable
and recyclable products and made from wood grown in sustainable
forests. The logging and manufacturing processes are expected to
conform to the environmental regulations of the country of origin.

Hodder and Stoughton Ltd
A division of Hodder Headline
338 Euston Road
London NW1 3BH

For my Mother

Also by Jasper Fforde

The Eyre Affair
Lost in a Good Book
The Well of Lost Plots
Something Rotten
The Big Over Easy

Because the forest will always be there
and anybody who is Friendly with Bears can find it.
– A.A. Milne

Author's Notes

The Nursery Crime Division, the Reading Police Department and the Oxford & Berkshire Constabulary in this book are entirely fictitious, and any similarity to authentic police procedures, protocol or forensic techniques is entirely coincidental, and quite unintentional.

The Fourth Bear has been bundled with **Special Features** including:
'The Making of' documentary, deleted scenes,
and much more. To access all these free bonus features,
log on to: **www.nurserycrime.co.uk/special/js2.html**
and enter the code word as directed.

Contents

I

A death in Obscurity

—————

'**Last Known Regional Postcode Allocation**. Obscurity, Berkshire. Pop. 35. Spotted by an eagle-eyed official and allocated its postcode (RD73 93ZZ) in April 1987, a matter of such import among the residents of this small village that a modest ceremony and street party were arranged. A bronze plaque was inscribed and affixed below another plaque that commemorated the only other event of note in living memory – the momentous occasion when Douglas Fairbanks (Senior) became hopelessly lost in 1928 and had to stop at the village shop to ask for directions.'
    – *The Bumper Book of Berkshire Records*, 2004 edition

The little village of Obscurity is remarkable only for its un-remarkableness. Passed over for inclusion in almost every publication from the Domesday Book to *Thirty Places Not Worth Visiting in Berkshire*, the small hamlet is also a cartographic omission, an honour it shares with the neighbouring villages of Hiding and Cognito. Indeed, the status of Obscurity was once thought so tenuous that some of the more philosophically inclined residents considered the possibility that since the village didn't exist then they might not exist either, and hurriedly placed 'existential question of being' on the parish council agenda, where it still resides, after much unresolved discussion, between 'church roof fund' and 'any other business'.

It was late summer. A period of good weather had followed on from rain and the countryside was now enjoying a reinvigoration of colour, and scent. The fields and trees were a vibrant green and the spinneys rich with the sweet bouquet of honeysuckle and dog rose, the hedgerows creamy with cow parsley and alive with cyclamen. In the isolated splendour of Obscurity the residents enjoyed the season more as they had fewer people to share it with. Not many people came this way, and if they did they were invariably lost.

The Austin Somerset that pulled up outside a pretty brick-and-thatch cottage on the edge of the village was *not* lost. A dapper septuagenarian bounded from the front garden to greet the only occupant, an attractive woman of slender build in her late twenties.

'Welcome to Obscurity, Miss Hatchett,' he intoned politely. 'Were you lost for long?'

'Barely an hour,' she replied, shaking his outstretched hand. 'It's very good of you to talk to me, Mr Cripps.'

'The gravity of the situation is too serious to remain unremarked for ever,' he replied sombrely.

She nodded, and the sprightly pensioner invited her into the garden and guided her to a shady spot under an apple tree. She settled herself on the bench and tied up her long blonde curly tresses. It was her single most identifiable feature and one that in the past had made her the subject of a certain amount of teasing. But these days, she didn't much care.

'Call me Goldilocks,' she said with a smile as she caught Cripps staring at her remarkably luxuriant hair, 'everyone else does.'

Cripps returned her smile and offered her a glass of lemonade.

'Then you must call me Stanley – I say, you're not *the* Goldilocks, are you? We have so few celebrities down this way.'

'I'm afraid not,' she replied good-naturedly, having been asked this question many times before. 'I think *that* Goldilocks was a lot younger.'

'Of course,' said Stanley, who was still staring at her hair, which seemed to glisten like gold when the dappled light caught it.

2

Goldilocks smiled again and opened her notepad.

'Firstly,' she said, taking a sip of lemonade, 'I must remind you that I am an investigative reporter for *The Toad*, and anything you say may well be reported in the newspapers, and you must be aware of that.'

'I understand,' replied Stanley, staring at the ground for a moment, 'I fully appreciate what you are saying. But this is serious stuff. Despite continued pleas to the police and evidence of numerous thefts, attempted murder and acts of wanton vandalism, we are just dismissed as lunatics on the fringes of society.'

'I agree it's wrong,' murmured Goldilocks, 'but until recently I never thought that . . . cucumber growing might be considered a dangerous pastime.'

'Few indeed think so,' replied Cripps soberly, 'but cucumbering at the international level is seriously competitive and requires a huge commitment in cash and time. It's a tough and highly rarefied activity in the horticultural community, and not for the faint-hearted. The judges are *merciless*. Two years ago I thought I was in with a chance, but once again my arch-rival Hardy Fuchsia pipped me to the post with a graceful giant that tipped the scales at forty-six kilos – a full two hundred grams *under* my best offering. But, you know, in top-class cucumbering size isn't everything. Fuchsia's specimen won because of its *curve*. A delicately curved parabola of mathematical perfection that brought forth tears of admiration from even the harshest judge.'

'Tell me all about your cucumbers but from the *very* beginning,' said Goldilocks enthusiastically.

'Really?' replied Cripps, whose favourite subject usually generated large yawns from even the most polite and committed listener.

'Yes,' replied Goldilocks without hesitation, 'in as much detail as you can.'

Cripps spoke for almost two hours, and only twice strayed from his favourite topic. He showed Goldilocks his alarmed and climate-controlled greenhouse, and pointed out the contenders for that year's prize.

'They're remarkable,' said Goldilocks, and so they were. A deep shade of bottle green with a smooth, blemish-free skin and a gentle curve without any kinks. If cucumbers had gods, these would be them. One cucumber in particular was *so* magnificent, *so* flawless, *so* perfect in every detail that Stanley confided to Goldilocks he was finally in with a chance to snatch the crown from the indisputable emperor of Cucumber Extreme, Mr Hardy Fuchsia. Unabashed rivals, they would doubtless lock antlers in the field of cucumbering at Vexpo2004, this year to be held in Düsseldorf.

'A shade under fifty kilos,' remarked Cripps, pointing at one specimen.

'Impressive,' replied Goldilocks, scribbling another note.

They spoke for another hour and she left just after eight, a notepad full of observations that confirmed what she already suspected. But of one thing she was certain: Mr Cripps was almost certainly unaware of the more sinister aspects of his hobby.

By 10.30 that night Stanley Cripps was tucked up in bed, musing upon the good fortune that would undoubtedly see his champion cucumber take all the prizes at everything he entered it for. He could almost hear the roar of the crowd, smell the trophy and visualise the cover story in *Cucumber Monthly* that would surely be his. As he sat in bed chuckling to himself with a cup of hot chocolate and a Garibaldi biscuit, the silent alarm was triggered and a cucumber-shaped light blinked at him from the control panel near his bed. There had been a couple of false alarms over the past few days, but his long-time experience of thieves had taught him to *always* be vigilant as wily cucumber pilferers often set alarms off deliberately so you would ignore them when they struck with real intent. He slipped on his dressing gown, donned his slippers and, after thinking for a moment, dialled Goldilocks' number on the cordless phone while he padded noiselessly down the stairs to the back door.

Even before he reached the greenhouse he could see that this was no false alarm – the door had been forced and the lights were on. Goldilocks' phone rang and rang at the other end, and he was just about to give up when her answerphone clicked in.

'Hi!' she said in a bright and breezy voice. 'This is Henny Hatchett of *The Toad*. If you've got a good story . . .'

Stanley was by now only semi-listening. He mumbled a greeting and his name at the beep then ventured forth into his inner cucumber-cultivating sanctum, stick in hand and apprehensive of heart. He stopped short and looked around with growing incredulity.

'Good heavens!' he said in breathless astonishment. 'It's . . . *full of holes!*'

An instant later Stanley's property exploded in a flaming ball of white-hot heat that turned the moonless night into day. The shock wave rolled out at the speed of sound in every direction and carried in front of it the shattered remains of Stanley's house and gardens, while the fireball arced and flamed up into the night sky. The property next door collapsed like a card house, and the old oak had the side facing the blast reduced to a foot of charcoal. Windows were broken up to five miles away and the blast was heard as a dull rumble in Reading, some forty miles distant. As for Stanley, he and almost everything he possessed were atomised in a fraction of a second. His false teeth were found embedded in a beech tree a quarter of a mile away, his final comment recorded on Goldilocks' answerphone. She would hear it with a sense of rising foreboding upon her return – and in just under a week, she too would be dead.

2

A cautionary tale

'**Most Under-funded Police Division**. For the twentieth year running, the Nursery Crime Division in the Reading Police Department. Formed in 1958 by DCI Jack Horner, who felt that the regular force was ill equipped to deal with the often unique problems thrown up by nursery-related inquiries. After a particularly bizarre investigation that involved a tinder box, a soldier and a series of talking cats with varying degrees of ocular deformity, he managed to persuade his confused superiors that he should oversee all inquiries involving "any nursery characters or plots from poems and/or stories". His legacy of fairness, probity and impartiality remains unaltered to this day, as do the budget, the size of the offices, the wallpaper and the carpets.'
              – *The Bumper Book of Berkshire Records*, 2004 edition

The neighbourhood in West Reading that centres on Compton Avenue is similar to much of Reading's pre-war urban housing. Bay windows, red brick, attached garage, sunrise doors. The people who live here are predominantly white-collar: managers, stock controllers, IT consultants. They work, raise children, watch TV, fret over promotion, socialise. Commonplace for Reading or anywhere else, one would think, aside from one fact. For two decades this small neighbourhood has harboured a worrying and unnatural secret: the occupants' children, quite against the norms of acceptable levels of conduct . . . *behave themselves and respect their parents*. Meals are always finished, shoes neatly double-bowed and cries of 'please' and 'thank you' ring clearly and frequently throughout the households. Boys' hair is always combed and cut above the collar, bedrooms are scrupulously clean, baths are taken at first request and household chores are enthusiastically performed. Shocking, weird, unnatural – even creepy. But by far and away the most strenuously obeyed rule is this: thumbs are never, repeat *never*, sucked.

'We used to call this neighbourhood Cautionary Valley in the old days,' said Detective Chief Inspector Jack Spratt to Constable Ashley, 'where vague threats of physical retribution for childhood misdemeanours came to violent fruition. Get out of bed, play with matches, refuse your soup or suck your thumb and there was something under the bed to grab your ankles, spontaneous human combustion, accelerated starving or a double thumbectomy.' He sighed. 'Of course, that was all a long time ago.'

It had been twenty-five years ago, to be exact. Jack had been a mere subordinate in the Nursery Crime Division which he now ran. Technically speaking, cautionary crime was 'juvenilia' rather than 'nursery' but jurisdiction boundaries had blurred since the NCD's inception in 1958 and their remit now included anything unexplainable. Sometimes Jack thought the NCD was just a mop that sponged up weird.

'Did you get any prosecutions back then?' asked Ashley, whose faint blue luminosity cast an eerie glow inside the parked car.

'We nicked a couple of ankle-grabbers and took a chimney-troll in for questioning but the ringleader was always one giant stride ahead of us.'

'The Great Long Red-Legg'd Scissor-man?'

'Right. We could never prove he snipped off the thumbs of errant suck-a-thumbs, but every lead we had pointed towards him. We never got to even *interview* him – the attacks suddenly stopped and he just vanished into the night.'

'Moved on?'

'I wish. Ever met a Cautionary Valley child?'

'No.'

Jack shook his head sadly.

'Sickeningly polite. A credit to their parents. Well mannered, helpful, courteous. We wanted to battle the Scissor-man and his cronies with everything the NCD could muster but were overruled by the local residents' committee. They decided not to battle the cautionaries lurking in the woodwork, but *use* them. They pursued a policy of "cautionary acquiescence" by promulgating the stories and thus ensured that their children never had cause to invoke the cautionaries.'

'Did it work?'

'Of course. Believe me, once the hands really *do* grab your ankles when you get out of bed or the troll up the chimney *does* try to get you for not eating your greens, you make damn sure to do everything your parents tell you. But they're still here,' added Jack as he looked around, 'waiting in the fabric of the neighbourhood. The stone, earth and wood. Under beds and in closets. They'll re-appear when someone is leaning back on their chair, being slovenly, not eating their soup, or – worst of all – sucking their thumb.'

They fell into silence and looked around but all was normal. The summer's night was cool and clear and the streets empty and quiet. They had been parked in Compton Avenue for twenty-five minutes and nothing had appeared remotely out of the ordinary.

Things at the Nursery Crime Division were looking better than they had for many years, Jack admitted to himself. The success of the Humpty Dumpty inquiry four months before had placed himself and the NCD firmly in people's consciousness. While not perhaps up there among the cutting-edge aspects of police detection such as murder, serious robbery or the ever popular 'cold cases', they were certainly more important than traffic or the motorcycle display team. There were plans to increase the funding from its ridiculously low level and a permanent staff beyond himself, DS Mary Mary and Constable Ashley.

'What's the time?'

Ashley glanced at his watch.

'10010 past 1011.'

Jack did a quick calculation. Eighteen minutes past eleven. It was binary, of course, Ashley's mother tongue. He generously spoke it as ones and zeros for Jack's benefit – full-speed binary sounds like torn linen and is totally unintelligible. Ashley had no problem with English or any of the other twenty-three principal languages on the planet; it was the decimal numbering system he couldn't get his head around. He was a Rambosian, an alien visitor from a small planet eighteen light years away who arrived quite un-expectedly along with 127 others four years previously. Every single one of the seventy billion or so inhabitants of Rambosia was a huge fan of Earth's prodigious output of television drama and comedy, and Ashley had been part of a mission to discover why there had never been a third series of *Fawlty Towers* and to inter-view Ronnie Barker. But when the mission got to see just how much filing and bureaucratic data management there was on the planet, all 128 elected to stay.

Ashley had been in uniform for two years as part of the alien equal opportunities programme and had found himself after much reshuffling at the Nursery Crime Division, where he could do no real harm. His real name was 10111001000100111011100100, but that was tricky to remember and even harder to pronounce. Get the emphasis wrong on the seventh digit and it could mean 'my prawns have asthma'. He was about five foot tall with slender arms and legs that bent both ways at the elbow and knee. His head was twice the width of his shoulders with big eyes, a small mouth and no nose. The UFO fraternity *had* got an alien's appearance pretty much right, which surprised them all no end. His police uniform had been especially tailored to fit his unique physique, with a special elasticised girth as Rambosians had a tendency to swell and contract depending on atmospheric pressure.

'So,' continued Jack, 'ten minutes to go. What stories do Rambosians use to terrify their children into behaving themselves, Ash?'

'Vertical stripes, mainly.'

'Why?'

Jack watched Ashley think. Owing to the Rambosian physiology, which comprised a translucent outer membrane filled with a blend of gelatinous liquid, Jack really *could* see his mind working. 'Amorous linguini' was how one unkind observer put it – but they weren't far wrong.

'It's the linear uniformity in the vertical plain,' Ashley explained with a shiver, turning a darker shade of blue. 'We don't much fancy bar codes, railings or pinstripe suits, either. Mind you, *horizontally* we have no problem with any of them – which is why we like to wear our pinstripes perpendicular to the norm.'

'I always wondered about that,' replied Jack slowly. Conversation was never easy with Ashley. There really wasn't much in common between humans and Rambosians – except for a passionate interest in order and bureaucracy. During his lunch hour Ashley could often be found indulging in his hobby of 'carspotting', which is like trainspotting, only with cars. At the weekends Rambosians would cluster around one of the town's many vehicle number recognition cameras, where they all got a bit tipsy reading the binary data stream. Other than that, they lived their own lives and didn't say very much. That's the thing about aliens that no one had ever really expected. They're a bit dull.

The walkie-talkie crackled into life.

'Jack, are you there?'

It was Detective Sergeant Mary Mary, Jack's number two at the

Nursery Crime Division. They had been together since the Humpty affair, and although there had been a few hiccups in the early days, they now got on well. She didn't know why she'd been allocated to the NCD but was glad that she had been. Despite it being a career black hole and the butt of many station jokes, she felt somehow that she *belonged*. She didn't know why. Jack picked up the radio and keyed the mike.

'NCD-1 in position front of house. All quiet.'

'I thought I was NCD-1?' replied Mary over the airwaves. 'I'm in the front line today.'

'No, you're NCD-2. Ashley's NCD-3 and Baker and Gretel are NCD-4 and 5.'

'I should be NCD-3,' cut in Baker. 'I've been working part time at the division longer than anyone.'

'Shall we stick to names?' asked Mary. 'It's going to be a lot easier.'

'Whatever. Spratt at front of house, nothing to report.'

'Good,' replied Mary. 'We have thumb re-entry in T minus . . . five minutes.'

This time, there'd be no escape for the Scissor-man.

Inside the house, Mary was briefing Conrad's parents for the last time. They stared at her anxiously, but with both Jack and Ashley at the front and Gretel and Baker at the back, it seemed as safe a sting operation as they could make it.

'Your backs are to be turned for Conrad's thumb to go in at 23.30,' explained Mary as she checked her watch. 'At the same time he should lean back on his chair, refuse to eat his soup and play with these matches. I'll be in the cupboard and on the radio, so if we can't catch the Scissor-man before he reaches the house I'll give the "thumb out" order and Conrad aborts all actions. Do you under-stand?'

Mr and Mrs Hoffman looked at one another and then at Conrad, who at seventeen was old enough to understand the risks. Like many of the children in the area he had lived in a condition of understated terror for so long that he now barely noticed. He had never had a brush with the cautionaries himself; the presence of Roland Snork in the neighbourhood was enough for most children. Roland's face was frozen in an ugly grimace because the wind *had* changed while he was pulling a face, and although the thirteen cosmetic surgeries had alleviated the problem somewhat, he was one of the more obvious warnings about uncautionary behaviour. But if all went well, children like Roland wouldn't suffer a lifetime of humiliation for a few injudiciously pulled faces. The parents of Cautionary Valley had banded together and unanimously voted for normality. For surly, grunty teenagers who dropped their clothes on the floor and stared vacantly out from behind lanky unwashed hair. For untied shoelaces, messy rooms, homework left until the last moment, inappropriate boy/girlfriends, and unregulated nose-picking. For brooding silences, funny smells in the bathroom, hours spent on video games and ignored calls to the dinner table. It all seemed so normal, so *blissful*. They had contacted the police, who gladly batted it down the line to the Nursery Crime Division.

'We're happy to go ahead, Sergeant,' said Mr Hoffman with a dryness in his throat. 'There are methods other than terror to instil discipline. We want to be like normal families where threats of mutilation and a sorry end to achieve good behaviour are met with a sarcastic "Yeah, Dad, like, way to go – you're such a zoid, like, y'know. Tight".'

He sighed deeply and turned to his son.

'Conrad? Are you happy to go ahead?'

The boy nodded his head enthusiastically.

'Yes, Father,' he replied good-naturedly, 'if it is for the good of everyone. Would anyone like a sandwich or a cup of tea?'

'No, Conrad. There'll be no more tea-making for you after tonight.'

'Are you sure? I could bake you all a cake, too – and then play the piano for your entertainment before taking the dog for a walk and repainting the spare room.'

Even Mary found him a bit creepy. She didn't have any children of her own – unless you counted her collection of ex-boyfriends – but children to her were meant to be something a little more than mindless automatons.

The Hoffmans hugged each other nervously, but when Mr Hoffman shook Mary's hand she noticed that his left thumb was missing.

'I was one of the first,' he muttered sadly, following her gaze. 'A life lived in fear is a life half lived. A life half lived is fear lived in half. A life half feared is fear half lived.'

Some people have a way with words, but Hoffman wasn't one of them.

'What exactly *is* the Scissor-man?' asked Mrs Hoffman, who found the idea of characters from cautionary tales made flesh and blood a little strange, as well she might.

'We call them PDRs,' explained Mary. 'Persons of Dubious Reality. Refugees from the collective consciousness. Uninvited visitors who have fallen through the grating that divides the real from the written. They arrive with their actions hardwired due to their repetitious existence, and the older and more basic they are, the more rigidly they stick to them. Characters from Cautionary Tales are *particularly* mindless. They do what they do because it's what they've always done – and it's up to us to stop them.'

'Are you sure the Nursery Crime Division is up to it?' Mrs Hoffman added, voicing a strongly felt suspicion within the community that the regular force weren't taking their concerns seriously.

'Of course,' replied Mary confidently. 'Only two months ago we successfully detained a ghoulie, a ghosty and a long-legged beastie.'

'And the bump in the night?' asked Mr Hoffman anxiously. 'What about that?'

'Ah,' returned Mary, scratching her chin thoughtfully. 'No, the bump got away – but I'm sure you would agree a seventy-five per cent success rate in that particular operation was a very good result indeed.'

Constables Charlie Baker and Gretel Brown-Horrocks were waiting in the back garden, covering the house from the potting shed in case the Scissor-man came from that direction. Unlike Ashley, Mary and Jack, Baker and Gretel were occasional members of the NCD, brought in only when the need arose. Baker had been designated a D-minus in 'public social skills' owing to his acute hypochondria and was used only for internal duties within the Reading Central police station.

'Want some Vicks?' he said to Gretel, offering her the small bottle after trying in a most noisy and unpleasant fashion to clear his sinuses, which seemed to be incessantly blocked with possibly the finest cold viruses that natural selection had managed to create.

'No thanks,' replied Gretel in her soft German accent. Her skills in forensic accountancy kept her much in demand not only in Reading but throughout most of the Berks & Wilts Constabulary. NCD work was meant to 'get her out more'. She was glad that it did. At the end of the Humpty affair she had met the man who was now her husband. He was seven foot three and she was six foot two and a quarter. It was a match made perhaps not in heaven, but certainly nearer the ceiling.

'Do you have to sniff constantly?' she asked him.

'The sniffing's *nothing*,' replied Baker. 'Do you want to see my rash?'

'You showed it to me already.'

'That was a tiddler. This new one covers two-thirds of my body and has raised pimples.'

'It does not.'

'It does so – or it will have soon, if my diagnosis is correct. What's the time?'

'One minute to go. We keep our eyes open – and for God's sake: *stop that sniffing.*'

Baker made one great big huge super-sniff that drew everything swilling around his lower sinuses into the space between his eyes, where gravity, being the force it was, would ensure it would not stay for long.

Back inside the house, Mary counted off the seconds on her watch. At five seconds to go she keyed the mike on her walkie-talkie and said:

'Thumb re-entry T minus five seconds.'

She climbed into the cupboard, shut the door to nothing more than a crack, and signalled to the Hoffmans. They nodded sagely and began the routine they had rehearsed down the road at Tesco's, where the Scissor-man had no influence. Mr Hoffman, in an overly dramatic fashion, said:

'We're going to leave you here to finish your soup on your own, Conrad. *Don't* play with those matches, *don't* lean back on your chair and don't you *dare* suck your thumb when our backs are turned!'

They sighed, walked out of the kitchen and closed the door behind them. Conrad was now alone in the kitchen with only Mary watching through a crack in the cupboard door. He stared at his thumb for a moment, having never even *contemplated* sucking it – not since he was first warned about the Scissor-man. His father had a missing thumb to prove the wisdom of this course, and Conrad was always careful to avoid getting his thumb anywhere *near* his mouth just in case the Scissor-man should make a mistake.

He paused for a moment, thumb outstretched, and looked at Mary again. She nodded to him and smiled. If they were to catch the Scissor-man, this was the only way. After wavering for a few more seconds, Conrad opened his mouth and in went the thumb. He paused for a few moments then obediently carried out the plan they had rehearsed. He leaned back on his chair, idly struck a match and said petulantly: 'I don't *want* my soup!'

Jack and Ashley were outside the car and looking about attentively at the time the thumb went in. There was a distant rumble of thunder and somewhere a dog barked. Other than that, nothing seemed unusual.

'What does the Great Red-Legg'd Scissor-man look like?' asked Ashley.

'Tall, red-legged – carries a huge pair of scissors. Believe me, you'll know him when you see him.'

Ashley looked down at his own hands. He had three fingers and two opposable thumbs on each hand, and any of them would grow back if lost. The idea of a thumb *not* growing back hadn't occurred to him until that morning.

Gretel and Baker were alert but like Jack and Ashley they found that this was to no avail. No Scissor-man – nothing. The night was clear and crisp and the moon had risen, so it was easy to see. There was nothing to be discerned in either the Hoffmans' garden or in any of the next-door gardens. There shouldn't have been, anyway. The entire neighbourhood had been evacuated for the operation. Only personnel involved in the sting were in residence.

'Gretel?' came Mary's voice over the radio. 'Anything your end?'

'Nothing,' she replied.

'Stay put,' came in Jack's voice, 'we wait. Mary, is Conrad still sucking his thumb?'

Mary looked out of the cupboard and confirmed that, yes, he was still sucking his thumb, not eating his soup and leaning back on his chair while playing with matches, something that he was actually finding great fun. They waited five minutes, then ten, then fifteen. Nothing. Mr Hoffman put his head around the door.

'Is anything happening?'

'No, sir. We must be patient.'

Mr Hoffman said: 'Okay,' and shut the door again. Every minute Mary would ask for a status report, and after twenty reports in as many minutes she keyed the mike and said in an exasperated tone:

'Jack, when *was* the last cautionary-related crime?'

Jack turned to Ashley. The alien had many talents, but only a few that might have been considered useful. One that definitely had its uses was his total recall.

'Five-day accelerated starvation due to soup refusal, 9 July 1978. Single thumbectomy on 23 December 1979. A fatal house fire on the night of 26 January 1985 may have been matchplay-related, but it was never proved.'

Jack relayed the information to Mary, who replied:

'Twenty-five years since the last definite scissoring – what if he's retired or inactive or something?'

'You mean Cautionary Valley has been living in terror for over two decades when they needn't have?' said Gretel from her position in the back garden. 'I'd be a bit pissed off if that was the case.'

'It's a possibility,' replied Jack, 'but only that. I say we give it another half-hour, then abort and go away for a rethink – Briggs will have something to say about the overtime as it is.'

Everyone radioed in their agreement and all was quiet again.

'Gretel?' said Baker in the potting shed.

'What?' replied Gretel, who was thinking about tall babies.

'You're a woman.'

'I know this.'

'Yes, well,' he said a bit awkwardly, 'I just wondered – do you think Pippa would go out on a date if I asked her?'

'You mean beautiful Pippa in the control room? No.'

'What do you mean, "No"?'

'I mean "No" as in "No, I don't think she'd go out with you".'

'You might have paused for thought or *something*,' said Baker in an affronted tone, 'or been ambiguous – to save my feelings, y'know.'

'Sorry. You ask a question and I answer it,' replied Gretel simply; she had a reputation for directness that sometimes didn't sit well with higher authority. 'I'll tell you why. Remember that time you sneezed on her?'

'It wasn't just her.'

'I know. It's just that girls don't really like that sort of thing.'

Baker nodded slowly. He'd suspected for a while that they might not. Still, he never thought it really fair to have a girlfriend, since he had only six months to live. The thing was, he'd had only six months to live for over thirteen years now.

'Hmm,' said Charlie, half to himself, 'I think I need a doctor who'll give me a year to live.'

'Do you like it here?' Jack asked Ashley. They were leaning on the car but still keeping a close lookout on the front of the house.

'Here, in this street?'

'No, Ashley, this planet.'

'*Most* agreeable,' replied Ashley happily. 'The filing is excellent, the sitcoms top notch and bureaucracy to die for. But by far and away the best feature is your digital mobile phone networks. We can taste the binary data stream in the air. It gives your cities a favourably congenial atmosphere – to you, something like the bouquet of a fine wine.'

Mary was beginning to get a bit uncomfortable inside the cupboard, and she looked at her watch with increased frequency, willing the hands to move faster so they could all go home. She shifted to get more comfortable, the door swung shut and there was a soft *click*.

'Blast!' she muttered as she gently pushed the door. It was no good. It was shut fast.

'Jack,' came Mary's embarrassed voice over the walkie-talkie, 'I've just locked myself in the cupboard and I can't see the kitchen any more. Can we abort?'

Jack looked around. The street was empty and quiet. He'd said they'd stay until midnight and he liked to be true to his word.

'No,' he said to Mary over the radio as he walked through the garden gate.

'Sir,' came Gretel's voice over the airwaves, 'it's just a thought but my mother told me *never* to hide in cupboards in case . . . I was locked in.'

Jack looked around again. It had been quiet before but now it seemed somehow even quieter. There was no distant hum of traffic – nothing. It was as though Cautionary Valley was suddenly an island, cast adrift from the rest of Reading, and the world. He'd felt it before in the same place twenty-five years earlier. He shivered with the onset of a cold breeze and his breath showed in the night air. He brought the radio to his mouth and whispered:

'He's here.'

He signalled to Ashley to stay put, ran a circuitous route to the front door and entered the house. When he opened the kitchen door he stopped short as there was a small conflagration on the kitchen table. The matches Conrad had been playing with had caught fire with an impossibly bright flame and were now rapidly burning a path up the table to where the boy sat, rooted to the spot with fear. They'd thought of this. Jack killed the fire with a handy extinguisher, opened the cupboard door to let Mary out, then barked to Conrad:

'The thumb – back in!'

In his panic the boy had stopped sucking his thumb, but obediently did as he was told. No sooner was the thumb back in when the back door was flung violently open, and before Jack and Mary could even blink a wild-eyed figure in crimson trousers leapt in brandishing a giant pair of gold scissors. With expert precision the tips of the scissors closed around Conrad's thumb and the Scissor-man would doubtless have snipped it off and been gone again in a flash if Jack hadn't shouted:

'HOLD IT!'

The Scissor-man froze. His bloodshot eyes darted towards Jack with a mixture of fear and insanity. He looked gaunt and pale with an untidy shock of nicotine-stained hair; a tailor's tape measure hung from the pocket of his bottle-green jacket.

'DCI Spratt,' continued Jack as he held up his ID. 'Nursery Crime Division. You're under arrest. STEP AWAY FROM THE THUMB.'

The Scissor-man glared at Jack, then at the thumb, then at Mary. His eyes twitched and his long bony fingers clasped the outsize scissors even more firmly. Jack could see that the tips of the scissors were clasped around Conrad's thumb; the flesh was white where the blades held it tight. Even the slightest pressure would take it off.

'I'm not kidding,' said Jack slowly in his best authoritarian voice. 'Drop the scissors. We can plea-bargain this down to possession of an offensive weapon.'

'Snip!' snarled the Scissor-man, a wild grin on his lips revealing several rotten teeth, 'snip-snap! The thumbs are off – alas, alack!'

He tensed, ready to cut.

'Cut that thumb off and you're doing serious time,' said Jack, hoping against hope that the others would initiate phase two without him. They should know what was going on; his finger had been pressed tightly on the 'transmit' button since the Scissor-man had so dramatically entered the kitchen. 'Put down the scissors and we can talk.'

In reply the Scissor-man made a wild *snip* in Jack's direction, then returned the scissors to Conrad's thumb. The whole movement took less than a second, and Jack didn't know what the madman had done until he saw that his tie had been neatly severed and was lying on the floor at his feet. If it came to a fight, they were in trouble. But at that moment, as Conrad's continued relationship with his thumb was looking at its most precarious, the floodlights came on in the front garden and Jack breathed a sigh of relief. The Scissor-man screamed in rage and shock. On the lawn outside were six *more* children, all waving at him with their thumbs in their mouths.

Jack and Mary didn't waste a moment. With the Scissor-man momentarily distracted Mary jammed her walkie-talkie in the jaws of the scissors as Jack pushed Conrad out into the hallway. The Scissor-man glared at Mary, gave an unintelligible cry and severed the radio in two with a metallic *snick* before bounding out of the front door – and straight into a pit covered with a sheet of painted brown paper in the front garden. In a vain attempt to save himself he had let go of his precious scissors, which flew through the air in a graceful arc before embedding themselves in a tree.

As the Scissor-man snarled and snapped and whined in the pit, jumping up and trying to scrabble out, Mary and Jack ran into the front garden at the same time as the neighbours appeared to take their children home. It had been an excellent plan, and unlike many other excellent NCD plans, it had *worked*.

'Have we missed something?' asked Baker as he and Gretel appeared from the back garden, where they had seen the grand sum of precisely nothing. Jack nodded towards the pit where the Great Red-Legg'd Scissor-man cursed at them in the most loathsome language imaginable.

'He looks kind of puny without the scissors, doesn't he?' said Jack as they all stared down at him. 'I'll toss you for who gets to put the cuffs on.'

The Scissor-man stopped yelling and screaming as he had suddenly noticed a small, accidentally self-inflicted cut on his hand.

'*Snip!*' he said to himself in dismay. 'Cut myself – bad – *wrong!*'

'How apt,' murmured Jack, 'Mr Red-Legg'd Scissor-man . . . you're nicked.'

3
St Cerebellum's

'**Most Outdated Secure Hospital**. St Cerebellum's, Reading. This woefully inadequate and outdated institution was constructed in 1831 and was considered modern for its day. With separate wards for unmarried mothers, milk allergies, unwanted relatives and the genuinely disturbed, St Cerebellum's once boasted a proud record of ill-conceived experimental treatment with curious onlooker receipts that surpassed even those of Bedlam. But the glory days are long over, and the crumbling ruin is now an anachronistic stain on Reading's otherwise fine record of psychiatric treatment.'

— *The Bumper Book of Berkshire Records*, 2004 edition

Dr Alan Mandible led the group of suited consultants along the peeling corridors of St Cerebellum's, Reading's premier secure hospital for the criminally insane. While perhaps not the newest, cleanest or driest, it did contain the most interesting patients. There are not many secure hospitals which can boast someone who thinks they are Napoleon, but St Cerebellum's could field three — not to mention a handful of serial killers whose names inexplicably yet conveniently rhymed with their crimes. Notorious cannibal 'Peter the Eater' was incarcerated here, as was 'Sasha the Slasher' and 'Mr Browner, the Serial Drowner'. But the undisputed king of rhyme-inspired serial murder was Isle of Man resident Maximilian Marx, who went under the uniquely tongue-twisting epithet 'Mad Max Marx, the Masked Manxman-Axeman'. Deirdre Blott tried to top Max's clear superiority by changing her name so as to become: 'Nutty Nora Newsome, the Knife-wielding Weird Widow from

Waddesdon', but no one was impressed, and she was ostracised by the other patients for being such a terrible show-off.

'We have funding to demolish the old nuthouse, Dr Maxilla,' explained Dr Mandible earnestly, catching sight of the Japanese delegate's obvious distaste at the mouldering fabric of the building, and adding quickly: 'I'm sorry, when I said "nuthouse" I actually meant "secure hospital".'

'It's an easy mistake to make,' replied Dr Maxilla cheerfully. 'I often refer to my patients as "the loons".'

Dr Mandible smiled. They understood one another perfectly.

There were five delegates following Dr Mandible's brisk pace down the corridors, each hailing from a different nation. They were visiting St Cerebellum's as part of an international exchange of ideas concerning the treatment of the dangerously criminally insane; Dr Mandible himself had attended Professor Frank Strait's specialist hospital in Ohio and would visit Dr Maxilla's clinic in Kobe at the end of the year.

'I understand one of your consultants was caught conducting unethical experiments,' said the French delegate, Dr Vômer. 'Such as grafting a kitten's head on to a haddock.'

'Dr Quatt? I barely knew her,' replied Mandible hurriedly, 'and her experiments were conducted without the knowledge or approval of the hospital governors or even of QuangTech, who own the hospital.'

'Oh!' said Vômer, who had once himself dabbled in the ethically grey area of grafting things on to other things for no apparent purpose, 'her work was much admired in Toulouse, where such experiments are permitted for gastronomic research.'

Mandible sighed.

'I wish our own medical council were as broad minded. She was one of St Cerebellum's most celebrated perverters of the natural order. But alas! She died earlier this year.'

'A great loss,' said Vômer sadly. 'I was hoping to speak to her – was it unexpected?'

'She was hit on the head with a shovel and then crushed by a falling beanstalk while being carried to safety by a bizarre genetic experiment gone horribly wrong,' replied Mandible thoughtfully, 'so I think it's safe to say it *was* unexpected – but what she would have wanted, nonetheless.'

'And her experiments?'

'Disposed of.'

'Even the monkey's brain kept alive in a jar?' queried Dr Maxilla, his voice tinged with disappointment.

'I'm afraid so. I mean, *mercifully* so. Ah! Security.'

He was glad to be able to change the subject. They had reached a steel gate. Behind it was a guard who was reading a copy of *The Toad* and looking bored.

'I'm afraid you must leave all sharp objects and personal possessions behind,' intoned Dr Mandible. 'For taking notes I will supply you with pre-softened crayons and notepads of damp tissue paper bound with mouldy wool.'

There was a sudden hush. The delegates looked at one another nervously. Dr Maxilla gave voice to their collective thoughts.

'Doctor, are you proposing that we are to wander amidst your inmates . . . unprotected?'

The other doctors nodded in agreement and started to mutter among themselves. Dr Mandible held up his hands in a conciliatory manner and smiled benignly.

'Here at St Cerebellum's we are trying to help the repeatedly violent offender by increasing *hospital* security to a maximum but reducing *individual* security to a minimum. The patients are allowed to wander relatively freely within the confines of the hospital's outdoor compound.'

'You mean, that it is to say, we are likely to face, I mean, without bars . . . *HIM*?'

Mandible smiled again.

'It *is* a radical treatment, I grant you, but we are more than happy with the results and I assure you that you will come to no harm. The patient to whom you refer is one of our greatest successes, and although transported from place to place within the hospital using the methods prescribed by law – in his case with straitjacket and bite mask – it is unnecessary, for he has renounced violence and freely accepted his loss of liberty as a just punishment for his crimes.'

Even though no name had been spoken, they all knew who he was talking about – the patient in question was the star attraction of the hospital, and the only reason any of them had bothered to visit Dr Mandible and his otherwise dull hospital in the first place. Even though St Cerebellum's secure wing was home to nine serial killers, three poisoners, one cannibal and an arsonist or two, only one of them had continued to command front-page status since his capture twenty years before. His name alone would cause a shiver to run down the spine of anyone who had even the slightest association with him.

Dr Mandible smiled at them but they did not smile back. Even the most committed of them had never had merely fresh air between them and their most dangerous patients.

'Did he really pull men's arms from their sockets?' asked Dr Maxilla, a slight tremor in his voice.

'Not at all,' replied Mandible. 'He pulled *anyone's* arms from their sockets. He was never gender exclusive and always the most egalitarian of psychotics – anything with a pulse was fair game for slaughter. He once saved the life of someone simply so he could kill him in a more imaginative fashion.'

'So the story about the guinea pigs and the kebab skewer is true?'

'*All* the stories are true,' replied Mandible, gesturing for them to follow, 'except the one where he showed mercy to a little old lady – it wasn't mercy at all; he had a dentist's appointment and was in a hurry.'

He led them through the steel gate, on the other side of which three burly orderlies were waiting to escort them. They walked down a short corridor and blinked as they stepped into a large outdoor area surrounded by a high wall. The compound was laid out as a spacious garden, and they could see patients tending small areas of their own. Dr Mandible led them down a concrete path to a beefy, neckless bull of a man who was weeding a vegetable patch.

'Hello, Martin,' said Dr Mandible calmly.

'Hello, Doc,' said the man cheerily. 'Carrots will be good this year.'

'Splendid!' replied Dr Mandible, patting the patient amiably on the shoulder and passing on.

'Martin Gooch,' whispered Mandible. 'Frustrated film director. Went mad and slaughtered a commissioning editor with an axe, then killed anyone who *reminded* him of the commissioning editor and, after that, anyone at all. Spent the first three years of his treatment in solitary because of his violent disposition. After six years of origami therapy we reclassified him from Category "B": "Dangerously Insane" to Category "D": "Functionally Bonkers".'

They nodded their heads agreeably and scribbled some notes with their soft wax crayons. They moved on, and Dr Mandible introduced them to several other mass-murderers, poisoners and pony stranglers, but it was obvious from their feeling of anticipation that these patients, while all remarkable examples of rehabilitation, were mere sideshows in comparison with the one patient in St Cerebellum's who made the rest seem like petty shoplifters.

Dr Mandible read the look on their faces, sensed their impatience and led them over to a small bed of rose bushes, each one sporting a dazzling selection of blooms. The delegates gathered behind Mandible as they approached, yet not even the orderlies felt they had much to worry about. The patient, despite the outrageous and often perverse violence of his crimes, hadn't lifted a finger against any of them during his two-decade stay at the hospital. The mellow figure snipping at the roses seemed somehow divorced from the savagery of his sadistic crimes. But it didn't help him. Liberty, in his case, could never be an option.

The patient in question had his back to the small group. He was dressed in pale blue denim trousers and jacket with *St Cerebellum's* stencilled on the back. The figure busied himself with his roses. He was stooped over a bloom, carefully trimming the plant with a pair of blunted plastic scissors firmly attached by a heavy chain to three anvils on the ground. He seemed not to be aware of their presence so Dr Mandible gave a polite cough. The figure stood up to his full height and turned slowly to face them. A faint whiff of ginger moved with him and Dr Maxilla took a sharp breath. Professor Palatine covered her mouth with her hand and uttered a small cry. The others all took a nervous step back, apart from Dr Vômer, who took three.

However many photos you see and however much news footage you watch of the Gingerbreadman, nothing can quite prepare you for seeing him in all his baked glory. He was a dark brown colour the shade of mahogany and seven foot tall, with weighty limbs and a large head. His jacket was open, revealing several large pink icing buttons that ran down his chest. He had large glacé cherries the size of grapefruits for eyes and a dollop of red icing for a nose. His mouth was two slivers of liquorice, the corners of which rose into a smile as soon as he saw them.

'Alan!' said the Gingerbreadman in a deep yet friendly tone. 'What a delightful happenstance! And most timely, too. See here, I have bred a new rose, which in honour of your work to cure me of my criminal tendencies I take great pleasure in naming after you. Behold, *Mandible's Triumph!*'

He offered the bloom to Mandible in his three-fingered gingerbread hand and the doctor accepted it gratefully. It was a flower that had blue, white and red petals on the same bloom.

'Thank you very much,' said Mandible as the Gingerbreadman gave a small bow and let out another whiff of ginger, 'it's magnificent!' He turned to the delegates. 'Ladies and gentlemen, allow me to introduce the Gingerbreadman, veteran of St Cerebellum's and one of our model patients.'

They relaxed slightly at the Gingerbreadman's apparent congeniality and stared at him as his glacé-cherry eyes darted eagerly among their faces. He recognised Frank Strait immediately.

'Professor Strait?' he asked as he took a step closer. 'I read your book on obsessional neurosis with great interest.'

'How . . . how did you know it was me?' stammered Strait, taken aback at the Gingerbreadman's powers of observation.

'That's easily explained.' The Gingerbreadman smiled. 'Your picture is on the book jacket.'

'Ah. Well . . . what did you think?' asked Strait, his voice high and tremulous with suppressed fear.

'I'll be frank with you, Frank,' replied the Gingerbreadman, adding hastily: 'May I call you Frank?'

'I'd prefer Professor Strait.'

'Very well. I'll be straight with you, Strait. I wasn't that impressed. The prose was dull, the research patchy. I thought that perhaps you had given over your time to listing case histories rather than proposing specific methods of treatment. It smacked of voyeurism. In a less enlightened age people like you would be given guided tours around lunatic asylums with people like me as the star attraction. Not that it's like that any more, eh, Alan?'

He winked at Dr Mandible as he said it, and gave out a cakey chuckle and another whiff of ginger.

Professor Strait twitched and raised an eyebrow, wondering how to reply to hearing his life's work so comprehensively trashed. He

31

paused too long; the Gingerbreadman's attention had moved on.

'Dr Lacrimal?' he asked, his cherry eyes flicking on to the German, who stood as straight as a poker to show that he was not in the least afraid, which he transparently was.

'I am,' Lacrimal answered, 'but there is no picture on my book jacket. How did you know?'

The Gingerbreadman chuckled another deep cakey laugh.

'Because you are the leading German expert on criminal insanity. Alan doesn't insult me by dragging along students; your bearing was unmistakably German and it seemed the most likely possibility. By the same criteria I suspect that is Dr Maxilla behind you, Dr Vômer is the one cowering in the distance, and I have at least a sixty per cent certainty that the lady is Professor Palatine, head of the Jordanian mental institute and as brilliant as she is beautiful.'

He gave another short bow and his liquorice lips rose into a radiant smile. The delegates all returned his bow and wrote more notes.

'I see you are surprised,' observed the Gingerbreadman, 'surprised that an evil spirit such as I, famed for my sadistic and murderous exploits, stands before you as an intelligent entity!'

Dr Mandible placed his hand on the Gingerbreadman's shoulder – which he had to reach up to do – and addressed the small group.

'When the Gingerbreadman first arrived here he was so violently deranged we had to invent a new category just for him – "A+++": "Throw away the key". He was brutal, dangerous and without a shred of human decency. He was, and I will beg your indulgence and use an unscientific term, a *fiend*. Unhelpful at first and contemptuous of authority, but the past twenty years have shown a remarkable change. Quite apart from utilising his not inconsiderable mental agility to become an expert on roses, he has also written several books on the criminal tendency, speaks seven languages, and has a degree in Philosophy & Ethics from the Open University. So you see before you, ladies and gentlemen, not a monster that was, but a useful asset to the society he once terrorised.'

The Gingerbreadman looked embarrassed and stared at his feet.

'Alan is too kind,' he said at last in a low voice, 'but what he neglects to tell you is that even though this is a hospital and not a prison, it is a confusion in words only. I will never be released despite the good doctor's work, because punishment and incarceration are but aspects of the penal system. We live in a society that values revenge, revenge for the victims and their families. It is for their sake that I must remain here.'

He lowered his cherry eyes and sighed, giving off another whiff of ginger. They all sensed that the interview was at an end, said their goodbyes and filed away. Dr Vômer was the first to say anything when they were safely out of earshot.

'I think I speak for all of us when I say how remarkable your rehabilitation of the Gingerbreadman has been,' he began. 'Perhaps you would like to give the keynote speech at LoopyCon next year?'

The other delegates nodded their agreement and Mandible tried to look unabashed and surprised by this sudden honour. He allowed himself a brief twinge of pride. The following year LoopyCon would echo with praise of the Mandible Technique for treatment of violent serial offenders. It would be a short leap, he thought, from there to his name being indelibly linked with the other great names of psychology: Freud, Jung, Skinner, Chumley – Mandible! He shivered as he thought of it.

The Gingerbreadman had returned to his roses after the small party left. He looked about him to make sure no one was watching, then cupped his hands around a small flower just coming to life. After thirty seconds or so he took his hands away and smiled to himself.

33

The small rose had undergone a transformation within his hands. Where before it had been alive and beautiful, now it was withered and brown. Dead, dried and decayed, rotten as the evil soul of the Gingerbreadman.

4

The Robert Southey

'**First (and Only) Bear Relocation.** Mr and Mrs Edward Bruin, 1977. With the passing of the 1962 Animal (Anthropomorphic) Equality Act, all talking animals won the right *not* to be exploited or hunted and instead live in the designated safe haven of Berkshire, England. Bears were fully expected to take up residence in small cottages in the middle of woods and eat porridge in a state of blissful quasi-human solitude, but they didn't. Most bears instead preferred to remain urbane city-dwellers, and shunned the notion of foraging in the countryside. Ursine elders deplore the situation, but secretly admit that Reading's proliferation of coffee shops, theatres and shopping opportunities is not without its attractions.'
— *The Bumper Book of Berkshire Records*, 2004 edition

Jack was being driven through Reading by Mary, and was studying that morning's copy of *The Mole* with a frown etched deeply on his brow. Despite the success of the Scissor-man capture six weeks earlier, and the Humpty triumph four months before that, a few well-publicised failings had sent them back to the pre-scissor/Humpty days of thankless obscurity, but annoyingly without the obscurity.

'How's it looking?' asked Mary.

'Not *exactly* favourable,' replied Jack, showing her a newspaper that sported the banner headline DOUBLE DEVOURING SHOCKS READING.

'I thought that was one of the better ones,' commented Mary, pointing to a copy of *The Reading Daily Trumpet*, which had NCD OVERSIGHT: WOLF EATS TWO emblazoned in large type

35

across the front page. *The Reading Daily Eyestrain* had been no better with RED-CLOAKED TOT IN SWALLOWING DRAMA. But *The Toad* had been the most scathing. Under a headline that read JACK SPRATT: INCOMPETENT BONEHEAD? it went on to list several well-argued reasons as to why he was.

'*The Toad*?' asked Mary. 'Must be our old friend Josh Hatchett.'

'Who else?'

Josh Hatchett was one of the Nursery Crime Division's more outspoken critics. He called himself 'the loyal opposition' whenever they met, but to Jack and Mary he was more simply 'that troublemaker'. It was he alone who had raised several questions over the ethical use of children as bait during the Scissor-man capture. The fallout from that hadn't been comfortable, and Jack had received an official reprimand.

Jack shook his head sadly as he read. The Riding-Hood investigation had admittedly gone a little off the rails and, okay, a few people had been eaten. The critical spotlight of the press had been swung brightly in Jack's direction and the hard-won prestige of the Humpty affair and everything else negated in less time than it takes to say 'what big eyes you have'. Jack sighed. The press had lauded him to the skies and now looked set to condemn him with equal enthusiasm. Mary shifted down a gear as Jack threw the newspaper on to the back seat.

'Our friend Hatchett isn't being very helpful, is he?' commented Mary.

'That's putting it mildly. What does he expect? The NCD isn't governed by the same rules as conventional police work – if it was there'd be no need for us.'

'It's all about readership and power, Jack,' observed Mary. 'They want the readers to know that they can break heroes just as easily as they can make them.'

'It's not as though it's even current news,' grumbled Jack. 'How long's it been since the wolf gig? A month?'

'A week.'

'Right – a *quarter* of a month, then.'

He thought for a moment.

'Speaking of which – heard anything about Red Riding-Hood and her grandmother?'

'Still catatonic. Fixed features, glazed eyes, no visible signs of mental activity. Post-traumatic stress, the doctors say – not surprising, being swallowed whole like that.'

'It wasn't a pretty sight,' agreed Jack, shuddering at the thought.

'What about you?' asked Mary, 'What did the quacks say when you saw them?'

'A completely clean bill of health.'

'You didn't go, did you?'

'No. Listen, I'm fine.'

'I thought Superintendent Briggs said—'

'Never mind what Briggs said. I'm NCD. I can handle this kind of surreal weirdness. Okay, so we screwed up a bit and a few people got swallowed. I mean, it's not as though they're dead, right?'

'*We* screwed up a bit?'

'Okay, *I* screwed up a bit. I just got sidetracked by the suppressed sexual overtones regarding predatory wolves and a little girl in a red cape lost in the forest. So I missed a few opportunities.'

Mary was silent. She had some opinions on the subject but decided to keep herself to herself. If she'd been there, she knew, things might have been different. Instead, she said:

'I still think you ought to go and see the counsellors. Delayed shock can be dangerous. My cousin Raymond was in the queue at a bank when armed robbers ran in. Very stressful. He thought he was fine but less than two hours later he was stone-cold dead.'

'Of shock?'

'No; he got hit by a truck crossing the road.'

Jack thought for a moment.

'I'll see the quacks *next* week. Did I tell you our request for extra funding has been refused?'

'It figures. What about increased manpower?'

'The same. It's you, me and Ash unless we get a big show on.'

'Doesn't seem fair, does it?'

Jack said nothing but Mary was right. Despite the trammelling they had received in the past few weeks, the division's record through the years had been sound. The closing down of Rumpelstiltskin's straw-into-gold dens, the Cock Robin murder inquiry, arresting notorious serial wife-killer Bluebeard, the detaining of the 'Emperor's clothes' confidence tricksters, the capture of the Gingerbreadman and the Scissor-man, the Humpty murder inquiry – it had all been good, solid, unconventional police work. Good and solid – until the Riding-Hood debacle. There had been other repercussions from the case which he hadn't told Mary about. The most worshipful Guild of Detectives had withdrawn its offer for him to join on the grounds of 'suitability issues'. It was good and bad news. He didn't want to join their stupid guild, but he liked them asking.

Jack stared out of the window. In the countryside the hot weather was glorious but here in the city the heat served only to make people bad tempered, the streets dusty and the pollution worse.

A Ford Transit van pulled up next to them at the lights. It was driven by a large figure in expensive Ferucci dark glasses. Within a few seconds the lights changed and the van turned left without the driver having looked at them.

'Wasn't that Tarquin?' asked Jack, swivelling his head to follow the van.

'I didn't see.'

'I'm sure it was. Let's follow. I want to see what he's up to.'

Mary pulled into the left-hand lane, ignored the glares of the other motorists and caught up with the van as it turned off towards the imposing art-deco-styled residential tower block that was the Robert Southey. She stopped the car and they watched as Tarquin's van drove down the ramp into the underground parking lot.

'What do we do?' asked Mary.

'What do you think? We take a look.'

'In the Bob Southey? Are you sure?'

Mary's reticence was not without foundation. Ever since the passing of the Animal (Anthropomorphic) Equality Act, Berkshire had become home to a growing band of talking animals who had sought refuge from persecution around the globe. The vast majority of these were bears, who had much to gain from moving to a designated safe haven, even if it was only Berkshire, a place not particularly noted for gushing mountain streams and countless acres of trackless pine forests. Not that this bothered the bears much; they had discovered to their chagrin that freedom to forage for wild honey and flick salmon from mountain streams was actually a bit tedious and might lead to multiple bee-stings and wet feet, so they had banded together their substantial fortunes and built the Robert Southey Tower. A luxury dwelling of almost two hundred separate apartments, it was strictly for non-humans unless by special invitation, something that suited the bears no end, as humans had not been particularly charitable to their species in the past, and if small cottages in the middle of woods weren't for them, then an apartment with views of the Thames and a well-appointed health spa, solarium, medical centre and gym fitted the bill admirably.

The conventional police gave the Bob Southey a wide berth as Nursery matters confused them, and even Jack thought twice before venturing in. Bears had a profound sense of unity and tended – like most animals, and with good reason – to treat humans with a degree of suspicion, especially with the threat of bile-tappers and illegal hunters still a very real one.

'If Tarquin is dealing in his garbage again I want him stopped.'

'Okay,' said Mary, hardly relishing the idea. Her lack of enthusiasm could be understood. Tarquin wasn't human, even if he acted like one. He was a bear, and in the strict hierarchical ranking of bear society was one of lowly importance – an *Ursa minor*. On the outer edges of ursine society, and eager to build a reputation, he and other bored minors dabbled in matters of dubious legality – and this was where Jack and Mary reluctantly entered the equation.

They got out of the car and walked down into the gloominess of the underground car park. It was used mainly for storage as bears generally only ride motorcycles if they drive anything at all, and as they searched they moved among the packing cases belonging to the many dispossessed bears of the world. Some were from aristocratic families that went back generations, but most were ex-dancers, circus performers and farm escapees who were only too glad to be away from exploitation and in many cases escaped with only the barest of possessions and a photograph album or two.

Mary and Jack trod silently through the crates and vintage Rolls-Royces beneath dust sheets until they found the Transit van, tucked away in a corner beneath the up-ramp and illuminated by the harsh glow of strip lights, one of which flickered annoyingly. They moved close enough to hear and see what was going on, but remained hidden – downwind.

The van's doors were open and several bags of contraband were heaped in the back, all taped up in clear plastic bags. A few of them had already been transferred to a waiting wheelbarrow. Tarquin was looking around furtively as another bear wearing faded Levi's and a Bearzone T-shirt cut open a packet of the contraband and carefully drew out a spoonful. He sniffed it suspiciously, mixed it with milk and heated it over a lighter before adding some brown sugar and salt, and then sipping the result.

'This is *good*,' he said at last in a deep voice, making a few lippy-smacky noises. 'How much you got?'

'Forty keys for now,' said Tarquin, his voice also a low baritone, 'plus as much as you can shift in the future. It's nine and fifty a key, Algy – non-negotiable.'

The bear named Algy laughed and scratched his head.

'Hey, Tarq, it's good but not *that* good. I can get this from Sainsbury's for half that price.'

'And who's going to march up to the checkout and buy it? You?'

'Sure. It's easy to pass for human. Just act like you own the place.'

'You wish it were that easy. Listen, you pay me nine and fifty for this and everything I can get in the future and I'll give you six pounds of honey just for you and the missus. Call it a sweetener.'

The second bear thought for a moment.

'Comb or jar?'

Tarquin opened his arms wide and smiled, displaying a mouthful of sharp white teeth.

'Algy! Who do you think I am? Comb, of *course*.'

Algy licked his lips and rapidly came to a decision.

'Then you've got a deal. Ninety-five pence times forty is – let me think – thirty-eight pounds.'

He pulled a wallet from his back pocket.

'Have you got change for two twenties?'

Jack told Mary to stay put and then stepped out from behind the concrete pillar. The two bears stared short-sightedly in his direction, flicked their ears down flat on their heads and growled until they saw who it was, then looked around innocently and tapped their claws together. If they could have whistled, they would have.

'Hello, Tarquin,' said Jack as he approached, 'up to your old tricks again?'

Tarquin winced and nodded a polite greeting.

'Private sale, Inspector. Nothing for you here.'

'Oh yes?' replied Jack, taking a handful from the opened bag. 'Planning a party?'

'For private consumption only,' replied Tarquin unconvincingly.

'Not even *you* could eat this much porridge,' said Jack as he let the rolled oats spill through his fingers on to the ground. 'Where did you get all this? Tesco's?'

'It's not for porridge,' announced Tarquin with a defiant air, 'we're going to use it to make . . . *flapjacks*.'

Jack looked into the van. Forty kilos of rolled oats was a reasonable-sized pile. Not huge, but enough.

'That's a lot of flapjacks.'

'I *like* flapjacks.'

Jack paused for thought. This was a new approach. Porridge was a restricted-quota foodstuff for bears along with honey, marmalade and buns, but rolled oats weren't classified at all. They were merely something the NCD called 'porridge paraphernalia', along with bowls, spoons, brown sugar and so forth. Legal to buy and sell, but generally used only for one purpose.

'Flapjacks, eh?'

'Yes, Inspector,' replied Tarquin innocently. 'Heaven forbid I would try and flog cheap porridge to Reading's bears.'

'Well, okay, then,' said Jack cheerfully, 'let's make flapjacks. How much honey you got?'

'What?' asked Tarquin, suddenly wary.

'Honey,' replied Jack as he opened the front door of the van and found half a dozen jars and six honeycombs. 'We're going to make flapjacks. Rolled oats and honey. Let's mix it all up here and now.'

Algy and Tarquin looked at each other in horror.

'Mix it . . . up?'

'Yeah. Come on, guys, you *said* it was for flapjacks!'

The bears watched with mounting horror as Jack picked up a two-kilo bag of oats and made to open it over Algy's wheelbarrow.

Algy muttered, 'Oh, lawks!' and put a paw over his eyes.

'WAIT!' shouted Tarquin. Jack stopped. 'Okay,' he said with a sigh, 'you've got me. Bloody NCD. You'd never try this if I was an *Ursa major*.'

'If you were a major you'd know better than to peddle porridge. So . . . where did you get this? Tesco's? Somerfields? *Waitrose?*'

'I can't tell you.'

'Have it your own way,' said Jack as he began to tear open the bag of oats over the wheelbarrow. Tarquin put up a paw to stop him.

'Okay, okay. I buy it wholesale from this person I've never met over in Shiplake.'

'How can you have never met him in Shiplake?'

'I'm sorry,' said Tarquin with a confused look. Like many bears he could be dense at times. 'You're going to have to ask me that question again.'

'What's their name?'

'I don't know. I pick the stuff up from a warehouse and leave the money in a biscuit tin.'

'I get it. How do they contact you?'

'By phone. About eight months ago. Said they needed to shift some merchandise and could I help them out. I've never met them.'

'Ursine?'

'No. Human.'

'Old, young, male, female? What?'

'I don't know,' said Tarquin with a shrug. 'You all sound pretty squeaky to me.'

'If you're lying to me—!'

'On my cub's life,' said Tarquin earnestly, crossing his chest, stamping one foot and then clicking a claw on one of his canines. 'I can give you the address and the code to get in.'

'Okay,' said Jack as he handed him his notepad. Tarquin jotted down an address and handed it back.

'Good. Now you – what's your name?'

'Algernon. Algy.'

'Okay, bear-named-Algy, Tarquin here is going to sell you these oats for sixty pence a kilo. Give him the money.'

Tarquin threw his arms in the air, opened his eyes wide and growled dangerously. Blabbing to the cops was one thing, but making a loss on an oat deal was quite another. He took a pace towards Jack and stared at him in the sort of way he'd stare at a leaping salmon, if he'd ever done such a thing, which he hadn't. Jack stood his ground.

'You are so out of order!' yelled Tarquin.

'No,' said Jack, '*you* are out of order. This is what happens to bears who smuggle over quota. I've got nothing against moderate porridge use but I don't take to bears like you seeking to capitalise on ursine weaknesses. I'll ignore the forty kilos this time but if I catch you with so much as an ounce in future you'll be sewing mailbags as a career.'

'Mailbags?'

'It's a euphemism for prison. Take the money.'

'No,' said Tarquin as he moved closer. 'What if I tell you to go take a running jump into a mountain lake somewhere?'

Jack stared at him and didn't waver for a moment.

'Listen here, Boo-boo,' he said slowly, 'you've been busted good and proper. Take it like a bear or I'll spread it around that you've been cutting the oats with Ready brek.'

'They'd never believe you,' he growled.

'Wouldn't they? Take a step closer and my associate hiding over there will tranq your fuzzy butt and we can talk it over at the station. Me with a cup of tea and a chocolate digestive, and you with a splitting headache and a numb arse. Your choice.'

Tarquin thought for a moment, sighed and then relaxed.

'Okay, Inspector,' he said with a forced smile, 'we'll play it your way.'

Greatly relieved at this, Algy gave Tarquin the reduced price and started to load the bags of oats into his wheelbarrow. He paused for thought and then asked: 'Do you really cut it with Ready brek?'

'Of course not.'

'But I still get the honey, right?'

'NO!'

'Here's to the day when they repeal porribition,' said Jack as they walked out of the car park and into the sunshine. 'The associated criminal element of supply far outweighs the harm that it does to the bear population.'

'What's the alternative?' said Mary. 'Unregulated porridge use? We'd have trippy spaced-out bears wandering around the town, hallucinating who knows what in the Oracle centre.'

'If I made the laws I'd let them,' said Jack. 'Porridge is a great deal less harmful than alcohol – and we seem to embrace and promote the sale of that almost *everywhere*.'

'I agree it doesn't make much sense,' replied Mary, adding: 'I thought calling Tarquin "Boo-boo" was a bit daring. You know how sensitive they can get on the whole Yogi issue.'

'Bears are big on dominance; I had to insult him. Besides, you had a tranquilliser aimed on Tarquin's arse the whole time, right?'

'The dart gun?' said Mary with surprise as she started the engine. 'Not me. I thought you had it. Where now?'

'Next time we're tackling bears,' pleaded Jack, who had suddenly turned a little pale, '*please* make sure you've got the tranquilliser gun. And we're off to Charvil. I need to buy a new car.'

5

The Austin Allegro Equipe

———

'**Feeblest British Car of the Seventies.** It was a close-run thing between the Morris Marina and the Austin Allegro, but the latter finally won out. Although originally designed as sharp and sporty, the Allegro (1973–82) was a victim of design and manufacturing compromises that conspired to dilute the original concept until the resultant car was utterly lacking in appeal, and the buying public responded in a lukewarm manner. When production was eventually shelved there were – tantalisingly – plans in the design office for a 420-horsepower V12 "Muscle" Allegro, a stretch "Allegrosine" and an RB-211 turbofan-powered version, with which it was proposed to break the Land Speed Record.'

– *The Bumper Book of Berkshire Records*, 2004 edition

Jack's last car, a very reliable Austin Allegro estate, had been written off when he ignored a complicated and little-understood – at least to him – procedure for setting the torque on the rear wheel bearings. The cost of repairing it far outstripped the value, so it had been scrapped. On reflection he should have just rebuilt it at any price, but at the time he hadn't realised how much he liked it. For all his sneering at other detectives owning classic cars such as Moose's Jaguar, Chyme's delightful old Delage-Supersport and Miss Lockett's wonderful pair of Bristols, he had begun to like the Allegro in a strange sort of way. It was his hunt for another in showroom condition which had led them here to Charvil on the eastern edge of the town.

They pulled up outside a shabby used-car lot that was *exactly* the sort of place you might expect to buy a used Allegro. It was decidedly low rent and displayed about a dozen well-used cars of dubious provenance. Faded bunting fluttered from light standards in the four corners of the yard. Jack rechecked the address before getting out of the car. Mary, passionately uninterested in Allegros like most other people on the planet, picked up the paper from the back seat and started to read the sports pages. Her mobile rang. She took one look at the screen and then put it back in her pocket, where it trilled plaintively to itself. Despite several subtle hints and a raft of unsubtle ones, her ex-boyfriend Arnold still hadn't figured out the 'ex' part of their relationship.

Jack walked up between the ranks of the cars, being careful not to touch them as they were all covered with a thin film of dust; it didn't seem as if the dealer sold that many. He was looking around for the Allegro when a young man stepped out of the office. He was impeccably dressed in a morning suit, bow tie, high collar and starched cuffs. From the blood-red carnation in his buttonhole to his shiny patent leather shoes, the young man carried with him the haughty air of undeniable superiority, and incongruity. He looked as though he were dressed for a society party – not selling cars. He regarded Jack with suspicion and then forced a smile on to his thin lips.

'Can I help you, sir?'

'I hope so,' replied Jack. 'I called yesterday. You had an Allegro—'

The car salesman's manner changed abruptly and a genuine smile supplanted the bogus one.

'Detective Chief Inspector Spratt?'

Jack nodded and the salesman put out a well-manicured hand for him to shake.

'Pleased to meet you, sir,' he said excitedly, giving off wafts of expensive aftershave as he moved. 'I followed the Humpty case with enthusiasm. *Extremely* impressive. My name is Gray, Dorian Gray –

but you *must* call me Dorian. I for one do not believe a word when Josh Hatchett refers to you as "a bad joke" or "a stain upon the good name of the Reading police force".'

'You're very kind,' said Jack a bit uneasily.

'Think nothing of it!' replied Dorian happily. 'I've wanted to meet you for *such* a long time, but my diary is *so* very full. It was lucky, in fact, that you caught me when you rang. Society is *such* a drain on one's energy. Would you follow me?'

He led Jack through the collection of battered wrecks which had nothing over £200 written on their windscreens and on to a small lock-up garage at the back of the lot. He smiled again, carefully donned white gloves and pulled the doors open with a loud *sqraunch* of long-forgotten hinges. Gray must have seen Jack looking doubtful, for he added quickly:

'It has been in storage for a number of years, yet I don't believe it has aged significantly.'

The garage opened to reveal an immaculate 1979 Allegro Equipe two-door saloon. It was painted silver with orange and red stripes down the sides and had alloy wheels and twin headlamps at the front. The paintwork glistened as though it had only just rolled off the production line. Dorian got in, started it at the first attempt and drove it into the sunshine.

'Remarkable!' said Jack after a pause.

'Isn't it just?' responded Dorian as he got out, unlatched the bonnet and revealed an engine bay that didn't have a spot of dirt or oil on it anywhere.

Jack smiled and got into the car. He could smell the freshness of the factory and the orange velour seats still had the fuzz on them. He looked at the odometer. It had only 171 miles recorded.

'Where did you find it?' asked Jack incredulously. 'This belongs in a museum. None would take it, of course, but it does.'

Dorian Gray looked to left and right and lowered his voice.

'It's not quite so strange as you think, Inspector. You see, every now and then I sell a car to a favoured customer with my own – *ahem* – unique guarantee.'

Jack sensed a scam of some sort and narrowed his eyes.

'Guarantee?'

'Yes. I guarantee that this car will never rust, or even age significantly.'

'Waxoil and underseal, eh?'

'Better than Waxoil, Inspector. Allow me to demonstrate.'

They walked round to the back of the car and Dorian opened the boot. Inside was a finely painted oil of the same car, but in much shabbier condition. The car in the picture had rust holes showing up through the bodywork, a peeling vinyl roof, the trim was missing and there was an unsightly scrape on the left rear which had taken the bumper off. In short, a bit of a wreck. Jack looked at Dorian quizzically.

'See the rear windscreen in the painting, Officer?'

Jack looked. It seemed normal enough. Dorian smiled again, removed the wheel brace from the boot and shattered the rear window of the Allegro with one strong blow. Jack took a shocked step back at this apparently motiveless act of vandalism. Dorian, however, merely smiled.

'Look at the painting, Mr Spratt.'

Jack frowned. He was certain that the car in the picture had *not* had a broken rear windscreen before, but now it did. His frown deepened, but Dorian had another surprise for him.

'Look at the car.'

The rear screen was intact.

'*How . . . ?*'

Dorian Gray put the wheel brace away, shut the boot and smiled the enigmatic smile of a conjuror who has just caught a speeding bullet in his teeth and no way on hell's own earth was going to let on how he did it.

'Everything you do to the car happens to the picture, Inspector. It never needs cleaning, repairing or servicing. It will stay new *for ever*. You may want to have rear seat belts fitted and replace the AM push-button radio, but I feel those are small inconveniences when you consider the vast savings this car has to offer.'

'For ever?'

Dorian stared absently at his perfectly manicured nails.

'*Nothing* lasts for ever,' he said carelessly, 'but yes, for the foreseeable future.' He smiled disarmingly. 'I've offered this warranty to only six other people and do you know, I've not had a single complaint.'

'How much?'

'Eight hundred guineas.'

'I'll take it.'

Dorian was quite happy to accept a cheque and moved several cars so Jack could drive out, the engine purring like a kitten brought up on cream. Jack was just signing a buyer's agreement in Dorian's red pen and thinking he had got the bargain of the century when Mary knocked on the window in a state of some agitation. She was holding her mobile and waved it at him.

'I need to speak to you as a matter of some urgency, sir.'

'Don't worry.' Jack smiled. 'I won't insist you drive it all the time.'

'It's not the Allegro. It's the Gingerbreadman.'

'What about him?'

'He's escaped.'

Jack laughed.

'Sure he has. I do this joke to Madeleine all the time and she . . .'

He stopped talking as he noticed that Mary was doing everything *but* laughing, and that Dorian Gray had turned on the television where a news bulletin was under way. The volume was off but it didn't matter; the grim face of the anchorman with a stock picture of the gingery lunatic said it all. Jack felt a heavy hand fall on his heart. Not *again*. He and Friedland Chymes had captured him the first time round. Jack and Chymes had survived, Wilmot Snaarb had not. Jack could still see Snaarb's look of agony as he had his arms torn from their sockets, his cries of pain and terror mixed with the maniacal cackle of the psychopathic snack. If Jack hadn't tricked him into a shipping container, the Gingerbreadman would have stayed at liberty for longer. He was delivered to prison still inside the container and it took fourteen men in riot gear to subdue him. It was nursery crime at its very worst.

'Who called you?' asked Jack, suddenly alert.

'Ashley,' replied Mary. 'He said the whole station was in uproar; Briggs was running around barking orders at people – and sometimes, just barking.'

'And that's what worries me,' said Jack, thanking Dorian and walking briskly from his office.

'That Briggs is rusty when it comes to panic?'

'No. I was the original arresting officer. The Gingerbreadman is clearly NCD – why didn't they call us first?'

6

The Gingerbreadman is out

'**Most Dangerous Baked Object**. A hands-down win for the Gingerbreadman, incarcerated at St Cerebellum's secure hospital for the criminally deranged since 1984. Currently serving a four-hundred-year sentence for the murder and torture of his 104 known victims. His crimes easily outrank those of the second-most dangerous baked object, a fruitcake accidentally soaked in weed-killer instead of sherry by Mrs Austen of Pembridge, then served up to members of the Women's Federation during a talk about the remedial benefits of basket-weaving. The final death toll is reputed to have been sixty-two.'

– *The Bumper Book of Berkshire Records*, 2004 edition

Jack insisted they take his new Allegro, and a few minutes later they were heading out of town to the south, and the little village of Arborfield. Mary tuned in the wireless and heard a news bulletin on RadioToadReading informing everyone exactly why they should be panicking, and what form this panicking should take. The wireless broadcasts were uncannily successful, and in a few short hours a state of fear had descended on the town, with normally sensible citizens running around like headless chickens and generally behaving like idiots.

Because of this the roads and streets were spookily empty. Mary and Jack passed almost no one until they arrived at a police roadblock just outside the village, where they parked the car and walked past TV network vans and police mobile incident trucks. They ducked under a *Do Not Cross* barrier and after a few hundred yards were met by such a scene of unrestrained violence and aggression that Mary, who never had the strongest stomach, had to do a rapid about-face and tell Jack she'd see him later.

The St Cerebellum's van that had transported the Gingerbreadman was lying on its side with the rear doors torn off. The bodies of the three victims who died instantly were still there, uncovered, being photographed. Already SOCO had started to record everything at the crime scene. The Gingerbreadman had undertaken the gruesome attack with a ferocity at least equal to or even greater than that displayed the last time he was at liberty. A torn-off arm lay in the street and the body of a man in a suit lay in an awkward position, half out of the passenger seat of the van. It looked as though he had been twisted until he broke.

'Shit,' muttered Jack under his breath. It was worse than he had imagined. The memories of twenty years came back in a flurry of painful, unwanted images.

'Spratt?' said a familiar voice behind him. It was Superintendent Briggs, Jack's immediate superior. A middle-aged man with a well-developed paunch, he had kindly eyes and one of those anachronistic 'sweep-over' hairstyles to disguise the fact he was going bald, but it fooled no one. Although Jack was head of the NCD, Briggs acted as his liaison with the rest of the force and had the power to tell him to drop any case he didn't feel it was worth pursuing. Their relationship usually swung between hot and cold, and Briggs had made it his sworn duty to suspend Jack at least once during any investigation, more for dramatic effect than anything else.

'Good morning, sir – we came as quickly as we could,' responded Jack, noticing that Briggs was with DI Copperfield, a contemporary of Jack's who worked CID at Reading Central.

'We?' asked Briggs, looking around.

'Mary's not too good with bodies, sir – I think she's honking up in the bushes. Good morning, David.'

'Jack,' replied Copperfield cheerily. He was the same age as Jack, but looked younger than his forty-five years. His boyish good looks and absence of grey hair meant he could easily pass for thirty, and frequently did.

'You caught him the last time,' Briggs said to Jack. 'Your experience in this matter might be invaluable.'

'When did he escape?'

'Ninety-seven minutes ago,' replied Copperfield. 'Killed two male nurses and his doctor with his bare hands. The other three orderlies who accompanied him are critical in hospital.'

'Critical?'

'Yes; don't like the food, beds uncomfortable, waiting lists too long – usual crap. Other than that, they're fine.'

This was big. Bigger than anything Jack had handled. The last time the Gingerbreadman was at large Jack was partnered with Friedland Chymes. But ex-DCI Chymes was now gone – retired under accusations of cowardice. This was up to Jack and Jack alone. Or so he thought. He took a deep breath.

'I'm going to need more manpower,' he began, counting off the items on his fingers, 'more than we've ever had on an NCD inquiry. Plus forensic resources, overtime and . . .'

His voice trailed off as he saw Briggs stare at the ground. He knew then why they hadn't called him.

'Jack,' said Briggs slowly, 'this won't be your investigation.'

Jack looked at Briggs, then at Copperfield, who looked away, faintly embarrassed.

'I don't understand.'

'Which part of "not your investigation" don't you understand?' asked Briggs with well-practised acerbic wit. He was learning it at night school.

'The "not your investigation" part. I'm Nursery Crime Division. This is the Gingerbreadman. *My* jurisdiction. The NCD has much experience in these matters.'

'Unarguably,' replied Briggs uncompromisingly, 'which is why I want you to give Copperfield all the help you can.'

'David is leading this?' asked Jack, the incredulity in his voice making the remark a question about ability. Copperfield was a nice guy and a good officer but he couldn't hack this sort of investigation, and Jack knew it. David gave a wan smile. He didn't want to play the political game and liked Jack personally, so wasn't going to make an issue of the lack of confidence. Secretly, he probably agreed with him, but he'd never run a murder investigation before and liked the sound of it – especially the vague possibility of promotion if he was successful.

'If I've anything to ask after I've seen the Gingerbreadman's original arrest report,' said Copperfield with a certain degree of vagueness, 'I'll be sure to get in touch.'

'Perhaps,' said Jack pointedly, 'you should be asking yourself why the Gingerbreadman was being driven around unsecured in a minivan rather than prison transport?'

Copperfield stared at Jack for a moment. Fully aware of his intellectual shortcomings, David compensated by doing everything by the book. Even reading the book he did by the book. Everything was orderly and logical and procedure-based in his world. He understood intuition and wild improbable hunches that turned out to be right, but he never used them – they were the tools he always left in the box during an investigation. Conversely, they were the ones that Jack used most. In the hazily preordained world of the NCD, it was almost obligatory. Even so, Copperfield made a mental note of what Jack said. He was right: the Gingerbreadman was a Category A+++ patient and he hadn't even been handcuffed.

Jack rubbed his brow. Copperfield as the investigating officer was madness even by NCD standards, which were by definition pretty broad.

'He's dangerously insane,' said Jack, 'but there are vague patterns to his behaviour. He usually violently ingratiates himself into someone's house or flat and stays there for as long as he thinks he can. His "hosts" generally don't survive the visitation, although he always makes a point of paying for any food he eats, does the laundry and then wallpapers the front room.'

'Pattern or plain?'

'Pattern – and lined, too. You might like to stake out DIY stores.'

'I'll bear that in mind.'

'He kills because that's what he does best,' said Jack. 'Don't take any chances.'

'We don't plan to. The SAS are on stand-by and armed to the teeth. They'll be called in the moment he's spotted.'

'The use of unnecessary and wholly unreasonable force,' added Briggs, 'has been approved. We're not planning for capture *or* containment.'

There was a pause and Jack stared at Briggs and Copperfield in turn, then at the crime scene, which was, he had to admit, far worse than anything he had seen either inside the NCD or out. Mr Wolff's scalding to death hadn't been pretty, and Wee Willie Winkie's evisceration wasn't exactly Sunday lunch conversation. But three at one go was something quite new even by Gingerbreadman standards. He had an annoying habit of raising the ante every time he drew breath. But Jack *still* wasn't satisfied.

'Sir—'

Briggs shook his head, took him by the arm and steered him towards a quiet spot.

'It's no use, Jack,' he said once out of earshot, 'Copperfield is running the hunt. And it's not just me. The Chief Constable has been on the phone already. With Friedland out of the picture and you busy getting citizens eaten, we need somebody to put Reading back on the detecting map.'

'But the Dumpty case—!'

'Humpty's tumble is past history, Jack. We've all got to think of the future – and with that Red Riding-Hood fiasco still ringing in our ears, you need to be on your best behaviour. Josh Hatchett is just itching to stick the knife in deeper.'

'Okay,' said Jack, 'so I screwed up. The bedroom was dark – how was I meant to know it was the wolf and not Red's gran? Besides, the woodsman's timely intervention saved the day.'

'With no thanks to you,' replied Briggs. 'And strictly speaking you should be on sick leave – have you seen the shrinks for some counselling?'

'All that weird shit goes with the NCD turf – it's business as usual.'

'Maybe to you,' returned Briggs with a sidelong glance to make sure no one could possibly be listening to this insanity, 'but I've got a grandmother and a small girl in traumatic shock. They'll probably sue the pants off us – if they ever come to their senses.'

Briggs lowered his voice.

'Jack, there's no easy way to say this, so I won't try. Your judgement has been called into question over the unconventional use of children as bait in the Scissor-man capture, and answers are already being sought about the Riding-Hood inquiry. The bottom line is that we need to be able to demonstrate that all our departmental heads are fully able to acquit themselves in difficult situations without any unpredictable or detrimental decision-making.'

'You think I might be insane?'

'I *know* you're insane, Jack – it's a question of whether you're *too* insane to run the NCD. It's a directive from on high. You're going to have to take a psychiatric evaluation to ensure you are still able to function properly as head of the NCD.'

'Sir—!' said Jack, knowing it would be almost impossible to get a doctor to say he *was* sane. In conventional policing a streak of madness could get you retired; in the NCD it was almost impossible to function without it. But Briggs was having none of it.

'The answer's still no, Jack. You've been doing a lot of very strange stuff for far too long. I'm worried that it's affecting your health, and judgement. DS Mary can be acting head of the NCD while you take it easy for a bit. Go home – put your feet up.'

'Sir,' replied Jack tersely, 'I should be out hunting for a seven-foot biscuit with a bad attitude – not watching reruns of *Columbo* on the telly.'

Briggs raised an admonishing finger.

'Don't underestimate *Columbo*, Jack – you might be interested to know that it's being used for training at police college, along with *Hawaii Five-O* and *Murder, She Wrote*. And . . . I think you'll find the Gingerbreadman is a *cake*.'

'Biscuit, sir.'

'Cake, but never mind. It's only because the Humpty gig was good PR that we're not seeing the NCD disbanded out of hand. Right now you'll do as you're told.'

There was a pause. Jack stared at the ground, unsure of what to say.

'And if I find you hunting for the Gingerbreadman on your own,' added Briggs, waving the admonishing finger, 'I'll, I'll . . .'

He paused for a moment, trying to figure out whether it was technically possible to suspend someone who was already on sick leave. And it wasn't as though he could be sent anywhere lower than the NCD, anyway.

'. . . I'll not be happy,' he said at last. 'Give Copperfield all he asks for, would you?'

He tipped his hat, mumbled, 'So long, Jack,' and rejoined DI Copperfield, who was directing proceedings from a 'murder procedure' checklist he had fortuitously brought with him.

7
Nursery Crime Division

'**Most Dumped Boyfriend**. It is reliably reported that Arnold Westlake (originally of Basingstoke, UK) has been dumped a grand total of 973 times in the past five years. Despite his being a self-confessed "sweet guy" and "good husband material" with a "fondness for starting a family", Mr Westlake's serial dumpings continue to surprise and confuse him, especially as 734 of those dumpings were from the same woman, a Ms Mary Mary of Reading, Berkshire. When asked to confirm figures, Ms Mary angrily enquired who the other women dumping him were, and added: "No one dumps Arnold but me – it's all over between us."'

– *The Bumper Book of Berkshire Records*, 2004 edition

Jack found Mary and they drove back into Reading. He was silent for most of the journey, trying to think which was worse: being consistently trashed by the press, having a superior who didn't trust his judgement, a prime NCD case allocated away from him or enduring the ignominy of having a psychiatrist ask him pointless questions and then going 'ah-ha' in a quasi-meaningful manner. He explained the news to Mary, who said:

'How about if we do a plot device number twenty-six and *pretend* not to look for him?'

'So you're suggesting we look for him against orders, catch him, cover ourselves with glory, and the by-the-book officers look like idiots?'

Mary nodded enthusiastically.

'Pretty much.'

'No, we're going to follow plot device number thirty-eight.'

Mary narrowed her eyes.

'Which one is that again?'

'We wait until they beg for our assistance, then save the day. For now, we follow orders. After all, do you think we'd get the support Copperfield is getting if it *was* an NCD inquiry?'

Mary thought about the forty or so officers milling around the Gingerbreadman crime scene. The SOCO crew, the incident vehicles, the tracker dogs, the armed response group, the catering facilities. Somehow, she doubted it. The largest quantity of officers on an NCD inquiry could be counted on the fingers of Ashley's hands, and he was a tridactyl – if you didn't count his four thumbs.

They arrived at Reading police station, parked the car in the underground car park and walked towards the elevators. As they approached, the doors opened and Agatha Diesel walked out. Jack groaned inwardly. Not because Agatha was Reading's most aggressive and efficient parking attendant, and not because she happened to be married to Briggs; no, it was because Agatha and Jack had once, many years ago, had something of a fling together and Agatha seemed intent that years, greyness, gravity and current marital status should not be a barrier to their conjoining in a tight knot of adulterous passion.

'Jack!' said Agatha in delighted surprise. 'I haven't seen you for a while – have you been avoiding me?'

'Why ever would I do that?' asked Jack as he walked past and pressed the lift call button repeatedly.

'Because,' she said with something that might once have passed for a coquettish smile, 'you have feelings too – but you're in denial.'

'I could only be living in de Nile if I was in de Egypt.'

'Eh?'

'Never mind.'

'Listen,' said Mary as she hid a smile, 'if you guys want to talk, I can take the stairs—'

'NO! I mean, no, I need to discuss something with you.'

'Well, listen,' said Agatha, moving closer to Jack, who backed away until he was pressed against the lift doors, 'you know you can always rely on me if you get bored.'

'The answer's no, Agatha,' said Jack, 'it was no twenty years ago, it was no yesterday, it's no now and it'll be no tomorrow and for the rest of recorded history. Get it?'

She laughed and tweaked his chin.

'You're such a tease!' she cooed. 'Any time. I'll be waiting. Whenever.'

The doors opened and Jack almost fell inside. Agatha was still waving at him as the lift doors closed.

'I'd get a restraining order on her if she weren't married to Briggs,' said Jack, rubbing his neck.

'Now you know how difficult it is with Arnold.'

'Perhaps we should introduce them to one another.'

'She'd have him for breakfast,' said Mary with a laugh, 'and spit out the bones.'

The lift ascended in silence for a few moments, then stopped. The doors opened.

'Good morning, Inspector,' said a shapely doe-like vision of uniformed loveliness who was waiting to get in the elevator, 'good morning, Sergeant.'

'Hello, Pippa,' replied Jack with a smile, 'how are you settling in?'

'Everyone's being *so* nice to me,' she said, bestowing a radiant smile on both of them. 'The control room here is a simply *wonderful* place to work.'

She got into the elevator and the doors closed.

'People that good looking shouldn't be officers,' said Jack as they walked down the corridor, 'it makes the rest of us look like gorgons – isn't Baker making a play for her?'

'I think it would be safe to say he's in the queue – and it's a long queue. Constable Pepper took her out for a drink, I understand, but I don't know how serious it was.'

They walked along the corridor in silence for a moment.

'You said earlier there was some good news?' said Mary.

'You've been promoted. You're acting head of the NCD while I'm on sick leave awaiting a mental health appraisal.'

'Does this mean I get to sit in your chair?'

'Incorrect response, Mary. I was hoping for something more along the lines of: "They can't do this to you, sir!"'

'Only joking. They can't do this to you, sir.'

'They just have. Briggs thinks I'm too disturbed to head up the NCD.'

'He should be worried about you not being disturbed *enough*.'

'Thanks for that – I think,' replied Jack doubtfully.

'Tell me,' said Mary slowly, 'despite your sick-leaveness, will I be able to consult you freely on matters regarding nursery crime at any time of the day or night and invite you along to enquiries in the capacity of observer or expert witness?'

Jack smiled as they stopped outside the office.

'I'm counting on it.'

When Mary first arrived at the Nursery Crime Division she was astonished at just how small the offices were. Barely room for a desk among the filing cabinets and stacks of papers, let alone three chairs. The walls were adorned by framed newspaper cuttings, a map of Reading and several pinboards but without the needless extravagance of a window. The filing cabinets were so full the metal bulged, and any available space that couldn't be more usefully employed for other purposes – such as standing or sitting – was stacked high with reports, notes and files. Case histories were still on card index, something that excited Ashley's innate filing instincts no end, but was generally a source of embarrassment to everyone else. There was another room next door which the cleaners had rejected on the grounds of 'too small, even for us' and this was also full of unfiled papers, a chair, a small desk and a coffee machine. They had computers and access to e-mail and the PNC, but the NCD database seemed to have been forgotten in the rush to centralise all police records. It didn't really matter as Berkshire was the only county with a Nursery Crime Division – travel beyond the county boundaries placed all Persons of Dubious Reality outside the protection of the law, so few troubled to do so.

It was no surprise to anyone that with Gretel and Baker on an inquiry the division spilled out into the corridor, even with Ashley working from his usual position stuck to the ceiling. Mary had got used to the size and chaotic nature of the office as soon as she figured out Jack's 'free-style' approach to filing, and Jack had been right about another thing: after a few months she could barely detect the smell of boiled cabbage that wafted in from the canteen next door.

Luckily, Gretel and Baker were engaged on other duties, and Ashley was the only incumbent, which made it feel positively roomy – sort of.

'Good morning, Ash,' said Jack.

'It is indeed,' replied the small alien with a joyous ripple of blue from within his semi-transparent body. 'I've got some good news for you both.'

'Briggs just called to change his mind about the Gingerbread inquiry?'

'No – much better. I've finally managed to complete my beer mat collection. I've got them all. *Every single one.*'

'That's . . . wonderful news,' said Jack in an absent sort of way.

Ashley was best humoured and, since he didn't really get sarcasm, never took offence. 'Any messages?'

'Of course. You've got one from the Force Medical Officer requesting that you attend a hearing with an independent psychiatric evaluator tomorrow, then another, *also* from the FMO, informing you that you shouldn't be at work to receive these messages, and suggesting you go home and watch a few reruns of *Kojak*.'

'Anything else?'

'No,' replied Ashley, 'but I think the FMO is wrong.'

'It's very good of you to say so, Ash.'

'Not at all. *Kojak* is entirely the wrong show to be watching for relaxation. We watched your TV a lot back home on Rambosia and *Kojak* was never our thing.'

'No?' replied Jack without humour.

'No; all that lollipop and "who loves ya, baby" – and the singing career? What was *that* all about? No, we always preferred Jim Rockford – especially Noah Beery, who played his father. I suggest you watch *The Rockford Files*.'

'You and Briggs should have a chat,' said Jack, glaring at the small alien. 'He thought I should be watching *Columbo*.'

'That's good too,' mused Ashley. 'A bit unusual for a whodunit since we always knew in the first five minutes who *had* done it; perhaps it should be called a howcolumbofindsoutwhodunit—'

'What about my other messages?' interrupted Jack before Ashley gave him a rundown of every single US cop drama of the seventies, a subject on which he was something of an expert.

'Nothing else. These are all for Mary.' He passed a large stack of yellow message slips to her and added: 'They're from Arnold.'

'Blast,' murmured Mary. She had been trying to dump Arnold for several years now but without success, despite trying almost everything from feigned death to pretending she had the bubonic plague, for which she was grateful to Baker for being able to furnish a complete list of symptoms. 'I thought I had it once,' Baker had said, mildly disappointed.

'Do you want me to speak to him again?' asked Jack.

'No thanks,' replied Mary, recalling the mess he had made of it the last time.

'Are we on the Gingerbreadman hunt?' asked Ashley.

'No.'

'Are we going to do a plot device number 11010?'

'No.'

'Would you like to see my beer mat collection?' asked Ashley, in a state of some excitement. 'It might cheer you up.'

'You wouldn't get them all in here, would you?' asked Jack, looking around at the diminutive offices.

'On the contrary,' replied Ashley, blinking laterally and producing a shoebox from under the table, 'they're in here.'

'How many do you have?' asked Jack, suddenly suspicious.

'100100001.'

'One hundred and forty-five?'

'Yes; every single one different – except an Arkley's Bitter 2003 Drink-Driving Warning special of which I have two.'

'You tell him,' said Jack wearily.

The phone rang and he picked it up.

'Spratt, NCD.'

He listened for a moment and then sat back and twiddled absently with his tie.

'Yes, there is some good news, Mrs Dish. Your daughter has turned up in Gretna Green . . . Gretna, yes, as in *Green*. Are you sitting down? Good. Well, she's married to Wallace Spoon.' Jack winced and held the receiver a little farther from his ear before continuing: 'No, there are no grounds for criminal proceedings unless you can prove to us that she was forced into marriage, which she *personally* told me she wasn't . . . No, Mrs Dish, I'm afraid not. The police have stopped "showing people a lesson" for quite some time now . . . This isn't a police matter, Mrs Dish. Yes, I'm sure the cow will be over the moon. Good day, Mrs Dish.'

He put the phone down and shook his head sadly.

'*How many?*' asked Ashley in a shocked tone.

'Perhaps more,' explained Mary apologetically, 'probably *tens* of thousands.'

Ashley opened his eyes so wide you could see the greens.

'But that could take years!'

Jack passed Mary the address that Tarquin had scribbled out for him.

'Check this out. See if it's for real, and who might be leasing the unit if it is.'

The phone rang again.

'Spratt, NCD.'

'It's for you, Mary.' He put his hand over the mouthpiece. 'I think it's Arnold.'

'Do you want me to speak to him?' asked Ashley.

'Would you? Tell him *anything.*'

'Anything?'

'Anything.'

Ash took the phone from Jack and said:

'Hello, Arnold, PC Ashley here. Mary can't have a date with you because she's going out with me. Yes, with me. No, we're going dancing that evening. She didn't want to tell you because she thought it might hurt your feelings. Yes, I am the weird alien chappie and no, this isn't some kind of sick joke – she'll confirm it herself. Mary?'

He held the receiver up and Mary yelled, 'Yes, it's true!'

'Sorry about that, Arnold,' continued Ashley. 'No, that's not true at all. It must have been someone else doing the abductions. And while we're on the subject, a saucer is *entirely* the wrong shape for interstellar travel – they were probably hub caps or something. Good day.'

And he put the phone down.

'How was that?'

'Very . . . straightforward.'

'Best way. I was kidding about the dancing, by the way – I dance very badly on account of my liquid-filled physiology; shake me up and I tend to hallucinate – driving over a cattle grid at speed has the same effect. But dinner would be pleasant. We'll arrange something, right?'

'Ri-ight,' replied Mary, unsure of whether he was kidding or not. She had never really known Ash to make a joke, so suspected not.

The phone rang again. It was Briggs, wanting to know what Jack was doing answering the phones at the NCD when he was on sick leave. Jack replied that he'd popped in to collect his things, and promised to be out of the station in ten minutes.

'Knowing Briggs he might come down here to check,' observed Mary.

'Right,' said Jack reluctantly, fidgeting and looking for some papers to shuffle or something.

'Ash and I can look after the office. If Copperfield calls with any questions over the psycho-cake I'll get him to call your mobile.'

'O-kay,' said Jack, 'we'll check out Tarquin's porridge contact first thing tomorrow – and just so there's no confusion, the Gingerbreadman's a biscuit.'

'Cake.'

'Biscuit.'

'A cake goes hard when it goes stale,' explained Jack as he got up, 'and a biscuit goes soft. That's the difference. He's pliable, so he's a biscuit – and I don't want to hear anything more about it.'

There was a pause as Ashley and Mary considered the feasibility of Jack's cake/biscuit definition.

'But it's not all bad,' Jack added from the door, 'at least the Gingerbreadman gives the papers something to write about other than the Riding-Hood debacle. So long.'

And he left the two of them staring at one another. Mary was thinking about how she'd never even *considered* going on a date with Ashley, and Ashley was thinking about how he'd been trying to pluck up enough courage for weeks.

8

Noisy neighbours

'**Most Noise Abatement Orders Served**. Heavy-metal-loving Mr and Mrs Scroggins and their seventeen hyperactively argumentative children have often been referred to as "the noisiest group of sentient beings yet discovered by man" and were moved to a special pro-noise council estate on the Heathrow flight path, until neighbours complained that they couldn't hear the jetliners any more. Their collective 179 noise abatement orders pale into insignificance, however, when compared to Mr and Mrs Punch of Berkshire, who have notched up 326 orders in the past forty-five years and also hold the record for "loudest argument in a restaurant" and the "non-stop bicker", which lasted for three hours and twenty-eight minutes at a sustained level of 43.2 decibels.'

– *The Bumper Book of Berkshire Records*, 2004 edition

Jack was right: the evening editions of *The Mole*, *The Toad* and *The Owl* covered little else but the Gingerbreadman's dramatic escape, along with lurid accounts of what he got up to the last time he was free. The scaremongering that had begun on the radio was thus reinforced, and by nightfall panic buying had occasioned the systematic emptying of every food store and petrol station in town, causing several shopkeepers to comment in private that they wished a dangerous homicidal maniac would escape every week.

Jack pulled up outside his house in the north of the town, and locked the Allegro. His neighbour Mrs Sittkomm was staring inquisitively over the fence as she pretended to take the washing in. But she wasn't looking at Jack, she was looking *beyond* him to the house attached to Jack's on the other side.

'There goes the neighbourhood,' she muttered with barely concealed venom.

Jack followed her look to where a removal truck was disgorging a procession of carefully taped cardboard boxes.

'Ah!' said Jack. 'Our new neighbours. Any idea who they are?'

Mrs Sittkomm stared at him and then ran through the gamut of severe English disapproval. She started with a slow shake of the head, went on to raised eyebrows and a glare, then ended with an audible 'tut'. She beckoned him closer and hissed under her breath: 'Nurseries!'

'Which ones?' asked Jack, more through professional interest than anything else.

'You'll see,' said Mrs Sittkomm scornfully. 'They've no right to be living with decent *real* people. They'll bring house prices down, you see if they don't.'

'Bears?' asked Jack curiously.

'Mercifully not,' replied Mrs Sittkomm with a snort. 'I had a bear as a lodger once; took six months to get the smell of porridge out of the spare room – and the honey out of the carpet . . .'

She didn't finish her sentence and just signalled that her contempt was total by rolling her eyes, shrugging and looking to heaven all at once, a curious manoeuvre that reminded Jack of a stage contortionist he had once seen.

Jack left Mrs Sittkomm to her twisted moral dilemma, walked along the street to his new neighbour's house and rang the doorbell.

A florid-looking woman in a flower-pattern dress answered the door. She had large exaggerated features, unblinking eyes and a shiny, almost *varnished* complexion. She also had several bruises on her face and one arm in a sling.

'Mrs Punch . . . ?' said Jack, recognising her immediately. She and her husband were well known to him and the NCD. Although their constant fights were no one's business but their own, Jack was always concerned that they *might* throw the baby downstairs, something they had been threatening for over thirty years, but fortunately they had not yet done so.

'Inspector!' screeched Judy, staring at Jack as though he were something you might tread on in the local park. 'What the bloody hell do you want?'

'I'm not here on business, Mrs Punch. I live next door – and keep your voice down; I'm only a yard away.'

'Nuts to *that*!' she screamed so loudly that several pieces of saliva exploded from her mouth with such force that Jack had to step aside to let them pass. '*Lazy-bastard-of-a-husband!*' she shouted over her shoulder into the house. She waited with extreme patience for perhaps a half-second for him to appear, and when he didn't she screamed, '*HUS-BAAAAND!*' so loudly that Jack felt his ears pop and one of the flower pots in the garden shattered. Presently, and with the slow, almost reptilian movement of the worst kind of loafer, Mr Punch appeared dressed in his traditional red tunic and hat. His features were more exaggerated than his wife's, his complexion more florid, shinier and *uglier*. He had a large hooked nose that curved down to almost touch his upwardly hooked chin, and his long thin mouth was curled into a permanent leer. He wore a small pointed hat and had heaped upon his back a hump that was as pointed as his chin, nose *and* hat. He also had several bruises on his face, and one eye was puffy and black. He had an infant clasped to his chest in a typical crossed-arms Punch pose and was rocking the baby back and forth in an aggressive manner. Jack stood and stared at Punch and Judy, trying to figure out which one he disliked least – it was a tricky contest.

'Bloody hell!' said Punch in an annoying high-pitched voice. He opened his glassy eyes wide in shock and grinned even more broadly to reveal two long rows of perfectly varnished teeth. 'The pig-bastard baby-snatcher! What the ****ing hell do you want?'

'I live next door,' said Jack, 'and keep your voice down. If I *ever* hear you swear without asterisk substitution, I'll arrest you for offensive and threatening language.'

'Like I g*ve a shit,' screamed Mr Punch, tossing the sleeping baby into a pram and picking up a handy baseball bat. Jack stood his ground.

'Drop the bat or you're under arrest.'

'It's not for you!' screeched Mr Punch. 'It's for my lazy scumbag of a wife. Where's my dinner, trout-lips?'

Judy expertly ducked the baseball bat that quickly followed. Mr Punch, thrown off balance by her quick manoeuvre, left his flank unguarded, an opportunity quickly grasped by Judy, who thumped him painfully in his already badly bruised eye. Mr Punch gave a scream of pain but Judy hadn't finished. She grabbed his arm, twisted it around so hard he had to drop the bat, which fell with a clatter to the floor, then stamped on his knee from the side. He collapsed in a groaning heap near the still-sleeping baby.

'I'll get your bloody dinner when I bloody feel like it!' she screamed, and trod on his hand as she stepped over him.

'Are you okay?' asked Jack.

'Never better!' he gasped, his painted grin not for one second leaving his face. 'Terrific lass, Judy. Very . . . *spirited*.'

'Very,' said Jack, thinking that if Judy hadn't ducked the baseball bat she would be unconscious, or worse. Still, this was what they did. What they had *always* done. For over three hundred years they had beaten the living blue blazes out of one another for the joyous edification of the masses. Of course, what with the changing attitudes to marriage, women and respect for the law, Punch couldn't actually *kill* anyone any more but the violent slapstick remained. He had for centuries been a source of light-hearted entertainment, but his star was now low on the horizon and he was seen more as a misogynistic social pariah than an icon of anti-establishment dissent – especially in any neighbourhood in which he lived. It wasn't his fault the world had moved on; today's Punch was a fly in amber, a fossilised pop-culture relic from a bygone era.

'I'm too old for this endless fighting crap,' he said mournfully, wincing as he struggled to his feet. 'Want to come in for a beer? We could chat about the good old days – do you still do your "Jack Sprat/eat no fat" routine?'

Jack's heart nearly bounced out of his chest. He'd hidden it for so long that he'd almost forgotten that he was *himself* a PDR – a Person of Dubious Reality.

'I don't know what you mean,' he said defensively. 'I'm as real as the next man. Besides, *that* Jack Sprat is spelt with one "T" – I have two.'

'Oh, *right*,' said Mr Punch with a smirk. 'In denial, are we? Got anything against PDRs?'

'No,' said Jack hurriedly, 'some of my best friends are PDRs. But I'm not and never have been – okay?'

'Okay, okay,' said Punch winking, 'your secret's safe with me.'

'There's no secret. I don't know what you mean, really I don't,' responded Jack, complaining perhaps a little too forcefully. 'Maybe another time for the beer – and keep the fighting down, yes?'

'I'll try,' said Mr Punch with all the conviction of a weak-willed recovering alcoholic being offered a shot of Jack Daniel's, 'but you know how it is.'

'Look what I've just found,' said Judy, returning to the door as though nothing had happened and holding a broken dinner plate. 'It's the first piece of crockery I ever threw at you. Look, I wrote the date on the back.'

They smiled and then hugged, gingerly trying to avoid the bruised areas on each other's bodies.

'Fish pie, sweetheart?' said Judy.

'Sounds perfect, my cherub.'

And she picked up the baby and walked back inside the house.

'Well then,' said Jack, still firmly rattled by Punch's comments on his PDR-ness. If Punch knew, how many others? His first wife knew because she'd been one too – the 'wife who could eat no lean' – but his second wife Madeleine had no idea, which on reflection was a big mistake. You can't and shouldn't keep those sorts of secrets from loved ones.

'So,' he added, swallowing a rising feeling of panic, 'enjoy your – um – evening.'

'Th-thank you,' said Punch, gently closing the front door behind him. Jack walked back down the garden path to the sound of breaking crockery and a scream from Judy that transformed midwail into a lascivious giggle.

Jack took a deep breath to calm himself, opened his own kitchen door and walked in.

'Honey,' he said, 'I'm home!'

'Wotcha, Dad,' said Ben, his nose firmly wedged into a copy of *Conspiracy Theorist* magazine, something in which he had a particular interest. He had been overwhelmed when he learned that his dad had an alien working for him, but underwhelmed when he actually met him. Instead of talking about faster-than-light travel and wormholes, Ash had droned on at length about seventies Datsun motorcars, collectible plates and who he thought was the best Cartwright in *Bonanza*.

'Hi, Ben,' replied Jack. 'Yeti populations holding steady?'

'Pretty much. Hear about the explosion up at Obscurity?'

'Let me guess,' said Jack, leaning backwards to avoid being struck by a spoon that little Stevie had hurled across the room, 'a governmental cover-up?'

However bad it got at the NCD, and no matter how many times

Briggs suspended him, Jack's home life more than compensated for it. His wife of five years was Madeleine, and they had each brought two children to the home: Jack's Pandora and Ben, and Madeleine's Jerome and Megan. To cement the union still further they'd also had Stevie, who was now eighteen months.

'This spoon-hurling is getting stronger and more accurate,' said Jack, selecting another from the draining board and sitting down at the table. Stevie gave a broad grin, took the new spoon and stared at it thoughtfully for a moment.

'Yes indeed,' replied Madeleine, who was in the process of making a pot of tea, 'the Olympic ladle-flinging team want to train him up for the 2020 Olympics.'

Jack smiled and looked at Megan, who was busy colouring at the other end of the table.

'What's that, princess?'

'It's the Blue Baboon.'

'I never knew the Blue Baboon was green.'

'Can't find the right crayon,' she said, and carried on colouring.

Madeleine and Jack were both on the second time round, marriage-wise. Unlike Jack, who was a widower, Madeleine's ex-husband Neville just turned out to be something of a dud. He had an eye for the ladies, too — a habit that Madeleine couldn't overlook during their marriage, much to the surprise of her ex-husband, who thought his roguish charm would have her forgiving anything. It didn't.

Jack loved Madeleine dearly, and he suddenly felt guilty that he'd not told her about his PDR-ness. But he would, right now — it was the right and proper thing to do.

He got up, kissed her and said with an emboldened heart:

'There's something I have to tell you.'

'Yes?'

'It's . . . that . . . I'm . . . Punch and Judy have moved in next door,' said Jack, losing his nerve entirely.

'I know. It should be quite a show,' replied Madeleine. 'I've had the residents' committee around already. They've opened a complaint book and want us to log every single problem we have with them.'

'I hope they've got a big book and several gallons of ink,' said Jack, giving up on confessions for the foreseeable future and fetching the milk from the fridge, 'but I don't think it will do much good. The pair of them have racked up so many Noise Abatement Orders they could wallpaper the toilet with them — and if the rumours are correct, have done so.'

'What do we do?' asked Madeleine. 'You know I can't stand all that residents' association curtain-twitching, protect-house-prices-at-all-costs stuff.'

Jack shrugged.

'Nothing, for the moment. Keep an eye out, and if you hear them threatening to throw the baby downstairs again, let me know and we'll get the social services involved. They won't do anything, but it might just calm them down a bit.'

'Fair enough. You know they've got a pet crocodile in the back garden?'

'It figures. There'll be a string of sausages, a beadle, a hangman and a dog named Toby involved somewhere, too.'

'How do you know?'

'It's a Nursery Crime thing. Punch and Judy are . . . PDRs.'

'I thought they might be,' replied Madeleine thoughtfully.

'You did?' asked Jack, suddenly worried. 'How? How did you know? What . . . was it something they said? The way they walked? What?'

'It was probably,' said Madeleine, giving him a 'how dopey do you think I am?' look, 'something to do with their heads being made of painted papier mâché.'

'Keen sense of observation you have there, pumpkin.'

'But why the ceaseless violence?'

'PDRs just can't help themselves. Ever have a song going round in your head all day and you can't shake it? Then find yourself humming it?'

'Yes.'

'It's the same with Punch and Judy and any other nursery character, but instead of a song it's *actions*. Look at it as a form of obsessive-compulsive disorder or a self-fulfilling prophecy. The Punches have toned down their act a lot since the seventeenth century – infanticide, wife-beating and multiple murder aren't generally considered entertainment these days.'

'Are *all* forms of compulsive behaviour a sign of PDR-ness?' she asked slowly.

'No, no, of course not,' replied Jack hurriedly, thinking about his own obsessional hatred of fat, 'there have to be several other factors as well.'

Stevie gurgled at him from his high chair and Jack, glad of the distraction, leaned over and affectionately tweaked his ear.

'Hi, Dad,' said Pandora as she walked into the kitchen with her fiancé, the Titan Prometheus. Having a daughter engaged to a four-thousand-year-old myth could be stressful at times, but Jack was determined not to be a flustery old hen of a father – and the union was improving her Greek no end. They were getting married in a month's time and there were still a lot of details to be ironed out.

'Do you think the record of the wedding should be a video, a tapestry, depictions on a Grecian urn or a twenty-eight-foot-long marble bas-relief?'

'I have a friend who can do urns at a discount,' added Prometheus helpfully. The budget for the wedding had long since spiralled out of control since Bacchus had taken over the reception arrangements.

'An urn, I guess,' conceded Jack.

'Oh, goody!' cried Pandora happily. 'I always saw my wedding recorded in profile. Now Dad, remember what you promised about not doing a plot device number fifty-two on the day of my wedding?'

'There's only the annual "Tortoise v. Hare" race on that weekend and there's never any trouble at that, Sweetpea,' he said, 'so there'll be no conclusion of a case near your wedding that results in an over-dramatic dash to the church.'

'Great!' said Pandora, and she and Prometheus walked out, talking about how they could stop Artemis and Aphrodite from squabbling, as they invariably did.

'Perhaps we should just let them fight in some mud and pretend it's part of the entertainments?' suggested Prometheus.

The large family and the expense of a wedding was a severe drain on Jack's salary, despite Bacchus's concession that they could drop Orpheus and go with a Santana tribute band instead. Madeleine had a limited income from her photography but insisted on concentrating on high-end limited-print-run photographic books. Good food for the soul, but famine for the wallet.

'How are things at work?' she asked, handing Stevie another spoon.

'Not . . . terrific,' replied Jack with a dash of understatement, stirring some sugar into his tea.

'I'm surprised you're back so early, what with Johnny Cake on the loose.'

'I'm . . . not on that case – and he's a biscuit.'

Madeleine stared at him quizzically and said:

'Listen, I don't know poo about police procedures, but even I know the Gingerbreadman is NCD.'

Jack helped himself to a ginger nut, smelled it, made a face and put it back in the biscuit barrel.

'Briggs gave it to . . . Copperfield.'

'*David?*' she echoed in surprise. 'He's a sweet guy but he couldn't find an egg in a hen house.'

Jack shrugged.

'Like it or not, there it is. Briggs thinks I'm overdoing it and that the Riding-Hood incident was beyond what any officer should have to face . . . he's made Mary acting head while I'm on sick leave.'

'Oh, sweetheart!' she said, giving him an extra-tight hug. 'I'm sorry to hear that. But don't worry, Briggs usually suspends you at least once during any investigation.'

'And that's what worries me,' responded Jack, returning her hug and kissing her tenderly on the forehead, 'I'm not on an investigation. And I won't be until I've passed some sort of mental review board.'

'Yikes. Being sane might render you almost useless at the NCD.'

'I know that. But you didn't have to say it.'

A spoon ricocheted off the back of Jack's head and hit a plant pot on the window sill.

'Was that you, monster?'

Stevie opened his eyes wide and shrieked with laughter.

Madeleine smiled, untangled herself from the embrace and stacked the tea things.

'So aside from losing a prime case that is clearly yours, being knocked from the top job at the division and the prospect of having to convince a complete stranger that you're not a drooling lunatic, how *else* was your day?'

'Peachy. I bought an Allegro Sports Equipe. Do you want to see it?'

'Maybe later.' She handed him a stack of plates to put in the dishwasher. 'Would you have a word with Jerome? I heard his pet sniggering to itself again this morning.'

Jerome was eight, and he wanted to be a vet. To get some practice he had taken to bringing strays home with him. First it was fleas with kittens attached, then it was puppies with fleas attached,

then it was fleas with fleas attached. All this could be vaguely toler-
ated until he brought something home that deftly escaped into the
void within the interior walls, and no one had seen it since.

Jack walked into the living room and bent down to listen at the
skirting. There was a sound a bit like someone blowing a raspberry.
He frowned, got up and walked into the hall. He opened the door
to the cupboard under the stairs and heard a faint rustling. He
quietly turned on the light and peered into the musty gloom.

'He doesn't mean any harm,' said a voice behind him. It was
Jerome, his face a picture of angelic innocence.

'You know your mother wants it out, my lad.'

'I asked him to go into the garden shed but he said his rheuma-
tism was troubling him again.'

'It can speak English?'

'And Italian, but his German is a bit rusty.'

Jack looked around the small cupboard and chanced upon a little
pile of glittery objects.

'What are my spare keys doing in here?' he asked, sorting through
the heap of shiny items. He also found a pair of cufflinks that had
been missing for a few days, a brooch, a couple of coins and the
Waterman pen that he'd thought he'd lost at work.

Jerome winced.

'He likes to collect shiny things. I try to get them back before
you notice. He must have been around the house last night.'

Jack started to rummage some more. There was a rustle and
something small and misshapen popped its head out of a cardboard
box, stared at Jack for a moment and then vanished through a hole
that had been gnawed in the plasterboard. Jack backed out of the
cupboard as fast as he could.

'Did you see it?' asked Jerome after Jack had not spoken for
some moments.

'Ye-es,' said Jack slowly, unsure of what he had seen but not liking it one bit. The creature was an ugly little monkey-like brute with hair that made it look like a black pig with psoriasis. What was worse was that it had a chillingly human-like face, and it had given Jack an impish grin and a wink before vanishing.

'Jerome?'

'Yes, Jack?'

'What *was* that?'

'His name's Caliban, and he's my friend.'

'Well, you can tell him from me he's got to live somewhere else.'

'But—'

'No buts. He's got to go.'

Jack left Jerome in the cupboard and rejoined Madeleine.

'The brooch you thought you'd lost,' he said, placing the jewellery on the table.

'Where was it?'

'Jerome's pet is a bit of a magpie. Have you seen it?'

'No.'

'It's a bit . . . odd. If anything else goes missing you'll probably find it in the cupboard under the stairs.'

He thought for a moment.

'Do we have to go out tonight? I'm a bit pooped.'

'I'd like you to accompany me,' she replied with a smile, 'but I can go on my own and flirt outrageously and in a totally undignified manner with young single men of a morally casual demeanour.'

'You know, I don't feel quite so pooped any more.'

'Good. We should be out of the door by seven-thirty.'

9

The Deja-Vu

'**Most Unreadable Modern Author**. Among all the pseudo-intellectual rubbish that hits the literary world every year, few authors can hope to compete in terms of quasi-highbrow unreadability than the accepted master in the field, Otis ChufftY. With unread copies of his books gracing every bookshelf in the fashionable areas of London, ChufftY's prodigious output in terms of pointless long-winded claptrap has few equals, and brings forth gasps of admiration from his competitors. Even after several million book sales and frequent appearances on late-night artsy-fartsy chat shows, ChufftY's work remains as fashionably unreadable as ever. "It's the bipolarity of human sufferance," Mr ChufftY explained when asked the secret of his success, "and the forbearance of wisdom in the light of the ultimate ignorance of nothing."'
– *The Bumper Book of Berkshire Records*, 2004 edition

'Remind me what we're doing here,' said Jack. 'You're a photographer, not an author.'

'The Armitage Shanks Literary Awards are sponsored by both the Quangle-Wangle and my publishers, the Crumpetty-Tree Press,' she replied as they queued up outside the Deja-Vu Hotel with an assortment of other guests, 'and I'm married to DCI Jack Spratt who quite apart from being tall and ruggedly handsome also happens to be the officer who cracked the Humpty case.'

They shuffled forward a few steps.

'I get it,' said Jack, sliding his hand around her waist, 'I'm your trophy husband and you're showing me off.'

'In one,' replied Madeleine, pushing his hand lower so it met the smooth curve of her bottom, 'and Crumpetty-Tree look on me favourably when I drag you along as it makes the event seem vaguely important and not a collection of pseudo-intellectual farts patting each other on the back.'

'I always suspected that. Are you going to raffle me at the end of the evening?'

She laughed.

'Only if I can buy all the tickets. Now listen: try not to be rude to the writers this year.'

'As if I would!'

The previous year's event had not been without incident. Jack didn't much care for what he called 'The Modern Novel' and had told the previous year's winner precisely that. It hadn't gone down very well.

The Deja-Vu Hotel was a popular venue in Reading for award ceremonies. It was big enough to service a good-sized crowd, had excellent catering facilities and coupled a congenial atmosphere with a fine opportunity for a few daft jokes.

'Have you ever been to the Deja-Vu before?' asked Madeleine as they entered the main doors. Jack looked around the entrance lobby.

'I don't think so,' he answered, 'but it does look sort of familiar.'

They joined the queue at the entrance to the ballroom. A liveried footman was reading the invitations and announcing the guests in a loud voice.

'Ladies and gentlemen, Lord Spooncurdle!' he boomed, giving an over-obsequious bow to Reading's most visible nobleman, who walked solemnly down the stairs, took a glass of champagne from a waiter and shook hands with someone he thought he knew, but didn't.

The queue shuffled forward.

'James Wheat-Reed Esq. and his niece Roberta – he says.'

James and his 'niece' smiled and descended the stairs. The footman continued introducing the guests in a respectful tone of voice.

'Mr and Mrs Croft and their fat daughter Erica.'

'The Dong – with his celebrated luminous nose.'

'Mr and Mrs Boore – by name, by nature.'

Finally it was Jack and Madeleine's turn. The footman read their invitation, looked them up and down in a critical manner, sighed and said:

'Inspector and Mrs Jack Spratt.'

They walked down the staircase to the ballroom as the band struck up a tune that they thought they recognised but couldn't quite place. A vaguely familiar waiter gave them a glass of champagne each and Madeleine looked around for anyone she knew. Jack followed her closely. He didn't really enjoy this sort of function but anything that made people remember Madeleine, he thought, had to be good for her exhibitions. Besides, there weren't many people he didn't know in Reading society. He had interviewed most of them at one time or another, and arrested at least a half-dozen.

'Hello, Marcus!'

'Madeleine, *dahling*!'

'Jack, this is Marcus Sphincter, he's one of the writers shortlisted for the prize this year.'

'Congratulations,' said Jack, extending a hand.

'Thank you, thank you, *thank you* – most kind.'

'So what's the title of this book you've written?'

'The terms "title", "book" and "written" are *so* passé and 2004,' announced Marcus airily, using his fingers in that annoying way that people do to signify quotation marks.

'It *is* 2004,' pointed out Jack.

'So *early* 2004,' said Marcus, hastily correcting himself. 'Anyone can "write" a "book". To raise my chosen art form to a higher plane I prefer to use the terms "designation", "codex" and "composed".'

'Okay,' said Jack, 'what's the appellative of the tome you've created?'

'The what?'

'Hadn't you heard?' asked Jack, hiding a smile and using that annoying finger-quotes thing back at Marcus, '"codex", "composed" and "designation" are out already; they were just too, too early evening.'

'They were?' asked Marcus, genuinely concerned.

'Your book, Marcus,' interrupted Madeleine as she playfully pinched Jack on the bum, 'what's it called?'

'I call it . . . *The Realms of the Leviathan*.'

'Ah,' murmured Jack, 'what's it about – a herd of elephants?'

Marcus laughed loudly. Jack joined him, and so did Madeleine who wasn't going to be a bad sport.

'Elephants? Good lord, no,' replied Marcus, adjusting his glasses. 'The Leviathan in my novel is the colossal and destructive force of human ambition and how it can destroy those it loves in its futile quest for fulfilment, seen through the eyes of a woman in London in the mid-eighties as her husband loses control of himself to own and want more. It asks the fundamental question: "*to be or to want?*" – something I consider to be the "materialistic" Hamlet's soliloquy. Ha-ha-ha.'

'Ha-ha-ha,' said Jack, but thinking: 'Clot.' 'Is it selling?'

'Good Lord, no!' replied Marcus in a shocked tone. 'Selling more than even a few copies would render it . . . *popular*. And that would be death knell for any serious *auteur, n'est-ce pas*? Ha-ha-ha.'

'Ha-ha-ha,' said Jack, but thinking: 'Even *bigger* clot.'

'But it's been short-listed for twenty-nine major awards,' continued Marcus. 'I'll send you a signed copy if you have a tenner on you.'

'If I gave you twenty you could write me a sequel, too.'

Madeleine pulled Jack away and told him to behave himself, while at the same time trying to stop herself having a fit of giggles.

'God, I love you,' she whispered in his ear, 'but *please* stop messing around and behave yourself!'

'Spratt!' boomed Lord Spooncurdle, bored with talking to writers and agents and not recognising anyone else.

'Hello, sir,' said Jack brightly. 'You remember my wife Madeleine?'

'Of course, of course,' he replied genially, offering his hand to Madeleine. 'Your husband did a splendid job on that Humpty lark. Never did trust Spongg, y'know; eyes too close together. Reminded me of a governess who ran off with the handsome young silver and half the family's boot boy.'

Madeleine excused herself with a whispered entreaty for Jack *not* to talk about his NCD work as it usually had a confusing effect on people, and went off to mingle.

'Been here before, Spratt?' asked Spooncurdle, waving a hand at the inside of the Deja-Vu. 'I'm sure I've seen that head waiter, but I'm damned if I know where. I say, old stick, do us a favour and ask him if he has a lion tattooed on his left buttock.'

'He hasn't,' replied Jack, humouring him, 'I asked earlier.'

'Did you, by George? Must have been someone else. I must say, I never knew you were a member of the Most Worshipful Company of Cheese-makers.'

'I'm not, sir. This is the Armitage Shanks Literary Awards.'

'A literary award for cheese-making? That doesn't sound very likely.'

'There's no cheese-making here, sir – I think you're confusing the event.'

'Nonsense, old boy,' said Spooncurdle amiably, having never know-ingly been mistaken once in all his sixty-seven years. 'I say,' he added, changing the subject completely and leaning closer, 'sorry to hear about that Riding-Hood debacle. Don't let it get you down, eh? We all drop a serious clanger sooner or later.'

'You're too kind,' replied Jack, wondering whether this was a good time to point out that Spooncurdle had himself 'dropped a clanger' on numerous occasions – and that shooting a grouse beater *was* illegal, despite the good lord's insistence that it wasn't, or shouldn't be.

Behind them the footman boomed out:

'Ladies and gentlemen, Admiral Robert Shaftoe. Never lost a ship, a man, or in retreat, a second.'

'Bobby a cheese-maker?' said Spooncurdle suddenly. 'How extraordinary. I must go and speak to him. You will excuse me?'

'Of course.'

Spooncurdle left Jack standing on his own near the bar. He ordered a drink but was not alone for long.

'Hello, Jack.'

A small man in his late forties and dressed in a black collarless shirt had appeared next to him. He was accompanied by a thin, gawky woman dressed in flamboyant mix-and-match clothes, a necklace of large orange beads and a huge pair of spectacles with matching frames.

'Hello, Neville,' said Jack coldly. He never felt easy speaking to Madeleine's first husband. He was, after all, supporting this man's children and loved them as he did his own, and Neville's continuing efforts to ingratiate himself with Madeleine and the children would have been acceptable – if he didn't try to do it at Jack's expense.

'This is Virginia Kreeper,' said Neville, introducing the thin woman to Jack. She nodded and stared at Jack with ill-disguised malevolence, as though Neville had said some disparaging things about him prior to their meeting.

'Hello, Virginia,' Jack replied pleasantly, and made a point of starting a conversation with her rather than Neville, 'what do you do?'

'I'm a counsellor,' she replied in a thin nasal voice.

'Really?' returned Jack. 'Reading council?'

'No, *counsellor*. I offer help to people who are suffering stress.'

'What sort of stress?' asked Jack suspiciously.

She stared him straight in the eye. 'Anything from police harassment to . . . being swallowed alive by a wolf.'

Jack felt himself stiffen defensively.

'You've been busy recently, then.'

'No thanks to you,' she replied sarcastically. 'Every time the NCD breaks a case I end up picking up the pieces. First the three pigs that you shamelessly pursued with the slenderest evidence imaginable, now the Riding-Hood disaster – it could take years of counselling before she and her grandmother can even *speak*, let alone dress themselves or have any sort of useful life skills.'

Neville was looking at Jack with obvious delight. He despised Jack with the lingering hatred of an idle under-achiever who had lost everything by his own stupidity and was now looking for someone to blame. Virginia was not a girlfriend, he had simply brought her along to try to humiliate Jack, something he seemed to treat a bit like a hobby. Jack sighed. He hadn't expected to have to defend his actions to anyone, least of all to some dopey friend of Neville's, but he wasn't going to take this sitting down.

'Ever been face to face with a serial wife-killer?' he asked her.

'No.'

'How about being chased by a deranged genetic experiment with murder on its mind?'

Kreeper sighed.

'No.'

'Staked out a grandmother's cottage for three weeks solid because you had a gut instinct something *might* happen?'

'No.'

'Walked unarmed into an illegal porridge buy?'

'No!'

'You run a relatively risk-free life, in fact. I don't. I put my arse on the line every time I go out there. Don't think that "nursery" in the title of my division makes it cosy kittens, fluffy toys and shades of pink – it's a violent and dangerous world full of murder, theft and cannibalism. When did you last make a life-or-death decision?'

Kreeper was unrepentant.

'That doesn't condone harassment of the three pigs or the reckless disregard with which you failed to protect Riding-Hood and her grandmother.'

Jack stared at her coldly.

'You don't get it, do you?' he said after a pause, his voice rising. 'In the world of nursery crime some things just *happen*, despite my best endeavours. Humpty takes a nosedive, the pigs boil the wolf – and Riding-Hood and her gran get eaten. In *my* world, the world of the vaguely pre-destined, you have to work five times as hard to involve yourself in the unfolding of the case, and ten times harder still to change the outcome. I couldn't stop the wolf eating them – but I did my best.'

'Your best?' said Kreeper with a contemptuous laugh. 'How can you have the cold arrogance to stand there and tell me you did everything in your power to stop them being eaten?'

'Because,' said Jack slowly, '*the wolf ate me, too.*'

Virginia's mouth dropped open. She didn't know about this; not many people did. Being swallowed whole wasn't something he'd like to repeat as it had ruined a perfectly good suit, but once past the oesophagus it hadn't been so bad. Strangely, it wasn't as dark as he had suspected – but certainly cramped with Red *and* her granny in there too. But Briggs had been right: without the woodsman's timely intervention they'd all be wolf shit by now, and Kreeper would be talking to a column of air. Fed up, Jack pounced.

'They didn't tell you that? Didn't tell you I went in alone and unarmed to face a murderous wolf as soon as I realised it wasn't Gran in bed?'

She shook her head.

'Did they tell you I grabbed Riding-Hood's ankles as she disappeared down his gullet? That I had my feet pressed against the wolf's jaws to stop her going down? That I couldn't save her and was gobbled up too?'

His voice rose. He'd been vilified in the press about this and he'd had enough.

'But get this,' he continued, 'I could have just legged it and called the regulars. But I didn't. I faced down the wolf and was devoured for my trouble. The first time, in fact, that a serving police officer in the British Isles has been eaten alive in the line of duty. Did Josh Hatchett write any of *that*?'

Jack stopped talking and looked around. Every occupant of the Deja-Vu ballroom was staring at him, hanging on his every word. Neville had a look like thunder. He had hoped Virginia would decimate his ex-wife's husband, but he had underestimated him. Again.

'What was it like?' asked a nearby guest, breaking the silence that had descended on the ballroom.

'The gastric juices burn your nose hairs, if you must know,' replied Jack, adding by way of explanation and giving a shrug, 'It's an NCD thing.'

Neville and Virginia took the opportunity to slip away. Partly because they felt defeated and deflated, and partly because Neville could see Madeleine approaching, and he was something of a coward in the presence of his ex-wife.

'Really,' said Madeleine, leading Jack to another part of the room as the conversation started up again, 'I leave you alone for *five minutes* and you start banging on about being eaten. Honestly, what did I tell you?'

'Sorry.'

Madeleine sighed and stared at him. She understood him, but the NCD thing could be confusing for anyone not used to it. Jack shrugged and took another drink from a passing waiter. He felt bored and tired. It had been a long day.

'I didn't come to an awards ceremony to have my professional actions judged,' he grumbled.

Madeleine gave him a hug.

'Never mind, sweetheart. Let's find our table.'

'Inspector?'

Jack turned to see the last person on earth he wanted to meet face to face. Someone who had made his life something very close to unpleasant for a long time. Someone who, if Jack hadn't been a policeman, would have deserved – and probably received – a punch on the nose. It was Josh Hatchett of *The Toad*.

'What do you want?' asked Jack, politeness not foremost in his mind.

'I heard you say you were swallowed alive,' said Josh, unable to contain his curiosity any longer. 'What was it like?'

'Ask an oyster. Good evening, Mr Hatchett.'

Jack turned to go but Josh stopped him with a hand on his shoulder. Jack stared at the hand and Josh quickly released him. The journalist sighed, leaned forward and lowered his voice.

'I'm not here to talk about the Red Riding-Hood . . . problem.'

'Magnanimity personified.'

'I'll come straight to the point.'

'It's what you seem to do best.'

'It's my sister. She's vanished.'

'Who is she? A magician's assistant?'

'I'm serious.'

'Try missing persons.'

'I told them yesterday. They instructed me to wait a month before reporting her as missing.'

Josh rubbed his face. He looked tired and haggard – even for a journalist.

'I need help, Inspector.'

But Jack wasn't in the giving vein.

'So did I – and I didn't get it. You might have given me the benefit of the doubt. I'm Jack Spratt the "incompetent bonehead" of the NCD who is now, almost wholly thanks to you, sidelined in his own department. Give me one good reason why I should even *listen* to you.'

'Her name's Henrietta,' said Josh, 'but she has long blonde hair.'

'So?'

'She's always been known as . . . *Goldilocks*.'

Jack raised an eyebrow.

'Are you saying this might have an NCD angle?'

'It's possible.'

'Had she been in contact with any bears recently?'

Josh thought for a moment.

'She's a journalist. She wrote a long piece about whether bears should be allowed to carry weapons for self-defence.'

'The "right to arm bears" controversy?'

'Yes. I guess she must have quizzed a few bears about it.'

'A few? Or three?'

'Is it important?'

'It might be crucial.'

Josh shrugged.

'I don't know. All I *do* know is that she's my sister and she's missing. Do you have a sister, Jack?'

'I have six. I could lose one without too much of a problem.'

Jack regarded the worried journalist in front of him and thought for a moment. On the one hand this man had caused him a great deal of trouble. Disrespectful headlines, awkward questions, press conference grillings. But on the other hand, with Josh's support the NCD might not get such a severe drubbing, and it might possibly even sway the Gingerbreadman case into his court. It smacked of sleeping with the enemy but all of a sudden doing Josh Hatchett a favour seemed to make the vaguest semblance of sense.

'Tell me,' said Jack, having a sudden idea, 'was she very particular about things? Not too hot, not too cold, not too hard, not too soft – that kind of thing?'

'How did you know that?' asked Josh, genuinely amazed.

He smiled.

'Call it a hunch.'

Jack looked at Madeleine, who stared at him in disbelief. If she'd been in a similar situation she would have just told Josh to sod off.

'I'll see you at the table, darling,' she said, glared hard at Hatchett and then departed. Jack and Josh walked over to the ornate marble fireplace where they could talk more easily.

'Your sister, eh?'

Josh sighed with relief, smiled and handed over a photo of an attractive woman in her late twenties with long, curly blonde hair. She had a large head and big eyes, which made her look quite young and a bit cutsey-ditsy – a bit like a character from a manga comic.

'I know what you're thinking,' said Josh, 'but don't be fooled by the bimbo looks. She's as hard as nails and just as sharp.'

'When did you last hear from her?'

'Did you hear about the events up at Obscurity?'

'Of course.'

'I spoke to her Tuesday morning, the day after the blast. She said she'd interviewed Stanley Cripps six hours before he died, and was going back up there as soon as the authorities reopened the site. She told me she *thought* she was on to something really big, and that I'd be proud of her. I next spoke to her on Thursday afternoon when she said she was *sure* it was something big and . . . well, I haven't heard from her since.'

'Was Stanley Cripps a bear?' asked Jack, ever hopeful.

'No. On Monday morning I went to her apartment to look for her. Her flat was empty and nothing seemed amiss. I found this in her desk drawer in the newsroom.'

He handed him a buff folder with 'Important' written in felt pen on the cover.

'Hmm,' murmured Jack, 'this could be important.'

He opened the file and idly flicked through the contents.

'What's it all about?' he asked, unwilling to study at length right now.

'Unexplained explosions – I think Goldy included the Obscurity blast somewhere in the list.'

'The Home Office report has the explosion as an undiscovered wartime bomb set off by Cripps himself with a rotavator or something.'

'It's not likely that he'd be using the rotavator at night, Inspector.'

'You never know,' mused Jack, 'they're all a bit funny in that area of Berkshire. Do you have any *suspicion* as to what's become of her?'

He sighed. 'Jack, I don't know anything. It could be the Easter Bunny for all I know.'

'It's not likely to be her,' replied Jack after a moment's thought. 'Kidnapping was *never* her MO. Did your sister have a car?'

'A green 1950s Austin Somerset,' replied Hatchett. 'It's not outside her flat or at *The Toad*'s offices. I don't know the number. This is her address, and these are her spare keys.'

'I'll see what I can do, Josh, but don't expect miracles. There's just one thing I'd like from you.'

'Anything.'

'Lay off the NCD, eh?'

'I'll give DI Copperfield my full support.'

That wasn't *precisely* what Jack had in mind, but to say so would have sounded disloyal, so he gave Josh a half-smile, passed him his empty glass and went to find Madeleine. He caught her eye across the crowded room and she beckoned him over.

'I want you to meet Mr Attery-Squash, my publisher. He's on our side so play nice, sweetheart.'

She steered him towards a large, friendly-looking man who seemed to be trying to avoid the many unpublished writers who milled around him like bees around a honey pot, hoping to be discovered. Attery-Squash was a sprightly octogenarian with a centre parting in his white hair and a matching beard decorated with a single red ribbon. He wore a suit of large checks of decidedly dubious taste, and had a jolly red face that reminded Jack of Father Christmas. He had run Crumpetty-Tree Publishing since he bought it from QuangTech in the sixties, and was reputed to be one of the few people who knew the Quangle-Wangle personally.

'Hello, Mr Spratt,' said Attery-Squash kindly, 'good to finally meet you. We were just discussing *Reading by Night*. Do you like it?'

'I love all Madeleine's work, but no one seems to want to buy photographic books these days.'

Mr Attery-Squash took a sip from his champagne.

'Publishing photography is a tricky game, Mr Spratt. Much as I love Madeleine's work, I'd be a whole lot happier if she'd start concentrating on the bread-and-butter of the photography world – celebrities misbehaving themselves and kittens in beer mugs.'

'Kittens in beer mugs?' echoed Jack.

'Yes,' continued Attery-Squash, eager to get Jack on board and somehow sway Madeleine away from her doubtlessly artistic but wholly unprofitable images, 'babies with spaghetti on their heads, ducklings snuggling up to kittens. That's where the *real* money is – that and puppies, lambs and calves shot with a wide-angle lens to give them big noses and make them look cuter, and chimpanzees dressed up as humans sitting on the toilet.'

'Babies with spaghetti on their heads?' said Jack, thinking of a typical mealtime with Stevie. 'Sounds like you might have something there.'

He nudged Madeleine, who said:

'Yes, I've often considered spreading my creative wings. I thought swans during sunset might be a good idea, too.'

'Mr Ottery-Squish?' enquired a young man dressed in a faded sports jacket and a necktie that looked as though it would have been better tied by his mother.

Attery-Squash smiled politely, despite the interruption.

'Yes?'

'My name's Klopotnik. Wendell Klopotnik. I have a novel that I've just written and I've chosen *you* to publish it for me.'

'That's very kind of you,' replied Attery-Squash, winking at Madeleine.

'I have a résumé somewhere,' Klopotnik muttered, rummaging through his pockets. 'It's called *Proving a Point* – a psychological thriller set in an all-night bakery.'

Jack and Madeleine excused themselves and walked off to find their table.

'What did Hatchett want?' whispered Madeleine as they threaded their way through the crowded ballroom.

'Help. His sister's gone AWOL.'

'I hope you told him to get lost.'

'On the contrary. Politically it could be a good move. I'll make a few enquiries and see what I can dig up – metaphorically speaking, of course.'

She shook her head and smiled at him. Jack rarely bore a grudge. It was one of his better features.

They sat down at their table and Jack introduced himself to his neighbour, a shabby-looking individual named Nigel Huxtable. He was, it transpired, another Armitage Shanks finalist and he jumped when Jack spoke as he had been trying to hide two bread rolls in his jacket pocket.

'So what's your book about?' asked Jack brightly.

'It's called *Regrets out of Oswestry*,' he said, fixing Jack with an intelligent gaze that was marred only by a slight squint. 'It traces one woman's odyssey as she returns to the place of her childhood in order to reappraise her relationship with her father and perhaps reconcile herself with him before he dies of cancer.'

Jack frowned. 'Didn't you submit that book to the competition last year?'

Huxtable looked hurt.

'No.'

'Oh. It just sounded familiar, that's all.'

Madeleine hid a smile.

'I know what you're saying,' said Huxtable in an aggrieved tone, 'but I tell you, more copies of my book have been stolen from bookshops than all the other Armitage Shanks finalists put together.'

'Do stolen books count on the bestseller lists?'

'I should certainly hope so,' replied Huxtable, thinking that it had been a colossal risk and a waste of his time if they didn't, 'but in any event, it's a modern benchmark of success, you know.'

Jack couldn't avoid a smile and Huxtable gave up on him, striking up a conversation along similar lines with his other neighbour.

In the end neither Huxtable nor Sphincter won. The first prize went to Jennifer Darkke's *Share My Rotten Childhood*. Lord Spooncurdle gave a pleasant after-dinner talk. He made several obscure puns about cheese-making and wondered why no one laughed.

That night Jack lay awake in bed, staring at the patterns on the ceiling. He was thinking about Goldilocks and the Gingerbreadman, the NCD, his career and the psychiatric assessment – and just how noisy Mr and Mrs Punch's lovemaking was next door.

'How long have they been at it now?' asked Madeleine sleepily, pillow over her head to block out the thumping, groans and occasional shrieks that penetrated the shared wall.

'Two and a half hours,' replied Jack. 'Go to sleep.'

10

Porridge problems

'**Most Illegal Substance for Bears**. The euphoria-inducing porridge ("*flake*") is a "Class III" foodstuff and, while admitting a small problem, the International League of Ursidae consider that rationed use does no real harm. Buns ("*dough-balls*") and honey ("*buzz*" or "*sweet*") remain on the "Class II" list and are more rigorously controlled, except for medicinal purposes. Honey addicts ("*sweeters*" or "*buzz-boys*") are usually weaned off the habit with Sweetex with some success. The most dangerous substance on the "Class I" list is marmalade ("*chunk*", "*shred*" or "*peel*"). The serious psychotropic effects of marmalade can lead to all kinds of dangerous and aberrant behaviour, and it is generally best avoided as far as bears are concerned.'

– *The Bumper Book of Berkshire Records*, 2004 edition

The day broke clear and fine. A light breeze in the night had cleared away the haze and the morning felt crisp and clean and sunny – the sort of morning that is generally reserved only for breakfast cereal commercials, where a nauseatingly bouncy nuclear family leap around like happy gazelles while something resembling wood shavings and emulsion paint falls in slow motion into a bowl.

No one was bouncy in the Spratt household that morning, but Jack dragged himself up and was out of the house at eight, telling Madeleine he was off to see the counsellor first thing. She'd replied: 'You're a lying hound. Good luck on the Goldilocks hunt and invite Mary and Ashley round for dinner one evening.'

Twenty minutes later he was driving down the unmetalled road to the lake where Mary lived. There were many flooded gravel pits dotted around the area, but only one had people living on it. Several boat-minded individuals had settled here in the thirties and started a precedent that couldn't easily be broken. Until Mary started living on the lake Jack hadn't known that residential moorings existed here at all. It was quiet at the lakeside and the houseboats, moored on the end of pontoons to stop them running aground, barely moved at all in the placid waters. The first boat was a converted Great War naval pinnace, her decks covered in plastic and in a constant state of conservation. She had been a Dunkirk 'little ship', so the enormous effort being expended on her rebirth, thought Jack, was quite justified. Beyond this was a Humber lighter, sunk at its moorings three winters earlier and abandoned by its owners. Next was the *Nautilus*, an ancient riveted iron submarine designed by its owner, an eccentric and reclusive millionaire by the name of Nemo, who was spending his retirement in the rusting hulk writing his memoirs and redefining the classification of sea creatures after a lifetime's research. The *Nautilus* was resting on the gravelly bottom with its large viewing windows on the waterline. No one knew how he'd got the submarine into the lake and he never gave anyone a straight answer when they asked.

Mary lived on the next mooring to Nemo in an old Short Sunderland flying boat, an ex-civilian version that she had bought from a bankrupt theme restaurant in Scotland, dismantled and shipped to the lake on the back of two low-loaders. She spent her spare time converting the inside to a comfortable home and had recently managed to get the number-three engine, the only one still in position, started. Madeleine and the children had come down for a barbecue that day and cheered as the old radial burst into life, belching clouds of black smoke, frightening a flock of geese and straining the old aeroplane at its moorings until Mary feathered the prop.

'Anyone home?' shouted Jack through the open door.

'I'm on the flight deck!' said a voice that echoed down through the flying boat. Jack stepped inside the hull and picked his way over the heaps of building materials and rockwool that were piled up inside the cavernous hull. She had, as yet, converted only the prow. Jack climbed the spiral staircase to the navigator's office that Mary used as a kitchen.

'There's some coffee on the stove!' she called out. He helped himself and joined her on the flight deck, a large room roofed in sun-clouded Plexiglas. Mary was sitting in the left-hand seat with her feet up on the remains of the instrument panel.

'Good morning,' said Jack, 'how's the acting head of the NCD?'

'She's fine,' replied Mary with a smile. 'How's the NCD's un-official full-time consultant?'

'He's all right.'

Jack sat down in the co-pilot's seat and balanced his mug on the throttle quadrant. They were at least twelve feet above the water level and were afforded a good view of the lake. To the left of them they could see Captain Nemo hanging up his socks on a makeshift washing line strung between the conning tower and tail of his rusty craft, and to their right was the lake, a full mile of open water, the glassy surface interrupted only by the marker buoys for the dinghy racing. It was quiet and peaceful and Jack could see why people would forgo the luxuries of land-based dwelling for a life on the water.

'Beautiful, isn't it?' murmured Mary. 'I wouldn't live anywhere else for all the money there is.'

Jack took a swig of coffee.

'I think you're right. Me, I'd worry about the kids falling in the drink.'

'If you brought them up to regard water the same way as they regard roads, I don't think you'd have a problem.'

'I suppose so. Everything okay at the office?' asked Jack.

'Fine. We were sorting through the statements for the Scissor-man's pre-trial hearing after you left. The CPS have asked for more witnesses and the thumbless victims of previous scissorings to try and create a cast-iron case against him.'

'Anything else?'

'I think Ashley was serious about that date.'

Jack shrugged.

'So? It only has to be a drink or something.'

'*Do* aliens drink?' she asked, not really knowing much about Rambosians, never having really considered them at all. 'I mean, what if he tries to kiss me or something?'

'Then call it off. After all, you're something of an expert when it comes to wriggling out of dates.'

Mary smiled.

'I am, aren't I? So . . . what's with this early visit, Jack?'

'I bumped into Josh Hatchett at the Deja-Vu last night.'

She pulled a face.

'What joy. I hope you wished him all the worst.'

'He has a missing sister.'

'If I were his sister I'd post myself missing, too.'

'And we're going to find her.'

Mary stared at him.

'We're going to help the person instrumental in your enforced sick leave and effective demotion? Who got you reprimanded over the Scissor-man case? Are you nuts?'

'"Yes", "yes" and "quite possibly", in that order. Look upon it as a long-term strategic operation to bring about a quantum change in press relations as regards the continuing effectiveness of the NCD.'

'We're cosying up to Josh to get better press coverage?'

'More or less. I think it might be an NCD case. Her name's Goldilocks.'

'So? She could be *a* Goldilocks, not *the* Goldilocks. There're probably hundreds of people with that name.'

'We have a vague bear connection – and she's fussy.'

'Ah. A "not-too-hot-not-too-cold-just-right" sort of fussy?'

'In one. She may have found some answers about the blast at Obscurity and three other unexplained explosions around the globe.'

He handed her the buff folder that Josh had given him.

'Hmm,' she said, looking at the 'Important' written on the front. 'This could be important.'

'I did that joke already.'

'Sorry.'

She opened the folder. It contained newspaper cuttings. The most recent, of course, concerned Obscurity, and contained a lot of competing theories from news sources of varying reliability. The Obscurity 'event' had been catnip for conspiracy theorists, who generally liked things going *bang* for no clearly explained reason. Mary flicked through the cuttings to find an article about a detonation in the Nullarbor Plain, a lonely area in the vast emptiness of the Australian desert.

'September 1992,' she observed, 'twelve years ago.'

'The Australian government denied that any tests had been undertaken,' said Jack, who had been reading the cuttings the previous evening, 'and no explanation was forthcoming.'

Mary turned over another clipping to reveal a faxed extract from the *Pasadena Herald* dated March 1999. It too described an explosion, this time in a neighbourhood on the edge of town. The detonation shattered windows up to three miles away and tossed debris over a thousand feet into the air. The owner of the house who died had been retired mathematician Howard Katzenberg. There were more clippings about a blast in Tunbridge Wells where someone named Simon Prong had perished in an unexplained fireball, and that was it. Four explosions with no link that they could see other than the fact that they were all reported as 'strange' or 'unexplained'.

'What do you think?' asked Mary.

'No idea. Josh seemed to think she was looking for a link between them.'

'And how is this related to bears?'

'I'm not sure. On Monday she meets up with Cripps in Obscurity. Six hours later he's dead in the blast. She tells her brother she's on to something big, and he last hears from her Thursday afternoon.'

Mary shrugged. 'She might be on holiday.'

'And she might not.'

They both sat in silence and watched a pair of swans attempt a long and slow take-off from the surface of the lake. As soon as they were airborne they landed again with a flurry of spray. It seemed a lot of effort to travel three hundred yards.

'I don't like station politics,' said Mary a half-hour later. 'I hope you know what you're doing.'

'Listen: the longer that twit Copperfield is playing hunt-the-biscuit, the more victims there will be. Look upon it as a back door to the natural order of things.'

'I don't like it, Jack.'

'It's NCD, Mary. It's what we do.'

'No, I mean I don't like your car.'

They were driving across Reading towards Shiplake and the industrial unit that Tarquin had told them was the place where he had picked up the porridge oats. It was the first time that Mary had driven the new Allegro.

'What's wrong with it?'

'Couldn't I explain what's *right* with it? It'll take a lot less time. Why don't you get a proper car?'

'A car without porous alloy wheels that let the tyres go flat overnight?' asked Jack, smiling. 'A car whose drag coefficient is better going forwards than in reverse? A car whose rear screen doesn't pop out when you jack up the rear?'

'Anything. I'd prefer to be seen in a wheelbarrow.'

'It could be arranged.'

They picked up Ashley, who was waiting for them at a pre-arranged street corner. He wished Mary a very good morning and enquired meticulously after her health, and Jack smiled to himself. Quite unlike Mary, Ashley was dead impressed with his new Allegro, and since he had memorised all the chassis numbers of every British car built between the years of 1956 and 1985, he could proudly announce that the car came off the production line at Longbridge on 10 September 1979.

'Really?' said Jack, amazed at Ashley's ability to recall utterly pointless facts. 'How do you remember all this stuff?'

'Very easily,' he replied. 'Humans rely on a pattern of electrically charged neurons to build up a picture that is revived by association. If the memory is not recalled now and again, it fades – if it is retained at all. Our memory works *quite* differently. Every image, fact or sound is translated into binary notation and then stored in molecular on/off gates within the liquid interior of our bodies. Since each teaspoon of *Rambosia Vitae* contains more molecular gates than there are visible stars, our memory is extraordinarily large. Best of all, we can erase what we don't need. Important memories are stored near our core but the boring stuff migrates to the extremities. If we run out of memory we simply reformat an arm.'

'You'd best be careful not to delete the wrong arm,' said Jack with a smile.

'Even if I did,' replied Ashley without seeing the joke, 'I'd be okay – I've got my core memories backed up at home in a jar.'

★   ★   ★

They pulled up outside the Shiplake industrial estate office a few minutes later.

'I'll have a word with the site manager,' said Mary, and climbed out of the car. Jack and Ashley sat there in silence for a while, Jack thinking about how he was going to pass the psychological appraisal he'd arranged for that afternoon. He'd only have to outline a typical case to a police shrink to be branded B-4: 'Unfit for duty on mental grounds'.

Ashley, on the other hand, had no particular worries – few Rambosians ever did. He amused himself by calculating to eight decimal places the cube root of every number under a million, and when he'd done that he said:

'Sergeant Mary is very attractive in a pink, fleshy, hairy, forgetful sort of way.'

'I never thought of Mary as hairy,' admitted Jack.

'Oh, it's strictly relative,' said Ashley, whose own skin was totally hairless, pliant and shiny, a bit like a transparent beach ball. 'Do you think she's really over this Arnold chap?'

'I don't know. All I know is that *he* doesn't seem to be able to understand "no" and *she* doesn't seem to be able to stop wanting to tell him.'

'It all sounds very complicated,' said the alien. 'Where I come from we just agree to a mutual memory erasure, and neither of us knows we've even met. In fact, it's possible to fall in love with someone you once hated – several thousand times.'

'Ash,' said Jack, unable to contain his curiosity any longer.

'Yes?'

'How do aliens . . . do it?'

'Do what?'

'You know. It. *Thing*. Have babies.'

'We don't have babies. Humans have babies.'

'You know what I mean – *reproduce*.'

'We swap egg and sperm sacs,' he said matter-of-factly and without the slightest trace of embarrassment. 'We can do it by post if we wish and the sacs will keep in a dry airing cupboard for anything up to nine centuries – it's very convenient.'

'It must be,' replied Jack.

'What about you?' asked Ashley. 'How do mammals propagate?'

As Jack told him, the few features Ashley did have scrunched into the vague semblance of a frown. When Jack had finished, Ashley gave out a laugh that was something very like the noise a squeaky toy makes when someone heavy sits on it, and he said:

'Get *out* of here! What utter nonsense – you think I was hatched yesterday?'

'It's true.'

'It is?' replied Ashley, his eyes opening wide in a mixture of wonderment and shock. 'And the baby comes out *where*?'

Luckily, Mary had returned to the car.

'Let to a company named Three Monkeys Trading. A "Mr Guy Gorilla" signed a three-year contract eighteen months ago.'

'Much traffic?'

'For all he's seen of them, he said, it might as well be the tooth fairy who leased it.'

'It won't be her,' said Jack after giving the matter some thought, 'she's doing four years in Holloway over that regrettable incident with the pliers.'

'What do you want to do?' asked Mary.

'We'll take a look.'

They drove on into the industrial estate. Unit 16 was sandwiched between a cut-price carpet showroom and a motorcycle repair specialist. The windows were grimy and unwashed and even up close it was difficult to see inside. Jack consulted the entry-code number Tarquin had jotted down and punched it into the keypad. There was a soft click and a buzz, and the door swung open.

They stepped into the gloom and Jack hit the switch. The strip lights flickered on to reveal a lot of not very much at all. The unit was deserted apart from a skip full of rubbish.

'If this is used as a distribution warehouse they're a bit low on stock,' murmured Jack.

'But they *were* here,' replied Mary, showing him a couple of rolled oats that had been trodden into the dust on the floor, 'so Tarquin wasn't lying.'

'Does this mean anything?' asked Ashley, who had been poking in the skip.

'No, that's just a bath – to wash in, you know?'

'I know what a bath is for,' said Ashley, 'but why would anyone want to throw away a perfectly good one?'

'People do that sort of thing all the time.'

'Can we take it?'

'No.'

'Look at this, Jack,' said Mary, who had also been looking in the skip.

'A sink?'

'No – empty porridge oat bags.'

Mary handed Jack a Bart-Mart plastic bag with *1Kg Value Porridge Oats* printed on the side. Jack looked into the skip, which held hundreds of similar bags. Either there had been a big shipment or someone had been doing this for a while. Next to the skip was a trestle table laid out with empty plastic bags and rolls of sticky tape, presumably for repacking the rolled oats to disguise provenance.

Suddenly, a shadow fell across the open door and a deep baritone boomed:

'Everyone turn round *really* slowly.'

They all slowly turned to look at the newcomer. He was a fully grown brown bear dressed in a well-tailored three-piece tweed suit. He was wearing a trilby hat, had a shiny gold watch chain dangling from his waistcoat and white spats that covered the tops of his shoe-less feet. And he was holding a gun.

'Police,' said Jack, 'DCI Spratt of the NCD.'

'ID?'

Jack very carefully retrieved it from his pocket and passed it across.

The bear looked at the card, raised an eyebrow and lowered his gun. His small brown eyes flicked between them.

'Then you must be Officers Mary and Ashley. Which one of you is the alien?'

'That would be me,' replied Ashley, putting up his hand.

'Right,' said the bear, returning the weapon to an elegantly tooled shoulder holster.

'Who are you?' asked Jack.

'Sorry about the weaponry,' said the bear without answering or even appearing to hear him, 'but I don't know who to trust these days. Since the bile-tappers got active in the area we members of the phylum *Chordata*, class *Mammalia*, order *Carnivora*, family *Ursidae* are not going to take any chances.' He walked over to the skip and looked in.

'Hm,' he said.

'It's a bath,' remarked Ashley. 'They're used for washing in.'

The bear looked at Jack.

'Is he for real?'

'I'm afraid so. Again: who are you?'

The bear took a calling card from a large wallet and handed it to Jack.

'The name's Craps, Vincent Craps. Folks call me Vinnie.'

Jack read the card and pocketed it.

'And the gun?'

'Licensed by NS-4,' replied Vinnie. 'I'm an investigator for the League of Ursidae. We take attacks on bears and ursine substance abuse very seriously.'

Jack wasn't convinced.

'I'm NCD, Mr Craps, and I've never heard of any League of Ursidae.'

'Then the NCD don't know shit, do they?'

He walked up close to Jack and towered over him in a very obvious display of dominance. He had a just-washed-dog smell about him laced with aftershave and just the vaguest hint of tomcat.

'Listen,' said Vinnie, tempering his overwhelming physical presence with a kindly fireside voice, 'I'd be happier if you left porridge problems to those who *really* understand them. Your well-intended but undeniably clumsy attempt to contain the problem yesterday did no one any favours at all. Do you understand my meaning?'

Jack thought for a moment, then the penny dropped.

'Tarquin is one of yours?'

'We have operatives on the ground looking after things, Inspector. Bullying Tarq into selling the flake cheap to bear-named-Algy was a classy move. But if you'd tried to shake him down I'd have . . . well, put it this way, the League of Ursidae don't generally consider the courts either efficient or fair in matters regarding bears.'

'I'll take that as a threat.'

'Come, come!' said Vinnie with a smile, and taking a few paces back to make himself appear less threatening. 'The NCD does an *excellent* job but bears are better policed by bears. Take it as a request to let us keep our own house in order without outside interference.'

'I'll leave you alone if you keep me in the loop, Craps. What's going on here?'

Vinnie thought for a moment and looked around the empty factory unit.

'This little set-up is nothing too special. Bears like porridge in the same way that humans like alcohol. Unhappily, the law regards porridge as not a harmless recreational pursuit but a potentially dangerous habit and regulates it with ration books.'

'I know how the system works, Vinnie.'

'Bears tend to blow their quotas in the first few days of each month. What you see here is a porridge "taster" undertaken by a couple of humans who see themselves as friendly to bears. They take forty kilos or so and dump it on the bear market mid-month through Tarquin. It's well meaning and pretty harmless but we like to keep an eye on this stuff rather than shut it down, just in case.'

'Who's doing it?'

'We cooperate closely with National Security and don't wish to jeopardise a good working relationship. I can't tell you.'

'Then why Bart-Mart and not, say, Waitrose or Somerfields?'

'I think we're about done here,' said Vinnie after a pause. 'I hope I can rely on your good sense to leave this up to us?'

'I won't ignore any law-breaking, Craps.'

'No one's asking you to, Inspector. It's a question of priorities. I'm just asking you to put porridge on a . . . *low priority*. Be seeing you.'

And without another word he walked briskly out of the factory unit and straddled a Norton motorcycle that was parked outside.

'Wait!' said Jack. 'What about . . .'

But he might as well have been talking to himself. Vinnie kicked the bike into life, revved the engine, clonked it into first and tore off up the road with a screech of tyre.

'You know what this means?' said Jack as Vinnie Craps vanished from view around a bend in the road.

'That the singular "screech of *tyre*" looks and sounds wrong even if it's quite correct?'

'No. It means there's a higher authority in ursine-related nursery crime than us.' He shook his head. 'I wouldn't mind but I'd like to have known about them.'

'So we cool off on the porridge thing?'

'Do we hell,' replied Jack. 'Ash?'

'Yes?' replied Ashley, who was still staring wistfully at the bath in the skip.

'I want you to get back to the office and call the biggest Bart-Mart in Reading and ask to view the security tapes covering the checkouts for the past five days. If the manager wants to know why, don't mention porridge or bears. And if you have to make up a story, make it a little less outlandish this time.'

'How much less outlandish?' asked the alien, whose understanding of the average human's perception of reality was patchy, at best.

'One that doesn't involve pirates and treasure,' said Jack. 'Just tell them we're looking for some thieves active in the area.'

'Right,' said the alien, and scampered off, only to return a few moments later.

'What am I looking for in the security pictures?'

'Anyone with a trolley full of rolled oats.'

'Okay,' said Ash, 'and no pirates.'

He dashed off again and Jack and Mary returned to the car.

'Where now?' asked Mary.

'It's time we found out a little bit more about . . . Goldilocks.'

I I

Goldilocks (absent)

'**Most Defeated British Parliamentary Bill**. Few bills before Parliament were ever so soundly rejected as the Ursine Self-Defence Bill of 2003, defeated by a record 608 to 1. Proposed to allow bears to protect themselves against illegal hunting and bile-tappers, the bill would have allowed adult bears to legally carry a concealed sidearm within the designated safe haven of Berkshire, UK. The defeat of this particular private member's bill brought to an end the previous record, set in 1821 when Sir Clifford Nincompoop's proposal to allow marriage to one's horse was defeated by 521 to 5.'

– The Bumper Book of Berkshire Records, 2004 edition

Twenty minutes later Jack's Allegro pulled up outside a large Georgian house that had once been a single residence but was now carved up into a number of uninspiring flats. They walked down the alley at the side of the house and, using the key that Josh had supplied, opened the door to Goldilocks' basement flat. The door opened against four days' mail and a lonesome cat. The latter entwined itself around Mary's legs and purred so loudly it almost choked.

'Josh asked us to feed it. It's not like a cat owner to go away and leave their pet unattended.'

'Poor puss,' muttered Mary as she tickled it behind the ears. 'Let's see if we can't find you some dinner.'

At the mention of dinner the cat darted off and Mary followed it into the kitchen. There was a rancid smell of rotting food and she cautiously opened the fridge. Her nose wrinkled as the smell grew stronger. She rummaged among the food and veg and picked out the stuff that was going off; chiefly the milk, which had turned to yogurt. She washed the remains down the sink, then fed the cat, which was rubbing itself against the cupboard where the food was kept.

'Check her bedroom, see if there's anything out of the ordinary,' called Jack as he picked up the mail from the floor. 'Y'know, girl's things – anything to point to a prolonged absence.'

Mary disappeared into the bedroom as Jack went through Goldy's mail. There were letters from disgruntled consumers wanting her to do an exposé on dishwashers, another from her bank complaining about her overdraft and several not-to-be-missed direct mail offers that seemed almost nostalgically warming compared to the barrage of spam e-mails that Jack received every day.

He dumped the mail on the living-room table and looked around. The entire flat was meticulously tidy, and if Goldilocks was *the* Goldilocks, exactly as Jack supposed it might appear. From the cushions on the sofa to the tins in the kitchen cupboard, the pictures on the wall and the books on the bookshelf, everything was arranged in threes, and where possible in descending order of size.

A work station was to one side of the open-plan living room. There was space for a laptop, and a power feed lay loose on the desk together with a printer cable. Her laptop, Jack decided, must be either with her or at *The Toad*'s newsroom. There were several snaps of Goldy and companions stuck on a pin board along with some Post-its. The top one grabbed his attention and he pulled it from the board. It mentioned someone named Mr Curry, and an invitation for dinner the previous Friday, the day after Josh had last heard from her. The drawers of the desk yielded nothing of interest, just personal matters regarding financial concerns and her membership of the Austin owners' club. Jack noted the number of Goldy's Somerset: 226 DPX.

'She's not away on a trip, Jack,' said Mary on her return from the bedroom. 'All her suitcases and toiletries are still here. It's a single woman's flat but she has a boyfriend who stays round on a casual basis. There's a second toothbrush and a pair of boxer shorts in the laundry.'

Jack showed her Goldy's passport.

'Not out of the country, then.'

'Well, well,' came a crackly Capstan-extra-strength voice from the doorway, 'Detective Inspector Spratt.'

They both turned to see a middle-aged woman in a black suit. Her features were pinched and pale to the point of cadaverous, and her clothes hung loosely on her bony body. She stared at them with the ease of someone who was used to giving orders, and used to having them taken. She wasn't alone. Her companion was a man who was twice as big and eight times the volume. He was dressed in an identical black suit that seemed too small for his bulk. He had a shaved head, a badly broken nose and shoulders that sloped at forty-five degrees from just below his ear lobes. Jack could just see a curly earpiece running up from his collar. They looked like bouncers with poor dress sense on a day-trip.

'Detective *Chief* Inspector,' corrected Jack.

'Congratulations, Spratt – have you met Agent Lunk?'

Jack nodded a greeting in his direction.

'Mnn,' said Lunk.

'Mary, I want you to meet Agent Danvers,' explained Jack, 'NS-4's finest. Remember the goose we gave to National Security after the Humpty inquiry? Well, it went through Agent Danvers here.'

'Oh,' said Mary, 'did you discover *exactly* how the goose laid all those golden eggs?'

Danvers' face fell.

'If I ever find out that you swapped the goose,' she growled at the pair of them, 'you'll both be finished.'

'Mnn,' said Lunk.

'We were just chatting to Vinnie Craps,' said Jack. 'He told us he'd been in contact with NS-4. Is that the reason you're here?'

'Never heard of him. NS-4 is a big department. We bully and intimidate a lot of people so it's hard to keep track of names. What's your interest in Miss Hatchett?'

'It's a potential missing-persons inquiry.'

'Do you know where she is?'

'No, that's what the "missing" in "missing persons" means.'

Danvers bridled slightly but Jack didn't care. He'd had dealings with Danvers and National Security before and he'd always come off worse. Most people did. He asked:

'Why do you want to know where she is?'

Danvers beckoned to Agent Lunk, who moved into the flat and started to look through the drawers and bookshelves in a half-arsed display of searching.

'What was the story she was working on?' asked Danvers.

'I've no idea.'

'Don't lie to me, Inspector,' she replied, removing her dark glasses to reveal two red-rimmed unblinking eyes, 'I'm the good side of NS-4. If you prefer I can ask Mr Demetrios to speak to your commanding officer. Do you want me to *make* you tell us?'

'If you want me to repeat myself with Briggs present, be my guest. Now: what's your interest in Miss Hatchett?'

'NS-4 is a one-way conduit of information, Inspector. I've told you too much already.'

'Too much? You haven't told me anything!'

'I've told you I don't know who Vinnie Craps was,' said Danvers. 'Consider yourself fortunate to get even that.'

'Really?' replied Jack sarcastically. 'Thanks for nothing – and you guys should get a better tailor.'

Danvers said nothing, Lunk reappeared empty handed and they both left without another word.

'Spooks,' murmured Mary as soon as the door had shut behind them. 'I *hate* spooks. Who was the Mr Demetrios she was talking about?'

'The *grand fromage* at NS-4. Not a pleasant chap, apparently. The story goes he's got so much dirt on everyone, no one dares fire him.'

'I see. It's a shame we didn't get anything out of them.'

'We did. Lunk was only searching for our benefit. They've already been through the flat.'

'So what's National Security's interest in Goldilocks?'

Jack shrugged.

'I don't know but they seem anxious to find out about the story she was working on. Intriguing, isn't it?'

They returned to the task at hand. It was possible that Goldilocks was on a road trip somewhere but no cat owner *ever* leaves a moggy with no one to feed it. Something was wrong, and by virtue of their profession Jack and Mary were inclined to think the worst. Jack was nosing through the kitchen when he came across two unopened packets of Bart-Mart value porridge oats as Mary walked back in. He held up the packages.

'Gifts for visiting bears, do you think? What have you got?'

'I found these,' said Mary, holding out several items. The first was a curt letter from the Department of Environment and Heritage in Australia denying that any sort of weapons tests – nuclear or otherwise – had been conducted on the Nullarbor Plain since 1963. The second item was more intriguing: a padded envelope that contained a fragment of what looked like a roughly fired mass of pottery with a thick layer of fused glass on one side. It smelled of freshly fired terracotta. Jack frowned and put the glassy mass back in the envelope.

'From the explosion?' asked Mary.

'Could be. Anything else?'

'This,' replied Mary, holding up a Dictaphone. She rewound the tape for a couple of seconds and then pressed *Play*. There was a beep and a message from Goldilocks' garage about her car being ready.

'Her answering machine,' said Mary, 'but listen to this.'

The next message was from a breathless and elderly man, who sounded as though he were hurrying somewhere.

'Hello?' said the voice. 'This is Stan Cripps and . . . wait a moment.' There were more sounds of shuffling, the creak of a door opening, then a crackle on the tape, a pause, and the voice again, this time in breathless wonder: 'Good heavens. It's . . . *full of holes!*' There was then a sudden blast of static and a constant tone.

Jack looked at Mary.

'Hardly famous last words, but last words none the less. Find out who is conducting the Cripps inquest and give it to him after making a copy. Where did you find all this?'

'Down the back of the sofa, wrapped in a handkerchief.'

'She wouldn't hide anything in her own flat unless she thought someone might break in and steal it. Best hang on to them.'

Mary carefully rewrapped the items in the handkerchief.

'Do I enter this as evidence?'

'We're not sure there's been a crime,' replied Jack, 'but Danvers makes me suspicious. Have a word with anyone living in the other flats – and check for any bears in residence close by. Most bears live in the Bob Southey, but you never know. I'm going to call Ash and see if he can't get a lead on Goldy's friend "Mr Curry" – he had a date with her the night she vanished.'

Mary walked around to the front door and read the names below the doorbells. One was marked 'Rupert' and the other 'Winston'.

Not *necessarily* bears' names, but all the same. She rang the door-bell marked 'Rupert' but there was no answer, so she peered in through the letterbox. The communal hall was deserted. She paused for a moment and then rang the doorbell marked 'Winston'. Again there was no answer, but she took a few steps back and saw the lace curtains on the upstairs window fall back into place. She returned to the door and pressed both buttons simultaneously and continu-ously for about five seconds, then released them. After a moment's pause, and without a sound from the entryphone, the lock buzzed. She pushed the heavy door open and entered. The communal hall led to the ground-floor and first-floor flats, the latter reached by climbing the open stairwell, at the top of which was another closed door. It stayed closed. No one came out and not a sound reached her. She sniffed the air. Was that the faintest smell of honey, or was she imagining it? The bears involved in NCD investigations were wholly anthropomorphised and not generally violent, but even so, a five-hundred-pound bear with a bad attitude – quasi-human or not – could be quite a handful. She thought about fetching the tranquilliser gun, but instead moved quietly to the bottom of the stairs and said in a loud voice:

'Hello?'

Mary's voice came out with a twinge of apprehension in it which triggered the hairs on the back of her neck to prickle, and she shiv-ered. The hot, sweet smell was stronger, and she took a deep breath and slowly climbed the stairs. When she reached the tenth step it creaked ominously and she stopped to listen. There was silence for a moment and then a strange sound of destructive tearing as though someone were undertaking some form of localised demolition. Then, silence – followed by the noise of water escaping under pressure. She frowned. This *definitely* wasn't right. As she stood on the stairs, undecided whether to return to Jack or continue up, the door upstairs exploded off its hinges as a cast-iron bath full of water was thrown through it. It was hurled with such force that the tub, taps, soap and several loofahs all sailed clean over her head and landed in the hall below with a teeth-jarring crash as the iron bath tub shattered, unleashing a flood of water across the parquet flooring. She was not so lucky with the bidet that quickly followed. It caught her on the shoulder and pitched her into a painful and untidy tumble down the stairs, at the bottom of which she ended up, bruised, winded and mildly concussed, in a pool of cold soapy bath water. She looked up but her vision was blurred and all she could see was a large brown object at the top of the stairs. Her assailant bounded down the stairs four at a time, landing with one large foot on Mary's hand. She winced, expecting pain, but none came. The foot that had landed on her hand was soft and spongy. And the smell. Hot and sweet but not honey – *ginger*.

Jack was sitting in the Allegro, speaking on his mobile.

'How many?'

There was a pause.

'1000100 Currys in Reading,' repeated Ashley. 'Now what?'

'That's sixty-eight,' Jack muttered to himself. 'Okay, we need to eliminate a few. Find out their ages and take out anyone under sixteen and over sixty-five. Sorry, that's – let me think – anyone under 10000 and . . . *whoa!*'

A movement in the house caught his eye and a second later the Gingerbreadman came bounding out and with a single stride from the middle of the front garden cleared both the garden gate and the Allegro. He landed in the street in front of a car that swerved violently and hit a postbox. He then ran off down the road in a series of large, powerful strides. Jack started the car and tore off in pursuit, shouting into the mobile to Ashley:

'Tell Copperfield I'm following the Gingerbreadman west down Radnor Road!'

Jack accelerated rapidly, the Allegro's more-powerful-than-usual-but-still-a-bit-crappy engine howling enthusiastically. The Gingerbreadman was running up the middle of the road at an incredible rate; Jack was hitting forty and still wasn't catching up. The Gingerbreadman didn't stop at the next road junction and Jack chanced it likewise. The Gingerbreadman was lucky, Jack less so. A car was approaching the junction at speed and clipped Jack's Allegro in the rear, causing him to career sideways; he over-corrected and slewed the other way, bouncing along a row of parked cars with the sound of tearing metal and the clatter of broken wing mirrors. He yanked the wheel hard over and recovered, dropped down a gear and floored the accelerator as the Gingerbreadman ran off round the corner.

'Turning left into Silverdale Road!' shouted Jack as he cornered hard, the tyres screeching in protest as they desperately tried to cling on to the asphalt. The Gingerbreadman ducked down an alley and Jack followed, oblivious to any damage that he might possibly inflict on the car. He caught a bollard on the way in and bent a suspension arm; the car vibrated violently as he turned left towards a block of garages and drove over a low brick wall that tore the offside front wheel off, shattered the windscreen and pushed the engine back into the scuttle with a metallic crunch. The car came to a halt on the rubble of the demolished wall, one rear wheel in the air. The engine died with a shudder. Ahead of him the Gingerbreadman had stopped running and just stood with his hands on his hips, regarding with detached curiosity the wreck of the car teetering on the broken masonry. There was an unnatural silence after the sudden excitement; the only sound to be heard was the hiss of the radiator and the tic-tic-tic of the engine as it cooled.

Jack fumbled with his mobile and gabbled into it:

'Garages behind Crawford Close, and get a car to seven Radnor Road for . . . ahhh!'

The Gingerbreadman had lunged forward, plucked the handset from Jack and crushed it between a massive thumb and forefinger. Jack looked up as the Gingerbreadman loomed over him. He was seven foot tall, broad at the shoulder and massively powerful, despite being less than four inches thick. His glacé-cherry eyes burned with unhinged intellect and his liquorice mouth curled into a cruel smile. He was enjoying himself for the first time in a quarter of a century and had no intention of returning to St Cerebellum's.

'Hello, Inspector,' said the Gingerbreadman, his voice a low, cakey rumble, 'how are things with you?'

'At this *precise* moment? Not terrific,' replied Jack, his hand feeling for the side-handled baton he always kept hidden between the seats. 'What about you?'

'Prison? Oh, I can take it or leave it.'

'So I see.'

'Aren't you going to arrest me?' asked the Gingerbreadman with a chuckle.

'Would there be any point?'

'Not really. You—'

Jack pulled out the baton and made a wild desperate swipe in the direction of the psychopath's head. The blow stopped short as the Gingerbreadman caught it in mid-air, wrenched it from Jack's grasp and snapped it like a breadstick. He was fast – astonishingly so.

'Any other bright ideas?' enquired the Gingerbreadman, raising his liquorice eyebrows questioningly and giving out a whiff of ginger.

Jack scrabbled across the passenger seat, kicked the door open, rolled out and made a run for it. He wasn't quick enough. The Gingerbreadman bounded across the car, grabbed Jack's arm and twisted it around into a half nelson.

'Although I swore to do unsfzpxkable things to you twenty years ago when you caught me,' he whispered in Jack's ear, the pungent smell of his gingery breath almost overpowering, 'I'm not going to.'

'Why not?' grunted Jack.

'Only the Sicilians know how to do vengeance properly,' he said. 'The rest of us are really just groping in the dark, to be honest. *Random* homicide, on the other hand, has a wonderful arbitrary feel to it, don't you think? The choice between giving or taking life is the ultimate exercise of power, and for you, today, here and now, I choose . . . *life*. Cross my path again and you won't find me so charitable.'

He then picked Jack up as though he weighed nothing at all and threw him bodily through the wooden doors of a nearby garage. He smiled again, gave a cheery wave and with a short run and a single leap cleared a nearby wall, then ran through the next five gardens as though they were a series of hurdles, vanishing over the last with a stylish Fosbury flop.

'Are you all right?' asked a kindly lady who had come out to see what the commotion was all about. Jack sat up among the remains of the garage door and blinked. He rubbed his neck and winced as his fingers discovered a painful cut at the back of his head.

'I'll be all right – thank you.'

The kindly lady smiled and patted him on the shoulder.

'I'll make you a nice cup of tea.'

The first of the squad cars arrived two minutes later as Jack emerged from the garage. It had been empty, which was perhaps just as well.

'Where did he go, sir?' asked Sergeant Fox.

'He's long gone,' murmured Jack, leaning on a corner of his Allegro. 'There's nothing here but a bruised DCI.'

He carefully unclipped his tie and threw it on to the back seat of the Allegro, then executed a neat double-take. *The car didn't have a single scratch on it.* The front wheel was back on, the windscreen mended and the side that had scraped down the line of parked cars had miraculously mended itself. The car was perfect in every detail, with no evidence at all of the gruelling punishment it had received not more than five minutes before. It seemed that Dorian Gray's 'guarantee' hadn't been an idle boast. Jack was looking at the oil painting in the boot – that of the even *more* wrecked Allegro – when Copperfield drove up with two other squad cars, which disgorged police marksmen in a seemingly never-ending stream.

'You look as though someone insane just threw you through a door,' said Copperfield without any sense of irony.

'Funnily enough,' said Jack, shutting the boot and sitting on the broken wall, 'that's exactly what he did.'

Copperfield whistled. He had read the reports about the Gingerbreadman's phenomenal strength, but it had to be seen to be believed. He started to arrange a search pattern in nearby streets but Jack wasn't confident of any success. He had seen the Gingerbreadman run at speeds of up to forty miles an hour and he hadn't even been out of breath.

'I thought you were on sick leave?' said Copperfield. 'And undergoing psychological assessment?'

'No secrets in the station, are there? It's called *counselling*. And I just happened to be in the area with Mary.' He suddenly remembered and sat bolt upright. 'Mary . . . ?'

Jack jumped in the Allegro and made his way back to Radnor Road, where he found her sitting in the back of an ambulance with a red blanket draped across her shoulders.

'You all right?'

She nodded.

'Bruised. He chucked a bathtub full of water at me.'

'How can he chuck a tubful of water?'

'With the bath still *surrounding* the water on most sides, quite easily. You?'

'He threw me into a lock-up garage.'

'Good job the doors were open.'

'They weren't. I lost him a mile away.'

He sat down next to her as she related what had happened.

'The owner of the flat?'

'She's dead – wallpapered over in the spare room. Good job, too. Despite the lumpiness all the pattern matched up and he'd bothered to line it first. No one does that any more – not even the really class decorators.'

Jack sighed. 'Another one for the Gingerbreadman. That makes one hundred and eight victims.'

He thought for a moment.

'Any bears living here?'

'None – not even a small one. If Goldilocks was *the* Goldilocks, she kept herself to a conventional neighbourhood.'

'Listen,' said Jack, 'where NS-4 are involved we can't trust anyone. We keep the Goldilocks thing to ourselves. I was cadging a ride and you were here checking on a potential Ursine Residential Licence infringement. You didn't find anything.'

'Got it.'

She shook her head sadly.

'Not really fair, is it?'

'How do you mean?'

'Getting the stuffing kicked out of us when it's not even our investigation.'

12

Gingery aftertaste

'**The Only Known Human Able to Speak Binary.** Owing to the complexity of binary, the speed at which it is spoken and the way in which the rules of grammar and pronunciation change almost daily and for no apparent reason, few humans have ever progressed beyond simple phrases such as "Hello", "Goodbye", "Can you direct me towards galaxy C-672?" and "My aunt is comprised chiefly of stardust". But utilising a "total immersion" system of learning, Dr Colin Parrot of Warwick University successfully mastered basic binary and can converse, but with a limited vocabulary and at only one thousandth the speed. "Colin did jolly well," said his teacher, friend and mentor, Adrian 100101011111101010. "His language skills are about on a par with a programmable toaster. Given a couple of years more and he'll be able to have an intelligent one-on-one with a dishwasher."'
    – *The Bumper Book of Berkshire Records*, 2004 edition

Jack and Mary were driven to casualty, where Jack had three stitches in his head. Copperfield and Briggs were waiting to question them when they got back to the station, the military and tactical firearms squads now very much in evidence. The first thing Briggs said was:

'I thought you were at home watching reruns of *Columbo*, Jack?'

'Mary was driving me to my counselling session and stopped off on the way – an NCD matter.'

Briggs turned to Mary.

'Is this true?'

'Yes, sir. A possible Ursine Residential Licence infringement.'

'The Gingerbreadman is *not* an NCD investigation, Sergeant, you know that.'

'It was a coincidence, sir,' she responded confidently. 'Do you think I would be crazy enough to tackle him on my own?'

'Perhaps not you,' said Briggs, glancing at Jack.

He thought for a moment and narrowed his eyes.

'This isn't a plot device number twenty-seven, is it?' he asked suspiciously.

'The one where my partner gets killed in a drug bust gone wrong and I throw in my badge and go rogue?' replied Jack innocently. 'I don't think so, sir.'

'No, not that one,' said Briggs in a state of some confusion. 'The one where you try and find the Gingerbreadman on the sly and make Copperfield and I look like idiots.'

'That would be a twenty-nine, wouldn't it?' put in Mary, who wasn't going to miss out on the fun.

'No, no,' said Jack, 'Briggs means a twenty-six. A twenty-nine is where the bad guy turns out quite inexplicably to be the immediate superior.'

'A twenty-six,' said Briggs, 'yes, that's the one.'

'What about it?'

'You're not doing one, are you?'

'No, sir,' replied Jack, 'I'm suspended awaiting a psychological appraisal, and I don't know what plot device *that* is.'

'Got to be well over a hundred,' suggested Mary helpfully.

Briggs looked at them both for a moment. He shrugged, seemingly satisfied. 'Okay. Copperfield has some questions.'

He left them to the inspector, who took infinitely detailed statements. The Gingerbreadman had been at liberty for less than twenty-four hours and had already killed once.

'Do you have any idea where he is now?' asked Jack, who wanted to keep abreast of what was going on.

'We're searching the local area,' replied Copperfield in a businesslike tone. 'He won't get far.'

'He's long gone,' said Jack with a sigh. 'He'll run and run and you won't catch him. No one will *ever* catch him. He has to make a mistake, or be tricked.'

'How would you know that?' asked Copperfield.

'I'm NCD. I know these things. It will take more than a platoon of highly trained killing machines to bring him down.'

Copperfield leaned closer.

'What then?'

'Get inside his head. Think what he thinks. Figure out what *you* might do if you were a Gingerbreadman.'

Copperfield stared at Jack then burst out laughing.

'You're kidding, right? Thanks for nothing. You can go.'

Ashley was waiting for them and when he saw them, he went even bluer than he usually was.

'I'm glad to see you're not mutilated in any way,' he said. 'A missing arm might ruin your symmetry. Personal asymmetry where I come from is a big taboo and brings great shame on the family and sometimes even the whole village.'

'Do you then have to kill yourself over it or something?'

'Goodness me, no! The family and village just have to learn to be ashamed – and nuts to them for being so oversensitive.'

'I see. Well, thanks for relaying the messages.'

Jack sat down and looked at the eighty or so pointless e-mails that were in his in-box while Ashley scuttled up to Mary.

'And you are well, too, Mary?'

'I'm fine, Ash. A bit bruised but I'll live. Um – were you serious about that date?'

He blinked again.

'Yes – weren't you?'

'Of course,' replied Mary, her nerve failing her.

Jack deleted the e-mails en masse and said:

'Ash, did you find out anything about Goldilocks' friend "Mr Curry"?'

The alien produced a sheet of paper covered with ones and zeros. Of course, he *could* write in English and readily agreed it was more efficient and helpful to do so, but he found binary more relaxing, despite the fact that it can take over two sides of closely written ones and zeros to ask for two extra pints from the milkman – and a single zero in the wrong place made it unintelligible, even to Ashley.

'1000100 Mr Currys,' read Ash, '100000 of which were either under 1000 or over 111100. 10 were in prison, which leaves 100010. I copied those addresses down in English – here.'

Jack scanned the thirty-four names closely. Sadly, none of them was a bear – which would have been a long shot, but worth a look none the less. He dialled Josh Hatchett's number but it was engaged.

'I called the Bart-Mart superstore about the security tapes,' said Ashley, 'and they told me they'd be happy to release them as long as we sent them a letter of request – it's for the QuangTech lawyers, apparently.'

'QuangTech? What have they got to do with Bart-Mart?'

'They own them,' remarked Ashley, 'everyone knows that.'

'It's not common knowledge, Ash.'

'I think it is. Mary?'

'Yes?'

'Who owns Bart-Mart?'

'QuangTech,' she replied without thinking, 'everyone knows that.'

'They do *not*,' replied Jack, reflecting upon the Quangle-Wangle's heavy financial cloak, which seemed to have fallen over most of Berkshire. 'It was a fluke you both knowing.'

Ashley handed him a sheet of paper.

'This was the request I was going to send. As you can see, *not one pirate*. What do you think?'

Jack quickly read it.

'Fine,' he said, handing it back, 'just leave out the bit about the elephants. And I need some info on Goldilocks' car. An Austin Somerset, registration 226 DPX. And we should consider tracing her mobile – and look through these explosions and see if you can find a link.'

He tossed the file marked 'Important' across the desk to him. Ashley picked it up and said:

'Somerset . . . mobile . . . link explosions . . . lose the elephants. Got it.'

He took the draft letter and walked up the wall to the ceiling, where he sat cross-legged and upside down at his work station. It was an efficient use of space in the small office, and by virtue of the ingenious use of Post-its and Velcro and a telephone screwed to the ceiling, usually quite safe.

Jack tried to dial Josh Hatchett again but the line was still engaged. He looked at his watch. He could still make his appointment at the shrink's, show them he wasn't a wild-eyed loon and be back on active duty by teatime. But something else was bothering him.

'Mary, can I show you something?'

They walked down to the car park beneath the station where Jack's Allegro was parked. As they approached they could see someone on their hands and knees peering intently at the pristine front wing of the car.

'What are you doing, Marco?'

Ferranti jumped up guiltily. He was a pale man with thin lips and very little hair covered by a bad wig. He was not in the force but worked for it – a claims assessor who looked into any damage inflicted by the police in the course of their duties. He tried to have any claims dealt with quickly and efficiently, sometimes irrespective of fault – lawsuits were in nobody's interest. He wasn't generally liked, for obvious reasons.

'My phone's been ringing off the hook all morning, Spratt. I've had fourteen claims for damages. One car wrecked, three with side damage, and another eight with broken wing mirrors. I've got a demolished wall and a smashed garage door. It could come to over eight thousand pounds. Eight thousand more than Reading can afford, Inspector.'

'The garage door I can explain. I was thrown through it.'

Ferranti grunted and conceded that perhaps that one wasn't *entirely* Jack's fault. He looked at Jack's spotless car suspiciously.

'Several witnesses attest to you damaging a lot of property with this car, Inspector. It *seems* they were mistaken.'

'Obviously.'

'I'm not convinced. How many other people chase Gingerbreadmen in silver Allegro Equipés?'

'Probably dozens, Ferranti. Can I ask you a question?'

'Sure.'

'Who owns Bart-Mart?'

'QuangTech,' he said, 'everyone knows that. Do you have *another* Allegro, identical to this one but covered in dents and scratches?'

'No.'

The assessor grunted, made a few disparaging remarks under his breath and then departed.

'What did you want to show me?' asked Mary.

'This car. I completely wrecked it and now . . . well, it's better again.'

'Are you sure?' she asked, not having seen Dorian Gray demonstrate the power of his unique warranty the day before.

'Yes. All that damage Ferranti claimed – it *was* me. I wrote the car off but then, as soon as my back was turned, it was all perfect again.'

Mary raised an eyebrow.

'That sounds kind of crazy, Jack.'

'*Sounds*, yes. But—'

'A car that can repair itself?' said a voice behind them. 'You should sell that idea to Ford.'

They turned to find Virginia Kreeper, who had been watching them from the shadows.

'Miss Kreeper,' said Jack without much enthusiasm, 'what a delightful surprise. Here to help some poor victim formulate a *really* good complaint against the service?'

'Not today, Inspector.'

'Having a break from trouble-stirring?' he asked sarcastically. He hadn't liked her the evening before at the Deja-Vu and he didn't like her now.

'No,' she replied, staring back at him coldly, 'I'm here to do an independent psychiatric evaluation.'

'Oh yeah?' said Jack with a laugh. 'And what poor cluck are you going to slap your snake-oil, leech-sucking voodoo magic on today?'

'Someone the doctors think might be suffering some form of delusional psychosis.'

'Such as?'

'Such as . . . cars that mend themselves.'

There was a pause.

'Bollocks,' said Jack in a quiet voice, 'it's me, isn't it?'

14
Virginia Kreeper

'**Most Confusing Word Association Examinee**. Jean Dimmock of Newbury, UK, holds the record for the most random answers in a routine word association test. Among her many utterly haphazard responses were such gems as: "Bird? Kneecap", "Banana? Bowling trophy" and "Great crested grebe? Disraeli". Her responses are spontaneous and unrehearsed, and make for much interesting study. She also holds the record for the most bizarre interpretations of a Rorschach ink-blot test, variously describing the meaningless and largely discredited test patterns as "A dog doing push-ups with an ant in attendance" and "Coco the clown in conversation with the Pope".'

– *The Bumper Book of Berkshire Records*, 2004 edition

'Of course, I was only kidding about that voodoo comment,' said Jack as soon as he was sitting in the Police Medical Officer's room. It was cold and sterile and cheerless and not somewhere you'd really want to be. It was here that officers were frequently told bad news about their failing health. Or in the hypochondriac Baker's case, bad news about his excessive good health. Kreeper was behind the desk looking through Jack's medical records and making annoying 'ah-ha' and 'mm' noises.

'. . . and the leech stuff was admittedly a bit infantile.'

'Your comments just now, although insulting and with intent to demean my profession,' muttered Virginia without looking up, 'have no relevance to your mental health, and neither did our conversation yesterday at the Deja-Vu. I get that sort of treatment a lot, so it is hardly indicative of your psychiatric state.'

'Ah!' said Jack, highly relieved.

'My evaluation will be based on objective and unbiased observation.'

'Well, that's good.'

'But,' she said, looking at him over her spectacles, 'give me any more of your sarcastic backchat and I'll recommend enforced retirement. Do you understand?'

'Perfectly.'

'Good,' she said, putting aside his file and picking up a pencil. 'I've been asked to conduct this appraisal as your commanding officer is concerned that too much exposure to unusual policing situations in a department requiring an open mind and imaginative thought processes might be aggravating a long-held psychosis which may render you incapable of distinguishing between reality and fantasy, and thus seriously compromise your abilities to conduct meaningful investigations.'

Jack frowned and said nothing for a few moments.

'Run that by me again?' he said at last.

'Briggs thinks you might be bananas.'

Jack leaned back in his chair and put his hands in his pockets.

'Now *that* I understand. Listen, Kreeper, I'm as sane as the next man.'

'Then I fear for the next man,' she said, tapping his record with an index finger. 'I am here to report on whether you are mentally fit enough to continue to work as an effective officer of the law.'

'Great!' said Jack, looking at his watch. 'Let's get to it.'

Kreeper stared at him again.

'Okay. I understand you are head of what you call the "Nursery Crime Division". Is this true?'

'Spot on.'

'And you were swallowed, alive, by a wolf a week ago?'

'Right again.'

'And this doesn't strike you as unusual?'

'Not at all. It's all pretty much standard operating procedure within the division. I've been in tighter spots than the swallowing, I can tell you.'

'Such as?'

'Probably the incident with the troll – or the attack by Dr Quatt's genetic experiment. Or the Gingerbreadman. Or arresting King Midas – and Rumpelstiltskin didn't take my closing down of his straw-into-gold dens too well.'

'And did any of these make you feel anxious, or worried?'

'Of course.'

'Feelings of delayed shock?'

'Nope.'

'Guilt?'

'Only for a failed conviction – guilty that I didn't present a robust enough case.'

Kreeper looked mildly disappointed and tried another tack.

'Your marriage is good?'

'Couldn't be better.'

'How do feel when you think of beautiful Pippa in the control room?'

'That she's very pretty and young enough to be my daughter.'

'And who do you think she's going out with?'

'Is this part of the test?'

'No, I was just interested like everyone else.'

'She showed an interest in Sergeant Pickle, but I'm not sure how far it's gone.'

Virginia showed him a picture of an ink blot.

'What does this look like to you?'

'It looks like a vagina. No, just kidding – it looks like a Rorschach ink-blot test.'

'And what about this?' she asked, showing him another.

'It looks like the test you just showed me.'

'And this?'

'Ditto.'

'O-kay. Word association. I want you to tell me the first word that comes into your head. Ready?'

'Brek.'

'We haven't started yet. Okay, here we go: Jack?'

'Yes?'

'No, we've started now. Jack?'

'Jill.'

'Dish?'

'Spoon.'

'Boy?'

'Blue'

'Baa–baa?'

'Black sheep.'

'Atishoo, Atishoo?'

'All fall down.'

'Porridge?'

'Bear.'

'Nursery?'

'Crime.'

'Bluebeard?'

'Crime.'

'Humpty?'

'Crime.'

'Crime?'

'Nursery.'

Kreeper wrote another note, leaned back in her chair and then asked:

'Being swallowed. What did it feel like?'

'Constricting to begin with, then quite warm and womb-like.'

'Ah–ha!' muttered Virginia triumphantly, leaning forward again. 'How do you get on with your mother?'

'She's a monumental pain in the arse, but I love her – I suppose.'

'When you were a little boy, did you ever walk into your parents' bedroom when they were making love?'

'No!'

'Beaten as a child?'

'No.'

'Humiliated? Other siblings favoured over you?'

'No.'

'Potty-trained too late?'

'No.'

'Potty-trained too early?'

'No!'

'Shame,' she said a little sadly, 'that would have made it all a *lot* easier. This car of yours. You say it mended itself?'

'No, I don't think I ever said that.'

'I distinctly heard you tell Sergeant Mary.'

'I meant it in . . . in . . . an *ironic* manner.'

'What sort of ironic manner?'

'I'm not sure,' said Jack, beginning to get a trifle annoyed and wanting to skip to the 'clean bill of health' part. 'Listen: I sleep well, eat well, have no problems with anyone except for people who . . . want to stop me doing my job.'

'Eat well?' asked Virginia, consulting Jack's medical records. 'That's what you said? "Eat well"?'

'Ye–s,' replied Jack, trying to figure where this was going.

'And your name is Jack Spratt?'

'You know it is.'

'Who eats no fat?'

'A lot of people don't eat fat,' replied Jack defensively, suddenly realising what Kreeper was up to. The interview had started out quite innocently but now she was probing right under his skin and he didn't like it – not one little bit.

'And your wife – your first one – she ate no lean, is that correct?'

'Do you have to bring my first wife into this?' said Jack, rubbing his hands together because they had begun to itch. 'You know she died?'

'I'm sorry, Inspector, but it might be important.'

'Yes, she only ate the fat. Only *ever* ate fat. What of it?'

'So together,' said Kreeper in a meaningful tone, 'you licked the platter clean?'

'Metaphorically speaking – you could say that,' snapped Jack, rubbing his brow. The room had suddenly grown hot, and he pulled at his collar to try to stop his shirt sticking to him.

'Are you feeling okay, Inspector?'

'Of course.'

'You don't want to stop and carry on another time?'

'No.'

'And none of that "eat no fat/eat no lean/platter clean" stuff strikes you as unusual?'

'Not at all,' replied Jack. He looked down at his hands and noticed a slight tremor. He tried to smile and clasped his fingers together, then felt an itch on his neck that he wanted to scratch but didn't in case Kreeper thought he was acting strangely. If this was a test to see whether he would crack and admit his PDR-ness, it was a good one.

'Have you heard of the Jack Sprat nursery rhyme?'

'Never,' he replied angrily. 'Is there one?'

'Yes. Do you want to hear it?'

Jack felt his heart thump heavily in his chest and his scalp prickled.

'No, I don't.'

'I see,' replied Virginia with infuriating calm. 'So, Jack, what is the meaning of all this . . . GIANT-KILLING?'

Jack jumped to his feet.

'Station tittle-tattle!' he exclaimed, more forcefully than he had intended. 'Yes, yes, there were three of them but only one was *technically* a giant; the rest were just tall. I was cleared of wrongdoing on every occasion.'

He found himself pacing the room, stopped, gave a wan smile, then seated himself with his hands under his thighs to stop them fidgeting.

'Is that all you need to know?'

'I'm only just beginning,' replied Kreeper with an unpleasant smile. 'Tell me about the beanstalk.'

'What beanstalk?'

'The one that grew in your mother's garden. The one that grew after you swapped the Stubbs' cow for the "magic" beans. The one you chopped down to destroy that giant . . . thing.'

'Oh, *that* beanstalk.'

'Yes, that one. Doesn't the whole scenario ring with even the slightest familiarity to you?'

'What do you want from me, Kreeper?'

'Nothing,' she replied evenly. 'I've just been asked to do a psychiatric evaluation to see if you are mentally fit enough to continue your duties, and I think it's important to understand why it is that you are so suited to nursery crime work.'

He stared at her, and she stared back. He took a deep breath and calmed himself. Something about her manner wasn't right. She had brought her own selfish agenda to the meeting. This wasn't an evaluation; it was simply a hurdle in the narrative. And as soon as he realised *that*, he knew he could go on the attack. He remembered some advice that DCI Horner had given him when he had passed the NCD reins across to him. 'Remember, m'boy,' his old boss had said, eyes twinkling, 'that if anyone tries to get the better of you, stand up straight and say to yourself with an imperious air:

"I am the new Mrs de Winter now!" You'll find it works wonders.'
Jack stared at Kreeper and narrowed his eyes.

'Mrs de Winter,' he murmured.

'I'm sorry?'

'Nothing. In answer to your question as to why I'm so suited to NCD work: after many years working among the nursery characters living in Reading I have grown to have an affinity with their way of thinking. Call it intuition if you like, but there it is, and I can't explain it.'

Kreeper's face fell at Jack's recovery. She thought she'd got him.

'Nothing else?'

Jack felt his heart stop thumping and was suddenly calmer.

'Nothing at all? Tell me, what kind of a parent named "Kreeper" gives their daughter a name like "Virginia"?'

She scratched her chin and looked away.

'Virginia Kreeper *is* a plant, isn't it?'

'Possibly. But this interview isn't about me, Inspector.'

'You're wrong. It's about *us*. And since you have to stand in judgement of me, I think I'm entitled to know just what sort of a person I'm dealing with and where you fit in the grand scheme of things. A tall, thin, beaky appearance with coloured-frame spectacles. Pointlessly aggressive, doubtlessly single and seemingly without a clue as to the proper procedure for a psychiatric evaluation. From where I'm sitting you look like a poorly realised stereotype; a one-dimensional character without backstory or future – and a name to match your bearing and position within the bigger picture.'

It was Kreeper's turn to be flustered. She ran a hand through her lank hair, trembled for a moment and then said:

'I . . . I . . . don't know what you mean, I'm sure. A stereotype? Bigger picture? What are you suggesting?'

'Let's put it this way,' said Jack, suddenly feeling a lot more self-assured, 'you and I have perhaps more in common than you think.

And you sitting behind that desk questioning my motivations smacks of the very worst kind of hypocrisy. Essentially, you're nothing but a vehicle for a series of bad psychiatric jokes and a plot device to stop me getting to the truth. A threshold guardian, whose only purpose in existence is for me to circumvent it – which I'm doing right now, if you haven't noticed.'

Kreeper stared back at him, trying to adopt a bemused air of condescension to disguise her sudden nervousness.

'A one-dimensional threshold guardian? No, no, you're quite wrong. Look, here . . . !'

She opened her purse and passed him a picture of a teenager in pigtails and wearing glasses.

'It's my niece,' she explained. 'I take her out on her birthday to all kinds of places. Last year we went to the Natural History Museum. So you see, I'm not poorly realised at all. I'm flesh and blood and fully in command of my own destiny – and having a recollectable past proves I'm not one-dimensional.'

She glared at him hotly, but Jack had enough experience of PDRs and incidental characters to know one when he saw one.

'What's her name?'

'Her . . . *name?*'

'Yes. Your niece has a name, I take it?'

Kreeper blinked at him, and tears started to well up in her eyes.

'I don't know,' she said at last, breaking out in a series of sobs. '*I just . . . don't . . . know!*'

Jack felt sorry for her. It can't be easy to have your entire life summed up in a few perfunctory descriptive terms, the sole meaning of your existence just a few lines in the incalculable vastness of fiction. Still, this was his career in the balance. If he didn't deal with her the Jack Spratt series was likely to stop abruptly at the second volume. No third book and *definitely* no boxed set. He passed her his handkerchief.

'The only question we have here,' said Jack without emotion, 'is this: am I sane enough to be back on active duty? Do we understand one another?'

But Kreeper was in no state to say or do anything. Her shoulders heaved with silent sobs and tears rolled down her cheeks. She buried her face in her notes and mumbled:

'*Why? . . . Why? . . . Why? Oh, the echoing void, the meaninglessness of it all!*'

Jack looked at his watch. This was becoming tiresome and he had a journalist to find.

'Her name's Penny,' he said in a quiet voice, 'Penny Moffat. She's your brother Dave's second daughter. They have another daughter called Anne who's at Warwick. You and Dave were brought up in Hampshire and once, when you were six and he was eight, you fell off your bike and cut your chin. That's how you got that scar.'

Kreeper stopped sobbing and looked up.

'Penny?' she said, picking up the photograph of her niece, then gently touching the small raised scar that had suddenly appeared on her chin.

'Yes. Your brother's wife is called Felicity and . . . she's the best friend you have.'

Kreeper's eyes filled with tears again, but this time they were tears of joy.

'She is, isn't she?'

'Yes. Last year you all went to Cadiz on holiday. It was hot.'

'Very hot,' agreed Kreeper. 'I got sunburned and had to spend the third day indoors.'

She smiled to herself, then at him.

'Thank you.'

'You're welcome. So . . . when do you put me back on the active list?'

She dabbed her eyes with Jack's handkerchief and took a deep breath.

'If it was in my power I'd do it here and now, Jack.'

He raised an eyebrow.

'But . . . ?'

'But the whole self-repairing car issue is a continuing sub-plot and completely out of my hands. The best I can do is ask you for some sort of *proof* the car is doing what you say it is.'

'I give you my word, Kreeper.'

She looked around and lowered her voice.

'Jack, you and I both know there are bigger forces at play here. If I don't have proof about your car I can't give you a clean bill of health. You know how it works. Besides, cars don't repair them-selves.'

'This one does. I bought it with a guarantee from this guy named Dorian Gray over at Charvil. Ever heard of him?'

'No.'

Jack stared at her for a moment. She was right – this *was* the best she could do. He snapped his fingers as an idea came to him.

'Come with me.'

A few minutes later they found themselves back in the under-ground car park, facing the shiny new Allegro Equipe. He showed her the oil painting of the busted-up Allegro but she wasn't impressed.

'So?' she said, hands on hips.

'I'll break something and you can see for yourself how it mends itself. Then you'll understand and I'm sane, right?'

'No; I'd be as mad as you – which is the same thing, relatively speaking.'

Jack took the wheel brace from the boot and with a single swipe took off the wing mirror and put a dent in the door skin. The mirror fell to the ground with a tinkling of broken glass.

'Watch carefully,' he said. 'The last time it happened the whole car repaired itself from a total wreck in under a minute so a wing mirror should be a doddle. Any moment now. Pretty soon. A few seconds.'

Kreeper folded her arms.

'Perhaps we shouldn't be watching it,' mused Jack after they had stared at it for more than a minute without the car giving even the *slightest* sign of repairing itself.

'Listen, I've been very patient over this—'

'Just turn around, Kreeper. We have to not be watching. That's when it works.'

Jack turned around and Virginia reluctantly joined him.

'I'm very busy,' said Kreeper, glancing at her watch, 'and if you want we can talk about this tomorrow.'

'It'll be fine,' said Jack, 'just give it a moment.'

They waited a minute and turned round. The mirror was still broken, the dent still showing clean and crisp in the door skin. Jack rubbed his head. This wasn't going so well.

'Listen,' said Virginia, resting a friendly hand on his shoulder, 'being swallowed by a wolf has probably stressed you out more than you think. You work in an area of policing that requires giant leaps of imaginative comprehension, and perhaps, well, you've been at it too long.'

Jack sighed.

'Then I'm not back on the active list?'

'No. Concede that this whole car-mending-itself nonsense was some sort of bizarre fiction-induced delusion and I'll suggest you return to work after a three-month rest.'

'What's the alternative?'

'I'll recommend retirement on grounds of mental ill health and they'll put you in front of a board of medics – and they'll be a good deal less understanding than me. It's a good deal, Jack – in effect, a paid holiday.'

She was right. It *was* a good deal. But he hadn't been seeing things.

'It happened, Kreeper.'

She sighed and stared at him.

'I'll leave you to think about it for a few days. My report doesn't have to be with Briggs until Monday next. If you change your mind,' she announced with the closest thing she had to a kindly smile, 'you know where to find me.'

And she walked off, leaving Jack staring stupidly at the door mirror he had just broken off. Perhaps Kreeper was partly right. Perhaps he *had* been overdoing it recently. But it didn't matter. He'd get Dorian Gray to explain the nature of his 'special' guarantee and he'd be back on the active list. He was just annoyed that his reality had been questioned twice in twenty-four hours, when no one had even suggested he was anything but genuine flesh and blood for over a decade. He turned and headed back towards the NCD offices, deep in thought.

'How did you get on with Virginia Kreeper?' asked Mary a few minutes later.

'Like two peas in a pod,' replied Jack sullenly, sitting down heavily on his chair, unable to shift thoughts of clean platters, beanstalks and Madeleine from his head.

'So she's going to give you a clean bill of health?'

'Not exactly. I've got to visit Dorian Gray again. Did you speak to the officer investigating Stanley Cripps's death?'

'Yes,' she replied. 'I told him about Goldilocks and the "It's full of holes" message and he was *very* interested. Goldilocks hadn't come forward after the blast and he'll be wanting to speak to her after we've found her.'

'It won't be the first time a reporter has committed the sin of omission,' mused Jack, dialling Dorian's number only to receive the 'unobtainable' tone.

'I've found several links between these explosions,' said Ashley, waving the folder.

'You have?' said Jack excitedly. 'What are they?'

'They all happened to humans – except the one in the Nullarbor Plain, which happened to sand.'

'Inspired. Anything else?'

'They all occurred on the planet Earth, the addresses all had an "A" in them, they all happened during the day except at Obscurity, none of them occurred in Antarctica, each was within a thousand miles of human habitation, all of them—'

'Any *useful* links. Like something Katzenberg, Prong and Cripps had in common.'

'Aside from them all being killed in unexplained explosions?'

'Yes.'

Ashley consulted his list for a moment.

'No. Not a single one. By the way,' he continued, 'I'm still waiting for Bart-Mart to come back to me and Goldy's car hasn't been reported abandoned or anything.'

'Thanks.'

'And Agatha Diesel dropped in to say "hello" while you were both out.'

'Did she?' said Jack, pulling a face. 'What did she want?'

'It was most odd,' said Ashley thoughtfully. 'She *said* she wanted to talk to you about a charity benefit in aid of distressed gentlefolk she was planning, but I think she just wants you to put your . . .'

He stopped, looked at Mary, gave a shrug and then placed a single sucker-digit on Jack's forehead.

'Yes, you're probably right,' agreed Jack after a moment, 'and most graphically realised, too.' He pushed Ashley's digit away. It detached itself with a faint *pop*. 'And please, don't do that mind-merging stuff on me, okay?'

'Sorry. Do you find it intrusive?'

'Not at all – it's just that I can see what you're thinking in the background.'

'Oops,' gulped Ashley, flicking a look towards Mary, who thankfully wasn't paying much attention, 'right you are, then.'

The phone rang.

'Spratt, NCD . . .'

It was Briggs so Jack just carried on talking.

'. . . isn't in right now, but if you'd like to leave a message when you hear the tone, please do so . . . *beeeeep.*'

'That old "pretending to be an answering machine" stuff doesn't fool me, Spratt,' said Briggs angrily.

'Sorry, sir.'

'What are you doing in the office?'

'I was with the quack for my psychiatric evaluation, sir – I just popped in to brief Mary about the Rumpelstiltskin parole hearing.'

'Hmm. Well, put her on.'

He handed the phone to Mary, who listened for a moment and then said:

'Yes, sir, I was very impressed you didn't fall for the answering machine gag.'

She looked up at Jack, who made a sign for her to call him and then crept out of the door. Briggs had been known to walk around the building on a mobile pretending he was in his office, and Jack had just about had his fill of threshold guardians for the day.

Jack walked down to his car and noticed that the door mirror had mended itself in his absence. He drove out of the car park, meaning to visit Dorian Gray and have a word with him in person. He'd called him several times but had continued to get the 'unobtainable' tone.

A few miles down the road, and after the brief annoyance of a checkpoint manned by soldiers looking for the Gingerbreadman, Jack's mobile rang.

'I'm going home to watch *Columbo*, sir,' he said without waiting to see who it was. 'Oh, sorry, Mary — what's up?'

He slowed the car as he listened, then pulled into a lay-by.

'Excellent,' he said at last. 'I'll meet you at the northern entrance in twenty minutes.'

He tossed his phone on to the passenger seat, indicated and pulled out into the afternoon traffic, heading rapidly off into the direction of Andersen's Wood. As he did so he noticed for the first time that the odometer on the Allegro was going *backwards* — and the fuel gauge was still on the three-quarters mark. He shrugged. Clearly a glitch of some sort.

15
Three bears

'**Largest Unmapped Area in the United Kingdom.** There are several areas of the UK which still defy any serious attempt at cartographic interpretation, but the largest by far is Andersen's Wood, a six-thousand-acre tract of forest to the south-west of Reading, Berkshire. The heavy oak canopy defeats conventional aerial photography, and cartographic expeditions have been known to become hopelessly lost, sometimes for weeks. A quick glance at the Ordnance Survey map of the area reveals only an irregular area of green with the legend: "here be trees".'

– *The Bumper Book of Berkshire Records*, 2004 edition

Andersen's Wood was remarkable not only for its mature hardwood, but for its *isolation*. Apart from one narrow asphalt lane running north to south there were no roads at all, just unmarked logging tracks meandering around the ancient woodland. It wasn't unusual for people to become lost while walking its leafy trails, and there were even rumours of a dilapidated and forgotten castle hidden somewhere beneath the heavy canopy, protected by an almost impenetrable wall of brambles.

Mary was waiting for him when he arrived outside the northern entrance to the wood and she jumped into his car as soon as he pulled up.

'So what have we got?' he asked.

'Mobile phone records,' she replied. 'Goldilocks had a "number withheld" call at 6.04 a.m. on Saturday morning which she answered. There was another one at 9.56 which she didn't, and several of the same all through the afternoon. Josh Hatchett's home number calls

155

her that evening and at regular intervals throughout the next five days. Seventy-six calls in total and about half with number withheld. None of them were answered.'

'Quite a few people withhold their numbers,' mused Jack, 'but her last *answered* call was the Saturday 6.04 one?'

'Yup. From there we can track her mobile as it began to move a half-hour later. It crossed eight coverage cells until it stopped in Andersen's Wood at 7.32. The signal faded three days later, probably as a result of a flat battery.'

'That doesn't really help us,' murmured Jack. 'Masts are few and far between in the country and cells can get pretty big – it will be like looking for the proverbial needle.'

'We got lucky,' said Mary. 'In the three days Goldy's mobile was doing nothing but firing off the occasional ident, it switched to another cell and back again six times.'

'It was moved?'

'I don't think so.'

She showed Jack a local map that had been faxed from Goldilocks' phone company with two intersecting polygons sketched upon it.

'Goldy's phone was at the *boundary* of a cell and the ident was bounced back and forth between two masts; by looking at where the cells potentially share coverage we can get a vague idea of where her mobile is.'

She showed him the approximate overlap of the two irregular cells and pointed to an area less than eight hundred yards wide and about three hundred deep which was on the western side of the wood.

'Let's just hope,' said Jack, 'she's still got her mobile with her.'

Jack started the car and drove slowly into the arboreal charm of the wood. He had often come here for picnics when a child. Its ancient splendour made it one of Berkshire's three jewels, along with the Sacred Gonga and the Castle Spongg.

They drove slowly down the main road and then took a grav-elled logging track, with Mary navigating, or trying to. She got them lost at least twice before they turned a corner and Jack abruptly stopped the car.

'Bingo,' he breathed.

'Gotta love those mobile phone records,' replied Mary.

Sitting by the side of the road, dappled with the sunlight filtering through the trees, was an immaculate Austin Somerset in all its 1950s curvy pressed-steel glory. The colour was green and the regis-tration 226 DPX. It was Goldilocks' car.

'We'll approach from the left in case this is a crime scene,' said Jack, getting out of the Allegro and walking slowly towards the Austin, which was covered with a smattering of leaves and broken twigs. There was a branch lying on the bonnet which had dented the panel.

'When was the last windy night?' he called over his shoulder.

'Sunday,' answered Mary. 'I feel them more than most on the lake.'

Jack nodded. The fact that a car could sit undiscovered for more than a week demonstrated the solitude of the forest. The interior of the car was dark and it wasn't easy to see inside, so with a heavily beating heart Jack tried the handle. It was unlocked and he opened the door, expecting the worst. He breathed a sigh of relief. The car was empty; Goldilocks was nowhere to be seen. Her mobile phone, its battery exhausted, was lying on the passenger seat.

'Anything?' called out Mary.

Jack checked the boot to make quite sure, but aside from a travel rug and a spare bottle of antifreeze, there was nothing.

'She's not here,' said Jack, and Mary cautiously approached from the same direction as Jack had.

'What do we do?' she asked. 'There's still no crime so I can't see Briggs agreeing to a search of the area. Not for the NCD, anyway.'

'Call Baker and Gretel,' he said, rummaging carefully in the glovebox, 'and see if they can't make an excuse to get out or something. Look at this.'

He handed her a receipt for fuel, neatly attached to several others in a bulldog clip.

'Theale services, dated last Saturday and timed at 7.02 a.m.,' murmured Mary. 'Theale's a thirty-minute drive from here, which puts her in the forest around 7.30 at the earliest.'

'And Theale is itself thirty minutes from her house,' added Jack. 'It all backs up the mobile phone record. She received a call at 6.04 and took – say – half an hour to get out of her house, half an hour to the services and then on to here. If I'm not mistaken, whoever called her on her mobile arranged to meet her here, in the forest – and as soon as possible.'

They looked around. All about them the forest stood heavy and lush in the summer's glorious embrace. It was like living in another world, or another age, when England was covered in lush oak forest, and humans were few. It would have been a haven for wild boar, elk and *bear*.

'Somewhere out there,' said Jack, 'is Goldilocks.'

'That sounded ominous,' remarked Mary, rummaging for her own mobile. 'I'll get on to Baker and Gretel.'

'Do that. I'm going to have a look around.'

He walked slowly into the forest, the crisp detritus underfoot sounding inordinately loud in the solitude. As soon as he stepped among the trees the high canopy of overlapping leaves shut out the daylight almost entirely, leaving just occasional spots of sunlight on the forest's ferny floor. Jack walked for a couple of hundred yards and then stopped. Not a bird stirred, not an animal dared show itself. He could see no sign of Goldilocks nor any sign of humans at all. There was nothing to be gained by meandering aimlessly in the forest so he walked back in the direction of the car. After five minutes, with no sign of the car, Mary or even the road, he realised he was lost. He'd heard the rumours about the forest's high lostibility index, but had not believed them until now. He continued walking in what he thought was the right direction, and after about ten minutes came across a small thatched cottage in the middle of a clearing.

It was a low building with a neat whitewashed façade and green door and shutters. The garden path was decorated with scallop shells and the humble abode had a cottage vegetable garden on either side. The whole was surrounded by a neat picket fence and a couple of fruit trees stood close by. There were several beehives near the back door, the gentle buzzing added a musical accompaniment to the idyllic scene. Neither telephone nor electrical cables led into the house. On the breeze there hung the unmistakable smell of freshly baked bread.

He opened the garden gate and walked briskly up the path, noticing that there was a hammock swinging gently on the veranda. But that wasn't all. Inside the hammock and snoring loudly with a brown derby hat over his eyes was a bear. A large male bear dressed in purple breeches and a blue waistcoat. Jack paused. He knew that a few bears lived in the wood but he'd never met them. These must be the traditionalists among them – most bears he knew preferred the comforts of the Bob Southey. The previous day's issue of *The Owl* was lying on the bear's massive chest and the remains of a honey sandwich and a huge mug of tea rested on a table near by.

'Hey!' said Jack, knocking on one of the wooden uprights that supported the roof over the veranda.

The bear didn't wake. He just yawned and displayed a huge set of sharp white teeth and a tongue the size of Jack's forearm.

'Hey, wake up!' repeated Jack, this time louder.

When this didn't elicit an answer he tapped the sleeping bulk with his foot. There was a grunting and a stirring and the bear licked his chops, coughed politely with his fist in front of his mouth and said, in a deep gravelly baritone:

'Is it dinner?'

'Police,' said Jack, holding out his ID. The bear pushed up the brim of his hat with one claw, squinted at the document and then looked up at Jack. He lowered his hat again and clasped his paws together over his stomach.

'So, Mr Policeman, what do you want?'

Jack put his ID away.

'The name's Detective Chief Inspector Spratt. I want to talk to you about a missing woman.'

The bear made no answer and Jack thought he had gone back to sleep. He was about to repeat the question when the bear said:

'You're a city cop, Inspector. I can smell the exhaust and concrete on your clothes. You had bacon for breakfast, buy your toiletries at The Body Shop and once owned a cat. You work closely with a woman who is not your wife, you did number twos less than an hour ago and you're lost – I can smell several different areas of the forest on you which tells me you didn't come here in a straight line.'

'You're very perceptive.'

The bear twitched his nose.

'The mighty sniffer never lies, Officer.'

'What's your name, bear?' asked Jack.

The bear chuckled and scratched his nose.

'Bruin,' he said, 'Edward Bruin.' He looked at Jack again and added: 'You can call me Ed.'

'How many of you live here in the wood?'

'It is not a *wood*,' retorted Ed pedantically, 'it's a forest. It's *always* a forest. Wood is something you make cricket bats out of.'

'Sorry. How many of you live here in the *forest*?'

'My good lady wife Ursula and Nigel, our son. The missus is indoors and Junior's at school.'

Jack nodded. There were *three* of them – things were looking better and better. He showed him Goldilocks' photo.

'Have you seen this woman in the forest some time in the last week?'

Ed donned a pair of spectacles and squinted at the snap, recognised her immediately and opened his eyes wide.

'That's her!'

'You've seen her recently?'

'Seen her?' echoed the bear. 'Why, she nearly wrecked the place.'

'When?'

Ed scratched his head and rolled off the hammock on to all fours, stood up to his full height, which was at least seven foot six, stretched, farted and then lumbered off into the house.

'Come inside, Inspector,' he said, beckoning Jack to follow, 'I want to show you something.'

The interior of the bear's house was austerely furnished but neat and tidy. There were only two rooms, one up and one down, and the downstairs comprised kitchen, dining and living area all in one. There were flagstones on the floor and the walls were finished in a pastel blue colour. A pretty pine dresser laden with crockery was against one wall and next to that was a small upright piano, the lid up and a book of hymns open on the music rest. In front of the hearth there were three stoutly built wooden chairs. A large one for Ed, a slightly smaller one for his wife and next to that a tiny chair that had recently been broken and remended. On the wall were various sepia-toned pictures of friends and relatives and above the mantelpiece was the Lord's Prayer embroidered upon a framed piece of cloth. The small dwelling was plain and no modern contrivances littered its simplicity. There was no television, stereo player or any modern appliance of any sort. The only artificial light was a large brass oil lamp in the centre of the oak kitchen table.

Mrs Bruin was at the range, taking a loaf out of the oven with a pair of oven gloves. She was smaller than her husband and wore a rose-patterned dress with a lace pinafore and a bonnet through which stuck her ears. She didn't take any notice of Jack at all.

'Darling?' said Ed in a low voice, holding his hat in his paws and blinking nervously. She looked up sharply and glanced at Jack.

'You've spilled honey down your front,' she said in a voice that was not quite as low as her husband's.

'Have I, my dove?' said Ed, looking down at the sticky stain on his blue waistcoat and rubbing at it ineffectually with a claw.

'You'll make it worse!' she scolded, and took a cloth to the offending stain. Ed gave an embarrassed smile in Jack's direction.

'What does the human want?' asked Mrs Bruin, again without looking at Jack.

'Police,' said Ed simply. Mrs Bruin stopped rubbing his waistcoat and looked at Jack suspiciously, placed her hands on her hips and said, in a weary tone:

'Okay, what's he done now?'

'Sorry?'

'What's he been up to? If I've told him once I've told him a thousand times. *Man is a bad influence*. I caught him wearing his baseball cap on backwards and he insists that the tongues of his sneakers stick out. He keeps on using terms like "Monster" and "Far out". Yesterday he sneaked a Gameboy into the house. He keeps on asking for an iPod and won't forage. He'll come to a sticky end and it's all *your* fault!'

She had directed the last sentence at her husband, who reacted as if he had been stung with a cattle prod.

'Mine, sweetness?'

'Yes, yours. If you'd been more firm after we adopted him we might not have a delinquent on our hands. "Clip him round the ear," I said. "Oh no," you said, "youth must have its voice," you said. Well, look what's happened. All *you* ever do is lounge around; I get all the meals and you won't lift a finger to help!'

Ed had been fiddling nervously with the brim of his hat, slowly backing away from the tirade.

'To think what I could have had!' she added, curling a lip at Ed and showing him a large white canine. She grunted and turned to Jack, smiled and said:

'He's really just a cub, Officer. I'm sure he was only under the influence of some of that human rabble from the village. What exactly has he done?'

'I'm not here about your son, Mrs Bruin.'

'Not?'

'No. I'm looking for this woman.' He held out the photo. Mrs Bruin glared at her husband, who shrugged. She wiped her paws on a tea towel and examined the photo closely.

'Ah,' she said, '*her*.'

'Perhaps you can tell me a bit more?'

'My husband will tell you all about it, Officer. He's the boss in this house.'

Ed stood up straight when he heard this and placed his hat on the bentwood stand. He led Jack to the other side of the room and offered him a chair.

'Have a seat, Inspector. Tea?'

'Thank you.'

'Honey sandwich? It's all quota – no substance abuse in this house.'

'Thank you, I've already eaten.'

'Do you mind if I have one?'

'Not at all.'

Ed licked his lips and shouted across to his wife:

163

'Two teas, pet – and a honey sandwich for our guest.'

He winked broadly at Jack and smiled slyly.

'So when did you last see her?' asked Jack.

'It must have been Friday morning—'

'Saturday,' said Mrs Bruin from the other side of the room.

Ed looked round. 'I think it was Friday, actually, dear.'

'Saturday,' she growled. 'We had to go to the vet about your worms.'

There was a ghastly pause. Ed looked at Jack with an expression of acute embarrassment etched upon his features. He smiled sheepishly.

'Thank you, darling,' said Ed sarcastically, 'I'm sure Inspector Spratt has better things to do than hear about my ailments.'

'If you hadn't been rummaging in the bins, you never would have got them in the first place,' replied his wife airily.

'I was *not* in the bins,' he said indignantly. He lowered his voice and turned to Jack. 'Worms can happen to almost *anyone*. Even,' he added, nodding in his wife's direction, 'to the trouble and strife.' He nodded his head triumphantly, checked to make sure she hadn't heard and then sat back in his chair.

'What were we talking about?'

'Goldilocks.'

'Oh yes; it was last Saturday. My good lady wife had made some porridge for breakfast – again, strictly quota – and we all went for a walk in the forest while it cooled.'

'Is that normal procedure?'

'Yes indeed; it's completely true what they say about bears and forests. Our morning *constitutional*, as it were. The forest speaks, you know, Inspector. Every morning it has changed in some small way. By the way the trees sway and the birds sing and the leaves—'

'That's very interesting, Mr Bruin,' interrupted Jack, 'but what happened about the porridge?'

'Oh, well, we came home to find that my son's porridge had been eaten. He was most upset about it.'

'Goldilocks?'

He held up a claw. 'Wait a minute. Then we noticed that my son's chair had been sat on and broken.'

'This one here?'

'Yes, I've tried to mend it but it's never quite the same, is it?'

'And then?'

'We went upstairs and found *that woman* asleep in my son's bed!'

The bear stared at Jack as though he should be as outraged as he was.

'Then what did she do?'

'Isn't that enough?' asked Ed angrily. 'You would have thought that finally, after two thousand years of being hunted, kept in grotty zoos, made to ride motorcycles and dance to some forget-table tune played by a repulsive and usually toothless eastern European, we members of the *Ursidae* family had won the right to be left alone.'

'She broke a chair, but surely that's not the end of the world?'

'It's the thin end of the wedge,' he replied indignantly. 'How would you like it if a bear wandered into your house when you were out, ate your breakfast, destroyed your property and then had the bare-faced cheek to fall asleep – *naked* – in your bed?'

'I see your point. Why didn't you report it?'

'What's the use? Most of the police I've ever met have been ursists.'

'Not in my department.'

Ed sighed.

'You may not *think* you're ursist, Inspector, but you are. You said to me earlier: "What's your name, *bear*?" Is that how you treat other men? "What's your name, *human*?"'

Jack could see his point. 'I'm sorry if I've offended you.'

Ed harrumphed. Since he occupied the moral high ground for the moment, he thought he would carry on.

'We've had a pretty chequered history with humans, you know. But the way I figure it, you lot can't seem to make up your minds about us at all. On the one hand you name constellations after us, make us deities and use us as strong national symbols, and on the other hand you hunt us to near-extinction.'

'Bears are not exactly alone in that category.'

'Agreed; but you also name athletic teams after us, create in our image tremendously popular characters like Winnie-the-Pooh, Paddington and Yogi, every child has a teddy bear of some sort, yet up until 1835 it was considered a fun day out to pay good money to see my kind either being torn apart by dogs or blinded and then beaten with a stick. Your first Queen Elizabeth liked nothing better than to watch us being tormented in some highly imaginative way.'

'I can only say that I hope we have made up for it,' replied Jack, unable to defend the indefensible but loyally trying to apologise for his own species' treatment of bears over the years, 'but the Animal (Anthropomorphic) Equality Act was quite far reaching.'

'Equality is *not* what we want, although it is a start,' said Ed slowly, flicking away a fly that was trying to get at the honey spilled down his front. 'Any creature that wants to be the equal of a human has set its sights way too low. We have an ursine saying, Inspector, which goes something like this: *If you crap with your arse in the mountain stream, the poo won't stick to your fur.* Do you see what I mean?'

'Not really.'

Ed frowned. 'Yes, I guess it loses something in the translation.'

'Tea?' enquired Mrs Bruin, placing a tray of steaming cups on the table in front of them. 'I'm sorry the mugs are a bit large, Officer, I won't be upset if you don't drink it all.' She smiled sweetly and tickled her husband affectionately behind the ear.

The mugs held about a gallon of tea each and Jack could hardly even lift his. As soon as his wife was back at the cooking range, Ed greedily ate up the honey sandwich that Mrs Bruin had put in front of Jack.

'Well, I'm sorry for all that, but my chief interest at the moment is Goldilocks.'

'Who?' asked Ed, who could be dense at times.

'The one who broke the chair.'

'Oh, *her*. Well, like I said, it's not the damage, it's the *principle*. An apology would help.'

'I'll see what we can do,' asserted Jack, wondering whether Goldilocks was in a fit state to apologise – or do anything at all. 'Why was she asleep in your son's bed?'

'Tired, I guess,' said Ed simply. 'We quizzed her, of course. She said that my porridge was too hot and Ursula's was too cold, but Junior's was just right.'

'So she ate it up?'

'Right. Then she said she tried my chair but it was too hard, my wife's but it was too soft, but Junior's, again, was just right.'

'And she broke it?'

'As you can see.'

'Then what happened?'

'Then she said she was tired so she went upstairs to bed. Again, my bed was too hard, my wife's too soft – so she fell asleep on Junior's. I've never heard of anyone so *fussy*.'

Jack paused for a moment.

'And she was asleep when you found her?'

'Right.'

'What time was this?'

'Half-eight.'

'And how long had you been out of the house?'

'Half an hour,' put in Mrs Bruin. 'We usually stay out for longer but we had to go to the vet.'

'Thank you for bringing that up again, dear,' said Ed meekly.

'Then what happened?'

'She got dressed and ran out of the house.'

'Did she have anything with her?'

'A bag. One of those work bag things.'

'And that was the last you saw of her?'

'Never saw her again, and good riddance. She had a damn cheek, Inspector.'

'But she was fine when she left here?'

He laid a claw over his heart. 'We never touched her. We were going to write a letter to *The Toad*. Their Henrietta Hatchett is a Friend to Bears and has done a lot for ursine equality.'

'Sorry?' said Jack, taken aback at this latest development.

'Miss Hatchett would have done something about it,' he replied. 'She has done a lot of good work for us in the past.'

'Had you ever met her? I mean, if you saw her would you recognise her?'

'No – why?'

'This,' said Jack, holding up the picture of Goldilocks, 'is Miss Hatchett.'

Ed's eyes opened wide and he looked at his wife, who dropped a teacup.

'That was Hatchett?' she said, turning from the sink.

Jack nodded and Ursula walked briskly over to them.

'YOU . . . *FOOL!*' she screamed at her husband, who looked terrified and tried to back away, which is tricky to do if you're already sitting down. He gave out a whimper and she replied with a snarl. There followed a protracted and very one-sided conversation in ursine which resembled a series of growls, whimpers and low barks. As they argued Jack looked out of the window, to see some cars pull up outside. Mary had arrived in his Allegro, and behind her Gretel and Baker bumped up the grassy track in the latter's Volvo.

'I'd like a statement from both of you,' said Jack, having to almost shout to make himself heard above the cacophony of growly noises. They stopped arguing and Ursula answered in a sweet tone.

'Of course, Inspector.'

Ed nodded an agreement and they both looked at the two cars unhappily. Machines, like humans, weren't that welcome in the forest.

Jack walked out of the house and met Mary on the garden path.

'Hello, sir,' she said. 'Any luck?'

'Goldilocks was here on Saturday morning – but ran away into the forest at about 8.30.' He turned back to Mr Bruin, introduced Mary and then said:

'Can you show me the bed you found her in?'

Ed shrugged a bit despondently and took Jack and Mary up the narrow stairs to the single bedroom, which was in the roof space. He nodded towards three beds of varying sizes.

'This one,' he said, pointing at the smallest.

'Did you wash the sheets?'

'Of course,' he said, shocked at the suggestion that they might not have.

Jack looked around. There didn't seem much more to be gained for the moment. They walked back downstairs.

'Baker, I'd like you to take statements from Mr and Mrs Bruin and wait for their son to come home, then do the same with him.'

Baker wrinkled his nose.

'Problems?' asked Jack.

'They're bears, sir.'

'I can see that.'

'Animals, sir.'

'So are we.'

'They've probably got fleas.'

Jack pulled him aside and whispered in his ear. 'Listen, Baker, I've been in there for half an hour and I'm not scratching. Tell the others and heed this yourself. If I hear of any ursism in my division, I'll have you up on disciplinary charges. Do you understand?'

Baker nodded.

'Yes, sir.'

'Which way did Goldilocks go?' asked Jack. Ed pointed a claw towards a small path leading up the hill to a ridge.

'Gretel?'

'Sir?'

'You and Baker should follow us up when you're done. Mary and I are going on ahead.'

They walked out of the clearing and back into the forest, this time following the path Ed had indicated. The trees were younger and smaller, letting in enough light to permit a thick carpet of grass to grow.

'How did you find me?' asked Jack.

'A woodsman told me he saw you over here. The bears' house is only five hundred yards from Goldy's Austin.'

Jack shook his head. He must have been walking in circles.

They followed the path up to the top of the ridge, where they found a high and very sturdy wire-mesh fence. Beyond this was a muddy landscape, a thousand acres of churned earth and stunted, shattered trees. A quarter of a mile away in the muddy wastes the remains of a small church nestled in a slight hollow near some leafless trees. On the hillside below the church the zigzag pattern of a trench was readily apparent, the web of rusty barbed wire an impenetrable barrier in front of it. Behind this first trench was a support trench and beyond this a battery of guns sat in supposed readiness. Behind them was the visitors' centre, unfinished and of modern brick and steel. The wasteland was totally incongruous in the green setting of Berkshire and an ugly scar on the land. Its construction had been fought at every step, but the theme park had gone ahead regardless. Jack and Mary looked up and read the threatening notice on the board that faced them. The message was clear:

SommeWorld
THIS THEME PARK IS OWNED AND
OPERATED BY **QuangTech.**
DANGER OF DEATH!
DO NOT ENTER. YOU HAVE BEEN WARNED!

'SommeWorld,' murmured Jack. 'That's all we need.' They walked slowly along the perimeter until Mary noticed a gap in the fence. She went and had a closer look as Jack forged on ahead.

'Jack, I think you'd better look at this.'

'It's probably kids,' he said, retracing his steps, 'wanting to have a look at the park before it opens.'

'Look,' said Mary, pointing at a small scrap of cloth stuck on the wire-mesh fence, 'it's a scrap of blue-patterned dress.'

'Goldilocks wore a dress of that sort,' murmured Jack as they both stared into the silent park. It wouldn't open for another three months. 'Thinking what I'm thinking?'

Mary nodded and they carefully climbed through the hole and looked around. The pockmarked damage of the shelling began about thirty yards in from the fence. The First World War theme park had been a major news story over the past six years. The biggest problem the designers faced was to make the park's 'guests' undergo a two-hour-long artillery barrage but with zero danger. No one knew how they managed it, but they had been testing for a number of months and all, apparently, was well. Jack and Mary picked their way across the freshly tossed earth and came across a large crater with battle debris scattered about and the remains of some barbed wire. The wire was real and it tore a hole in Jack's trouser leg. He was just surveying the disjointed landscape and thinking that perhaps Goldilocks was sunning herself on a foreign shore somewhere when Mary reached down and pulled something from the freshly pulverised earth.

'What do you make of that?'

It was not from the First World War, or even close. It was a small piece of white plastic the size of a Scrabble tile with the letter 'M' printed on one side. But it wasn't a Scrabble tile. It was a computer key.

'Her laptop?'

'Could be.'

They had both started to search the ground for anything more when there was a loud *whompa!* noise and a plume of earth shot high in the air less than thirty feet away. They ducked as the soil and debris fell around them and coughed in the cloud of dust that drifted across.

'What was *that*?' said Mary, rubbing her eyes.

Before Jack could answer there were two more dull thuds and two more plumes of earth shot skyward, this time with greater force – and closer. The search momentarily forgotten, they dashed for the fence amid a barrage of increasing violence with earth, roots and small stones cascading down around them.

Jack reached the fence first and threw himself through the gap.

'Well, Mary, that was . . .'

He stopped. Mary wasn't with him. He stared back into the barrage, the rising columns of soil and the pebbles bouncing on the ground in front of him. The dry dust in the summer heat drifted like a smokescreen and made him blink, hiding the scene from his view. He had run over his previous sergeant with his wife's Volvo and killed him. It was an accident, of course, but to lose one sergeant is a misfortune. To lose two would be considered . . .

He was just about to dash back towards the destruction to look for her when a small figure stumbled from the barrage which was now beginning to wane. She was covered in dirt, her hair was sticking almost straight up and she had lost a sleeve off her jacket. She fell to the ground quite out of breath but with a smile on her face.

'What happened to you?'

'I . . . saw . . . this,' said Mary in between breaths. She passed him a large section of broken laptop. 'I . . . thought . . . it . . . important!'

Jack turned the casing over. Written on the bottom, in indelible marker, was Goldilocks' name and phone number.

16

Somme World

'**Most Pointless Loss of Life in the First World War**. The
Somme offensive makes a good claim to this title, but competition is pretty stiff. Begun along a fifteen-mile sector of the
Western Front at dawn of 1 July 1916, the attack followed a week-
long artillery bombardment of an unprecedented 1.5 million
shells which achieved little except to warn the German High
Command of the impending attack. There were 19,240 British
dead on that first day – for a gain of only 1,000 yards. Despite
numerous "pushes" to attempt a breakthrough, little was accom-
plished aside from more loss of life, and the battle was abandoned
three months later. There had been a Franco-British gain of five
miles for a total casualty list on all sides of 1.3 million. An obscenely
profligate waste of human life? Undoubtedly. *Totally* pointless?
Maybe not. Historians agree that the German army never recovered from the losses and it is likely that "the foundations of the
final victory on the Western Front were laid by the Somme offensive of 1916".'

– The Bumper Book of Berkshire Records, 2004 edition

Jack and Mary drove into the car park at SommeWorld a half-hour
later and parked in front of the theme park's buildings. Most of the
visitors' centre was finished, but the roof was not yet in place on
the auditorium and the canteen hadn't even been started. Builders
were toiling round the clock in order for the construction to be
over by Christmas. That was four months away, but there was still
a lot to do. Two years behind schedule and ten years in the planning, the bizarre theme park was the long-time personal dream of
the Quangle-Wangle, the reclusive industrial, computer and shipping billionaire whose own experiences on the Somme had been

the basis of what he called 'the only safe real-life war experience in the world'.

They parked the car, entered the impressive dome-roofed visitors' centre and were directed up the stairs to the base of park operations. They walked along the partially finished corridors until they found the correct door, and Mary pressed the entry buzzer. She stuck an index finger in her ear and waggled it.

'I don't know how those explosions work but the concussion is for real. One went off a couple of yards from me and I felt my ears pop like a champagne cork.'

The door opened to reveal a young man of about twenty with a goatee and matching SommeWorld T-shirt and baseball cap. He looked at them both in turn.

'Can I help you guys?'

'Police,' said Mary. 'We want to see whoever's in charge.'

'Sure,' said the young man, leading them into the spacious control room perched on the upper floors of the visitors' centre. 'What's this all about? Someone complaining about the noise again?'

Inside the room were a dozen or so Quang-6000 computers with technicians hunched over them, doubtlessly trying to debug whatever problems troubled SommeWorld. In front of the consoles a large window assured the operators an unimpaired view across the battlefield. As they watched a squadron of low flying Sopwith Camels buzzed across the smoking battlefield as three separate explosions went off near the ruined church.

'No, no, no,' said the supervisor into a microphone. 'We can't get away with a simulated bombing run unless you actually *drop* something. Land and we'll try something else.'

'Mr Haig?' said Jack and Mary's guide quite timidly. 'The police would like a word.'

Haig looked up and strode over. His manner was abrupt but helpful.

'Good afternoon, Officers.'

He caught sight of Mary's tattered state.

'My goodness! What happened to you?'

'I'm DS Mary Mary, head of Reading's NCD, and this is Inspector Spratt. I want you to shut down the park.'

Haig knew better than to ask why. The park was a legal nightmare in terms of public liability, and everyone had been told to cooperate fully with authority. He turned to the operators:

'Code red shut-down, disarm all air mortars.'

Within a couple of moments the operators were leaning back from their terminals and stretching. To them, this was a welcome break from a long and tiresome day.

'As simple as that,' said Haig, the impromptu emergency procedure having been a deft display of safety. 'My name is Stuart Haig, overall supreme commander of control operations. We're in the middle of a test firing. Is there a problem?'

'I need to search your park where it borders Andersen's Wood.' Mary walked over to a large map that was hanging on the wall and tapped it where she'd found Goldy's laptop. 'Just about *here*.'

Haig did not display any emotion.

'Can I ask why?'

'We believe,' said Jack slowly, 'that someone might have wandered on to the park last Saturday morning.'

Haig frowned and tapped a few keys on a nearby keyboard.

'Saturday?' he echoed, staring at the screen. 'There was a test firing that morning at nine. An hour's barrage at one hundred per cent efficiency. I'd not like to think what might happen to someone caught in *that*.'

'We were caught in one ourselves over there not more than an hour ago.'

Haig scowled angrily, seemingly more concerned about the future of the park than their safety.

177

'Didn't you see the signs? How did you get in?'

'The fence has been breached. We were looking for someone when the barrage began.'

His manner abruptly changed.

'I'm sorry about that, Officer. Thank heavens you're unharmed. I can see we are going to have to increase perimeter security. I'll take you out there and we'll have a look around.'

He picked a Motorola radio out of a rack, handed them each what looked like a large wristwatch and a hard hat, then led them out of the control room, back down the corridor and out through the turnstiles, which led them through a farmhouse, ingeniously built to look half shelled and with a camouflage net over the badly damaged roof. On the dusty road outside was the debris of battle. Old guns, shellcases, rolls of barbed wire, scrap dumps, wood, cartwheels, everything. The whole park had been dressed with meticulous care and the smallest attention to detail. Even the road signs had been made out of wooden shell crates. Haig jumped into a mud-spattered Daimler and invited them up. The car started easily and they were soon driving along the bumpy road towards the bombed-out church.

'Kind of an odd idea for a theme park, isn't it?' asked Jack.

'*Unusual* is more the word I would choose, Inspector,' replied Haig. 'It's been a personal dream of the Quangle-Wangle for quite some time now. As you probably know he served with the Kent Fusiliers on the Somme and the experience never really left him. "If this facility allows people to really understand what war was about," the Quangle-Wangle once told me, "then we are one step closer to a peaceful planet."'

'Very noble words,' commented Jack, 'but won't a theme park dedicated to the battle of the Somme just attract those wanting to glamorise war?'

'Those are *precisely* the people we want to attract, Inspector,' replied Haig with a smile. 'It will be a sobering experience. All our visitors are dressed in uncomfortable and badly-fitting standard British issue uniform and sent up to the front with a full pack of supplies and a Lee Enfield rifle. They are accompanied by an RSM and two officers. We shell their position for two hours and then send them over the top. Nobody ever comes back wanting to glamorise *that*.'

'I see your point. What does the Quangle-Wangle say about it?'

'As far as I know he's pleased. We often send him videotapes of the progress here, but as far as I know he has never visited. The Quangle-Wangle is an intensely private man. The joke goes that a group of recluses start to talk and one of them says: "Hey, has anyone seen the Quangle-Wangle recently?"' Haig laughed at his own joke and then added: 'I've been working for him for fifteen years, and have only seen him once.'

'How do you do the artillery barrages?' asked Mary, who now had some first-hand experience and wanted to know just how dangerous it had been.

'We use air mortars,' replied Haig. 'A sort of large funnel pointing straight up with an air reservoir attached. The whole battlefield is networked with high-pressure air pipes. We arm the mortar by filling up the reservoir with compressed air at anything up to five hundred atmospheres, then release the mortar as we wish. We can control the blast almost infinitely, calculating the pressure against the size of the blast required and the weight of soil over the mortar. Don't be fooled by the fact that it's just air,' added Haig grimly. 'A ten-atmosphere mortar can take your arm off.'

'How do you stop fatal accidents, then?' said Mary, looking around nervously.

Haig smiled and drove on. 'The wristwatch thing I gave you is a proximity alert. No air mortar will arm or fire with one of these within fifteen feet. It means that you can be in the front lines under heavy fire, be showered by soil, smell the cordite, experience the battle – yet be in no *real* danger.'

The Daimler drove past the abandoned church and on up the hill to the area where Mary and Jack had been earlier. The terrain had changed since they had been there and several new craters had opened up. At the bottom of one they could see the air mortar itself, a cylindrical iron tube half filled with soil.

'Do you have any idea who wandered on to the park?'

'We have some ideas. We're going to have to sift through this soil, Mr Haig. It may take some time.'

Haig seemed unperturbed. It wasn't his theme park, after all.

'I'd better alert QuangTech,' he said, taking out his mobile and pressing a few keys. 'They like to know what's going on.'

He turned away to speak on the mobile and Jack and Mary started to look around for any sign of Goldilocks. After twenty minutes Jack made the first discovery. It was a woman's shoe, with the foot still inside it.

Mary called Briggs and he reluctantly agreed to send in the whole forensic machinery. Within an hour the area was crawling with paper-suited crime-scene officers, who divided the ground into sections and started a minute search while Jack and Mary stood by and watched. In two hours they had found several parts of her bag, assorted scraps of clothing, eighty-seven parts of her laptop and sixty-two pieces of gristly bone, the only recognisable parts of which were her foot, a finger and half a jaw, all of which had been sent to the labs.

'Will you be in early tomorrow?' asked Jack as he and Mary prepared to part for the evening.

'At sparrow's fart,' she replied. 'I've asked Mrs Singh to expedite that identification and I'd like to have the news as soon as possible.'

'Will you tell Josh as soon as you have confirmation?'

'Of course.'

'In charge of your first NCD murder inquiry. How does it feel?'

'We don't *know* it was murder, Jack.'

'It's murder all right,' he replied, 'take my word for it. Grown women don't wander into well-signposted and extremely hazardous theme parks accidentally.'

'Do you think the three bears have told us the truth?'

'Yes. It's all turned out pretty much as expected. I wasn't sure if she was *the* Goldilocks to begin with but I was in good company: neither did she. One thing's for certain, though: the moment she entered the three bears' house everything just started to slot into place. She couldn't have stopped the trail of events even if she'd wanted to. Her visit could only end in one way: with her running out of the bears' house and into the forest, never to be seen again.'

17
Home again

'**Worst Newspaper (Berkshire)**. *The Toad* appears at first glance to be the worst, but since it can't be strictly classed as a "newspaper" owing to its obsession with celebrity exposés and shameless tittle-tattle, the mantle of "worst newspaper" falls to *The Reading Daily Eyestrain*, which uses the "news" stories of road traffic accidents and law court reports merely to give some sort of vague notion of informed credibility to the pages of adverts for escort agencies, premium-rate chatlines and dodgy loan shark operations.'
  – *The Bumper Book of Berkshire Records*, 2004 edition

'Hello, sweetheart,' said Madeleine as Jack walked in the door, 'what did your psychiatric evaluator have to say?'

'I'm only mad if my car isn't. If my car is mad, then I'm sane – but I have to *prove* my car is insane for me to be seen as sane. Is that clear?'

'As mud.'

'And I think we've found Goldilocks – or bits of her, anyhow.'

'Murder?'

'Possibly. Have you seen Jerome's pet whatever-it-is today?'

'There was a gnawing sound from behind the hot water tank,' she replied, 'but I didn't see anything.'

'And the Punches?'

'They are the neighbours . . . from hell,' she replied coldly.

Jack looked at the partition wall. All was silent.

'They seem pretty quiet to me.'

'They're taking a breather,' replied Madeleine, consulting the kitchen clock. 'Since they got in from work I've noticed they have a strict rota to their arguments – fifty minutes of violent squabbling, then ten minutes' rest. Regular as clockwork.'

'Oh, come on!' said Jack. 'No one fights to a *rota*.'

'Three seconds from now,' said Madeleine, donning a set of ear defenders. Megan, who was doing her homework on the kitchen table, did the same. Almost immediately there was a thump and a crash from next door, all the pictures on the wall shook and tiny trails of dust fell from the ceiling. There was silence for a moment, then a scream of laughter and another crash.

Madeleine looked at her husband and raised an eyebrow.

'See?'

'I wonder how they got rid of them in their last neighbourhood?'

'Sorry?' said Madeleine, lifting one side of the ear defenders.

'I said: I wonder how they got rid of them in their last neighbourhood?'

Madeleine raised a finger in the air.

'Good point. I Googled them and found "www.hatepunch.co.uk", which is a website dedicated to assisting anyone unlucky enough to live near them.'

'And?'

'The Punches are pretty canny and know how to keep quiet as soon as the law or social services come round, and can drag noise pollution proceedings out for months – sometimes years. The only sure way to get them out quick is to pay them off with a cash "gift" of twenty grand.'

'That's extortion and possibly demanding money with menaces,' announced Jack. 'I can have them for that.'

'Apparently not,' replied Madeleine. 'They never ask for the money and deny they want it if asked – you just push it through their letterbox and a week later they decide to move on.'

'Hmm,' said Jack with a grudging respect, 'good scam.'

'It's the *perfect* scam. The residents' association have already raised half the fee. They want to act quickly before word gets around that Punch is in the neighbourhood.'

'Property prices!' snorted Jack. 'Sometimes I think they think of nothing else. But listen: all we're doing is passing the problem on to somebody else.'

'I think the residents' association know that, sweetheart. And what's more, I don't think they care.'

'I care,' he replied. 'There must be *something* we can do.'

There was another crash from next door which set the ceiling light swinging.

'On the other hand,' he added, 'they are pretty annoying.'

Jack had to ring the doorbell for a long time as Punch and Judy were having a fight and couldn't hear the bell for all the screams, swearing and breaking of furniture. When the door finally opened it was Judy, who had a cut lip and a nosebleed.

'Yes?' she said, holding a handkerchief to her nose and clearly annoyed at being disturbed during her leisure time.

'If Mr Punch did that to you I can have him arrested for assault,' said Jack, wondering whether perhaps Judy wasn't quite as much of a willing partner as she made out.

'Sod off,' she said, and slammed the door in his face. There were more sounds of crockery breaking as Jack rang the doorbell again and after another ten minutes the door opened once again. This time it was Mr Punch, who held an ice pack over his still-damaged eye.

'What?' he asked irritably.

'I just want you to know that I'm on to your little scam and I'll use every—'

'Get *real*,' said Punch cruelly, 'and *then* sod off.'

And he slammed the door.

'How did it go?' asked Madeleine when he got back.

'I had an interesting exchange of views with both of them,' he replied, 'and I'm sure we can come to some sort of amicable solution to the whole sorry business.'

'They told you to sod off, didn't they?' said Madeleine, who knew her husband pretty well.

'Yes. But I'm not out of ideas yet. That's not to say I have any, but I'm sure I can deal with them without having to buy them out. Besides . . .'

Jack was thinking about his session with Kreeper and his PDR-ness. Punch and Judy were not just neighbours, they were something closer to *family*. And besides, this was what they did. For Punch and Judy there was nothing else – just uncontrolled and pointless violence directed at one another.

'Besides . . . what?'

'Nothing.' He took a biscuit out of the tin and nibbled it. 'How was your day?'

She shrugged.

'It was dandy until the Punches got home.' She thought for a moment and looked confused. 'Jack, Punch said something odd.'

'He did?' asked Jack warily.

'Yes. I asked him why they insisted on beating the crap out of one another and he said that *you'd* understand because they'd beat each other up *as long as you continued not eating fat.*'

Jack's heart missed a beat and he felt a hot flush rise within him which seemed to burn his cheeks.

'He was just having a joke,' he replied in an unconvincing voice.

'You're hiding something from me,' she said. 'I know when you're lying, Jack, and you're doing it now.'

'Because . . .' began Jack, unsure of how to put it. He had hidden it from her for so long that he couldn't predict how she would react when he told her.

'Because what?'

'Because I'm Jack Sprat,' he said at last.

'I know that,' she replied, her voice dropping as she saw the pain in his face.

'Yes, but I'm not *a* Jack Spratt, I'm *the* Jack Sprat, as in *who could eat no fat.*'

She looked at him with a furrowed brow, unsure of what to say.

'. . . *whose wife could eat no lean?*'

Jack nodded. Madeleine's eyes widened at the sudden acquisition of this new knowledge.

'Your first wife ate nothing but fat,' she said slowly. 'That was what killed her.'

'I know.'

'You mean, you're a . . . a . . .'

'Yes,' said Jack softly, laying a hand on her arm, '*I'm actually a character from a nursery rhyme.* I'm a PDR, sweetheart, and have been from the moment I was born.'

Madeleine looked at him unsteadily. She felt confused, hurt, uncertain. She pushed his hand off her arm.

'How long have you known?' she asked in a quiet voice.

'Ever since I married for the first time and then started work at the NCD. DCI Horner said I was just the man for the job. I felt I *belonged*. It seemed too much of a coincidence.'

'And the beanstalk and all that giant-killing?'

'I think it's a question of economy.'

She leaned against the door frame, her mind whirling. She'd had no idea, no idea at all, yet now it all seemed so obvious.

'Why didn't you tell me?' she gasped at length.

Jack shrugged.

'I didn't want to lose you. I thought you might not marry me if you knew.'

She looked at him for a moment, then asked in a subdued tone:

'Am I one?'

Jack smiled.

'Of course not, darling.'

'How can you tell?'

'It was my *first* wife who "ate no lean" – you'll eat anything put in front of you.'

'Why does it always have to be about you? Can't I be a PDR in my own right?'

It was a good point.

'It's not likely. In the nursery world, surnames nearly always make good rhymes. Horner/corner, Sprat/fat, Hubbard/cupboard. Your maiden name of "Usher" doesn't rhyme with much except "gusher" and . . . "flusher".'

She said nothing but stared at the ground, trying to make sense of this unexpected news. They had been married for five years and she had never suspected it for one moment. Not *once*. She felt betrayed, and *angry*. Angry that the man she loved and trusted had been hiding something so fundamental from her.

'Nothing's changed, Madeleine,' said Jack soothingly, 'I'm still the same Jack Spratt—!'

'You might have told me you weren't real!' she blurted out.

'I *am* real,' he implored, 'in a collective-consciousness, post-modern Zeitgeisty sort of way.'

'What on earth does that mean?'

'I don't know. But what I do know is that . . . I love you.'

'Do you?' she asked, tears of anger and hurt welling up inside her. 'Do you really? Or maybe it's only because you're *written* that way.'

The barbed remark was like a dagger in Jack's heart, but before he could comment further Pandora chose that moment to walk into the kitchen with Prometheus. They were carrying a much-annotated seating plan for their upcoming wedding.

'Medusa has agreed to come with a pillowcase on her head after all,' she said. 'Do you think it would be awkward to sit her next to Athene?'

'Is he?' mouthed Madeleine to Jack. Jack mouthed back 'kind of' and Madeleine left the room at a brisk trot. There was a distant bang of a door from upstairs and Jack realised that it was going to take more than just careful words to undo the damage.

'Have you and Madeleine been having a row?' asked Pandora.

'Not really,' replied Jack unconvincingly, and went upstairs. The bedroom door was locked and he knocked on it very gently.

'Go away,' came a voice from inside, so he went downstairs to look after Stevie, who had discovered the dusty delights of the coal scuttle.

'Hi, Dad!' said Ben, who had just walked in. 'How's it swoggling?'

'I think your brother wants to be a chimney sweep,' replied Jack, attempting to put a cheery face on matters. 'How are things with Penelope?'

Ben was sixteen and awash in an almost toxic cocktail of hormones; the object of his unrequited love was Penelope Liddell, who played the harp in the school band. Despite his hard-worked best intentions he had utterly failed to convince her he was worthy of a date.

'Not that good,' he replied. 'About a month ago I overheard her saying she always looked forward to Laurence Sterne, so I spent the next three weeks reading nothing but *Tristram Shandy* and then quoted several passages and made a few obscure jokes of a Shandean nature to try and impress her.'

'What happened?'

'She asked me what I was talking about. I told her and she said: "Laurence Sterne? Who's he?" and there's no real answer to that except to say that he was an eighteenth-century pastor who wrote very strange books. Then she said she didn't see how pasta could write books, and any pasta *that* old would be inedible anyway and that Sterne couldn't be half as strange as me, and walked off. It was only later I found out what she *really* meant was how she always looked forward to Lawrence's turn . . . to go to the shops, as he usually had a few extra bob in his pocket.'

Jack patted him on the arm.

'This reminds me of the time when you heard her say she loved Keats – only to find out she wanted to have two: a boy and a girl.'

'Yes,' he replied mournfully, 'life is full of little misunderstandings. I'm now an expert on Sterne and Keats when a £1.20 investment in a Snickers bar and a can of fizz would have at least got me a cheery "thank you" and a peck on the cheek.'

At that moment Pandora walked back into the living room in a state of high dudgeon.

'No, no and no,' she said, 'we won't be having *any* live animal sacrifices.'

'Oh, come on,' said Prometheus, who had entered after her, 'it's *traditional*.'

'So was the Black Death,' she retorted, 'but I'm not having it at my wedding.'

'Just one teensy-weensy bull – barely a seven-hundred-pounder. You'll hardly even notice it.'

'No!' said Pandora, putting her foot down. 'I'm not having any animals put to death at my wedding. You'll be inviting Zeus next.'

There was silence.

'You've invited him, haven't you?'

Prometheus shrugged.

'I had to. Hera called and said the God of Gods was down in the dumps when he didn't get an invite. He was right off his smoting and hadn't even *looked* at a dusky handmaiden to ravage for over a week.'

'This is because I invited Aunt Beryl and you don't like her, isn't it?'

'I have no problem with your Aunt Beryl,' replied the Titan, 'it's that dog of hers that gets right on my tits.'

'What's wrong with Frubbles?'

'What's *right* with Frubbles? That's not a dog – it's a skeleton with hair. And why does it shiver all the time?'

Pandora thought for a moment. The shivering annoyed her, too.

'I'll speak to Beryl and tell her that Frubbles shouldn't attend because . . . because Cerberus will be part of the wedding procession, okay?'

'Okay,' said Prometheus sulkily.

'But no Zeus, no sacrifices, and *definitely* no sirens. Dad, will you back me up?'

'I'm with you on this one, sweetpea.'

'Very well,' said Prometheus, who regarded Jack's word as law, 'but Zeus will only cause trouble. Forget reason – he acts like a three-year-old in charge of the US Marine Corps.'

Jack bathed Stevie and put the younger children to bed after dinner, telling the kids when they asked that Madeleine 'wasn't feeling well'. He tapped on the bedroom door but there was no answer, so he went to bed in the spare room. After tossing fitfully for an hour he finally fell asleep, only to wake with a start. He patted the bedside table for his watch but couldn't find it, so got up and tiptoed down the hall to the bathroom. He looked in on Megan, who was wrapped up in her duvet like a dormouse huddled in a knot of straw. Jerome was asleep on the floor of his room next door, surrounded by Lego and Meccano.

Jack was just pondering whether to knock gently on Madeleine's door when a movement on the edge of his vision made him stop. He turned slowly, the hairs on his neck rising. At the far end of the corridor, staring at a large gold-painted vase that was sitting atop an occasional table, was the small ape-like creature he had seen the previous day in the cupboard under the stairs. It was not more than two foot high and was covered with a smattering of brown hair. It couldn't reach the vase and looked around for something to stand on. As it turned, the moonlight caught its features and Jack shivered. A large snout surrounded a mouth that was filled with brown teeth that were anything but straight. Small eyes stood below a wrinkled brow, and its ears, pixie-like, stuck out at odd angles from the side of its potato-shaped head. This, Jack knew, was Caliban.

He disappeared around the corner and reappeared a moment later pulling Stevie's trike. He placed it under the table and stood precariously on top, the trike wobbling dangerously. Caliban put out two hands, picked up the shiny vase and looked at it admiringly. He stepped off the trike with some difficulty as the vase was large and he couldn't see round it, then took several uncertain steps towards where Jack was watching. Jack waited until the little ape was almost on top of him and then plucked the vase from his grip.

'Ah-ha!' said Jack with a triumphant cry.

But Caliban wasn't so easily dispossessed of his property, and with an 'Ah-HAH!' he jumped up and grabbed it back, then ran off as fast as his short legs would carry him. Jack yelled 'Stop!' and ran after the small figure. The farce could end in only one way. The creature tripped over a fold in the carpet, fell flat on his face and dropped the vase, which then rolled towards the head of the stairs. Caliban put a paw to his mouth as he watched the vase escape him and Jack, more concerned now for the vase than interested in capturing the ugly little ape, raced past the creature, took a running leap, fell headlong on the carpet and just managed to touch the vase as it rolled out into space, bounced on the second stair, smashed on the fifth and scattered pieces of gold-painted porcelain all over the hall downstairs. Jack lay on his stomach at the top of the stairs and watched the pieces settle on the floor below.

'Craps,' he muttered. The vase was Madeleine's, and had been until very recently a priceless and much-loved family heirloom.

Caliban walked up to where Jack was lying at the top of the stairs and looked forlornly at the remains of the vase.

'Oh dear,' he said. 'Was it valuable?'

Jack closed his eyes as he heard a door open behind them.

'More than you know,' he answered in a low voice.

'Who did this?' asked Madeleine as soon as she realised what had happened.

'He did,' replied Caliban and Jack in unison, each pointing an accusing finger at the other.

'What?!' said Jack in outrage. '*You* stole the vase, pal.'

'I wouldn't have dropped it if you hadn't been chasing me.'

'I wouldn't have been chasing you if you hadn't stolen it!'

'I wasn't stealing it.'

'What, then?'

'I was *borrowing* it.'

Madeleine interrupted them both.

'I don't care who's to blame; you can *both* clear it up. My grand-mother gave me that vase; *before* she died.'

Caliban giggled at the non sequitur, but tried to make it sound like a cough when Madeleine glared at him.

'What's so funny?'

'Nothing,' he replied meekly.

Madeleine walked angrily back to the bedroom and shut the door with a bang.

'Thanks a bunch,' said Jack to the misshapen little ape as they both sat on the top step, 'you troublemaking little ignoramus.'

'I'm *not* an ignoramus,' retorted Caliban crossly. 'Ask me anything.'

'All right, smart-arse. Who owns Bart-Mart?'

'QuangTech,' said Caliban without a pause. 'Everyone knows *that*.'

18
Early morning

'**Most Suspended Police Officer (UK)**. As of writing, the most suspended officer in England and Wales remains DCI Jack Spratt of the Nursery Crime Division in Reading, Berkshire. Since beginning his career in 1974, he has been suspended from duty over 262 times, with only one of them leading to further action, a reprimand, in 2004. The next highest is ex-DCI Friedland Chymes (also of Reading) with 128 suspensions, with no further action taken on any of them. In consequence of this, the senior officer who holds the record for suspending the most officers is Chymes' and Spratt's immediate superior, Superintendent Briggs. Upon being told of his dubious distinction, he growled ominously: "You ain't seen nothing yet."'

— *The Bumper Book of Berkshire Records*, 2004 edition

Jack didn't get back to sleep at all that night and eventually got up at six. He had a bath, then went downstairs to have a cup of coffee and listen to the early news, which didn't carry any bulletins about the Gingerbreadman, so he figured he must still be at large. He thought of going to speak to Madeleine but decided against it, took his keys off the hook and glared at Caliban, who had somehow overcome his initial shyness and was sitting on the window sill, picking his nose and staring out of the window.

'Hey,' said Jack, 'you'd better be out of the house by the time I get back.'

'Yeah, right,' replied Caliban with a reproachful sneer, 'and what if I'm not?'

Jack jabbed a finger in his direction but for the life of him couldn't think of anything either vaguely threatening or even intelligent.

'Oh, nuts to you,' said Jack and made for the door.

'Nuts to you, too,' murmured Caliban, and continued to stare out of the window.

Jack got into his car, slotted the ignition key in, then stopped. Where was he going? His department wasn't his any more, and Briggs would almost certainly have something to say if he turned up there. He sighed. He wanted to stay out of Madeleine's way, but he didn't actually have any work to go to. He thought for a moment, tuned the radio to something mindless and settled back to think about Goldilocks. They had a victim but no obvious cause of death, no suspect, no motive, and no particular leads apart from the mysterious 'Mr Curry' and QuangTech, who seemed to be cropping up a lot. NS-4 were somehow interested and it seemed that Goldy had been doing a story about unexplained explosions. Then there was the Gingerbreadman, and Vinnie Craps, who seemed to think he was above the NCD's jurisdiction. And it was with thoughts like this that Jack drifted off to sleep, a lot more successfully than he'd been able to manage in the spare bedroom. He was just dreaming about the Dungeness nuclear power station and his Aunt Edith when the plaintive trill of his mobile phone roused him to confused wakefulness.

'Yuh?' he said.

'It's me,' said Mary.

'What's the time?'

'Ten past nine.'

Jack rubbed his face. He'd been asleep for over two hours, and noticed that Ben had written 'Working hard, Dad?' on the driver's-side window as he'd slept. Madeleine must have seen him sleeping and he half hoped he'd have a message from her, too – but he didn't.

'What's the news?'

'Positive ID from Mrs Singh – it's Goldilocks, all right.'

'What did Briggs have to say about it?'

'He said he wasn't going to elevate this to a full-level NCD murder inquiry without some sort of proof that she was killed unlawfully, but that I should continue "rigorous enquiries" with my current level of resources.'

'Which is you and Ashley,' observed Jack, 'a woeful lapse of responsibility, even for Briggs – he must be stretched thin with the hunt for the Gingerbreadman. Have you spoken to Josh?'

'I've just told him. He'd been expecting it but the confirmation was still a shock. I showed him the list of "Mr Currys" to see if he knew which one Goldilocks had been having dinner with the night before she died.'

'And?'

'He didn't even look at the list. He said it was a code name – and that Goldilocks had made him swear not to reveal who it was.'

'I've a feeling this is *seriously* bad news.'

'You'd be right. "Mr Curry" was . . . Bartholomew.'

Jack was suddenly wide awake.

'Bartholomew? *Sherman* Bartholomew?'

'The very same.'

'Why the secrecy? Was she investigating him?'

'Josh said we should ask Bartholomew.'

'He's right,' said Jack, 'we will.'

'Shouldn't I okay it with Briggs first?' asked Mary nervously. 'This could be a hot potato.'

'I've had hotter,' said Jack. 'Besides, Briggs said this wasn't a full murder inquiry yet.'

They agreed to meet at the council offices where Bartholomew was holding a surgery that morning. But Sherman Bartholomew wasn't a doctor. He was Reading's representative in the House of Commons: the Right Honourable Sherman Oscar Bartholomew, MP.

19

The Rt Honourable Sherman Bartholomew, MP

'**European Nation with Highest Politician/Lover Ratio**. Few European states can hope to compete with France and Italy in this department, and the two nations have been battling for European political Lothario supremacy for over thirty years. The contest has been increasingly acrimonious since 1998, when France was initially the clear winner, but somehow "lost" sixty-eight illicit lovers in the recount and had to concede defeat. The following year was no less rocked in scandal when the Italians were disqualified for "stretching the boundaries" of their elected representatives to include senior civil servants – and the crown was tossed back to France. No one was quite prepared for the disgraceful scandal the following year when it was discovered that one French minister had no mistress at all and "loved his wife", a shock revelation that led to his resignation, and ultimately to the fall of the government.'

    – The Bumper Book of Berkshire Records, 2004 edition

'I'm sorry we always have to meet under such disagreeable circumstances,' said Jack to a well-dressed handsome man in his late fifties. 'This is Detective Sergeant Mary Mary, also of the NCD.'

'I was the defence lawyer for the Gingerbreadman,' explained Bartholomew for Mary's benefit. 'No one else would handle it.'

'You put up a robust defence,' replied Jack with a smile.

'I'm always relieved it wasn't robust *enough*, Inspector. He got better than he deserved – have you caught him yet?'

'We're not on the chase. I shouldn't worry – you're the last person he'd want to attack.'

'I'm very relieved to hear it.'

Sherman Bartholomew shook their hands with a firm grip and offered them a seat in his office. He was that rare thing in politics, a free-thinking and radical MP who wasn't sidelined by his party to the anonymity of the back benches. He was an asset to the city and took his job seriously. The constituency surgery took place once a week in the council offices, and Jack and Mary had managed to jump the queue of disgruntled bears and other assorted citizens who sat grumbling in the waiting room. Bartholomew, in keeping with the strongest parliamentary tradition, shunned the possibility of any kind of scandal and agreed to see them straight away.

'Perhaps you might tell us what you know about Goldilocks, Mr Bartholomew?'

He didn't answer and instead drummed his fingers on the desk for a moment.

'It's a situation of the utmost delicacy,' he said without making eye contact.

'Was she investigating you about something?'

'No.'

'Extortion?'

'No!'

'Blackmail?'

'No, no – it was nothing like that.'

He stood up and paced nervously backwards and forwards behind his chair.

'Sir,' said Jack, this time more forcefully, 'I have to tell you that this morning we positively identified the remains of a woman we found up at SommeWorld.'

Bartholomew looked at Jack with a pained expression.

'Goldilocks?'

'Yes.'

'I need to sit down if you don't mind,' he mumbled, and sat heavily in his chair.

'We know,' continued Jack, 'that you dined with her the evening before she vanished. If you have been involved in any sort of parliamentary impropriety that Goldilocks was investigating it will almost certainly come out in the fullness of time.'

He looked at them both and rubbed his forehead.

'We were lovers,' he said in a quiet voice.

'*What?*' exclaimed Jack in undisguised astonishment. He was expecting any explanation but this one.

'Lovers,' repeated Bartholomew, 'Goldilocks and I. For over a year now.'

'Wait, wait,' said Jack in a state of some confusion, 'you were, to great fanfare, Westminster's first openly gay MP and have remained a vociferous mouthpiece for all kinds of minority-rights issues for the past twenty-five years, and now you're telling me . . . you're *straight?*'

Bartholomew covered his face with his hands and his shoulders shook with a silent sob.

'You don't know what it's like,' he said miserably, 'living a lie. I'll be ruined and disgraced if this gets into the papers. My parliamentary career will be finished and my hard-fought pink credentials reduced to tatters.'

'What about Douglas?' asked Mary, equally shocked by Bartholomew's confession. 'Your long-term relationship and much-publicised adoption of two children have always seemed so . . . perfect.'

'I did it for appearance's sake,' he mumbled sadly. 'Doug knows what I am and will stand by me if any of this gets out.'

Jack and Mary looked at one another as Bartholomew rubbed his temples and stared at the blotter on his desk, as though the dark smudges might reveal some sort of answer to his dilemma. He blew his nose and tried to compose himself.

'Mr Bartholomew,' said Jack after a pause, 'it won't be the first time I've had to investigate a potential crime that has involved sensitive issues of a strictly personal nature. But you must understand that our prime consideration at this point is to find out what happened to Goldilocks.'

'Potential crime?' Bartholomew said, looking up at him. 'What do you mean?'

'We don't know precisely how she died.'

'Are you saying she might have been . . . *murdered*?'

'No, I'm saying we don't know precisely how she died. I need to know more about the circumstances surrounding Miss Hatchett's death before we can decide one way or another; I'm not here to ruin anyone's career.'

Jack meant it. Bartholomew was a good MP and Jack didn't want to see him ousted over something as meaningless as his utterly conventional sexual orientation. Bartholomew served Reading well, and represented many of the nursery figures that Jack worked with. In many ways, the concerns of Jack's were Bartholomew's too.

'I think I knew deep down something terrible had happened to her,' said Bartholomew unhappily. 'It was unlike her not to be on the end of the phone. The police's involvement was predictable, too – but I must confess I was expecting a more – how shall I put it? – *conventional* branch of the service – no offence meant.'

'None taken. There appears to be a nursery crime angle to this.'

'Ah,' said Bartholomew. '*Bears*. I knew my support of them might be my undoing.'

'Bears?' echoed Jack. 'I never mentioned anything about bears.'

'I think you'll find that Goldilocks and bears are inextricably linked, Inspector. It was bears that brought us together, in July of last year. Since all the anthropomorphised animals in Reading are my constituents, I have a duty to promote their interests in Parliament – I met Goldilocks when she came to my office to press for a law to allow lethal ursine self-defence.'

'The "right to arm bears" controversy?'

'Yes; it seemed pointless to have given bears equal rights, only for them to be unable to defend themselves against illegal hunting and the bile-tappers who still stalk their community. If a hunter takes a rifle to kill a bear, it seems entirely just and proper to me that a bear should be able to obtain an identical rifle in order to defend itself.'

'The hunters claim it is not anti-bear or ursism, but tradition.'

'Prejudice is a product of ignorance that hides behind barriers of tradition, Inspector. We got to talking and before I knew it I had asked her out to dinner. We worked closely to draft the Ursine Self-Defence Bill. It was my fifth private member's bill and met with general approval, although the final vote was disappointing – six hundred and eight against and one for.' He sighed. 'A lone voice in the wilderness.'

'When did you last see her?' asked Mary.

'We had dinner at the Green Parrot last Friday. Do you know it?'

'I've *heard* of it,' returned Mary, knowing full well that it was one of the most expensive and exclusive restaurants on the Thames. It was *so* exclusive, in fact, that most nights the guests never attained the necessary high criteria, and it remained empty.

'What time did you part company?'

'About 11.00. We spoke again a little after midnight. I wished her good luck and . . . that was the last time we spoke. I called her at about 10.00 on Saturday morning but she didn't answer.'

'At 10.00 on Saturday morning?' queried Jack. 'You're sure it wasn't before?'

'Definitely.'

'And you withheld your number on your mobile?'

'Yes.'

'Sorry, please continue.'

'I tried the rest of the day to call both her mobile and her home but only got her answering machine. When I hadn't heard anything by Sunday evening, I went round to her flat. It was locked and dark, so on Monday morning I called her brother to see if he knew where she was. He didn't.'

'And he speaks to me four days later at the Deja-Vu,' observed Jack. 'You're the last human we know to have seen her alive. Did she seem normal on Friday night?'

'Excitable, I would say. She said she was close to an important breakthrough in a story.'

'About unexplained explosions?'

'No,' replied Bartholomew, somewhat surprised, 'it was about *cucumbers*.'

'Cucumbers?'

'Yes. Something big going down in the world of *extreme* cucumber growing. She said that her story would have major consequences.'

'And she didn't mention explosions?'

'Only in relation to that Stanley Cripps fellow's death. Other than that it was cucumbers, cucumbers, cucumbers. She spoke about record-breaking examples, the international cucumber-fancying fraternity, the fact that a cucumber is a fruit and not a vegetable, a member of the pumpkin family – that sort of thing. Bit boring, really – but it makes a change from parliamentary procedure and . . . I just like listening to her talk.' He paused for thought and his eyes glistened.

'Did she mention anyone else in connection with this story?'

'Yes,' said Bartholomew, snapping his fingers, 'she was going to have lunch with a contact on Saturday who she said would "reveal all". McGuffin was his name. *Angus* McGuffin. She said he was the key to the whole business.'

'Did she say why?'

Bartholomew shook his head. Jack and Mary looked at one

another. Perhaps Goldilocks had been working on *two* stories.

'Can you tell us where you were on Saturday morning?' asked Mary.

'At my house here in Reading. Doug had taken the kids up to his mum's for the weekend – I didn't expect them back until Sunday. I was alone until Agent Danvers picked me up at 11.00 to take me to the Sacred Gonga's visitors' centre for a lunch with the mayor and the Splotvian ambassador.'

'Did you call anyone, or did anyone call you?'

'Doug called me at about 9.30 and I must have fielded a dozen or so calls until Agent Danvers arrived.'

'So you can't account for your whereabouts until 9.30 in the morning?'

'No.'

They questioned him further but gained little else that was useful. He knew of no one who would want to hurt Goldilocks except a few disgruntled hunters and bear farmers. He regarded the notion that she might have committed suicide or ignored warning notices to wander over SommeWorld as 'laughable', and described her as 'fussy' and 'methodical', but quite obsessive and single minded.

'You've been very helpful,' said Jack finally. 'I may ask you some more questions when we know more. I'll let you get back to your constituents.'

Bartholomew rolled his eyes skywards.

'More complaints about the roads and hospital waiting lists, I shouldn't wonder. If you ever think you might want a career in politics, Inspector, think again. It's merely a continuous and mostly vain attempt to keep several groups of people with opposing needs and agendas happy, and knowing in your heart of hearts that you cannot, and being lambasted for your hard work into the bargain.'

He paused for a moment before continuing:

'Please keep me informed, Inspector – she meant a great deal to me.'

Jack drove by a circuitous route back to the office. He still wanted to get Dorian Gray to explain to Kreeper the nature of the Allegro's guarantee. On the way there, Mary said:

'Bartholomew genuinely seemed to have cared about Goldilocks.'

'I agree. It also explains NS-4's interest. They must realise that his days as an MP are numbered if even a whiff of his straightness gets out, and are trying to protect him.'

'I'd like to know the story she was working on,' mused Mary.

'So would I.'

'Sorry to trouble you,' said a young officer who had just waved them down at another police checkpoint, 'but I wonder if you have seen this person any time recently?' He showed them a picture of the Gingerbreadman.

'We're NCD, Officer,' said Mary, holding up her ID.

'Beg pardon, ma'am,' said the officer. He saluted, and waved them on. As they drove off they could see that the armoured car parked next to the road was full of heavily armed troops. Copperfield was clearly trusting in superior firepower to bring the Gingerbreadman down.

They fell silent until they reached Dorian Gray's used-car lot, or to be more precise, Dorian Gray's *ex*-car lot. He had done a runner. There was a mini-skip full of old brochures and headed notepaper, cheap furniture and a few old Leyland posters. The lock-up where Gray had kept the Allegro was open, and empty. On the forecourt, where the cars had stood less than two days earlier, a smattering of oil stains was the only evidence that there had even been a used-car lot there at all. Of the cars, the Portakabin, Dorian Gray himself and even the bunting, there was no sign.

'Blast,' said Jack, 'another missing person.'

20

Taking stock

'**Most (and Only) Successful Alchemical Experiment.** The experiments undertaken by Rumpelstiltskin in Reading between 1997 and 1998 have been the only successful transmutation in recorded history, whereby straw was spun into gold using a technique that is still not fully understood. Rumpelstiltskin, who is currently serving ten years in Reading gaol for his part in the illegal undertaking, has so far refused to divulge how the dried stem of a common form of wheat made chiefly of cellulose could be transmuted into one of the most valuable metals on the planet. For other unlikely gold-related records, see: Midas, King.'
— *The Bumper Book of Berkshire Records*, 2004 edition

'Ash,' said Jack as they walked into the NCD offices, 'see if you can get an address for a car salesman called Dorian Gray and someone named Angus McGuffin.'

'Will do,' replied Ashley cheerfully. 'I faxed that request off to Bart-Mart and they said I could go round any time. They were very keen to assist but had to confess they'd not appreciated how big a problem elephant theft was these days.'

'You didn't take the elephants out, did you?'

'I took *some* of them out.'

Jack shook his head and sat down. If they got hold of the security tapes it didn't really much matter about elephants anyway. He leaned back in his chair and thought about what they knew, which wasn't much, and what they didn't know, which was a lot. Then he remembered about the upset with Madeleine the previous night and suddenly felt guilty that he hadn't thought of it all morning.

He hastily dialled home but got only the answering machine. He didn't know what he was going to say to her anyway. He took a deep breath. He was what he was – a PDR – and he wasn't going to feel ashamed of it. He'd have to argue it out with her that evening.

'Okay,' he said, standing up. 'This is what we've got so far: Henrietta Hatchett, aka Goldilocks and "Friend to Bears", was talking to Stanley Cripps the Monday before last about cucumbers. At 10.37 p.m. that night a fireball rips through Obscurity, killing Cripps but not before he's called Goldilocks and left a message about something being "full of holes".'

'Are you suggesting Cripps was killed for his cucumber?' asked Ashley.

'Vegetable growers are not *generally* noted for being violent,' observed Mary.

Jack nodded his agreement and continued.

'Goldilocks returns to Obscurity to investigate, and calls her brother to say she's on to something "big". On Friday she meets up with her lover Sherman Bartholomew but doesn't mention explosions at all, and instead tells him that her story involved cucumbers. She names Angus McGuffin as someone with "information to impart", and is last contacted by Bartholomew shortly after midnight.'

'There was a call to her mobile at 6.04 the following morning,' said Mary, 'and the caller withheld their number. Sherman said it wasn't him.'

'I'm not convinced Bartholomew is our man,' replied Jack slowly. 'It's an easy shot to always assume the worst of politicians. I say we keep an open mind. Okay. She parked up in Andersen's Wood at around 7.30 and wandered into the three bears' house at approximately 8.00, after they had left for their morning walk. There is then the regrettable incident with the chair and the porridge and she goes to sleep in Junior Bear's bed. At 8.30 the three bears return, she runs off into the wood after trying to explain herself and then—'

'The test firing at SommeWorld was at 9.00,' said Mary, 'one hundred per cent efficiency for one hour. As Haig told us: "I'd not like to think what might happen to someone caught in *that*".'

'Right. And we find her six days later. Mrs Singh can't put a clear estimate on her time of death, nor tell if she was dead when the barrage started, or whether it killed her.'

There was a moment's silence.

'And that's pretty much all we know. Any questions?'

'Yes,' said Ashley, 'can you make "lightning" into a verb? I mean, it doesn't really sound right, does it? "It was lightning*ing*".'

'I meant about the inquiry.'

'Oh.'

'Why not suicide?' suggested Mary. 'The fact that she was working for *The Toad* and not *The Owl* shows she wasn't an A1 reporter. She'd been there for a number of years with nothing more remarkable than a few pro-bear articles to show for herself. And every journalist on the planet claims to have a world-beating story in their desk drawer.'

'What are you saying?'

'She may not have had any stories at all,' replied Mary, 'and just up and legged it rather than have to face the reality of her own failings. She could have been walking along the perimeter fence at SommeWorld, saw the barrage going on, found the gap in the fence and just . . . wandered in.'

'It's *possible*,' said Jack, 'but her bag was destroyed with her. She would have had to have taken it *off* her shoulder to get through the gap, and then put it back *on* again to walk in. No, I'd have left the bag at the fence.'

Mary nodded. Jack's scenario was the more feasible of the two.

'I've got another question,' said Ashley, raising his hand.

'A proper one?'

'Yes. What's the deal with QuangTech and the Quangle-Wangle? They seem to be popping up a lot in this inquiry and so far we don't know anything about them at all.'

'Good point,' said Jack. 'I'll tell you both what I know, since QuangTech does fall under the NCD's jurisdiction. It's the biggest corporation run entirely by PDRs.'

'I never knew that,' said Mary.

'It's not generally known. They don't spread it around in case it affects the stock values. James Finlay Arnold Quangle-Wangle was the brains behind a group of nine undergraduates who all left Oxford in 1947. Each one contributed to the Quang business empire, and all aside from Horace Bisky-Batt fell out of favour as time went on. They all made a fortune, of course, but nothing approaching the net worth of the Quang himself.'

'These nine,' said Mary. 'Anyone we know?'

'All movers and shakers in the world of high finance and business. Mr Attery-Squash owns *The Owl* and several publishing companies. He and the Quangle-Wangle had a bust-up in the early eighties over copyright disagreements. The Quangle-Wangle gave Mr Attery-Squash Crumpetty-Tree Press as a pay off.'

'Who else?'

'Aside from Horace Bisky-Batt they all left under a cloud. The Dong with the Luminous Nose looked after their finance division and now lives near Oxford. He's under a cloud of his own most days – an alcoholic one. Mr and Mrs Canary run a chain of hotels in the Far East, the performer and record producer Blue Baboon lives in Los Angeles and George Fimble-Fowl who ran the QuangTech weapons division shot himself. The computing arm of QuangTech and the responsibility for the hugely successful Quang-5000 series of personal computers was Roderick Pobble, who now lives the life of a hermit on his own island off the Hebridean coast. Finally, the textile designer known only as "the Orient Calf from the land of Tute" died in a car accident three years ago.'

'Did you ever meet the Quangle-Wangle?' asked Ashley.

'Several times,' replied Jack. 'He used to be very visible in the town. Always sombre, always philanthropic. As he grew older he went out less and less until he just stopped going out altogether. I've heard he lives in the QuangTech facility. Never had any family; just devoted his life to making money – and did pretty well at it, too, which is why I suppose he can afford to spend nearly two hundred million on SommeWorld.'

'Are you still here?' said a voice from the door. It was Briggs.

'I was just going over my Scissor-man testimony with DS Mary, sir.'

'Sure you were,' replied Briggs, clearly not believing a word. 'Did you talk to Dr Kreeper?'

'Yes, sir.'

'Funny – she hasn't spoken to me about it.'

Jack breathed a silent sigh of relief. Kreeper was keeping her promise. He still had a few days to prove that the Allegro was self-mending before the metaphorical straitjacket began to tighten.

'Any news on the Gingerbreadman, sir?'

'Not that it's any of your business, but yes, Copperfield cornered him in the menswear section of Marks & Spencer.'

'And?'

Briggs looked at the floor for a moment.

'He fought his way out using extreme levels of concentrated violence, then returned ten minutes later because he wanted to exchange the zip-up cardigan he'd stolen for a grey macintosh with removable liner. He leapt through a plate-glass window to escape and ran into the Oracle centre, where we lost him in the car park. I thought the newspapers would tear into us at the press conference but that Josh Hatchett fellow asked how he and his readers could *help*. How strange was that?'

'Very,' replied Jack. Hatchett, also true to his word, was supporting an NCD inquiry. If only it had been one that Jack was on, he might have cause to thank him.

'Right,' said Briggs, 'off you toddle, then – I've got to speak to the head of the NCD.'

He said it without malice, but it didn't sound good, or right. Jack left the office but he didn't go far – he just locked himself in the NCD annexe next door; the one they used for additional filing which was too small even for the cleaners. He needed the peace and quiet to make a few enquiries of his own. Stuart Haig of SommeWorld was first on the list. Jack wanted to know why they had chosen that *particular* sector for the test firing on Saturday morning. Haig told him it was chosen automatically by the central QuangTech mainframe, based on a simple algorithm to ensure the park was pulverised equally all over, ostensibly to keep the soil soft for the air mortars to work effectively. Jack thanked him and hung up. Vinnie Craps was next, but his voicemail told him he was in Cologne on business. He then called QuangTech to make an appointment to see the CEO and was politely informed that *no one* saw the Quangle-Wangle – not even members of the board. He then asked for an interview with the vice-president and was told 'to drop in at any time'.

'So, Acting NCD Head Mary, what have we got?' asked Briggs, who had taken a sudden and unhealthy interest in the Goldilocks inquiry, given the absence of progress on the only other case gaining the public's attention at the time.

'Very difficult to say,' replied Mary, thinking she'd not mention the bit about McGuffin, Bartholomew or the explosions – or anything at all, in fact. 'We have a positive ID but with Goldilocks' body in such a fragmented state it's impossible to tell whether she was dead before the barrage, or whether it killed her – or even to establish a cause or specific time of death at all.'

'On reflection it might be a good idea to find out that she was murdered,' said Briggs matter-of-factly, 'and for you to then foul it all up. I've got a PR disaster over the lack of progress on the Gingerbreadman case and I was hoping a bit of well-publicised incompetence by the NCD might draw the flak, so to speak.'

'I'll see what we can arrange,' said Mary agreeably, trying to act how she thought Jack might.

'Splendid, splendid.'

He gathered up his papers and prepared to leave.

'Goodness gracious me!' he exclaimed as Ashley walked in. 'What's that?'

'That's Constable Ashley,' replied Mary. 'He's part of the alien equal opportunities programme.'

'PC Ashley is a *real* alien?' echoed Briggs incredulously. 'I thought he was just from Splotvia or something. What sort of misguided lunatic puts little blue men in the police force?'

'The Chief Constable,' replied Mary, hiding a smile.

'Fine idea,' said Briggs with a volte-face that was rapid even by his own exacting standards. 'Does it talk?'

'It talks very well, thank you,' said Ashley indignantly, offering his hand for Briggs to shake.

Before Mary could stop him Briggs's hand had been enveloped by Ashley's warm and sticky digits. Mary had shaken hands with Ashley once before, and his inner thoughts had transferred themselves to her – a slimy embrace in an alien marsh, if memory served.

'Oh!' said Briggs in a shocked tone as Ashley stared at him and blinked his large eyes twice. 'No, I didn't realise that, I'm sorry.'

Ashley relaxed his grip and released Briggs, who stood up straight and strode from the room without another word.

'What did you say to him?'

'The *truth*. Do you know what his greatest fear is?'

'I've got a feeling I shouldn't know. Promotion? His budget?'

'Neither,' replied Ashley. 'He worries . . . that his wife doesn't love him.'

'Agatha?' mused Mary. 'I wonder where he gets *that* idea. Still, I suppose it softens him a bit, don't you think?'

Mary gave her first NCD news conference at 10.30 to a hushed response from Reading's journalists. There were no questions; just a comment from Hector Sleaze that Mary could expect to receive all possible help and cooperation from everyone present. There was a chorus of approval for this sentiment, and Mary asked anyone who knew what stories Goldilocks was working on to contact her. No one did. Later on she fielded a call from Jeremy Bearre of the *Ursine Chronicle* who wanted some facts for an obituary, but at the same time confirmed that, yes, Goldilocks had written several pieces for the *Chronicle* in the past, mostly about issues regarding the iniquity of the quota system, the urgent need to protect wild bears and advocating stricter controls over marmalade availability. Her 'Friend to Bears' status had been conferred upon her over a year earlier.

'It's a very special honour and one not given lightly,' explained Jeremy. 'It bestows protection on the holder from any bear, without question, even unto the Forest.'

'The Forest?'

'When bears die it is known as "returning to the Perpetual Forest". The magnificence of that unsullied forest can be yours, too – but you have to be friendly to bears to find it.'

'That's very lyrical,' said Mary.

'Forests are like that,' answered Jeremy.

'Oh-ho!' murmured Ashley a few minutes later. He knocked twice on the wall and Jack emerged shortly after, looking about warily for Briggs.

'What have you got?'

'I just found Angus McGuffin,' said Ash, staring at his VDU. 'And he's in Reading: municipal cemetery plot 10010101-B1001.'

'He's dead?'

'Killed in a lab accident 10000 years ago,' continued Ashley. 'I've got a copy of his death certificate.'

'10000? That's . . . sixteen years, 1988. Was he big in cucumbers?'

'No; he was big in physics. He was *Professor* McGuffin and died in a lab accident at QuangTech.'

'QuangTech,' murmured Jack, 'again. What kind of lab accident?'

'A violently explosive one. There weren't any parts big enough to identify, so the coroner had to pronounce death without a body.'

'How convenient. See if you can't get a full transcript of the inquest.'

He turned to Mary.

'Why do you suppose Goldilocks would tell Bartholomew that she'd be meeting a dead man for lunch on Saturday?'

'I've no idea.'

'Me neither. Ash, I want you to find out more about McGuffin. In particular his work and the possibility that he's not dead – and any news of Dorian Gray?'

'None, sir.'

'Keep on it.'

'What now?' asked Mary.

'We retrace her steps. Start at the very beginning.'

'The three bears' cottage?'

'Earlier.'

21
Driven to Obscurity

'**Largest Unexplained Explosion (UK)**. Unofficial sources credit the sixteen separate explosions at the QuangTech facility in Berkshire between 1984 and 1988 as the largest *series* of unexplained explosions, the last and strongest of which resulted in the death of the supposed instigator, Professor Angus McGuffin. The blast was heard all over Reading, broke windows within a two-mile radius and even disturbed the peace at the Reading Gentlemen's Club, where they responded by penning a stiff letter of reproach, which was then forwarded to the Quangle-Wangle.'
– *The Bumper Book of Berkshire Records*, 2004 edition

'Welcome to Obscurity,' said the vicar kindly, shaking their hands.

Jack and Mary had arrived at the village – after becoming hopelessly lost – two hours later. The damage to Obscurity was readily apparent before they even reached the edge of the small hamlet. Fallen trees and hedges blackened by fire guided them the last half-mile or so.

'As you can see not many buildings were spared the damage of that night,' explained the vicar, waving his arm in the direction of the vicarage. The windows had been boarded up and blue plastic tarpaulins were draped across the roof. 'I'm five hundred yards from Stanley's house and this is the result. Would you like some tea and a scone?'

'Maybe later,' Jack replied.

'They're very good scones.'

'I'm sure they are. But this is a matter of some urgency.'

'Then I'll show you around.'

They walked past the church, which had lost the top of its steeple and all its windows. The yew in the churchyard had burned where it stood, as had many of the surrounding trees, hedges and crops. This and the blackened texture of the stone walls and buildings gave the whole area a scorched hell-on-earth look.

'Large graveyard,' observed Jack as he peered over the wall.

'You'd be surprised by the number of people who die in Obscurity,' observed the vicar. 'The gravediggers are rarely out of work.'

'What was Stanley Cripps like?' asked Mary.

'Quiet fellow. A brilliant man in his day, I understand – something big in the power industry. After his wife died he immersed himself in vegetable-growing in general and cucumbers in particular; he rarely showed anyone what he was doing but I was once granted access to his cucumbertorium. This year's effort was a *remarkable* sight.'

He stretched his arms out wide in the manner of a hyperbolic fisherman.

'I've never seen anything quite like it. He said it would take the world championships by storm.'

'They *have* cucumber world championships?'

'Indeed they do,' replied the vicar. 'He took his vegetables extremely seriously. After almost twenty years of work, it was a very great tragedy that Stanley didn't live long enough to enjoy the fruits – or should I say *vegetables* – of his labours.'

He laughed at his own joke for a moment, noticed that Jack and Mary hadn't joined him and turned the laugh into a cough.

'Who knew him best? You?' asked Jack.

'I wish I could boast that, but no. As I understand it he was closest to Mr Hardy Fuchsia, his old colleague and only serious competitor in the Cucumber Extreme class. Despite Mr Fuchsia's pre-eminence in the field, I understood they spoke frequently. If you want to know more about Stanley, best call on Hardy.'

'They never found Mr Cripps, did they?' asked Jack, who had read several accounts of the incident that morning, everything from the official government report to misinformation and half-truths in the self-appointed journal of the conspiracy world, *Conspiracy Theorist*.

'They found his dentures embedded in a tree a quarter of a mile away,' replied the vicar. 'It took a crowbar to get them out. But they don't think he was wearing them at the time; his bedside lamp was also found close by.'

They walked past another house that had completely lost its roof and was abandoned, ready for demolition. The damage was considerably worse here, even though they had walked less than a hundred yards.

'The *devastation* increases *exponentially* the closer we get to the *epicentre*,' explained the vicar, who had spent the days after the event talking to curious onlookers and had learned a few destructive buzzwords. 'It was an unexploded "Grand Slam" wartime bomb, apparently. Look at the trees.'

They passed another house, this one almost flattened. The trees were indeed a good indication of the centre of the blast – they all had been felled in straight lines radiating outwards.

'Mr Cripps's last words were "Good heavens, it's full of holes!",' said Mary. 'Do you have any idea to what he was referring?'

'Most puzzling,' confessed the vicar. 'He might have been referring to anything – the greenhouse, his cucumber, the plot – anything.'

'The plot?' echoed Mary.

'I mean the *vegetable* plot,' he said hurriedly. 'A slip of the tongue. Vandals may have dug it up – holes, you know. Hm.'

There were quite a few tourists wandering around although there was precious little to look at, but this didn't seem to bother them. Quasi-scientific-looking people dressed in lab coats were conducting experiments of an entirely spurious nature on anything they could find, and a local farmer was doing a brisk trade renting out a field for parking. On the verges and the village green an eccentric and brightly coloured collection of tents and yurts had been set up, offering refreshments and advice on spiritual matters. There seemed to be quite a few Druids kicking around, too.

They had reached the village's one and only street lamp next to its one and only telephone box, or what was left of them. The cast-iron lamp standard had melted like a soft candle and the phone box had collapsed gently in on itself in the same manner.

'The glass from the phone-box windows had melted and then cooled in mid-flow, like icicles,' explained the vicar. 'It was quite lovely – but most of it was taken by souvenir hunters. Neither of these will be replaced; we want to keep them as a memorial to Stanley.'

They walked on for a few moments into an increased density of aimless milling crowds.

'We've had thousands of people through here but it all seems to be slackening off, praise the Lord.'

'This is "slackening off"?' asked Jack, looking at the crowds.

'You should have seen it last week,' said the vicar with a smile. 'There was a mile-wide no-go zone while the area was made safe. As soon as the cordon was lifted it was like a plague of locusts. For a moment we thought we might have to change the village's name to "Popularity".'

The vicar chuckled at his own joke.

'Well, this was Stanley's property,' he said, waving his hand at a flat piece of hard-packed soil which had been roped off and contained nothing except a white-coated individual who was passing some sort of humming sensor over the ground. 'That's Dr Parks. He'll answer questions if you find him in a good mood. Do drop in for tea before you go, won't you? My wife does a mean scone.'

He smiled, shook their hands, and was gone.

Jack and Mary stared at the expanse of well-trodden ground among a group of forty or so others doing exactly the same.

'It's not the original soil,' said a man dressed in tinfoil overalls and holding a crystal.

'No?'

'No. The crater was fully excavated by government inspectors who then filled in the hole with eighty tons of new topsoil.'

'That was charitable of them,' remarked Jack.

'Charitable be damned,' said their new friend. 'All it did was hamper the investigations of the *independent* scientists who arrived as soon as they could.'

They learned from several other passers-by who seemed to be in the know that the government's interventions had given the conspiracy theorists a field day, and six books with equally bizarre and implausible explanations were being hurried to the bookshops. The most popular concept was of some sort of modern battlefield-sized nuclear device delivered accidentally by a fighter-bomber, although the lesser theories were still considered quite seriously: a meteor strike, an unprecedented ball-lightning explosion, the planned arrival of an asteroid made entirely of sapphire, an attack by French cucumber terrorists intent on nobbling the opposition, the arrival of Lucifer to cleanse man's wickedness or even – if you *really* stretched your imagination – an overlooked wartime 'Grand Slam' bomb that spontaneously detonated.

They walked over to Dr Parks, who was absorbed in his work and didn't hear them approach. When Jack spoke he jumped, and then glared at them testily. He was aged about thirty and looked tanned and fit, for an academic. It was soon apparent that he didn't hold government agencies, police included, in very high esteem.

'Dr Parks?' asked Jack. 'May we have a word?'

He looked them both up and down.

'Police?'

'Well, yes,' replied Jack, a bit miffed that it should be so obvious. 'I'm DCI Spratt; this is Sergeant Mary.'

The scientist chuckled to himself.

'You're a bit late. I got here as soon as the government would let me and even *then* I was too late. Which theory do you guys adhere to?'

'We're not so much interested in the phenomenon as in a journalist who was investigating it.'

'Which journalist? There must have been dozens.'

Jack showed him a photo of Goldilocks. Dr Parks stared at it for a moment, then at Jack and Mary.

'Yes, I remember her. She was one of the first in once the government lifted the cordon on Wednesday morning. She sticks in my mind because she didn't treat any of us out here on the outer fringes of science as loonies and geeks. Everyone else does.'

'Did you know she was talking to Cripps the day *before* the explosion?'

'If she was,' replied Parks, 'there're a lot of people who'd like to speak to her.'

'They'll be disappointed. She died on Saturday morning.'

'Murdered by the government?' he asked excitedly, his conspiratorial leanings springing to the fore. 'Now that *would* be good.'

'From my experience of government departments,' said Jack, 'they couldn't order the right size of staples, let alone succeed in anything as bizarrely complex as a murder and then a subsequent cover-up.'

'Yes,' agreed Parks sulkily, 'it's where that particular mainstay of conspiracy theory falls down. I hate to admit it, but governmental deviousness is usually better explained by incompetence, vanity and the need to protect one's job at all costs. Still, I liked her.'

'What else can you remember about her?'

'Not much,' said Parks after a moment's thought, 'except . . .'

'Except what?'

'Except she was the only one who asked me about . . . *McGuffin*.'

'Professor Angus McGuffin?'

Parks registered surprise that they knew about him.

'You've heard of him? Not many people have outside the pseudo-science elite. He's been dead these past sixteen years; a great loss to the conspiracy industry. When Guff was around there was always lots of wild conjecture to try and dress up as serious scientific study.'

'What sort of work did McGuffin indulge in?' asked Jack.

'We don't know for sure,' replied Parks, putting away his equipment and walking back to his van. 'That's what made him such catnip for the conspiracy industry. What we *do* know is that he liked blowing things up – big bangs, fireballs, that sort of stuff. He lost two fingers to a batch of nitroglycerine when he was still in the sixth form. He was eventually expelled for blowing up the gymnasium with a form of home-made plastic explosive. By the time he was twenty-two he had moved from rapid chemical decomposition to the power within the atom. He shared a Nobel prize for physics when he was only twenty-eight. He was brilliant, outspoken, daring. Best of all, he died while claiming he was "on the brink of a quantum change in atomic theory". Mind you, I suppose they all claim that.'

'Do you think his death at all mysterious?'

'Sadly, no,' replied Parks. 'Fittingly, he blew himself up.'

'I heard. And his work at QuangTech?'

'The official story is that he was transforming grass cuttings into crude oil, but it's doubtful someone as savvy as the Quangle-Wangle would fall for that. His work was top secret but even now he still holds the record for blowing up laboratories – thirty-one in under twenty years if you count his school experiments.'

'What about farther afield?' suggested Jack. 'Such as the Nullarbor in '92, Tunbridge Wells in '94 or Pasadena in '99?'

Parks stopped and stared at them both.

'Hoo-eey. Not even the staunchest theorist would connect *those* with Guff.'

'He was too under-qualified?'

'He was too *dead*. Those happened after his accident. No one seriously doubts that he died, Inspector. If you're after truth I'm not sure the conspiracy fraternity is the place to find it.'

Jack looked around at the fresh topsoil and said:

'Do you want to see a part of Mr Cripps's garden before it was taken away?'

Parks's eyes nearly popped out on springs.

Jack took the package from his pocket and passed it across. Dr Parks led them to the back of his van, donned a pair of latex gloves and delicately removed the small piece of fired glassy earth from the jiffy bag.

'This is good,' he said quietly, '*really* good. Do you have any provenance for it?'

'Sadly, no.'

'Excellent. Reliable provenance has always seriously damaged the conspiracy industry. Do you see how smooth and glassy one side is while the other side is fired into a hard terracotta?'

'Yes?'

'This is the remains of one of Mr Cripps's gravel paths. The sand has fused into glass, the soil beneath it into a ceramic. The principle of firing pottery is the same, only instead of several hours at a relatively low temperature, this was done in a fraction of a second – but at several hundreds of thousands of degrees. No wonder they didn't want us to see it.'

'Why?'

'Because it proves it wasn't a conventional explosion. The damage you see around you could easily have been done by an unexploded wartime bomb, but with this evidence of associated heat' – he waved the piece of fired earth at them – 'it's *quite* impossible. Conventional explosives just don't match the heat generated by . . . *nukes*.'

'Wait, wait, wait,' said Jack, who was willing to take a few steps into the conspiracy world, but not the several hundred yards Parks was suddenly demanding, 'you're saying someone was using a nuclear weapon in Berkshire? Surely cucumber fanciers aren't *that* concerned about the opposition?'

'Extremism comes in all shapes and forms, Inspector. But you're right to be sceptical. Let's see what we can find out about this object of yours.'

He opened a small wooden box and took out a device that began giving out random clicks when he switched it on.

'This Geiger counter measures radioactivity,' he explained. 'The more clicks, the higher the levels – the odd clicking you can hear is just background radiation.'

He passed the instrument over the sample and there were a few extra clicks, but nothing wildly dramatic.

'You see?' asked Parks.

'No.'

'The nuclear blast theory *seems* sound until one looks for evidence of radioactivity – and there's hardly any at all.'

'I'm no expert in nuclear weapons, Dr Parks,' admitted Jack. 'Perhaps you can explain that in more simple terms.'

Parks took a deep breath.

'Atom-*splitting* reactions are called fission devices; the A-bomb. Atom-*fusing* reactions are called fusion devices. A nuke small enough to do the limited damage you see here would have to be a fission device.'

'Why?' asked Mary.

'Simply stated, an A-bomb is the bringing to critical mass of a quantity of fissile material, say uranium-235. A lump of uranium-235 the size of a football would be critical, a lump the size of a golf ball would not.'

'I get it,' said Jack. 'Just add two uncritical masses together and *bang*, right?'

'In essence. However, you can ignite even *smaller* lumps of fissile material by bringing them together very rapidly. In theory you could make an A-bomb to fit into a suitcase. A mini-nuke with a limited destructive power.'

'And that was what hit Cripps?'

'No; A-bombs give out large quantities of radioactive fallout. There is nothing at the site, nothing downwind, and only a small amount on this sample. This could *not* have been a fission device.'

'What, then?'

'A *fusion* reaction with the heavy isotope of hydrogen as the fuel would give a waste product of only helium and a small amount of localised radioactivity caused by an excess of neutrons. However, there are problems here, too.'

'Such as?'

'To start a fusion reaction you need a huge amount of heat – two million degrees or more. To get that you need either a plasma chamber the size of a house consuming vast quantities of power, a ball of gas the size of the sun, or—'

'An A-bomb?' suggested Mary.

'Precisely. A fission trigger to set off the fusion device – but that would also leave large quantities of detectable radioactive fallout.'

He waved the Geiger counter over the fused earth again and it clicked in a desultory manner.

'This is only mildly radioactive, so it *suggests* that there may have been a fusion blast of a very small size. Since nuclear fusion only exists in the heart of stars, an A-bomb or a plasma chamber, I think this was something else entirely – a ground burst of a type we have yet to fully understand.'

There was a brief silence as Jack and Mary tried to figure out just what Parks was talking about. As far as Jack could make out,

Cripps and his garden were destroyed by a destructive force that Parks couldn't explain, and which the government was keen on hiding – they had removed nearly eighty tons of topsoil before allowing anyone in.

'Do you know the significance of this shape?' asked Parks, indicating the rectangular block of fired earth. Jack and Mary said nothing, so he continued: 'If this *did* come from here it was cut when the glass was still hot. There was only a time window of twenty-six minutes before the area was cordoned off. The first officers on the scene saw no one but confused villagers. If that's correct then we have a witness to the event. Find him and you'll answer a lot of questions.'

Jack thought for a moment. Up until ten minutes ago he hadn't entertained the possibility of McGuffin being still alive *or* heavily involved at Obscurity, but now he was reasonably convinced of both.

'If you think of anything else I'd appreciate a call,' said Jack, giving Parks his card, 'but keep all this under your hat. It seems Goldilocks found a link between the explosions and McGuffin, and she's dead.'

'Better and better,' replied Parks cheerfully. 'No conspiracy is worth a button unless someone is murdered over it – preferably with clandestine overtones and with just enough ambiguous facts to be tantalising – yet not so many that it's possible to resolve it one way or the other.'

They all stood and stared in silence at the bare earth that had once been Stanley's property.

'A mess, isn't it?' murmured Parks. 'If this is linked to McGuffin it would explain QuangTech's interest.'

'QuangTech?' asked Jack sharply.

Parks looked at them both slightly oddly.

'Yes; they undertook the initial investigation here. I thought that was common knowledge.'

'Not to me. Does QuangTech usually do investigative work for the government?'

'I have no idea. All I know is that their trucks and personnel were swarming over here for the first week after the blast. They were the ones that took all the topsoil.'

Jack thanked Parks and walked back along the road past the scorched hedgerows to the car. The presence of QuangTech might have been nothing but a coincidence but it had to be looked into. Within ten minutes they were back on the road, the vicar's increasingly aggressive offers of scone and tea notwithstanding.

They were both silent until Mary had driven them on to the main road back to Reading, when she said:

'That's odd.'

'You're not kidding,' replied Jack, who had been making notes since the moment they left. 'I wonder if Parks was talking any sense at all when he thought Obscurity was an explosion of a type "unknown to science".'

'No, I mean it's odd that your odometer is going backwards.'

'I noticed that too. This is how I see it: McGuffin is still alive and conducting secret tests of some sort. In Pasadena, Tunbridge Wells, the Nullarbor – and now here. He's going to reveal everything to Goldilocks but then something happens – and she has to be silenced.'

'Where do the cucumbers come into it?' asked Mary.

'I'd forgotten about them,' replied Jack with a frown. 'Perhaps they don't. In any event, I think we need to start getting some answers out of QuangTech – perhaps we should even try to speak to . . . the Quangle-Wangle himself.'

22

QuangTech

———

'**Biggest Fictional Multinational Corporation**. Largest of all imaginary mega-companies is the Goliath Corporation, with an illusory net worth of 6.2 quip-zillion pounds. Despite falling under the brief control of the Toast Marketing Board in 1987, Goliath resumed control of its own affairs and by the beginning of the fifth Thursday Next novel was once again ready to bully and cajole anyone who dared stand in its way. Claims that a larger and more oppressive fictional corporation had been dreamt up on a word-processor in Oregon were dismissed by several illusory Goliath executives as "fanciful nonsense".'

  – *The Bumper Book of Berkshire Records*, 2004 edition

The headquarters of QuangTech Industries were a series of large and generally low-lying buildings built within the boundaries of an old aerodrome. They had been based here since the early fifties, and QuangTech's rapid expansion had seen the company's buildings, offices and manufacturing facilities spread in every direction on the seven-hundred-acre site, and then to satellite factories dotted around the Home Counties. When you factored in all the smaller companies that operated under the umbrella of QuangTech, it was easily Berkshire's biggest employer.

Mary parked the Allegro and they walked across to reception. They announced themselves to an attractive receptionist, were given visitors' passes and then escorted into the main office building, where they were met by Mr Bisky-Batt himself. He called the receptionist by her first name, and the receptionist did likewise. They noticed that he was carrying a cup of coffee from the vending machine in the lobby. Clearly, QuangTech's reputation for egalitarian business practices was not without foundation; Bisky-Batt was second only to the Quangle-Wangle himself, and he fetched his own coffee.

The vice-president was a tall, heavyset man with massive hands that enveloped Jack's and Mary's as they shook.

'Welcome to QuangTech,' said the giant, whose voice seemed to rumble on after he had spoken. He smiled at them both, his heavy brow and large jaw reminding Mary of a model Neanderthal she had seen in a museum once. 'How have you been these past few years, Jack?'

'I've been good.'

'Impressive work on the Humpty Dumpty inquiry,' Bisky-Batt said with another smile. 'I was particularly glad the Jellyman came to no harm.'

'Us too.'

'I always think our *lack* of association with the NCD is something we can be justly proud of,' Bisky-Batt said after a moment's reflection. 'You haven't questioned us since that unfortunate business concerning the Dong's luminous nose.'

'Eight years,' said Jack. 'How's the Quangle-Wangle these days?'

'Still going,' replied Bisky-Batt, 'although now *extremely* frail.'

He opened a door and led them into his office. They had visited vice-presidents of other corporations in the past, but Bisky-Batt's office was the most modest they had seen. Completely unostentatious, it was almost austere. A collection of old-fashioned dial phones sat on his desk next to the very latest Quang-6000 desktop computer, the only piece of modern or high-tech equipment that could be seen. He indicated chairs and they all sat down.

'You're very kind,' said Jack, 'and I hope not to take up too much of your time, but QuangTech's name has been flagged several times in a recent inquiry and I was hoping you could offer me some information.'

Bisky-Batt held up his massive hands.

'Ask whatever you wish, Inspector. QuangTech has no secrets from the police, but you must understand that we are a vast company with subsidiaries in thirty-one countries and every major city of the world. The Quangle-Wangle has interests in food, wine, engineering, electronics, software and construction all over the globe. More than a million people worldwide are somehow employed by the corporation either directly or indirectly, and we can't be held responsible for every one of them.'

'I understand that,' answered Jack, 'but I have to ask. It's about a woman named Henrietta Hatchett.'

'Ah, yes,' replied Bisky-Batt, 'the unfortunate woman who was caught in the barrage up at SommeWorld. Most upsetting. Are you satisfied with the extra precautions we have taken to ensure that this sort of tragedy does not happen again?'

'I have heard the Health and Safety Executive are more than happy with your efforts. I was just wondering if Ms Hatchett had ever approached QuangTech Industries for information?'

Bisky-Batt frowned.

'Indeed she did. She was most insistent on speaking to the Quangle-Wangle, but as you know, he sees no one. She was *so* forceful I agreed to see her myself.'

'What did she want?'

'She wanted to know about an ex-confederate of ours named Angus McGuffin.'

Jack said nothing and Bisky-Batt continued:

'During the eighties the Quangle-Wangle followed a policy of funding projects on the very fringes of science on the basis that if they *did* work, then the profits might be very substantial indeed. He called it Project Supremely Optimistic Belief. We had a few mild successes. Pumpkin transmogrification was one of them, but in general the project was a failure. McGuffin's time here at QuangTech was a particularly *expensive* failure. He arrived in 1984 with claims of being able to synthesise oil from grass cuttings; it was an idea the Quangle-Wangle found irresistible.'

'There are many people who say the grass-cutting story is a myth to cover his true intent.'

'If only it were.'

'So you're saying McGuffin was a charlatan?'

Bisky-Batt shrugged.

'Charlatan would be a polite term. Personally I would have had him drummed out asap, but the Quang calls the shots. We gave McGuffin a laboratory. He blew it up. We gave him another. He blew that one up as well. We rebuilt the lab for the third time a little farther away from the other buildings and he blew that up too.'

'He was making progress?'

'No, I think he just liked blowing things up. He destroyed at least two labs a year until even the Quangle-Wangle began to see that he was pouring money down the drain, and McGuffin's contract was terminated in 1988.'

'And his death?'

'The day before he was due to leave. A parting shot, we think, and although the coroner recorded an open verdict, we considered it suicide. It was his biggest explosion to date. Despite our isolating his laboratory on the far side of the plant, he still managed to blow out all the windows in the village.'

'But you never found the body.'

'We never found the *laboratory*, Inspector.'

'Might he have escaped somehow?'

'No. We had CCTV of him right up until the moment of the blast; it was all played at the inquest. It wasn't just him, you know.

He took three lab assistants with him. He cost us over thirty million pounds and all for nothing. Project Supremely Optimistic Belief was abandoned soon after.'

'What else was Miss Hatchett asking about?'

'I think that was pretty much it.'

'Did she mention other explosions she was looking at?'

Bisky-Batt thought for a moment.

'No. It was McGuffin she was after. We get a lot of requests about Angus, so I have most of it at my fingertips. I understand he's become the patron saint of the conspiracy movement.'

'And what about Obscurity?'

'Somewhere the Quangle-Wangle shall never be, Inspector.'

'I meant the village.'

'You're not the first to ask. Yes, I can confirm that we were requested by the Home Office to do a detailed examination of the site. The results were sent on to NS-4 and published the same day – a wartime bomb, detonated accidentally.'

They sat in silence for a while.

'Tell me,' said Jack, 'does QuangTech have an interest in genetically modified foodstuffs?'

'Owing to the almost blanket ban here in Europe,' replied Bisky-Batt after considering the question briefly, 'GM foodstuffs are not a market worth the very great expenditure and stringent regulations. However, we do have a cross-pollination seed division which does generate a good deal of income. High-yield crops are big business. Unlike many of our competitors we have a rigorously applied ethical policy, so that we are not exploiting those least able to defend themselves. It's a contentious subject, and despite our very best intentions we are still lambasted for our efforts. Sadly, globalisation and multinational business are seen as a great evil in many people's eyes, despite the good that we do.'

'What about cucumbers?'

Bisky-Batt raised an eyebrow.

'In what respect?'

'Genetically modified or cross-pollinated over-size vegetables to – I don't know – feed the hungry masses or something?'

'With *cucumbers*?' asked Bisky-Batt, a lean smile crossing his impassive features. 'The most remarkable thing about cucumbers is that they have the *least* calorific value of any vegetable. Good for the crunch in a salad, but otherwise pretty useless. We concentrate on those foodstuffs which are *themselves* a staple – such as rice, maize, oats, wheat and so forth.'

'I see,' said Jack thoughtfully, 'so the financial sense in breeding a giant cucumber is . . . ?'

'Not very high, although there may be value to the competitive veg-growing industry. Cucumbers are technically a fruit and in the same family as pumpkins, melons and squash, so it may benefit those markets, although to be honest giant melons don't strike me as potentially that commercial. But it's not something we go in for, so my knowledge is a little sparse on the subject. May I ask why?'

'Just something that has come up in the course of our enquiries.'

There was another pause. Annoyingly, Bisky-Batt was being disarmingly candid.

'Can we interview the Quangle-Wangle?'

'I can certainly ask him, but I shouldn't hold your breath. He grants me an audience every morning. I am, to all intents and purposes, his arms and eyes and voice. The Quangle-Wangle is old and frail. He has fought in two world wars and built an empire that straddles the globe. His body is wasted but his mind is still keen. He told me once, although I think he was paraphrasing Carnegie, that a man who dies rich dies without honour. He has spent the last ten years of his life giving away more than fifty million pounds to needy institutions through his various charitable trusts. All requests are considered on their own merits by a table of eight consultants, but the Quang makes the final decision. A request for a new scout hut in Wantage is taken with the same seriousness as a diphtheria inoculation programme in Splotvia. As I recall, both were approved.'

'And SommeWorld?'

Bisky-Batt smiled and leaned back in his chair.

'Ah yes, SommeWorld. The Quangle fought as a foot-soldier in the Great War and was in the third wave at the battle of the Somme. He knows more than most the horrors of war. The theme park was an idea he had been toying with for a while. He wanted to demonstrate to the world the hideous conditions and pointless loss of life in warfare but didn't want to be seen as a hypocrite, so sold QuangTech's weapons division and poured the proceeds into SommeWorld. What did you think of it?'

'Very impressive – but none too cheap, I should imagine.'

'Too true. The land alone cost over a hundred million. Can you imagine trying to buy a single two-thousand-acre tract in the Home Counties? He had to purchase an entire village to make it. The park itself cost another hundred million to build. Even with five hundred thousand visitors a year it will take seventy years to break even.'

'Hardly good business.'

Bisky-Batt shrugged.

'The Quang's like that. But even with the vast cost of SommeWorld he's still one of the wealthiest men on the planet.'

There was more small talk but nothing of any relevance, and after another twenty minutes Jack and Mary rose to leave. They had heard enough for the moment and could easily return. Bisky-Batt showed them back to the entrance lobby and shook them by the hand once again. He was the vice-president of a major corporation and had given them an hour of his time without being the least bit obstructive. He had given straight answers and volunteered information. QuangTech's ethical policy was well known and perhaps, thought Jack, his own prejudices against big corporations were clouding his judgement. Then again, if someone's behaviour is too good to be true, it generally is.

'What do you think?' asked Mary as they walked back to the car.

'He seemed straight enough,' replied Jack, 'but I'd still like to have interviewed the Quangle-Wangle personally.'

'By the way he spoke you'd think it would be easier to speak to the Easter Bunny.'

'Almost certainly. Why, do you think it would help?'

'No, Jack – I mean, aren't you taking all this missing scientist and mysterious explosions stuff a little bit too seriously?'

'How do you mean?'

'Okay, devil's advocate here. We have a dead journalist with no sign *whatsoever* that it was anything but an accident. She was trying to link – as the conspiracy theorists have been doing for years – a doubtlessly insane and almost certainly dead scientist with un-explained explosions around the globe which on the face of it appear to have no link at all. QuangTech is a big corporation, sure, but that doesn't necessarily mean it's bad. The Quangle-Wangle has built SommeWorld as a graphic lesson on the horrors of war and they haven't indulged in any sort of weapons development in over a decade. I just think it all sounds a little far fetched – even by NCD standards.'

'I see your point,' replied Jack slowly, 'but what about the nature of the blast at Obscurity?'

'Jack,' said Mary, 'Parks based his *entire theory* on that one piece of baked ceramic. It could have come from *anywhere*. He could have sent it to Goldilocks himself.'

'And the radioactivity?'

'The radium from an old watch would have done the trick.'

'Is that likely?'

'Why not? It won't be the first time that an over-keen journalist has been given the run-around by a source more eager to receive fifteen minutes of fame than deliver facts. Conspiracy nuts are always looking for mainstream outlets for their rantings. Perhaps Goldilocks was just being *used*.'

'And her death?'

'I don't know. It's possible we're not even *close* to the real reason.'

'Maybe you're right,' said Jack with a sigh. 'I always tend to look for the more bizarre aspects of a case. Perhaps I should take a page from Copperfield's book and concentrate on purely objective, relevant and sensible matters.'

There was a pause.

'Right, done that. Let's drop in on Hardy Fuchsia and learn something about giant cucumbers.'

Mary laughed.

'You're the boss, boss.'

23
Extreme cucumbers

——————

'**Largest Cucumber**. The official heavyweight in the cucumber world is the 49.89-kilo monster grown by Simon Prong in 1994. Cultivated after many years of patient cross-breeding and nurturing, Prong's champion may have grown even larger were it not for the attentions of a gang of murderous cucumber nobblers, who destroyed the cucumber two days after the record was officially set, an attack that tragically cost Prong his life.'

– *The Bumper Book of Berkshire Records*, 2004 edition

Mr Hardy Fuchsia was editor, publisher, proprietor and founder of *Cucumber World* all rolled into one. They found him in the greenhouse of his modest semi-detached house in Sonning. The day was hot and the glasshouse's vents were all open to keep the heat down inside. Hardy Fuchsia was a cheery man with a limp; he was about eighty, retired and obviously thought cucumbers were the be-all and end-all. He came out of the greenhouse, mopped his brow with a handkerchief and shook them warmly by the hand.

'Tragic,' was all he could say when they mentioned Stanley Cripps. 'Tragic, tragic, tragic.'

'Had you spoken to him recently?'

'The evening – um – before he died,' said Fuchsia, 'he was wildly excited over this year's possible champion. We might be competitors but we still talk a great deal. Premier-league cucumbering is a lonely pursuit, Inspector, brightened only by the arrival of another with a similar high level of skill. I hope – ah – you appreciate that?'

'Of course. What did you talk about?'

'His challenger for the nationals. He and I were the only

competitors in the Cucumber Extreme class – for anything weighing over twenty-five kilos. If he beat me he'd automatically win the world championships. His champ was about to pass the magic fifty-kilo mark; not even I've managed that, although size isn't everything. A fine curve can speak volumes – and a smooth unblemished skin is worth thirty per cent of the judge's – ah – marks alone. Would you care to have a seat?'

He indicated an upturned water butt for Mary and a garden roller for Jack.

'How long have you known Mr Cripps?' asked Mary.

'Well, that is to say, I – oh – over thirty years. We both worked in the same department although he is my senior by, er, well – um – more years than he would have cared to remember. Would you like to see Cuthbert and the family?'

'I'm sorry?'

'Oh! An – um – petty foible of mine. Quite – er – childish. Cuthbert, well, and the family – my cucumbers, you see.'

He led them into his ancient wooden greenhouse, the wood almost black with layers of creosote and the roof curved downwards in the centre with age. The rewards in cucumbers, Jack noted, were not of the monetary sort. Mr Fuchsia led them past radishes the size of basketballs, then some tomatoes and a few parsnips growing in a length of downpipe. His champion cucumbers were green monsters about six foot long and the thickness of a small barrel. The plant that had spawned the beasts was seemingly quite small and forlorn next to them. Even though there were seven of similar size, it wasn't hard to figure out which one was Cuthbert. The others were excellent but this one was *perfect*. The skin was smooth and shiny and blemish free; it was quite a vegetable – or fruit, if you want to be pedantic.

'Very nice,' murmured Jack. 'What do they taste like this size?'

Mr Fuchsia looked shocked.

'Taste like? You don't *eat* them, Inspector. These are for – um – *showing*.'

Mary pointed to a passive infrared alarm in one corner.

'You take this seriously?' she asked.

'I certainly do,' replied Fuchsia. 'Many cucumberistas have suffered loss and damage at the hands of . . .' He looked around and lowered his voice. '. . . the *Men in Green*.'

'You're kidding, right?' said Mary, somewhat rudely.

'Well, I've never seen them *myself*,' conceded Fuchsia, 'but the cucumber world is awash in stories of mysterious men turning up at night to steal prize cucumbers and to conduct *experiments*.'

'What sort of experiments?'

'Bizarre and unseemly experiments of a horticultural nature. Core samples and cuttings taken, probes inserted, skin removed, that sort of thing. Have you ever seen a flayed cucumber, Inspector? It's not a pretty sight. The Men in Green are rarely seen, but when they are, they seem to wear nothing . . . but green.'

'That's quite far fetched, if you don't mind me saying so,' said Mary.

'I don't mind at all,' replied Fuchsia evenly, 'and you're probably right. But *true* cucumberistas are a superstitious and somewhat obsessed group of people – many consider us insane, and rightly so.'

'So what do you think happened to Mr Cripps?' asked Mary.

'Cucumber-nobblers, without the shadow of a doubt,' said Mr Fuchsia without even drawing breath, 'the Men in Green. Probably French. They've been jealous of *le concombre anglais* ever since the Hundred Years War, which was mostly about the right to buy and sell cucumbers in Europe.'

'Of course it was,' said Jack, humouring him, 'but isn't blowing Cripps and his house to kingdom come a little over the top?'

'It's in their blood,' replied Fuchsia with a hefty whiff of xeno-phobia, 'from the days of the Resistance. Why use a pound of

Semtex when a ton will do the job with a much more impressive bang? Besides, no one would suspect it a cucumber crime with such a blast – it's a smokescreen, Inspector, mark my words.'

'And you?' asked Jack. 'Might you want to nobble Mr Cripps's cucumber?'

'Good Lord no!' said Fuchsia in a shocked tone. 'What a suggestion! Cucumber growing is the best fun a man can have, I grant you, but the *really* exciting bit is the competition. And now that Stanley has joined Simon Prong and Howard Katzenberg in the great greenhouse in the sky, I am on my own in the Cucumber Extreme class – and there is no fun to be had in a one-cucumber race.'

'Wait, wait,' said Jack. 'Katzenberg and Prong were both cucumber growers?'

'Of course!'

Jack and Mary exchanged glances. There *had* been a link after all – but cucumbers?

'Katzenberg was one of our colleagues who had emigrated across the – ah – water,' explained Fuchsia. 'A loss to the European cucumber fraternity, but we always kept in touch.'

'And Prong?'

'Again, a good friend and colleague. Like Cripps and Katz, his greenhouse, garden and cucumber strain were all destroyed. When he died he'd just reported a one-hundred-and-ten-pound corker. Mind you,' he added, 'I've always gone for curve and colour rather than out-and-out weight. That'll all change,' he said, patting the smooth hide of his cucumber affectionately, 'once Cuthbert here gets into his stride. Three more ounces and he'll have equalled Stanley's record.'

Fuchsia seemed entirely unconcerned by the risk that he seemed to be facing. The fact hadn't been lost on Mary, though.

'Has it struck you,' said Mary slowly, 'that *all* your fellow cucumberistas have died in blazing fireballs?'

'Goodness,' said Fuchsia thoughtfully, 'I'd never even considered it before. Do you suppose the Men in Green are after me, too?'

Mary looked at Jack.

'Protective custody?' she queried. 'Or just section him?'

Jack shook his head.

'Can you imagine trying to run this request past Briggs? We'll try but I think I know what he'll say.'

They turned back to Fuchsia.

'It's likely you're in very grave danger,' said Mary. 'Is there anyone you can stay with for a few weeks?'

'Impossible!' spluttered Fuchsia, waving a hand in the direction of Cuthbert and his family. 'A gap in the continuity of care right now could set me back decades. Four people might have died in explosions, but this is something well worth the risk!'

'Four?'

'What?'

'You said *four* had died. Who was the fourth?'

'Cripps, Katzenberg, Prong and . . . McGuffin.'

'You knew McGuffin?' asked Mary.

'Indeed!' he said jovially. 'Myself, Howard, Prong, McGuffin and Cripps began this whole cucumber thing together in the sixties. It was Simon's idea, I suppose, the growing of heavy cucumbers. A distraction from the – ah – rigours of work.' He thought for a moment and added: 'To be honest I don't think McGuffin loved cucumbers half as much as he loved blowing things up. He left us in the early eighties to conduct his own experiments over at QuangTech.'

'What sort of a man was he?'

'Mad as a barrel of skunks. Brilliant, but impetuous. He wanted to grow heavy cucumbers like us but he was always too impatient. He said he'd like to fast-forward the years of cross-breeding and grow a champion to beat all champions in his retirement.'

243

Jack thought about this. If McGuffin *were* alive, perhaps he was planning on doing precisely that.

'Has . . . anything been stolen from you recently?' asked Mary.

'Indeed it has!' exclaimed Fuchsia indignantly. 'Someone broke in here two nights ago and stole my fledgling Alpha-Gherkin.'

'Your . . . what?'

'My Alpha-Gherkin. It's the progeny of Cuthbert here and will develop into an even *finer* specimen. Mind you, the Alpha-Gherkin is worthless without the skills to make it develop. In untrained hands it will be good only for . . . salad.'

After that, they showed him Goldilocks' photo to ascertain whether he had seen her, but he hadn't. He couldn't throw any light on the blast on the Nullarbor Plain, either. Deserts, he told them, were not great places in which to grow cucumbers. They asked him again if he would move somewhere else, but once again he refused, stoically declaring that he would, as an Englishman, defend his cucumbers to the death. Quite how much fight Jack and Mary thought an octogenarian would put up was questionable, but McGuffin, if alive, would be sixty-eight, so perhaps Fuchsia was in with a chance after all.

'What do you think?' asked Jack as they took the road back to Reading.

'I don't know. What do you think?'

'No idea. Winning a cucumber championship where the first prize is twenty quid and a trophy seems the slenderest of motives for a triple murder. And if Goldilocks' "scoop" was about deceit, skulduggery, murder, faked death and high drama in the world of competitive cucumber growing, would it really be necessary to kill her too? I must say, I'm pretty flummoxed by it all.'

'I'm the same,' retorted Mary, 'but more so. No matter. I'll use my feminine wiles on Briggs to see if we can't get some sort of protection for Fuchsia. I'm sure he'll agree to it.'

24
Over-quotering

'**Most Overdue Manuscript**. Although many writers have been known to be late with manuscripts, and the dialogue between editors and writers can sometimes reach a fevered pitch of cordial dispute, the lateness of Gerald of Frome's celebrated audit of the Reading Cathedral repairs of 1364 took 640 years to reach the publishers. Gerald's successive ancestors cited many reasons over the delay, such as not having enough ink, the wrong sort of vellum, noisy peacocks and the dissolution of the monasteries. The descendants of the original publishers who commissioned the work were overjoyed to finally receive the beautifully illu-minated manuscript handwritten in copperplate and bound in leather, and returned it with a note saying that they "totally loved it" but suggesting the emphasis of the work be moved *away* from a spider-vaulted North Arcade suffering from subsidence, and more *towards* a single career woman obsessed with boyfriends and her weight.'

– *The Bumper Book of Berkshire Records*, 2004 edition

'Let me get this straight,' said Briggs. 'You want me to sanction the overtime for a twenty-four-hour surveillance operation on a *cucumber?*'

'Not just any cucumber,' said Mary, who was standing in front of Briggs's desk an hour later, 'this one is a world champion, and if you read the report on the blast at Obscurity—'

'It was an unexploded wartime bomb, Mary. Official. You don't honestly expect me to believe that someone is going around bumping off the competition solely to win a cucumber championship?'

Mary bit her lip. It was almost *exactly* what Jack thought he'd say, but she had to try.

'I'd like your refusal to be noted, sir.'

Briggs looked up at her.

'That's very impertinent, Sergeant.'

'It reflects my certainty that Fuchsia's life is in danger, sir.'

'Your passion in this matter is certainly intriguing,' replied Briggs thoughtfully. 'Tell me, is there a lot of money in cucumber championships? A six-figure pay-out or something?'

'A twenty-pound book token, sir – and a dented cup.'

He shook his head sadly.

'You're as mad as Spratt. Perhaps madder. Sonning isn't far – if this Fuchsia fellow gets suspicious he can call us. Just speak to beautiful Pippa and have him put on "expedite" in the control room.'

'But, sir—'

'Before you go, Sergeant, one other thing. There seems to be a bizarre rumour making its way around the station that you're going on a date with that alien. Is this true?'

Mary scratched her nose nervously. She still wanted to wriggle out of the date if she could, but she didn't like Briggs's attitude. Despite a few obvious failings, Ash was a good officer, and part of the team.

'Yes, sir,' she said defiantly, 'it's all true. And his name's Ashley.'

'Well,' said Briggs with a patronising air, 'I hope you know what you're doing.'

He returned to several reports on his desk.

'Yes, sir.'

When Mary got back to the office she found Jack in conversation with Copperfield, who had aged five years since the Gingerbreadman inquiry had begun. His eyes were dark rimmed and hollow and he was chain-smoking again. There had been several near-misses but the Gingerbreadman had remained tantalisingly out of his reach, despite the build-up of almost three hundred troops and armed response groups from as far away as Newcastle. You couldn't walk anywhere in Reading without seeing somebody armed and in uniform standing on a street corner.

'Any leads on the crazy biscuit?' asked Jack.

'No . . . and he's a cake.'

'I don't *think* so,' replied Jack firmly, 'a biscuit goes soft when—'

'And it's not getting any better,' added Copperfield, who hadn't the inclination to listen to Jack's biscuit/cake debate. 'We've got nothing, but *nothing*, to go on. We're getting these twice a day, all posted from the centre of town – look.'

He passed a photocopied note to Jack, who read it carefully.

'*I'll run and run and jump with glee, I'm the Gingerbreadman – you can't catch me.*'

Jack passed it back to Copperfield, who said:

'He's taunting us, Jack. Posted in Friar Street at two-thirty yesterday afternoon. Broad daylight, centre of town. We've been staking out postboxes but somehow he always finds a way round us.'

'He wants you to know he can do what he pleases, and that he's still around. He's also telling you that he's smart. And he is. Smarter than you or me.'

'That's comforting to know. Listen, I know I've been a bit of an arse for not seeking your advice, but now I really need some help. You've been NCD for years – how would you go about this?'

'Well,' Jack said slowly, glad that Copperfield had finally seen sense, 'we need to know more about him so I'd start at the very beginning. First, I'd be looking for an oven big enough to have baked him. Second, there can't be many rolling pins large enough to have rolled him out, and someone must remember building a cutter that size and shape. Perhaps a local steel fabricator might know something. And you'd need a bakery with an overhead crane to lower the cutt—'

Copperfield gave an indignant snort and stood up.

'Thanks for nothing, Jack. I *plead* with you for help and all you do is start taking the piss. Good day.'

And he left without another word.

'Some people just don't want to be helped,' said Mary as she sat down in the chair vacated by Copperfield.

'He'll come round to us eventually,' said Jack slowly. 'I just hope the gingery lunatic hasn't killed too many people before he does. Let me guess: Briggs told you to stick the cucumber stake-out in your ear?'

'In one. Did you really think he'd go for a twenty-four-hour cucumber stake-out?'

'To be honest, no. Have a look at these.'

He pushed a couple of photos across to Mary.

'This is a picture of Stanley Cripps and this is McGuffin. I thought they might be the same person, but they're not.'

'Do you think McGuffin's alive?'

'If he is he's bloody well hidden.'

'Hellooo,' said Ash as he walked in carrying a buff envelope, 'want to see what I've found?'

He laid a photograph on the desk. It was from the security cameras at the Coley Park Bart-Mart, and the date in the bottom corner showed that it had been taken ten days earlier. The picture was slightly grainy and a bit blurred, but the figure pushing the shopping trolley piled high with bags of value-pack porridge oats was unmistakable.

'Bartholomew,' breathed Jack. 'An MP involved in over-quotering to bears?'

'He gets it at discount, too,' said Ashley. 'Bart-Mart is the family business. Although it's controlled by QuangTech, the Bartholomew family still hold thirty-eight per cent.'

Jack rubbed his head.

'I suppose it makes some kind of sense,' he said finally. 'Perhaps he felt he was somehow indebted to them for not being able to pass the Ursine Self-Defence Bill.'

'There's more,' said Ashley, laying down another picture. The relevance of this one wasn't so clear until he pointed it out.

'This was taken two minutes before the one with Bartholomew – that's Goldilocks' Austin Somerset parked in the background.'

They peered closer. It was. This complicated matters.

'Anything else?' asked Jack.

'Only this,' said Ashley, laying a third picture down on the desk and pointing at someone astride a motorcycle near the trolley park. They were so far in the background they were barely a smudge. A blow-up that Ashley had printed didn't really help. 'It's *possible* that this motorcyclist is Vinnie Craps,' said Ashley, 'but I couldn't say for sure – it might just be someone very bulky.'

Jack leaned back in his chair and twiddled absently with a pencil while Ash and Mary stared at him.

'What does it mean?' asked Mary.

'I'm not sure,' said Jack. 'Goldilocks and Craps in the car park while Bartholomew is on a porridge buy. It might mean a lot of things – or nothing.'

Jack put down the pencil, placed his hands behind his head and stared at the ceiling. Explosions, cucumbers, porridge, missing scientists, QuangTech. Nothing seemed to make any sense at all.

'Anything on Gray?' he asked, still hopeful.

'No,' replied Ashley, 'he isn't on the electoral register. I went through the births, marriages and deaths records and I'm not sure he really *is* Dorian Gray – the only person I could find of that name was born in 1878.'

'A false name?' muttered Jack. 'That's all I need. Without Gray I'm almost certainly up for the "retirement on mental grounds" review board. Perhaps I should cut my losses now and take the three-month sabbatical Kreeper so kindly offered me.'

'Hm,' said Mary, glancing at Ashley, who blinked twice at her. Privately they had talked about this. Although they trusted Jack's judgement, there was a strong possibility he had been overdoing things. Neither of them truly believed the Allegro *could* mend itself.

The phone rang.

'Spratt, NCD . . . Good afternoon, Mr Bruin,' said Jack. 'Yes, I imagine it must be very difficult to dial with claws.' He grabbed a piece of paper and, with the telephone jammed in the crook of his shoulder, started to scribble as Mary looked over his shoulder. 'Okay . . . but why don't you tell me now? . . . Right. We'll be over as soon as we can.'

He put the phone down.

'Ed said he didn't know it was Goldilocks and would never have scared her out of the house if he'd known. He wants to tell us something — something he felt bad about and has to tell us in person. Hold the fort, Ash — Mary and I are heading back into the forest.'

25

Back to the forest

'**Most Attractive Police Officer at Reading Central**. In a
recent poll, PC Philippa Piper (AKA "Beautiful Pippa in the control
room") was voted the most attractive officer at Reading Central.
Her delightful temperament and bubbly personality coupled with
her fresh-faced youthful good looks have made her not only the
most sought-after prize of anyone currently without a partner at
Reading Central, but also the subject of fevered bets as to whom
she might eventually choose as her consort.'

– *The Bumper Book of Berkshire Records*, 2004 edition

Within minutes the silver Allegro was bowling down the road,
heading for Andersen's Wood as quickly as Mary could drive. Jack
was worried. Ed had sounded scared, and when a 550-pound male
bear with nothing above it in the food chain is frightened, then
you are sure to take notice. The sun went behind a cloud as they
entered the forest and the whole world seemed to darken. Mary
slowed down instinctively but hit a speed bump anyway. Everything
loose in the car was tossed in the air as they landed.

'Er, right here, isn't it?' said Mary as they counted the turnings
off the tarmac road.

'Next one, I thought.'

'Are you sure? I recognise that broken branch.'

'Did you? What about the fertiliser bag?'

'Probably blew away.'

Mary stopped and backed up, ignored Jack's advice and bumped
down a forestry track. They found the three bears' turning after
about half a mile and drove up the grassy track. The cottage was

exactly as they had last seen it, except for the absence of any smoke from the chimney. They stopped the car and got out.

'Wait!' said Jack in a soft voice. Mary paused.

'What?'

'Hear that?'

Mary strained but no sound could be heard.

'No.'

'Exactly,' murmured Jack, and moved on. The forest was deathly quiet. Mr Bruin had told Jack that the forest could speak and he realised now what he meant. A drum beating is ominous, but ominous changes to threatening when it stops. A sense of foreboding closed over both of them, a feeling of danger that seemed to roll in from the forest like a wave.

'Shall I call for back-up?' whispered Mary.

'Not yet. They might just be out.'

Jack knocked at the front door as Mary went around the back. There was no answer so he lifted the wrought-iron latch and pushed the door open. The sun came out as the door swung open and a shaft of light illuminated the large room through the front windows. Amid the mess of what looked like a flagrant act of vandalism, smashed chairs and emptied drawers, Ed was lying in a heap beside the fireplace, a mountain of brown fur. A lake of dark blood had formed next to him, and was still moving slowly outwards. By the piano was another mound of fur, this one dressed in a pretty floral dress. It was Ursula. Jack quickly unlocked the back door and let Mary in.

'Oh my God!' she murmured.

Jack ran back to Ed's bulk and pressed his hand into the thick fur at his neck. He'd never felt a bear's fur before; it would have been unthinkably rude to do so uninvited. It felt warm, but coarser than he had imagined.

'I can feel a faint pulse. Call the Bob Southey Medical Centre and get a trauma team out here *immediately*.'

She flipped open her mobile and dialled a number as Jack looked at Ursula. Her eyes were open and she was breathing in short gasps. He patted her paw and told her it would be okay, but she made no sign that she'd heard.

'Who'd want to kill the Bruins?' asked Mary, waiting for the phone to connect.

'Look over there,' said Jack grimly.

He pointed to the wall above the fireplace. In red aerosol someone had written:

Bears are for hunting

'Ursists!' said Mary angrily.

'Get on to Control and have roadblocks set up on all roads leading out of the forest. We didn't pass a car on the way in and this crime is less than ten minutes old.'

Jack found the entrance wound on Ed's lower back. It was large-calibre – a hunting rifle. He was still alive, but Jack didn't rate his chances. Illegal hunters and bile-tappers: the scum of the earth.

'This is DS Mary of the NCD,' said Mary into the phone. 'We've got two bears shot and wounded in Andersen's Wood . . .'

Jack had returned his attention to Ed and was about to feel for his pulse again when he noticed something. He peered more closely. Ed hadn't lost consciousness immediately. Next to his right claw were some letters traced with his own blood on the scrubbed flag-stone floor. They didn't read very well, but the meaning was clear:

SOB dnt trst

'Back-up will be here in twenty, always supposing they can find the place,' said Mary as she flipped her mobile shut, 'and the Bob Southey are dispatching a trauma team. What have you found?'

Jack pointed.

'"SOB don't trust"? Who's SOB?'

'Son of a bitch to our friends across the Atlantic. Ed's a grizzly. They're North American, aren't they?'

'I'm not really an expert on . . .'

Mary stopped mid-speech as Jack raised a finger to his lips.

She mouthed 'What?' to him and he pointed at the ceiling. A thin trail of dust was falling from between the floorboards and the wood creaked as someone upstairs shifted their weight.

'Baby Bear?' whispered Mary.

It seemed likely, and Jack was about to call out to him when there was the delicate metallic ring of a spent cartridge falling on the floor upstairs. If it *was* Baby Bear, he was armed – and dangerous.

'What weren't you an expert on?' asked Jack, trying to pretend all was normal but still staring at the ceiling.

'Bears,' she replied, pointing at the door leading upstairs. 'Who do you think did this?'

'I don't know,' replied Jack as he moved across to the sturdy wooden door, which he discovered, to his relief, could be secured by a peg.

'We had better leave the crime scene,' said Mary as she noticed that the thin trail of dust was now falling from an area closer to the door. There was also the sound of a footfall and the unmistakable *clack* of a breech being surreptitiously locked. They couldn't do any more for the bears, so retreat to safety seemed the best and only course of action. Jack ran the last two strides to the door, slammed it shut and dropped the peg into the hasp. There was an enraged cry from upstairs and they both headed for the safety of the car. They heard two muffled gunshots in quick succession as the door exploded into splinters. They reached the car, threw themselves in and started it up. There wasn't time to turn around, so Jack slammed the Allegro into reverse and backed down the lane as fast he could.

A tall mahogany-toned figure stepped nonchalantly from the door of the cottage, then jumped from the veranda to the cabbage patch with a single leap. He watched as they backed hurriedly out of the clearing, and Mary shuddered. He looked dangerous enough on his own, with the cruel liquorice mouth and his piercing glacé-cherry eyes, but what made him look even *more* dangerous was the massive Holland & Holland heavy game sporting rifle he was cradling in his arms. He had sawn the barrels short and wielded it as though it were a handgun. Mary knew from experience that it weighed at least thirty pounds, could stop a rhinoceros and had a kick like a carthorse.

The Gingerbreadman, laconic as usual, was in no hurry. He eyed the car reversing down the grassy track away from him, smiled to himself and broke the gun, which ejected two steaming brass cartridges that landed in the asparagus bed behind him. With slow deliberation he withdrew two more shiny rounds from a belt slung over his shoulder and closed the gun with a deft flick of his wrist. He raised the weapon as though it weighed almost nothing, then aimed and fired in one smooth movement. The Allegro swerved as it hit a dip in the road and the shot went wide, shattering the trunk of a silver birch next to them as they sped past, the felled tree dropping into the road behind the rapidly receding car.

'Blast,' said the Gingerbreadman and, surprised by his own poor marksmanship, took aim again.

'What was that?' asked Jack above the scream of the engine, the tachometer needle edging into the red although the car was not wanting to go much faster than fifteen or twenty miles an hour. He hadn't seen the figure; his attention was dominated by the need to keep the car on a straight course down the track.

'Gingerbreadman,' shouted Mary. 'Keep going.'

The Gingerbreadman decided that they were too far away and started to run towards them in long, measured strides. He held the

Holland & Holland with one hand as he strode after them, the Allegro bouncing in and out of the bumpy track as Jack floored the accelerator.

'Faster!' cried Mary as the Gingerbreadman started to gain, his long strides swiftly eating up the distance between them. He fired at them as he ran, a slug the size of a king-size marble passing through the windscreen between them and vanishing through the rear seats with a scattering of velour and kapok stuffing.

The Gingerbreadman cursed again and reloaded as he ran, the Allegro's over-revving engine howling in protest. As he took aim for the third time they hit the logging track, and before Jack could even think about braking, they had crossed the road and slammed straight into a large beech tree, the sudden stop knocking the wind out of them both and entirely demolishing the rear of the car. The boot was pushed into the area where the rear seats had been and the two swing axles were twisted outwards, causing the two rear wheels to bend at an impossible angle. The rear screen burst and a steel ripple rode through the roof, ultimately relieving the stress by popping out the front windscreen and deforming the two front wings. But both the front seats held in the impact and neither of them was hurt.

Jack and Mary were not the only ones to be caught unawares. The Gingerbreadman, unused to running fast during his twenty-year incarceration, had forgotten the rules governing the inertia of moving bodies. He attempted to stop but skittered on the gravel track and ran straight into the car, tripped on the front bumper, bounced off the roof and hit the tree with sufficient impact to knock the heavy game rifle out of his hand and send it tumbling end over end into the undergrowth.

The Gingerbreadman was only slightly stunned. He sat up on the forest floor and rubbed the back of his neck.

'Wow!' he murmured to himself, then chuckled, shook his head and looked around to see what had become of the sporting rifle. At the same time, not more than ten feet away on the other side of the tree, Jack and Mary cautiously pushed the twisted doors of the Allegro open and looked around warily to see what had become of the Gingerbreadman. They all quickly noticed one another.

'Inspector Spratt!' said the Gingerbreadman cordially. 'We meet again! And you *still* not even attached to this inquiry. Briggs and Copperfield *will* have something to say!'

He got to his feet and started to look around for the Holland & Holland more seriously, talking as he did so. 'I do so wish you were on the hunt for me,' he said with a grin. 'I really don't think that Copperfield chap is up to it.'

Jack rolled out of the car and grabbed a stout branch, swung it above his head and swiped the Gingerbreadman on the back of the head. The blow bounced off his cakey body without effect. The Gingerbreadman turned back to him, oblivious to the impact.

'If he thinks a massive display of firepower will bring me down, he's badly mistaken. This is the second time you've found me, Jack. People will think you have a hidden agenda.'

'Why shoot the Bruins?' demanded Jack, giving up on the branch and joining in the hunt for the Holland & Holland. Mary was putting out a call to the station to upgrade her back-up to *armed* back-up, although it would take a squad car at least twenty minutes to get there, and that was always supposing they could find them.

'I needed a place to hole up, Jack,' replied the Gingerbreadman in a deep dough-like voice, his cherry eyes flicking this way and that as he searched the undergrowth for the gun. 'You may not have noticed but I'm public enemy number one at the moment.'

'It hadn't escaped my attention,' replied Jack. 'But why here and now? And blaming the attack on hunters. Since when were you *ever* ashamed of taking the rap for some utterly mindless display of violence?'

'You ask a lot of questions for a very puny and insignificant human, don't you?' said the Gingerbreadman as he stopped the search for the gun and stared at Jack with just the kind of look you wouldn't want from a psychopath.

'It's my job,' replied Jack, sensing that if he didn't find the gun and gain the high ground, he might be pushing up the daisies quite soon.

'Who needs a gun anyway?' asked the Gingerbreadman, catching Jack by the wrist. He tried to pull away but was held fast in the biscuit's iron grip. The Gingerbreadman smiled cruelly as he placed his other hand on Jack's body, meaning to pull his arm off, just as you might dismember a roast chicken on the dinner table.

'I like this bit,' he announced, his cherry eyes flashing wickedly. His grip tightened around Jack's wrist and he started to pull. He smiled. He *was* having fun. Jack's face contorted with the pain and he gave a cry of agony as he felt the tendons stretch tight in his arm.

But the Gingerbreadman didn't pull his arm off. Abruptly, he relaxed his hold. Jack looked up at him but the Gingerbreadman was looking past Jack, his liquorice eyebrows raised in exclamation.

'Careful,' he said to Mary, who had found the Holland & Holland and was now pointing it at him, 'you might hurt someone.'

Mary slid the safety catch to off with a loud *click*.

'That's the idea.'

The Gingerbreadman's liquorice mouth drooped at the corners.

'Be careful, miss,' he repeated as he let Jack fall in a heap at his feet. 'That's a point-six-hundred-calibre elephant gun loaded with Nitro Express cartridges. It has a muzzle energy of over eight thousand foot-pounds; the recoil can dislocate a shoulder!'

'I'll be careful,' replied Mary evenly. 'Just step away from Jack and lie face down on the ground with your arms outstretched.'

They were less than ten feet apart and Mary couldn't have

missed. The Gingerbreadman took a step back but didn't lie face down. He stared back at Mary and narrowed his eyes, wondering what course of action to take.

'Have you ever killed anyone, miss?'

'JUST LIE FACE DOWN ON THE GROUND!!'

'No,' said the Gingerbreadman simply. 'I've been locked in St Cerebellum's for twenty years and I'm not going back. If you want to stop me, you're going to have to fire.'

Mary's finger tightened on the trigger. She was in no doubt that the Gingerbreadman would have killed her after he had dealt with Jack and would kill again, given the chance. There was no decision to make. She *would* shoot him. In the back, if necessary – and to hell with procedure.

The Gingerbreadman, despite his resigned attitude, was not out of tricks. He turned and jumped to one side, leapt back again and then ran away, zigzagging crazily. He knew, as Mary soon found out, that a heavy elephant gun wasn't designed to follow a fast-moving object, and by the time Mary had him in her sights, he had jinked out again. Mary gave up following him and held the gun still, waited for the Gingerbreadman to leap back into her sights and then squeezed the trigger.

There was a concussion like a thunderclap, and for a moment Mary thought the gun had exploded. She was pushed violently backwards, caught her foot on a tree root and fell over in an untidy pile. When the smoke had cleared the forest was empty. She had missed; the Gingerbreadman had escaped.

'You all right, sir?'

'Fine,' said Jack, rubbing his shoulder and standing up as the distant wail of sirens brought the outside world once more into the forest. 'What about you?'

'Pissed off I didn't kill him, sir.'

'I can understand that.'

Mary reloaded the rifle from the cartridge belt the Gingerbreadman had discarded, and walked slowly up the road to make sure that he wasn't wounded and lying out of sight. She looked around carefully, satisfied herself that he was long gone and then picked something up from the ground before she returned to Jack.

'I didn't miss after all,' she announced, showing Jack what she'd found. In her hand was a single gingerbread thumb.

26

Jack's explanation

'**Most Coincidence-prone Person**. Mrs Knight (née Day) of Wargrave, Berks, holds several world records for the quantity and quality of the coincidences that assail her every waking hour. "It's really more of a burden," she replied when interviewed. "Every wrong number I get turns out to be a lost relative or something. I can't walk in the street for fear of bumping into an endless parade of long-forgotten schoolfriends." Her powers of coincidence question the very dynamics of time, leading some scientists to theorise that cause and effect are actually two sides of a cosmic scale that have to be in balance – and that Mrs Knight may be a beacon of effect where orphaned causes flock, like moths to a lamp.'

– *The Bumper Book of Berkshire Records*, 2004 edition

'You'd better have a good explanation for this, Spratt – how many times do I have to tell you the Gingerbreadman is *not* your inquiry?'

Briggs wasn't in a terribly good mood. True, he was never *really* in a good mood, but right now he was less so than usual. He liked to think that there existed a strong feeling of trust between his officers, and they wouldn't go against what he had told them. He had trusted Jack more than most, which annoyed him especially.

'I know this might seem a bit hard to swallow, sir, but this is a coincidence as well.'

'Oh yes?' replied Briggs. 'And give me one good reason why I shouldn't arrest you for working while suspended?'

'Because you like me and I'm good and I'm the only chance you've got to catch the Gingerbreadman.'

Briggs fell silent. He'd begun to think exactly the same.

They were standing outside the three bears' cottage. The trauma team from the Bob Southey Medical Centre had turned up promptly and without getting lost; they were an immediate blur of action upon arrival at the scene, successfully stabilising Ed and Ursula before gently transferring them into ambulances and vanishing back to Reading in a blare of sirens.

Copperfield and the rest of the human contingent took a little longer to get there as they *did* get lost, but wasted no time as soon as they arrived: police photographers covered every angle of the two shootings as the white-overalled SOCO officers went through the small cottage to find anything that might show either where the Gingerbreadman was going, or where he had been. Jack sat and glowered at all the activity; if the Gingerbreadman hadn't been involved then Mary would have had to go begging to Briggs for resources, as usual.

As if the whole thing wasn't bad enough already, NS-4 had turned up in a shiny black Ford Scorpio, and Agent Danvers insisted her 'associates' had a good look around. Even more annoyingly, Danvers also wanted to hear Jack's appraisal of the situation. Briggs declared that this was a police matter but was swiftly overruled by Danvers, who called the Chief Constable personally.

'How is the attempted murder of two bears a national security issue?' asked Jack.

'It just is,' replied Danvers shortly. 'Mr Demetrios *himself* has requested that we attend.'

'No good can come of squabbling,' announced Briggs, 'so why don't you tell us what you know, Jack, and we can take it from there. Let's face it, this is one hell of a mess. Berkshire has the best record of ursine equality in the European Union. When the Animal Equality Federation get hold of this the shit's really going to hit the fan.'

'At least you know who did it.'

'I suppose so. What were you doing out here anyway?'

'Ed Bruin called me. He said he wasn't happy and needed to talk.'

Jack felt Danvers' eyes bore into him, but pretended not to notice.

'About the Gingerbreadman?' asked Briggs.

'About Goldilocks.'

'Her death wasn't an accident, was it?'

'No, sir.'

'Sir,' said Mary as she walked up and handed Jack two clear plastic envelopes. One held a note handwritten in highly distinctive ursine-styled cursive script, the other a photograph. 'I thought you'd better see these – I found them on Ed Bruin's desk.'

Briggs and Copperfield leaned over his shoulder to read the note.

'*Mr Curry, Sat, 8.15 a.m., Andersen's Wood*,' read Briggs. 'What does that mean?'

'It means,' said Jack slowly, thinking carefully, 'that "Mr Curry" was to meet Goldilocks the morning she died.'

'And who's Mr Curry?' asked Copperfield.

'It was a code name for Goldilocks' boyfriend. A man named . . . Sherman Bartholomew.'

Briggs started as though stuck with a cattle prod, and Danvers beckoned to one of her minders and whispered something in his ear.

'Are you nuts?' asked Briggs. 'That's one of the least likely things I've ever heard.'

'I thought so too,' replied Jack slowly, 'but it's true – they'd been seeing one another for about a year.'

'Why meet here?'

Jack showed him the photograph Mary had just passed him. It was of Mr and Mrs Bruin with Baby Bear as a cub-in-arms. They were outside the cottage with a grinning Sherman Bartholomew. It had been taken over ten years ago and beneath was written: '*Feb*

4th 1977, the Ursine Suitable Housing Act gives us a home shortly after adopting Junior. L–R: Ed, Ursula, Nigel, Bartholomew.'

'Sherman was their barrister in his pre-parliamentary days, sir. It was hardly surprising they let him use their house for his little trysts. They *owed* him.'

'Okay, you've got a link with the Bruins and a note from Father Bear *without* Bartholomew's name. That's not a burning bush, Jack.'

'There's more, sir. Bartholomew can't account for his movements until 9.30 on Saturday morning, and Ed Bruin's note on the floor in his own blood read *SOB dnt trst*. SOB: Sherman Oscar Bartholomew.'

Briggs rubbed his temples. Bartholomew was close to the mayor and the Chief Constable, and if there was any sort of error, the repercussions would ripple down the ranks like dominoes.

'So . . . how does the Gingerbreadman fit into all of this?' asked Copperfield, who wasn't pleased that Jack's inquiry had significantly progressed while his hadn't.

'Bartholomew defended him at his trial. Perhaps he felt he was indebted in some way.'

'He got four hundred years without parole,' said Briggs. 'How would you thank your barrister for that?'

'Bartholomew had the sentence reduced from five hundred. It's not much, but Ginger must have taken it to heart.'

'Okay,' said Briggs, 'you've got a dying bear who etched Bartholomew's initials in blood, a note placing him in the forest at the same time and a cake who owed him favours – it's a bit circumstantial and you know how the CPS has trouble understanding NCD cases. Give me something *concrete*, Jack – like a motive.'

Jack sighed, and thought quickly. Danvers' eyes were still riveted on him.

'It's all about . . . porridge quotas, sir. Uncooked rolled oats, if you want to get technical. We found two kilos in Goldilocks' apartment that were part of a shipment we chanced across a few days ago. Bartholomew had been aggressively pro-bear almost his entire career. He argued for the Ursine Suitable Housing Bill, and tried and failed to secure the right to arm bears. His pro-bear leanings led him beyond the law, and he took it upon himself to buy oats from the family discount store where he has a generous staff discount, repackage them at a warehouse in Shiplake and then sell them to a middlebear, who flogged them down at the Bob Southey. Bartholomew and Goldilocks may have been lovers, but Goldilocks was going to blow the whistle on his pro-bear over-quota porridge-pushing. The scandal would have destroyed his career. So . . . she had to go.'

Briggs, Copperfield and Danvers said nothing, so Jack continued:

'He arranged to meet her that Saturday morning but it all went wrong – the bears came back early and Goldilocks ran from the house. I don't suppose we'll ever know what happened up at SommeWorld, but you can see the results. Bartholomew knew Goldilocks had been investigating cucumber-nobbling and spreads it around that this was her "big story". It all seems to be going fine and I'm chasing my tail around scorched areas of Berkshire when Ed Bruin gets an attack of conscience. He *knew* that Bartholomew was due to meet Goldilocks that morning, and felt bad about it. Goldilocks had been a good friend to bears, too – her exposure of the illegal bile-tappers sent shivers of relief through the bear community. Bears despise lies and deception, so he *had* to see me. Bartholomew gets wind of this and he calls in the Big Bad Biscuit.'

'Isn't he a cake?' asked Danvers.

'I thought so,' muttered Copperfield.

'And me,' added Briggs.

'Biscuit or cake, he attempts to kill Ed and Ursula and tries to make it appear that hunters did it. If Mary and I hadn't got here as fast as we did, no one would be any the wiser.'

Danvers broke the silence that followed.

'This is a very serious accusation,' she murmured, 'and even if you're wrong the investigation will destroy Sherman's career. He has much good work still to do.'

'No one is above the law,' said Jack pointedly, 'no one.'

'I'm forced to agree,' replied Danvers. 'This is now a police matter and I leave it with reluctance in your capable hands. If you will permit me, I would like to be present at Bartholomew's questioning. Good day to you, gentlemen.'

Danvers climbed into her car and it bumped out of the clearing.

'Well,' said Briggs, 'you'd better pull Bartholomew in – but be warned. There's going to be a shitstorm over this.'

'Not from NS-4, sir,' said Jack, pulling his mobile out of his pocket. 'Looks like they just dropped him like a hot potato. And besides, when it comes to shitstorms, I think I'm something of an expert.'

He dialled a number and stepped away from the small group to make one of the hardest phone calls of his life. If he was wrong, there really *would* be a shitstorm – and he'd be right at the centre of it. The call made, he dialled again, and then returned to the group.

'Done,' he said. 'Uniform are on their way to Bartholomew's house right now.'

The light of the dying sun was filtering low through the trees as the last squad car drove away. The forensic examination had finished and quiet had once more descended on the forest. Jack and Mary stood at the door and watched as the pool of dried blood went from dark red to black in the failing light.

'Not fair, is it?' said Mary.

'No,' replied Jack, deep in thought. 'Just ordinary bears trying to lead a life of peaceful solitude. Ed should have spoken out when he could. Any news?'

'Ursula's stable and out of danger but Ed's still critical. The surgeon told me that if he can survive the next forty-eight hours he's in with a chance. Baby Bear is staying with relatives in the Bob Southey.'

It was nearly two hours after Jack had given the order for Bartholomew's arrest, but he wasn't yet in custody. When the uniformed officers arrived to pick him up, Sherman Oscar Bartholomew, Member of Parliament for Reading and prime suspect in a murder investigation, had gone.

The news had filtered back to everyone waiting at the cottage. Briggs had blamed NS-4, something that Jack encouraged. Briggs had returned to Reading after telling Jack that the search for Bartholomew was far too important for the NCD, and that the multi-force hunt could be better managed by an officer with more experience – such as himself. Clearly, there were headlines to be had, and in Reading positive headlines were in short supply.

'It's not good,' said Mary, shaking her head sadly.

'Yes; who'd be a bear?'

'No, I mean it's not good that the last squad car has gone – how are we going to get back into town?'

'In the Allegro.'

'It's a wreck.'

'Trust me.'

They walked down the grassy road to the logging track, where Jack's car, as predicted, was as pristine as the day it had been built.

'I'm sorry I doubted you,' said Mary as Jack showed her the fine oil painting in the boot, a picture of the car that now resembled a barely recognisable heap of scrap. She looked at the Allegro suspiciously.

'Seems a bit, well, *diabolical*, doesn't it?'

'Nah,' replied Jack reassuringly, '*every* car should be made this way.'

'I'll write a report out for Kreeper explaining that the Allegro *does* heal itself. You'll be back on the active list in a jiffy.'

'Do you think she'd believe you?'

'No,' conceded Mary.

Mary got into the car a little anxiously and glanced around at the interior as though she thought it might bite her. She took a surreptitious look at the odometer, which now read only thirty-eight miles. The car started on the first attempt and Jack drove slowly out of the forest, the approaching night changing the face of the wood from one of arboreal beauty to one of insufferable gloom. The forest was once more exclusively the domain of its children.

27

What Mary did that night

———

'**First Extra-terrestrial Marriage.** Although there have been a few instances of alien/human dating, no actual marriage or civil union has so far taken place. Pre-emptively condemned by all the world's leading religions as an "abhorrence to nature" and "an affront to all social values", pro-alien sympathisers were quick to point out that visitors from distant worlds are *not* covered by any divine texts, which was an interesting omission by the Almighty, and leads to all manner of theological debate over galactic deity jurisdiction. But if such a union comes to pass, *The Bumper Book of Berkshire Records* will faithfully record it.'

– *The Bumper Book of Berkshire Records*, 2004 edition

Ashley was waiting for them at the NCD offices when they walked in. His uniform had been freshly pressed and his transparent skin buffed up to a high shine. He looked expectantly at Mary, who smiled uneasily in return. It was the evening of their date, and Mary had yet to think up a believable excuse.

'What's that smell?' asked Mary, wrinkling her nose.

'It's Windolene,' explained Ashley cheerily. 'It shines up my outer skin a treat.'

'What did you do?' asked Jack. 'Take a bath in it?'

'If only,' replied Ashley wistfully, adding: 'Bartholomew's still not been found and Briggs wants you to meet the press first thing tomorrow to discuss Bartholomew and the Goldilocks case.'

Jack picked up the phone and asked to be put through to the Super.

'Hello, sir – it's Jack. No, I'm not doing the press. I'm taking sick leave as requested. Yes, I know I'm already on sick leave but now I'm *really* on sick leave. I'll be gone for three months – perhaps longer. Maybe I'll retire. Yes, really. The head of the NCD can take the press conference tomorrow.'

He looked up at Mary and raised an eyebrow. Mary shook her head.

'No, she's not here. Yes, I agree the situation is not at all favourable. Goodnight, sir, and if you're thinking about getting me a gold watch, I'd rather you didn't.'

Jack put the phone down and looked up at Ashley and Mary, who were staring at him incredulously.

'Don't worry,' he said, 'I'm not retiring – that was for Briggs's benefit. I don't know what I'm going to do.'

'About what?'

'About finding Goldilocks' killer.'

'I thought you said Bartholomew murdered her?'

'If you believed all that crap I was spouting up at Andersen's Wood,' said Jack unhappily, 'you'll believe *anything*.'

'Then why did you say it?'

'I had to say something. NS-4 are in this up to their armpits and I needed them to *think* we're as stupid as they believe.'

Mary thought for a while, trying to figure out what she'd missed – Jack's explanation of Goldilocks' death and Bartholomew's porridge-pushing had *seemed* plausible.

'But we're not, are we?' she said, a mite confused.

'Not at all,' he said, trying to force a smile. 'I know Bartholomew didn't have a hand in it, but I'm really not sure who did. I need to sleep on it. Better than that, I need to *sleep*.'

'Wait!' said Mary. 'If Bartholomew *is* innocent, why have you got half the force out looking for him?'

'To give me some breathing space, and quite possibly save his life.'

'Jack,' said Mary, 'are you sure you're all right? You seem to be acting a bit . . . weird.'

'I'm fine, Mary. But listen: if it all goes pear shaped I'll take full responsibility. Have a pleasant evening.'

He took a deep breath, managed a tired smile and walked out of the door, leaving Mary and Ashley staring at one another.

'Mary?' murmured Ash, whose taut and usually expressionless face seemed to be cast in the vaguest semblance of a frown. 'I'm completely and *totally* confused.'

'Join the club,' she retorted. 'He's either fantastically brilliant or he's gone completely off the rails. I hope it's the former – I really don't think I can handle the NCD on my own.'

Ashley looked at her and blinked.

'Sorry; I really don't think *we* can handle the NCD on *our* own.'

'If we have to I suppose we just will,' he replied with commendable optimism.

'It must be a double or triple bluff or something,' mused Mary, 'a plot device the reason for which we probably won't figure out until tomorrow morning.'

'A what?'

'Never mind. The thing is – business as normal.'

'What's all this about a self-healing Allegro?' asked Ashley, who thought it sounded a lot of fun.

'Exactly,' said Mary, trying to stall the inevitable date, 'I think Jack's in danger. Get on the PNC and bring up the details of every single car that has ever been registered to Dorian Gray or had him as previously recorded keeper. I know that might take a while, and if it means we have to cancel our date, then so be it. Duty first, Ash.'

'Duty first,' he agreed, and scuttled off to tap into the PNC while Mary put her feet up on the desk. Dorian would doubtless have sold thousands of cars and the two of them could be wading through the list for hours. Ashley was right about running the

NCD. It would be tricky, but they'd get the hang of it eventually. She leaned forward and logged her user name in on Jack's computer in order to start a report for Briggs on—

'Done it!' interrupted Ashley. 'How about dinner?'

'You can't have,' said Mary with a sinking feeling. 'How many were there?'

'Five.'

'Five?'

'Yes. I don't think he was that good at selling cars.' He showed her the list, and Mary scanned the details carefully.

'One every three years, regular as clockwork,' she murmured.

'And,' said Ashley, who was more adept at spotting patterns, 'every single one was scrapped between two and nine weeks after purchase. How does all this fit into the Goldilocks inquiry?'

'It doesn't. I've just had a hunch.'

She tapped the most recent name on the list.

'We can interview this Mr Aldiss fellow right now. No time to lose.'

'No time to lose,' repeated Ashley, reading the address. 'Good – it's on the way to my parents' place.'

'Oh, rats,' said Mary with a sigh, finally resigning herself to the inevitable. 'Okay, okay, you're on – listen, you don't eat bugs or anything, do you?'

'Bugs? Why ever would we do that?'

'Well, I thought your antennae made you kind of – I don't know – *insectoid.*'

Ashley gave out a high-pitched squeak of a laugh and said:

'Insectoid? The very idea!' He squinted up at his stubby antennae before continuing, 'These don't do anything at all, really – as much use and purpose as your eyebrows. No, of all the many strange and barely related phyla you have on your planet, you know which body type most closely resembles ours?'

Mary shrugged as she looked at Ashley's curious semi-transparent, liquid-filled appearance. 'I don't know. A cross between an amoeba and a crème brulée?'

'Not even close. I'll tell you: none of them. The closest thing to our physiology is seven live jellyfish stuffed inside a balloon designed to fit only two.'

He pinged his cheek with a digit and the shock waves in his elastic skin rippled round his head and back again before he added: '*Intelligent* jellyfish, mind you. We'll take my car. Shall we go?'

'These old things are a rarity these days,' explained Ashley, driving through the darkened streets at exactly twenty-two miles per hour in his meticulously restored 1975 Datsun 120A coupé. 'My brother rebuilt it for me.'

'You have a brother?'

'And a sister, although the concept of gender is a tricky one to understand, even for us. That reproduction stuff of yours sounds pretty messy. Does the man really—'

'Yes, yes he does,' said Mary quickly. 'It's all true.'

'And is that *really* a satisfactory method? I've got a couple of ideas for improvements if you want to hear them.'

'No, no, please keep them to yourself. It seems to have worked very well for quite a few years now.'

They drove on slowly in silence for a few minutes, while drivers behind them attempted to pass where they could, and honked their horns in annoyance. Mary consulted the list of ex-Dorian Gray car owners and guided Ashley to a very ordinary-looking street in Tidmarsh.

'Do you want me to come in with you?'

'I'll be fine,' said Mary, fully aware that some people still couldn't get their head around the fact that there really *were* aliens, and on occasion would start screaming uncontrollably – sometimes for hours.

273

'Right-o,' said Ashley, who generally didn't like people screaming, especially at him. 'I'll sit here and listen to the Delfonics on my eight-track.'

Mary climbed out of the car and walked up the garden path of number sixty-two. Even though Dorian's car had been consigned to the breaker's yard almost exactly three years previously, the owners, she reasoned, might still be living in the same house. They were. Or at least, Mrs Aldiss was.

'Oh!' she said when Mary explained the reason for her visit. 'I'm sorry, but I thought I'd answered all the questions back then – do I have to go over it all again?'

'What questions were those?' asked Mary. 'After all, it was only about a car your husband once owned.'

'It was more than that, Officer,' she replied softly. 'It was the one he . . . died in.'

Mary apologised and Mrs Aldiss invited her in for a cup of tea. Her husband had been something of a seventies car nut, too, and the pristine 1976 Austin Maxi had been too good to resist.

'He was initially very happy with it,' said Mrs Aldiss, staring at the carpet, 'but after a few weeks I think he began to grow *suspicious* of it.'

'In what way?'

'It's difficult to say precisely. I used to see him stand outside the house staring at it. He tried to take it back but Dorian Gray had vanished.'

Mary felt herself shiver.

'He used the car as normal after that, and then one night they found it crushed on the eastbound lane of the A329. It had been hit by a truck, apparently, although the other vehicle was never traced. Brian died instantly.'

She fell silent and wiped a tear from her eyelash.

'I'm sorry to ask you these things,' said Mary. 'Did you ever drive it yourself?'

'Once. I didn't like it.'

'I know the feeling. I have a colleague with an Allegro I have to drive.'

'It wasn't that. There was something else. Something *malevolent* about the car.'

Mary knew what she meant.

'The odometer went backwards, didn't it?'

'Yes,' said Mrs Aldiss quietly, 'yes, it did.'

'What news?' asked Ashley, turning down the volume on 'Didn't I (Blow Your Mind This Time)'. Mary sat in the passenger seat and opened her phone.

'The driver was killed and the car destroyed in an accident on the A329 three years ago. The odometer went backward on that car, too.'

She texted Jack: 'Caution Allegro mileage approaches zero Mary' and then snapped her mobile shut.

'What does it mean?'

'I've no idea. Have a look at the other owners first thing tomorrow,' said Mary. 'I'd like to know how many of them are still with us.'

'I'll get on to it. So . . . my place?' he asked, positively – and literally – swelling with expectation.

'Yes,' said Mary absently, 'your place.'

They drove the short distance to Pangbourne and pulled into a very ordinary-looking estate, the proliferation of seventies Japanese saloon cars giving it a very time-warped appearance.

'Is the whole neighbourhood alien?' asked Mary.

'Pretty much,' he replied. 'Very few people want to live next to us although I've no idea why; we make good neighbours.'

Ashley got out, ran across the roof and opened the door for Mary before she could do it herself.

'Thank you,' she said graciously.

'My pleasure,' said Ashley, 'and *please* don't make fun of my parents' attempts to be human.'

'I wouldn't dream of it.'

28

What Jack did that night

'**Seediest Hotel in Reading**. The thirty-eight-room Bastardos on Station Approach holds this dubious distinction, having been awarded the coveted 'five bedbug' award by *Clip-joint* magazine every year since records began, except in 1975, when an accidental change of linen raised the hotel's ranking from "nasty" to "shamefully grimy". Currently under investigation by the area health authorities but kept open owing to an obscure statute of 1845 relating to the conditions of workhouses, the Bastardos has recently added a restaurant where food poisoning is almost a certainty, and death a distinct possibility.'

        – The Bumper Book of Berkshire Records, 2004 edition

Jack parked the Allegro in the street a few doors down from his house and tried to catch a glimpse of Madeleine through the kitchen window. He could see shadows moving around behind the curtains, but little else. He hadn't spoken to her at all that day and wondered whether she would still be pissed at him for being a PDR and, worse, not telling her. It was the least of his worries. If Bartholomew really *had* murdered Goldilocks, Jack could be up for some very serious charges indeed. He frowned to himself. Up until the Red Riding-Hood debacle, everything seemed to be going so well. It had all just spiralled downhill from there, both professionally and personally. He fortified himself with the thought that it couldn't possibly get much worse. He looked next door. Mr and Mrs Punch were having a fight as usual, and the muffled thumps and sounds of breaking crockery punctuated the peace of the night.

His mobile rang.

'I have information for you,' said a woman's voice on the other end.

'Really?' responded Jack, well used to crank calls.

'Yes, really. About Goldilocks. Hotel Bastardos, room twenty-seven, half an hour, *alone*.' There was a click and the line went dead. He frowned again and looked at his watch. It was a little past nine. He thought of calling Mary to back him up, but she and Ash were on a date and he didn't really want to disturb them. He thought of calling Madeleine, then decided not to. It was the wrong decision, of course, but he had made up some very compelling arguments for it in his own head. He thought he'd go and see what his mystery caller had to say for herself, and put off the fight that Madeleine would surely give him for at least an hour.

The Hotel Bastardos was the grottiest hotel in a series of grotty hotels located near the railway station. It was in a shabby state of disrepair. The interior was grimy and smelly, cheap and nasty, badly decorated if at all. The rooms were small and cheerless, the windows cracked and grimy, the curtains stained and torn. The hot water supply was patchy, the electricity unreliable and the food lamentable. Rooms could be hired for the month, week, day or hour, and the only room service anyone got was the sort that usually follows a call to a number on one of those brightly coloured cards you find in telephone boxes. It was *exactly* how the clientele liked it, and the proprietors expended a lot of time, energy and money maintaining just the right level of sleazy decrepitude.

Jack trotted up the stairs, past the landing where the Easter Bunny had once held him at bay with a stream of hot lead from her M-16. It had been over a decade earlier, and she'd done her time. People were often fooled, he mused, by the one day in the year on which she did charitable work – the rest of the time she was the rabbit from hell. He topped the stairs and turned left down the hallway, walking along the threadbare carpet to room twenty-seven. He stood to one side and rapped on the door. There was a muffled 'Enter!' from within and he pushed open the door.

The room was poorly furnished and dimly lit; a forty-watt bulb was burning in a lamp on the sideboard, a scarf lying across the shade to diffuse the light. A neon light flashing outside the window and the hum of the air-conditioning units on the roof next door gave the room a certain degree of noir charm. Jack had arrested a murder suspect in this same room seven years previously but it might have been yesterday; the room hadn't changed a jot. The same old wallpaper, the same badly painted woodwork.

There was a figure on the bed.

'Hello, Jack.'

'Goodbye, Agatha.'

Jack turned on his heel and walked back out of the door and down the staircase, seriously pissed off. Why couldn't she leave him alone? He'd heard that Briggs and Agatha had marital difficulties but he didn't see why he had to be dragged into them. He'd have to make some sort of official complaint, but he didn't know how Briggs would take it. Not well, he presumed. He stepped out of the front door of the Bastardos and walked back towards his car, reading Mary's text. He wondered what she'd found out but wasn't worried – the odometer on the Allegro still had twenty-eight miles to go before it hit zero.

A familiar voice said: 'Where have you just been?'

Jack stopped. There was a figure in the shadows of the bus stop outside the hotel entrance. His heart froze. It was Briggs, and he looked a bit drunk – and not at all happy.

'Good evening, sir. A contact called me with information but it was nothing.'

'You expect me to believe that?'

'Sir, I just want to go home.'

279

Briggs looked up at the hotel and gave a mournful sigh.

'Agatha is in there and I think she's waiting for someone. Who do you think it is?'

'I've no idea, sir. Why don't *you* go home?'

Briggs nodded agreement, and the whole sorry chapter might have ended right there and then had not Agatha, in a masterful display of bad timing, appeared out of the entrance of the Bastardos yelling: 'Jack, come back . . . !'

Briggs scowled angrily and before Jack could even try to explain punched him painfully in the eye, then strode off. Jack staggered backwards under the blow and momentarily saw stars. He'd been avoiding Agatha for years, but had never reported her continual pestering in order not to cause trouble and to help her help herself. If there was a situation that had 'unfair' stamped all over it, this was it.

'Are you okay?' said a passer-by, helping him to his feet. 'I can call the police.'

'I *am* the police,' said Jack, who'd always wanted to say that, but preferably in a better set of circumstances, 'and so is he. Thanks, I'll be fine. I'm going home.'

When he got to the house it was locked and bolted. He was about to knock when a small voice said:

'I shouldn't bother, if I were you.'

It was Caliban. He was sitting on a dustbin reading a copy of the *Beano* by the outside light.

'What did you say?'

'I said,' repeated the small misshapen ape, 'I shouldn't bother if I were you.'

'Oh? And what makes you say that?'

'I heard what she said she'd do to you if you dared to show your face.'

'And what was that?'

The door was suddenly flung open. Madeleine marched out, struck Jack a glancing blow on the head with a rolling pin and went back inside in one swift movement. Jack fell over, more through surprise than as a result of the blow itself.

'She said she'd do that.'

'Why?'

'She got a call from Briggs about something.'

'*Shit*,' he murmured. Implausibly, things *had* got worse. Much worse.

29
What Ashley did that night

'**Least Likely Alien Abduction Suspects**. The Rambosians, who, when asked whether they'd been involved in reported medical experiments on "abductees", replied: "You must be joking. If we wanted to know about your physiology – which we don't – we'd just watch BBC2 or read *Gray's Anatomy*." When pressed, they had to admit they couldn't think of any life form bored enough to want to travel halfway across the galaxy to push a probe up an ape's bottom, nor what it might accomplish – apart from confirming that in general apes don't like that sort of thing.'
    – *The Bumper Book of Berkshire Records*, 2004 edition

The front door to Ashley's house opened and two almost identical aliens stood in the hall and blinked rapidly at Mary. To the untrained human eye, every alien is identical to every other alien – in much the same way as all humans seem identical to aliens. Indeed, to the more unobservant alien all *mammals* looked pretty much the same. 'It's the backbone that's so confusing,' explained an alien spokesman, when asked how a sheep might appear indistinguishable from a human in a woolly jumper. The reason Mary could tell Ashley's parents apart at all was that one was wearing a large and very obvious brown wig, had a folded newspaper under its arm and was wearing slippers, and the other wore a blue gingham dress with an Alice band perched precariously on its shiny high forehead.

'Hello,' said Mary politely to the one in the slippers, 'you must be Ashley's father.'

'No, that would be me,' said the one in the gingham. 'Roger's the name. This is Abigail, my wife.'

'Hello,' said the one wearing the slippers, proffering a three-fingered-double-opposable-thumb hand for Mary to shake. Mary did so with some trepidation, as Rambosians tend to transmit their thoughts through touch. Still, she thought it would be rude not to, and her hand was enveloped in the warm dry stickiness of Abigail's grip. Almost instantly the image of a wedding popped into Mary's head, complete with a large white Rolls-Royce, church, confetti, and with Mary herself dressed in a quite *stunning* white wedding gown, with Ashley in a morning suit.

'Sorry about that,' said Abigail, hurriedly letting go of Mary's hand.

'It's quite all right,' she replied, her close contact with Ashley having prepared her for almost anything, 'but just out of interest – where did you see that dress?'

'At Veils R Us,' replied Abigail wistfully. 'Wasn't it just the most beautiful thing ever?'

'Why did you assume I was the father?' asked Roger, who had been thinking about this for several moments.

'It's the dress and Alice band,' explained Mary. 'They're *usually* considered female gender apparel.'

'I told you the sales assistant didn't seem that bright,' he said to Abigail. 'We'd better swap.'

Mary half expected them to strip off in front of her but they didn't. They just placed a sticky digit on each other and trembled for a second or two.

'Right,' said the one who used to be Abigail, 'I'm now Roger. Why don't you come in?'

Roger led her into the living room, which was decorated as though from the seventies. Earth's TV signals had taken eighteen years to reach distant Rambosia, so it was understandable that this was the era in which they felt the most comfortable. The furniture was dark coloured, the wallpaper and carpet patterned, the music centre one of those combined radio-cassette-turntable things, and the obligatory plaster ducks flew across the wall next to a print of *The Haywain*.

'How long have you had this bad knee?' asked Abigail, rubbing the offending joint of her body-swapped partner.

'A few days,' replied Roger.

'You should look after yourself better – and your arms feel a bit low. When did you last have a pressure test?'

'This always happens when we swap bodies, doesn't it?' replied Roger with a baleful glare. 'Nag, nag, nag.'

'If you looked after yourself I wouldn't have to.'

'Maybe I *like* having a dodgy knee – ever thought of that?'

'Sorry about this,' said Ashley.

'You're a pompous old windbag sometimes, aren't you?' said Abigail. 'Give me back my body.'

'It would be even *more* confusing for our G-E-U-S-T, dear – show some manners, eh?'

'Manners?' replied Abigail, opening her already large eyes still wider. 'I'll give you 10100101 001, you 1001 010011.'

'Oh yes? Well you can 1001001 00101010 010001 00101010 1001011111100110100111 000000010 010101101 0111001000100 10001111111001100 01001001 01110 010010 10010 010010010111011,' replied Roger, lapsing into pure binary in his anger.

'100101010101011111001110010010101011111,' yelled back Abigail. '11 1 1001 0101001 1000010101011.'

'Why don't you just swap your thoughts back and then your *clothes*?' suggested Mary. 'I'd not be confused – and you could then have your own bodies, and be dressed human gender specific.'

They stopped their argument and stared at her, blinking, for some moments.

'Brilliant . . . !' gasped Abigail.

'Such wisdom,' added Roger in awe, and they both ran off upstairs without another word.

'Good move,' said Ashley, clearly impressed. 'We'd not have thought of *that* solution in a million years.'

Mary was going to ask how it was possible *not* to think of that solution when a car horn sounded outside and another alien came running down the stairs holding a spotted bow and a glue gun. Ashley looked to heaven.

'My sister,' he muttered out of the side of his mouth, '*total* bimbo – IQ barely crawls into the double-century.'

'Ash!' she exclaimed in a state of extreme fluster as she handed him the bow and glue gun. 'I'm sooo late! Stick this on, would you? Hello, you must be Mary. I'm Daisy. Ashley told us all about you.'

She put out her hand and Mary shook it, catching a glimpse of a great number of aliens all crammed into a Honda Civic and chanting Monty Python's dead parrot sketch in unison.

'Stand still,' said Ashley as he squeezed a blob of glue on to the top of Daisy's translucent head, then placed the bow on top and held it while the glue dried.

'Is Ash a good policeman?' asked Daisy, wincing in reaction to the heat of the glue.

'Yes, he is.'

'Then why is he data-crunching down at the NCD and not out on the beat?'

'Training,' said Mary.

'Really?' replied Daisy scornfully. 'I thought it was because no one wanted to work with him.'

'You're done,' muttered Ashley, taking his hands off the bow, 'and try and keep your 101011101010 closed, why don't you?'

Daisy showed Ash the finger, skipped off to the front door, and went out.

'You put her bow on backwards on purpose, didn't you?' asked Mary.

'Yes. Come and meet Uncle Colin. He fought in the first Zhark Wars, you know.'

Ashley led Mary through to the living room, where a smaller alien with a slightly wrinkled appearance was watching *Man about the House* on the TV.

'Hello!' he said. 'Who's this?'

'This is Mary, Uncle. *Mary* Mary.'

'No need to repeat yourself, young fella-me-lad. What do you think I am, deaf?'

'How do you do?' said Mary.

'Not at all,' he said genially, '*quite* the reverse.'

Mary frowned and looked at Ashley, who crossed his eyes and rotated a finger next to his head.

'I fought in the Zhark Wars, you know,' Uncle Colin continued, his eyes going all dreamy as he stared off into the middle distance. 'I've seen things you would not believe. Zharkian battle cruisers massing near the Rigella cross-over—'

'Here we are!' said Abigail and Roger, who had just scampered back down the stairs. 'Would you like a drink?'

'Thank you.'

'We've got most types of hooch,' said Roger cheerfully, opening the top of a globe that tastefully doubled as a drinks cabinet. 'I like to keep the house well stocked. We've got diesel, castor, olive, groundnut, multigrade or sunflower.' He looked among the bottles. 'I think we might even have some crude somewhere – that'll put hairs on your chest.'

'I told you all this earlier,' said Ashley in a strained tone, 'humans don't drink oil – at least, not on its own, and only organically derived.'

'Are you sure?' replied Roger, sorting through the bottles in the cabinet again, as though hoping something suitable might miraculously appear. 'We're a bit short on everything else.'

'A glass of water would be fine for me – I could have one of those.'
She pointed to an array of jars on the mantelpiece.

'Ah,' said Roger with an embarrassed cough, 'those are our memory jars. We like to have at least one back-up.'

'Oh,' said Mary, blushing at the faux pas.

'I'll get you a glass from the kitchen,' said Abigail, and scampered off.

'. . . and seen the Dorf army scatter in the wake . . .' muttered Uncle Colin, still to himself.

'A toast,' announced Roger as soon as Abigail had returned with Mary's water, and everyone had been handed an oil of some sort, and Ashley told he couldn't have multigrade but would have to stick to olive 'until he was older'. 'A toast,' Roger said again, 'to the excellent bi-species understanding we currently enjoy.'

'1000101011o,' said Abigail, raising her glass and downing it in a single gulp.

'1000101011o,' said Ashley, doing the same.

'1000101011o,' said Roger, winking at Mary.

'1000101011o,' said Mary, and they all stared at her and blinked for some moments in silence.

'Well, I think you're mistaken,' said Abigail eventually, 'my mother *never* would have done that, and certainly not to herself.'

'What did I say?' asked Mary, looking at Ashley for support.

'. . . and fought through the spice mines of Kessel . . .' droned on Uncle Colin.

'Dinner, anyone?' said Roger as a pinger went off in the kitchen, and everyone sprinted for the table, leaving Mary to bring up the rear.

'Has anyone seen Daisy?' asked Abigail, bringing in a large basket full of chips.

'She went out earlier,' said Ashley impishly, 'with that 1001011111o1o1 rabble from across the road.'

'She'll come to a sticky end,' said Roger.

'I think that was her intention,' replied Ashley with an amused squeak.

'Ashley,' scolded Abigail, 'I won't have that sort of gutter-talk at dinner. Mary, be a darling and pass the toothpaste.'

Mary picked up what she thought must be the condiment basket and passed it up the table. Abigail carefully chose some Colgate and squeezed it on to her chips with some diesel oil out of a jug.

'Would you like some more?' asked Roger.

'I haven't had anything yet,' pointed out Mary.

'I mean, would you like your more *first*?' replied Roger with a trace of annoyance.

'Do you like Marmite?' asked Abigail quite suddenly.

'Not really.'

And they all applauded by tapping their sucker-digits together. It sounded like twelve popguns all going off in unison.

'Is this what Rambosians eat?' asked Mary politely. 'Chips?'

'Goodness!' said Abigail, suddenly rising from the table and running into the kitchen, only to return a few seconds later with another plate, 'I almost forgot the pop-tarts.'

Mary didn't eat any pop-tarts but found some vinegar to put on her chips. The conversation was pretty mundane, and centred around Roger and Abigail's jobs in the library, with Uncle Colin's recollections occasionally rising above a murmur in the background.

'. . . so we put it in "over-sized books", which is a *highly* unsatisfactory way of categorising anything . . .'

'. . . outran a supernova in the Crab Nebula . . .'

'. . . So I memorised every word in every book, so customers can ask for anything with even the vaguest reference to their subject . . .'

'. . . suggested we taught binary as part of the Open University's language programme – I ask you . . .'

'. . . binary keyboards are much simpler, of course – only one key . . .'

'. . . seen fusion bursts above the plain of Squrrk . . .'

The conversation moved around to *Big Brother* after that, and the news that cousin Eric had applied to be on the show, but had been turned down because he *lacked* severe mental problems, and it might have had a bad influence on the others.

'Pudding?' asked Abigail.

'Yes, please,' said Mary, who didn't think she could eat just chips. Abigail vanished into the kitchen and then returned with *another* basket of chips.

'Dessert!' she announced to an approving chorus from the family.

'*More* chips?' said Mary, leaning closer to Ashley.

'Yes,' he replied, 'only eaten this time with a spoon – does anyone want to play Ker-plunk! after dinner?'

'Can I show you something?' said Ashley once the meal was over, and they had played Ker-plunk! twice, and Binary Scrabble, which was fundamentally flawed since every possible combination of ones and zeros made a word, and it was impossible *not* to put down all your tiles, anywhere you wanted and in any order, every single go.

'Sure.'

Ashley took her outside, opened the garage door and beckoned her inside. He flicked on the lights to reveal a double garage that had most of the usual junk one might expect to find: a discarded weight-training machine, a bicycle or two, a motor mower, tools and a workbench. It was all aligned, precisely, of course – order pervades every aspect of a Rambosian's life. In the middle of the garage was a large object covered with a bedsheet.

'I tinker with this in my spare time,' announced Ashley, pulling off the sheet to reveal a translucent sphere about ten feet in diameter. It was entirely smooth, was floating about six inches off the floor, had no apertures and did not seem to contain anything at all.

'Amazing!' said Mary. 'What is it?'

'Step aboard,' said Ashley. 'If you think my Datsun is the last word in personal transportation, think again!'

And so saying he stepped through the translucent covering and into the sphere. The surface just seemed to part when he touched it and then close again as soon as he passed through. Mary stared at it a little apprehensively and put out a hand to touch the surface, which felt soft and warm, and parted away from her fingers.

'You're not going to abduct me and then conduct medical experiments or something, are you?' she asked.

'It's a distinct possibility.'

Mary smiled and stepped into the bubble, which parted and then reformed around her. She felt the whole thing sink slightly, a bit like the suspension on a car.

'Have a seat,' said Ashley.

Mary looked around; there didn't seem to be one.

'The ship is made of a living predictive polymer,' explained Ashley. 'It will form itself under you.'

Mary went to sit down and sure enough the surface of the bubble expanded and merged to form a seat beneath her.

'How does it work?' she asked, awe-struck.

'I'm not entirely sure.'

'I thought you guys were some sort of advanced super-race or something?'

'I don't know where you got *that* idea,' he replied with an amused squeak. 'Do you know how a mobile phone works?'

'Not really. Something digital and radio waves, masts . . . and stuff.'

'It's the same with this. There's anti-gravitons and bio-conducive plastoids in it somewhere, but I'm not too clear on the details.'

Ashley placed his central sucker-digit on the only control that could be seen anywhere inside the strange craft – a single push-button switch.

'One button to control all this?' said Mary. 'That's it?'

'It's a new development,' explained Ashley, pressing the button on and off so fast it sounded like a staccato bumblebee. 'We used to have two buttons – one for on and one for off; but then after about forty thousand years someone pointed out you could actually do the same job with one. It destroyed the switch industry on Rambosia almost overnight. Hang on.'

The globe rose another six inches off the floor and rotated slowly to the right, then reversed into the tool bench, knocking over a half-built bird box that Roger had told them all about earlier.

'Oops!' said Ashley. 'Sorry. We left Rambosia before I could take my test.'

He made another series of rapid clicks on the button and the globe rotated again to the right and floated out of the open garage doors, hovered over the tasteless fountain feature in the front garden for a moment and then shot high into the air like an express lift.

'Whoa!' murmured Mary as the lights of Reading receded rapidly below them. In a few seconds the estate street lamps had become a long chain of fairy lights which merged with another chain at the main road, which itself joined to another until the pattern of roads could no longer be seen and Reading seemed like just a dense concentration of twinkling lights with radiating arms of jewels stretching away to other, smaller prickles of illumination that were the outlying towns. They continued to rise rapidly in the night sky and pretty soon the lights joined up with other towns, cities and conurbations until Reading was lost in the anonymity of distance, and the whole nation came together in one glittering network of light that seemed to breathe and pulsate beneath them. A few moments later only a narrow ribbon of darkness separated England from the Continent, where an identical smudge of randomly clumped lights continued to the edge of the horizon.

'Look over there.'

To the west the curved edge of the planet was a feast of colours that ran through the spectrum in a never-ending parade of infinitely subtle hues. As their altitude increased the sun rose miraculously in the west; a glorious light show that bronzed the visible atmosphere and the clouds, blood red below them.

'Your eyes are leaking.'

'It's so . . . *beautiful*,' exclaimed Mary, wiping away a spontaneous tear. 'The horizon over there – it's like it's on fire!'

'I come up here just to watch the sunset,' explained Ashley. 'By ascending as the earth rotates away, I can watch it as many times as I want. I can even keep pace with it, and hold the final dying rays of light in my hand for as long as I wish.'

Mary took Ashley's hand and smiled at him.

'Not many people get to see this.'

'Yes,' replied the small alien thoughtfully, 'which is a bit strange, considering we're only a couple of hours' drive from Reading in the average family saloon.'

Mary laughed.

'If there were only a road . . . !'

He shrugged.

'Perhaps you're looking at the problem in the wrong way. There's an easier way to do pretty much anything.'

They watched the sun set again as the earth rotated away from them, the small globe hovering in the near-vacuum of space eighty miles from the earth's surface.

'Hang on,' said Ashley, clicking on the switch again. Mary felt the globe move, and once more the sun rose, and Europe moved away to the east as they travelled around the earth. Ashley looked about, trying to see something. 'It should be along soon.'

'What?'

'You'll see.'

They didn't have to wait long. Ash saw it first, a large dark object that was almost invisible against the inky blackness. As it moved towards them Mary could see that it was big, and angular, and had long flat plates pointing out in two directions. When less than five hundred yards away it broke into the sunlight, the rays of the sun bouncing off the turquoise solar panels. The craft was painted white and seemed to be a series of knobbly sections stuck together in a haphazard manner. After the tidy simplicity of Ashley's globe, it seemed almost shabby by comparison.

'The International Space Station,' said Ashley. 'We can wave if they're looking out of the portholes. It perks up their day a bit.'

As it turned out they *were* watching, and they waved, and Ash and Mary waved back.

'Hey,' said Ash impishly, 'show them your breasts.'

'No!'

'Oh, go on. It would be funny. I won't look.'

Mary smiled. It seemed infantile but she thought it actually *would* be funny, so while Ash covered his eyes with his hands, Mary rolled up her top and showed her breasts to the occupants of the ISS, who *also* thought it funny, and gave her the 'thumbs up' sign and waved some more as the space station drifted past and on.

'Have you put them away?' asked Ashley, eyes firmly closed.

'Yes.'

He uncovered his eyes.

'Tell me,' said Mary after they had watched the earth move beneath them for a while, the shape of the North American land masses easily recognisable by the delineating inky blackness of the oceans, 'do you find humans at all odd?'

'Not really,' replied Ashley after a moment's reflection, accelerating the globe on and moving round into the midday region of the planet to make a full orbit before returning home, 'but your obsession with networks takes a bit of getting used to. Still, it's understandable.'

'How do you mean?'

'Because networks are *everywhere*. The road and rail systems, the postal service, the Internet, your friendships, family, electricity, water – *everything* on this planet is composed of networks.'

'But why understandable?'

'Because it is the way you are built – your bodies use networks to pass information; your veins and arteries are networks to nourish your bodies. Your mind is a complicated network of nerve impulses. It's little wonder that networks dominate the planet – you have modelled your existence after the construction of your own minds.'

Mary went silent for a moment. She hadn't thought of this.

'And you don't?'

'We most certainly do. But we are wired more sequentially. Every fact is compared with every previous fact and then filtered to find the differences. Our mind works like an infinite series of perfectly transparent glass panels, with all our experiences etched on to them. Where clusters of certain facts appear, then we know what importance must be attached.'

'You remember everything?'

'Of course. I remember every single word you have said to me. Where you said it, and when, and what would have been showing on TV at the time.'

'That must make lying very difficult.'

'On the contrary; it makes it very easy. Since I can recall every lie I tell, I repeat the lie in every context in which it is required. Humans are such poor liars because they have poor memories. The strange thing is that everybody knows everyone else is lying, and nothing much is done about it.'

'You're right about that,' said Mary, gazing up at the sable blackness above them. 'Which is your star?'

'That one there,' said Ashley, pointing in the vague direction of Cassiopeia. 'No, hang on. Over there. No . . . goodness,' he said at last, 'they all look so similar from here.'

And they both fell silent for a while, staring at the sky, deep in thought, with Mary resting her head on Ashley's shoulder, his thoughts and memories seeping into her like a warming stew on a cold day. She saw a green sky with a moon hanging low and dominant in the heavens, and small houses like igloos dotted about a rocky landscape.

'Do you ever think about going home?' she asked in a quiet voice.

'Reading's my home,' he replied.

They returned only ten minutes after setting out, before Mary's exhaled carbon dioxide had time to make itself known. Ashley piloted the small craft back to the same estate in Pangbourne, where, after knocking the head off a garden gnome and hitting the sides of the garage several times, he finally managed to park.

'That was *amazing*,' said Mary, giggling like a schoolgirl.

'Oh-oh.'

'What?'

'We've got a problem. I think that gnome has damaged a thermal exhaust port . . . or something. Quick!'

He grasped her hand and they jumped out of the pliable skin of the globe to the dusty floor of the garage, then outside. They had got as far as the other side of the street when there was a *whoomp* noise and they were knocked over by a blue ring of light that shot out in all directions as the globe exploded.

'Oh dear,' said Ashley as he picked himself up and walked back to his parents' house, which had been badly shaken by the concussion. The walls had cracked and the roof had lost several dozen tiles. The garage itself had ceased to exist – except for a few tattered walls. Of the globe, there was nothing. Isolated fires had been set alight on the lawn, which helpful neighbours were already stamping out.

'Was that you, Ashley?' asked Roger, who was standing at the off-kilter doorway of the house, wig askew and one slipper blown off.

'I cannot tell a lie, Father – Mary was driving. She wanted to have a go so I let her but her binary is a bit rusty and, well, there you have it.'

'Is this true?' asked Roger, staring at Mary.

'No,' said Ashley before Mary could answer. 'And I think I broke your bird box, too.'

Ashley's father turned a paler blue.

'You're *banished*, young man,' he said sternly, jabbing the remains of his pipe in Ashley's direction. 'I think you'd better take Miss Mary home and not return for at least a week.'

Ashley bowed low.

'I take my punishment with good grace. Thank you, Father.'

He looked at his Datsun, which had been blown on to its side. 'I think we'd better take the bus.'

'Wait a minute,' said Mary, picking her way across the wreckage to the front door and inside, where Abigail was staring sadly at the plaster ducks, now in several pieces. 'Thank you for dinner, Mrs 100111100100010011101110010o, it was most enjoyable.'

'Oh!' said Abigail happily. 'Well, you must come again. It's been a pleasure meeting you.'

'Yes indeed,' added Roger kindly, 'our house is your house. Sorry about Ashley. He's always been a bit difficult.'

'The last one out of the egg-sac,' added Abigail with a sigh, by way of explanation.

'. . . saw the first launch of *The Proteus* . . .' muttered Uncle Colin, speaking from beneath the print of *The Haywain*, which had fallen on top of him.

'What did she call you?' whispered Roger as they stood at the front door and waved goodbye.

'I'm not sure,' Abigail whispered back, 'something about how her prawns have asthma.'

'So,' said Mary as they walked away from the smouldering ruin of Ashley's parents' house, 'where are you going to stay tonight?'

'I'll sneak back and sleep in the potting shed,' he said after a moment's reflection. 'It's relatively undamaged.'

'I've a spare ceiling,' said Mary. 'You can stick yourself to that if you want.'

'Well, o-kay,' said Ashley suspiciously, 'but if you're trying to invite me home for sex on a first date, I don't have a penis so you might be a bit disappointed. Then again, you haven't got a 10101110101, so I might be, too.'

Mary hid a smile.

'I'll try and resist the temptation to jump you, Ash.'

But then he saw the funny side and relaxed, and made several of those squeaky-toy-being-sat-upon laughs.

'Your offer is very generous,' he replied, and went several different shades of blue in rapid succession. 'I accept.'

'You know what?' asked Mary as they walked towards the main road and the bus stop.

'What?'

'That was the best date I've ever had.'

'All of it?' asked Ashley in surprise. 'Even my dopey parents? And the wig and the Binary Scrabble and exploding Travelator and stuff?'

'*All of it.*'

'I'm very glad,' he said at last. 'Do you want to come on another date some time? Somewhere better and classier and more fun?'

'I'd like that a lot,' replied Mary. 'Where are we going? The moon? Venus?'

'Somewhere *much* better,' replied Ashley happily. 'Some of the original members of the Stylistics are re-forming, and my dopey sister reckons she can get tickets.'

30

The Punches make peace

'**Most Successful Tooth Fairy**. The most active fairy ever in the Berkshire regional milk-tooth harvesting department was Grundle Arturo Pipsqueak VIII (licence number: 6382/6Y), who collected a grand total of 6,732 milk teeth during 1996 at a total cost of £2,201 36p (less expenses), an average unit cost of 32.7p. The record remains unlikely to be beaten owing to 1: the declining demand for maracas, the chief end-use product of milk teeth, and 2: stiff competition from Far Eastern tooth fairies, who can procure the same quantity for almost one fiftieth the cost.'

— *The Bumper Book of Berkshire Records*, 2004 edition

Before Jack had even had a chance to recover from the blow with the rolling pin, the back door opened again and Madeleine came out, her face crimson with anger.

'You miserable unreal piece of crap!' she screamed at the top of her voice, tears streaming down her cheeks. 'I *trusted* you.'

Jack tried to say something but she cut him short.

'Don't try and explain yourself. If I were you I'd start looking for a good divorce lawyer.' She went back inside and banged the door shut after her.

'Phew!' said Caliban as he hopped down from the dustbin. 'Kind of serves you right. I mean, swapping Madeleine for Agatha Diesel? You must be nuts.'

'*I didn't.*'

'What the sodding hell is going on out there?' said Mr Punch, who had just come out of his house. 'Judy and I can barely hear ourselves shout.'

'Nothing,' said Jack.

'He screwed the boss's wife,' piped up Caliban.

'I did no such thing – and who asked you?'

'Hang on,' said Punch, 'I'm coming round.'

In a couple of minutes he had reappeared, dressed in pyjamas and a bed-hat, and still grinning crazily with his varnished leer, which Jack thought even more galling in the present situation.

'Well,' he said, 'infidelity, Mr Sprat? That doesn't sound like you at all.'

'It's not me. And it's none of your business. And it's two "T"s in Spratt, not one.'

'But it *is* my business,' retorted Punch. 'I'm your neighbour and we PDRs have to stick together.'

'Huzzah!' said Caliban in enthusiastic agreement.

'*You're* a Person of Dubious Reality?' asked Jack of the little ape. 'From where?'

'*The Tempest*,' replied Caliban with a twinge of pride, adding: 'You know, Shakespeare?' when Jack didn't seem to understand.

'Oh,' he said, 'right.'

'Your problem is *our* problem,' said Punch kindly.

But Jack was still angry.

'What makes you think Punch and Judy – *of all people* – are qualified to give advice on marriage?' sneered Jack.

'Nothing really,' explained Punch in a calm and patient voice, 'but we've been married three hundred and twenty-eight years next Wednesday and not a single day goes by without us arguing and fighting. But despite all that we find it in our hearts to forgive because the bottom line is that we love one another dearly, and it is that love which binds our relationship together, regardless of the violence and the quarrelling.'

Jack sat on the garden wall. He ran a hand through his hair. His head was tender where Madeleine had hit him, and was starting to come up in a bump. He looked up at Punch and Caliban, who were staring at him with quiet concern.

'Madeleine found out I was a nursery rhyme character,' said Jack at last, sighing deeply.

'*You never told her?*' asked Punch. 'How can you keep that a secret from her?'

Jack shook his head.

'I don't know. I didn't want to lose her. Perhaps it was because I want to be a *real* person.'

'I'm told it's overrated,' replied Punch. 'Think you could do what you do and help the people you help if you *were* real? You'd never have found out who killed Humpty Dumpty, and Bluebeard would still be killing his brides. And what about Red Riding-Hood and her gran?'

'Yeah – what about them?'

'Okay,' Punch conceded, 'that was a bad example. But you see what I mean. You're good at this weird NCD shit precisely because you're *not* real. Besides, what's so great about "real" these days anyway?'

'It's all right for you,' said Jack after a pause. 'At least you've got a long, performance-based traditional backing to your existence.'

'More of a curse than a blessing,' replied Punch with a sigh. 'We'd love to retire back home to Italy but they keep on updating the act and dragging us out again. We bought a house in Tuscany a few years ago when we thought political correctness would end the show, but it didn't. The Punchinistas think they're doing us a favour, restoring the tradition, but they're not.'

'Tuscany,' mused Jack, who had never been out of Berkshire in his life, 'that could be nice.'

'Yes,' replied Mr Punch dreamily, 'Judy and I were going to spend our twilight years beating each other senseless under the warm Mediterranean sun. We'd sip Chianti through broken teeth and grapple at each other's throats as the orange orb of the sun set on another perfect day. Then, after a truly excellent *spaghetti vongole*, I would jam my thumb in her eye and she would kick me hard in the gonads – and we would go to bed, tired but happy.'

They all fell silent for a while until Jack said:

'Yes, but that doesn't help me right now.'

'Perhaps not,' replied Punch, 'but we can probably do something. Who was this woman you slept with?'

'I didn't,' insisted Jack. 'Briggs's wife has had her eye on me since a fling about twenty-five years ago.'

'Agatha Diesel?' asked Punch.

'You know her?'

He didn't answer, and instead knocked on the back door. It was opened by Prometheus.

'Hello, Punchy,' said the Titan cheerfully, 'how's it cooking?'

'Madeleine needs to come out and speak to Jack.'

Prometheus looked at Jack and then back to Punch.

'I don't think she really wants to.'

'Please? It's important.'

The door closed and Punch winked at Jack while dialling a number on his mobile.

'Are you Voda or Orange?' he asked Jack. 'I get a hundred free min— Agatha? It's Punch. I know your next appointment isn't until Tuesday, but I've just heard about the regrettable incident with Mr Spratt.'

There was a pause as Punch listened to a tearful babble of Agatha's woes.

'I disagree,' he said as soon as he could get a word in, 'the whole situation is a long way from irredeemable. You're to tell your husband *everything* when he gets home, but for now I need you to talk to Mrs Spratt and tell her precisely what happened – or didn't happen – between you and Jack.'

302

There was a pause.

'It's the right thing to do, Agatha. You'll feel a lot better for it. Here she is.'

Madeleine had appeared at the door and glared at Jack. She reluctantly took the proffered mobile and went back inside.

'Now what?' asked Jack.

'Agatha will sort it out – unless you really *did* screw her, in which case you're in such deep shit even I can't help you.'

'I didn't. How do you know Agatha?'

'Judy and I run a marriage guidance centre. Mr and Mrs Briggs have been seeing us for several years now. It's bad. Separate-bed bad.'

The door reopened a few minutes later and Madeleine came out, wiped a tear from her eye, handed the mobile back to Punch and hugged her husband.

'I'm sorry,' she whispered.

He held her tightly.

'And I'm sorry I never told you I wasn't real. People don't change just because you know more about them. I'm still the same Jack Spratt that you knew yesterday and I'll be the same Jack Spratt tomorrow and the day after. You can hold this against me if you want, but it doesn't alter anything that I've ever said to you or take any of the happiness out of the times we've spent together. I'm just an ordinary plod trying to support his family in the only way he can. I may not ever make superintendent, but I'll always be standing beside you.'

She kissed him and said: 'That was a *really* crap speech, sweet-heart, but thank you. Did the rolling pin hurt?'

'It's only painful when I think.'

'If you hadn't made me love you so much I wouldn't have hit you so hard.'

'I had a feeling it might be my fault.'

She laughed and they rested their heads on one another's shoulders, and rocked gently from side to side.

'That's the way to do it,' said Punch with an air of satisfaction of a job well done.

'Oi, shitface!' said Judy, popping her head over the garden fence and interrupting the romance of the moment in a most disagreeable fashion, 'are you going to yabber all night or give me a good ******** like you promised?'

'Hold your tongue, viper!' yelled Punch.

'You're dead meat, you stinking heap of trash!' she screamed back. 'I'll . . .'

But then she suddenly noticed Jack and Madeleine embracing under the yellow glow of the outdoor light.

'What's going on?' she asked in a quiet voice.

'A misunderstanding, sweetness – but it's all right now.'

'Ahhhhh!' she murmured, watching them both and holding her hand out towards Mr Punch, who took it and caressed it gently. 'I like an argument with a happy ending. Actually, I just like an argument.'

She looked at her husband with a coquettish smile and said:

'It's still early. Why don't you and I get all togged up and have a meal, an excellent bottle of wine and then a stand-up row and a punch-up down at the Green Parrot?'

He reached over and kissed her affectionately.

'That sounds like a beautiful idea, Pookums. Can it be a really *serious* punch-up? Like we used to have in the good old days?'

'You're just an old romantic at heart, aren't you?' she replied tenderly. 'I'll ring up the Green Parrot for a reservation, book a couple of beds at the hospital and alert the finest emergency trauma team in Berkshire – and it's my treat.'

Jack and Madeleine went back inside and upstairs to bed, shooing Caliban out of the room when he tried to follow them. They were both fast asleep a half-hour later, the best and deepest sleep for them both in many weeks. And as they slept, Mr and Mrs Punch donned their evening dress and knuckle-dusters, Agatha had a heart-to-heart with her husband, and below on the street outside a single rust bubble popped up on the paintwork of the otherwise pristine Allegro.

31
The Truth is out there

'**Largest Flying Boat Ever**. In 1934 the Soviet Union decided
to enter the global travel world with the mighty Iluyshin-95.
With a wingspan of 520 feet and weighing in at almost 200 tons,
this monstrous behemoth of the skies was powered by no less
than sixty-eight "Vokspod-87" 290HP radial engines. The first
and only attempt to fly her was on 15 June 1934, when she was
tugged out into the Caspian Sea, filled with fuel and the pilot
and crew told not to return until "they had brought glory on
the motherland". With all engines roaring the flying boat vanished
over the horizon and into legend. Nobody knows what became
of her, but it is thought that after failing to become airborne she
made landfall in Turkey, where the crew, too worried about the
repercussions of failure, quietly sold her for scrap.'

– *The Bumper Book of Berkshire Records*, 2004 edition

Jack woke with a start at 5.30 a.m. He and Madeleine were still
entwined, and he carefully unravelled her sleeping form from his
before donning a dressing gown and walking into the bathroom.
He examined the bruise round his eye where Briggs had thumped
him, the cut on his scalp from the incident with the Gingerbreadman
and the garage doors, then the one on his head from the rolling
pin. He swallowed a couple of paracetamols, relieved himself, and
went downstairs.

Jack sighed deeply. He had told Briggs he was on a three-
month leave of absence, but in reality he was anything but. There
were at least two murderers loose in Reading, a mother of all
conspiracies was unfolding unseen in front of him, and if what

he thought was true, the geopolitical future of the world was very much in the balance. Perhaps. He made some coffee and tapped into toadnews.com to see whether the Gingerbreadman had been caught or shot. He hadn't.

'Can I come to work with you?'

It was Caliban, sitting on the kitchen table.

'I'm on leave.'

'Sure you are.'

'I am. And get off the table.'

'Please?' implored Caliban as he jumped to the floor.

'There is no place for you in . . . Hang on,' he said, suddenly thinking of something. 'You're a thieving little swine, aren't you?'

'One of the finest,' replied Caliban proudly, puffing out his chest.

'Then I may have a job for you.'

'Sorry,' said the little ape, wagging a finger at him, 'I never steal to order – that would be immoral. I only do it for fun.'

'Okay, then – do you want to have some seriously good fun?'

Caliban nodded vigorously and Jack ran upstairs to get dressed. He kissed Madeleine, who mumbled something in her sleep along the lines of 'Knock 'em dead, tiger'.

Forty minutes later Jack was bumping down the track to the gravel pit and Mary's Short Sunderland flying houseboat. It was still not yet 6.30, and the lake was flat calm. Not so much as a ripple broke the broad expanse of silver, and when Jack walked along the jetty he could see fish feeding in the gin-clear shallows. It was almost idyllic and hard to believe that, as likely as not, a ten-mile radius would encompass not only this picture of calm and tranquillity but also a raging psychopath and a fugitive Member of Parliament wanted for murder.

Jack knocked twice on the hull door and after a few minutes it was opened by Mary, who was wrapped up in a dressing gown. She blinked sleepily.

'Shit, Jack, what's the time?'

'Early.'

'What happened to your face?'

'This one was Briggs,' he said, pointing to his eye, 'and this one was Madeleine.'

'Madeleine?'

'It's all right – we made up. Can I have some coffee?'

'You know where it is. I'll get dressed.'

Jack walked through the main part of the hull and up into the flight deck, where he lit the gas and put on the kettle. He sat in the co-pilot's seat and stared absently at the view. There were still a lot of unanswered questions, but he hoped he could fit all the pieces together before the shitstorm *really* began.

Mary reappeared a few minutes later, drying her damp hair with a towel.

'You have an alien stuck to the ceiling,' observed Jack.

'I know,' said Mary, pouring some coffee, 'he needed somewhere to stay.'

'How did the date go?'

'Probably the oddest I've ever been on. I think our two species are so fundamentally different that any form of physical bond between us is almost insurmountable. Still, he's fun to be with – and his family are completely nuts. His brother's called Graham, he has a dopey sister named Daisy and he . . .'

Mary realised that she had been gushing a little too much, and stopped. Jack hid a smile, and Mary took a sip of coffee.

'So . . . what's going on, Jack?'

'Everything. If we don't get to the bottom of it all within the next twelve hours then I'm a dead man.'

Mary's eyes narrowed.

'You were serious about all that "Bartholomew being innocent" stuff last night?'

'Absolutely. Bartholomew wasn't anywhere near the three bears' cottage that morning, and he certainly didn't meet her there for trysts. There's something rotten in the city of Reading, and it's up to the NCD to do something about it.'

'So where does the twelve-hour death thing enter into it?'

'Because that's how long it'll be before Danvers or Briggs starts checking Bartholomew's phone records and . . . and . . . finds out that it was me who tipped him off.'

Mary was stunned. She couldn't quite believe it.

'You called him so he could escape?'

'I did.'

'Jack — that's not good. In fact, it's very much worse than not good — it's illegal. *Really* illegal. You'll be bounced out of the force and banged up into the bargain.'

'I had to do it to save his life. He didn't kill Goldilocks. He's the patsy; the fall guy. And like all fall guys in a frame-up, he won't live twenty-four hours. If I hadn't told him to run we would have found him hanging by his pyjama cord with a convenient confession close by. Everyone walks away and Goldilocks' murderer goes free. More importantly, the *reason* for her death remains secret.'

'So . . . she wasn't killed over illegal porridge quotas?'

'Of course not. They were *both* good friends to bears; they were into that harmless little scam *together* — easing the burden of the average bear by free handouts of porridge mid-month. They were working together when photographed at the Coley Park Bart-Mart — and with Vinnie Craps in the background, monitoring them.'

'I get it. So who framed him?'

Jack paused for a minute.

'NS-4. I thought at first they were protecting him but they weren't; they were setting him up to take the blame for Goldy's death. They planted the Post-it note in the three bears' house about

Bartholomew meeting Goldilocks on the Saturday morning, and they knew he wouldn't have an alibi for that time period.'

'How did you know it was a plant?'

'Easy. The note referred to "Andersen's *Wood*". Ed never called it a wood. It was *always* a forest.'

'As you say,' breathed Mary, feeling a bit stupid that she hadn't spotted it, 'easy. But NS-4? That means this is all wrapped in that dodgy beast known as *national interest*.'

'National interest be damned,' replied Jack. 'Goldilocks is dead and the Bruins are fighting for their lives. I tell you, someone's going to go down for this.'

'Are you going to take it to Briggs?'

Jack sighed.

'I can't. He's a good cop but he's politically motivated. He'll blab to the seventh floor and the shutters will bang down tight. As long as NS-4 *think* we've bought into the whole Bartholomew/porridge scenario, then we're safe. Any hint that we're not and the pair of us could find ourselves in a trillion pieces in SommeWorld – or somewhere equally imaginative.'

'Good morning,' said a voice from the door. It was Ashley, dressed only in a pair of yellow boxer shorts. 'The short pauses and nervous intakes of breath woke me up.'

'There's some cooking oil in the cupboard,' said Mary. Ash poured himself a glass of oil and sat down.

'So if Bartholomew didn't kill Goldilocks,' said Mary, 'who did?'

'There was *someone else* in the cottage that morning.'

'Why do you think that?'

'Because of the porridge temperature differential. It's been bothering me for days. How could the three bears' porridge be at such widely varying temperatures when it was poured at the same time?'

'I don't know,' said Mary. 'Because . . . of the different bowl sizes?'

'The guv'nor's right,' remarked Ashley. 'From a *thermodynamic* point of view that's just not possible. The bowl with the smallest volume would cool fastest – making Junior's the coolest – yet his was warmer than Mrs Bruin's.'

'Perhaps it's about surface area?' suggested Mary.

'If that was the case then Ed's would have been cooler,' replied Ashley.

'*Exactly*,' said Jack. 'This is the scenario as I see it: Goldilocks is investigating the murder of champion cucumber growers around the globe. She is talking to someone who may or may not be a long-dead scientist named McGuffin, who aside from taking a cheery delight in blowing things up also dabbled in cucumbers and was connected for a time to QuangTech. Every serious world championship contender has had their cucumber strain destroyed and themselves with it. She is about to go public with what she found out – but someone wants to keep her quiet at all costs and lures her to the three bears' cottage on Saturday morning by telling her Bartholomew will be waiting for her.'

'How do you know they used Bartholomew as the lure?'

'She was naked in bed when the three bears found her.'

'Of course. And the porridge?'

'I'm coming to that. Her assailant tells her to be there at 8.15 and he arrives just *after* the three bears left for their walk but just *before* Goldilocks arrives. He waits – but the smell of porridge is too tempting, and he eats the coolest porridge – Baby Bear's. Then he refills the bowl. But he's still hungry, so he eats Father Bear's porridge too. And then he refills *that* bowl.'

'I get it,' said Mary. 'So when Goldilocks arrives and tastes the porridge, Father Bear's is too *hot* because it's just been poured, Mother Bear's is too *cold* because it was the original pouring, but Baby Bear's was just right – and that's the one she ate.'

'But then . . . who *was* there that morning?' asked Ashley.

'Who can't resist porridge?'

'Bears.'

'But there's a problem,' observed Mary. 'Bears are essentially peaceful and Goldy's "Friend to Bears" status would have protected her. And besides, why didn't they tell you about him? His scent would have been all over the house.'

'Because . . . he was sleeping with Ed's wife.'

'You can't tell that from the porridge, surely?'

'No. Do you remember the three bears all had their own beds? I didn't think anything of it at the time but Punch mentioned it last night and all of a sudden it made sense. Mr and Mrs Bruin were sleeping separately because there were *serious* marital problems within the bear family. The interloper in the cottage that morning was another bear, a *fourth* bear. *He* was the one that ate and repoured the porridge, *he* was the one sleeping with Ursula Bruin. *He* was the one waiting for Goldilocks, *he* was the one who killed her – and *he* was the one Ed wanted to tell me about.'

'Then it was the fourth bear and not Bartholomew who ordered the Gingerbreadman to kill the Bruins?'

'I believe it was. And if he was diddling Ursula under Ed's nose without being killed, he's dominant. *Very* dominant.'

'Ed Bruin was ranked sixty-eight in the Reading Ursa Major Bear Hierarchy,' said Mary. 'They're very big on male dominance. Which leaves us with sixty-seven more suspects than we need right now.'

They all sat in silence for a moment, digesting the latest revelations.

'So . . . continue your scenario,' said Mary.

'Okay. Goldilocks arrives at the cottage about 8.10 and she's hungry so she eats the porridge, accidentally breaks a chair and then undresses to wait for Bartholomew in bed. She falls asleep because she has been up all night working on her story, and might have been dispatched there and then *except* the three bears return half an hour early because of Ed's appointment with the vet. They don't realise who she is, she gives a truthful account of herself and runs off into the forest.'

'And was never seen again – at least, not alive,' murmured Mary.

'Precisely. Her flight from the cottage is watched by her assailant, who has seen the three bears return and elects to stay hidden – they don't know he's arranged this little meeting. He follows her, kills her and dumps the body in SommeWorld, where it is hoped either she will not be found or it will be assumed she died accidentally.'

'Then what?' asked Mary.

'It all goes fine until we start to ask questions and connect Goldy with Obscurity and the cucumber-related deaths. But Ed Bruin is deeply disturbed that a "Friend to Bears" has died and is suspicious about the fourth bear being in the cottage that morning. He decides to call me but the fourth bear acts quickly: he orders the Gingerbreadman to kill them and plant the note about meeting Bartholomew on Ed's desk. If all had gone to plan we would have arrested and charged Bartholomew and he'd have been silenced shortly afterwards, and the killings would have looked like an un-related ursist attack.'

'Had we not got to the forest as quickly as we did.'

'*Exactly.*'

'Are you saying the Gingerbreadman, the fourth bear and NS-4 are all connected?'

'I'm not sure, but muse on this: Ginger's been on low-security transportation for over six years yet chooses to break out at *exactly* this time and place. He's being controlled by someone, I'm almost positive.'

'How do you control a Gingerbreadman?'

'I don't know. He was in St Cerebellum's when Goldilocks died, so that rules him out as regards the actual murder.'

They all went silent for a moment.

'This is the plan,' announced Jack. 'We find out the story Goldilocks was working on. If it was big enough to have her killed, then it's as big as she boasted. Four unexplained fireballs with world-class cucumber growers in the centre of three of them.'

'You think Cripps and the other cucumberistas were murdered and their champions stolen?'

'I do. Cripps must have entered his greenhouse that night and come across an empty sight – holes where his plants had been.'

'*Good heavens, it's full of holes,*' murmured Mary, 'his final words. Bisky-Batt said the nutritional value of a giant cucumber is almost zero, but perhaps Cripps and the others were working on giant cucumbers to then cross-pollinate with other foodstuffs that *would* be useful. Since GM research is banned in the UK, maybe QuangTech were having a bunch of well-meaning amateurs do their work for them – and occasionally "lending a hand" with visits from the Men in Green.'

'You're right,' replied Jack. 'Fuchsia mentioned something about the MiG taking core samples and clippings and so forth – and if McGuffin didn't die and is supervising the research . . .'

They thought about all this for a while as it was quite far fetched, but then NCD investigations generally were, as a rule.

'It's a good theory,' said Jack finally, 'but we need to know more – and we've got a good place to start.'

'Where?'

'The Gingerbreadman. Find him and with a bit of luck he'll lead us to the fourth bear.'

'We're going to do a plot device number twenty-six after all,' observed Mary with a smile. 'One small thing: how do we find Mr G when Copperfield and six hundred officers are running around Reading without a clue?'

Jack said nothing but took a paper evidence package from his jacket and showed it to her.

'What's that?'

'It's the gingerbread thumb you shot off.'

'You *removed* evidence from the evidence store? How the hell did you manage that?'

'I have a good friend who steals things for me. This is what we'll do: Mary, you'll be with me and we'll take this broken biscuit to Parks. Ashley, I want you to go into the office and pretend everything is as normal. If Briggs or anyone else asks what's going on you're to tell them that Mary is looking into a minor domestic bear incident down at the Bob Southey.'

'You mean lie to a ranking officer?'

'Yes,' said Jack, 'and do it well. But remember: no elephants, no pirates.'

He was halfway out of the door before Jack called him back.

'What?'

'You'd better get dressed if you're going to work.'

'Of course,' said Ashley, and dashed off into the hull of the flying boat.

32
Parks again

'**Strangest Degree Course**. Gone are the days when only traditional academic disciplines were offered for further study. A quick
trawl of UK prospectuses reveals that Faringdon University offers
a three-year BA in 'Carrot husbandry', a course that is only mildly
stranger than Nuffield's 'Correct use of furniture' or Durham's
'Advanced blinking'. Our favourite is the BA offered by the
University of Slough in 'Whatever you want' in which you spend
three years doing . . . whatever you want. Slough has reported,
perhaps unsurprisingly, that the success rate is 100 per cent.'
     – *The Bumper Book of Berkshire Records*, 2004 edition

It was mid-morning when they found Dr Parks at Reading
University's Charles Fort Centre for Cosmic Weirdness. He was
giving a lively lecture to a packed auditorium. Pseudo-science had
become a popular degree subject in recent years and Reading
University, always eager to provide popular coursework and with
their finger hard on the pulse of the Zeitgeist, had added the three-
year master's to their roster of unconventional BAs, along with
crypto-zoology, crop circles and the study of extra-terrestial life,
which went down quite well with Rambosians, who knew most
of the answers anyway – except what all those previous UFO things
were, as it certainly hadn't been them, or anyone they knew.

Jack and Mary stood near the door and let the talk go over their
heads. It was mostly about the feasibility of using the solar wind as
a power source for telekinetics, the theoretic possibilities of the
existence of a chrono-synclastic infundibulum, and the likelihood
of capturing ball lightning in large glass jars to use as an indefinite

light source. Jack and Mary applauded with the others when the talk ended and they approached Parks as the students filed out.

'Inspector!' said Parks with a friendly smile. 'I was meaning to call you.'

He shook them both by the hand and started to pack up his notes and the carousel of slides that had accompanied his talk.

'You were?'

'Yes; I found some information about the blast on the Nullarbor Plain. In October 1992 a seismic survey on a routine oil exploration reported an explosion of some sort to the National Parks Authorities. They sent out a survey team, expecting to find a meteorite strike. Instead they found glass.'

'Glass?'

'Glass. Fused sand, to be precise. Circular in shape, about the size of a football pitch; the glass was four inches thick in the centre and thinned out towards the edge. Subjected to a few hundred thousand degrees for a very short time.'

'What do you think it was?'

Parks took the small piece of fired earth from the jiffy bag.

'I think it was the same type of blast we saw at Obscurity. Intense heat, very little radiation. Some form of advanced thermal weapon, tested clandestinely in the Nullarbor. If you wanted to sterilise an area of land quickly and easily, a heat bomb of the description I've given you would be just the way to do it; and if you didn't want your competitors to figure out what was going on, you'd make damn sure you removed the evidence.'

'QuangTech,' murmured Jack. 'Perhaps they didn't disband their advanced weapons division after all.'

'That would be good news for the conspiracy industry if true,' said Parks excitedly, adding after a moment's thought: 'Or even if not true. Did you want to see me about something?'

'Yes,' replied Jack. 'Do you have a scanning electron microscope?'

'Not officially – but the SEM operator here is heavily into the whole yeti/bigfoot/sasquatch non-controversy, so could probably be swung.'

Jack showed him the gingerbread thumb, still in the evidence bag.

'Is that what I think it is?'

'It certainly is. I'd like you to see if there is anything unusual about it on the granular level. On the face of it, Gingerbreadmen are usually passive victims at teatime and not homicidal maniacs, so I need to know more – and I need to know it *now*.'

'I'll get on to it straight away.'

They thanked Parks and walked out of the centre.

'Why didn't Copperfield think of doing that?' said Jack.

'Because he's not NCD?' suggested Mary. 'Or because he's a twit?'

'Probably both.'

He pulled out his mobile and called the NCD office.

'Hello!' said Ashley cheerfully. 'Guess what?'

'What?'

'The office has been bugged. When I got there I could hear the buzz of the encoded binary radio transmission.'

'Tell me you're not still in the office—?'

'No. I'm in the roof space just behind the third-floor toilets reading the phone traffic as it leaves the exchange. It's made me a bit tipsy. Did you know that Pippa is up the duff?'

'You're kidding!'

'No; she was talking to her mother all about it. And what's more,' continued Ashley, 'the father is Peck – you know, in Uniform with the pockmarked face and the twin over in the Palmer Park?'

'What's going on?' asked Mary.

'Pippa's pregnant by Peck.'

'Pippa Piper picked Peck over Pickle or Pepper?' exclaimed Mary incredulously. 'Which of the Peck pair did Pippa Piper pick?'

'Peter "pockmarked" Peck of Palmer Park. *He* was the Peck that Pippa Piper picked.'

'No, no,' returned Mary, 'you've got it all wrong. *Paul* Peck is the Palmer Park Peck; Peter Peck is the pockmarked Peck from Pembroke Park. Pillocks. I'd placed a pound on Pippa Piper picking PC Percy Proctor from Pocklington.'

There was a pause.

'It seems a very laborious set-up for a pretty lame joke, doesn't it?'

'Yes,' agreed Mary, shaking her head sadly. 'I really don't know how he gets away with it.'

Jack turned his attention back to Ashley.

'Has Briggs called the office?'

'Several times. I told him Mary was down at the Bob Southey and I didn't have a clue what was going on as I am merely window dressing for better alien–sapien relations. More interestingly, Agent Danvers has called Briggs on several occasions.'

'You eavesdropped on Briggs's private telephone conversations?'

'Not at all,' replied Ashley. 'I've eavesdropped on *everyone's* conversations. How did you think I found out about Pippa and Peck?'

'Well, that's all right, then,' said Jack, whose interpretation of the Police and Criminal Evidence Act was becoming more elasticated by the second. 'What did Danvers want?'

'She wanted to know where you were so she could have a chat. Briggs was commendably evasive – said you were dangerously insane and safely on leave where you could do no real harm except possibly to yourself.'

'Did he now? Did you get anything on Hardy Fuchsia?'

'And how. Before he retired he spent forty years in the nuclear power industry.'

'He referred to Prong, Cripps, McGuffin and Katzenberg as colleagues,' observed Jack thoughtfully.

'Precisely. They *all* worked together at various times – in nuclear fusion R&D.'

Jack told him he was a star, Ashley asked him which one, Jack said it didn't matter, and then rang off.

'Let's get over to Sonning and talk to Fuchsia,' said Jack. 'It looks like our scatty and mostly dead cucumber fanciers were all retired nuclear physicists.'

33
Hardy Fuchsia and Bisky-Batt

'**Least Mysterious Mysterious Visitors**. Following on from the UFO fraternity's much-envied and highly mysterious "Men in Black", other minority groups have also begun to claim visitations by "mysterious" groups of men. First the barely mysterious "Men in Tartan" spotted either singing or insensible on Burns Night. Next comes the hardly mysterious "Men in Red" who are usually sighted near talent contests at Butlins, and then the only mildly mysterious "Men in Yellow" who gather around partially completed buildings. Least mysterious of all, and the winners in this category, are the "Men in Blue" who tend to gather around football matches and other potential areas of public disturbance.'

— *The Bumper Book of Berkshire Records*, 2004 edition

There was no answer when they knocked on Fuchsia's door.

'Keep trying,' said Jack. 'I'm going to check round the back.'

After the third attempt Mary entered the garden by the gate at the side and thumped even more loudly on the back door, then peered through the kitchen window. There was no sign of life and the door was firmly locked.

'Over here,' yelled Jack from the greenhouse. She found him kneeling near the empty bed that had once held Fuchsia's collection of champion cucumbers.

'Stolen?'

'Worse,' said Jack, pointing at the freshly disturbed earth. Mary shivered. Poking up from the dirt were eight fingertips. They were held out in front of whoever was buried there in a position of terrified supplication. Jack donned a latex glove and scraped away at the dry earth with his fingertips. It was Fuchsia, barely six inches below the surface. His eyes and mouth were still open and the earth was dark and heavy with blood.

'Damn and blast that Briggs!' cried Jack. 'Why can't he ever believe us?'

He stood up and they quietly left the greenhouse.

'Cucumber extremists?' suggested Mary. 'The Men in Green?'

'Except they didn't blow it up. You'd better speak to Briggs while I do some house-to-house. If only he'd agreed to the twenty-four-hour surveillance . . . !'

Mary spoke to Briggs, who told her – a bit sternly, she thought – to stay *exactly* where she was. She sat in the warm sun and stared at the body of Fuchsia until Briggs arrived. And he was in a seriously bad mood.

'Where's Jack?' was the first thing he said, looking around.

'I'm not sure,' said Mary, trying to remain deniably ambiguous. 'On leave, I think.'

'You,' he continued angrily, 'are in deep trouble, Sergeant.'

Mary's heart went cold. If Briggs could prove that she knew about Jack's call tipping off Bartholomew or the theft of the gingerbread thumb from the evidence store, she'd be as guilty as he was. The correct procedure would have been to arrest Jack, but that had been out of the question. They'd triumph or fall together.

'Have you found Bartholomew, sir?' she asked brightly, trying a spot of misdirection.

'It's not your concern any longer. You are suspended from duty facing disciplinary action. I was a fool to think you might be responsible enough to head the NCD.'

She felt her shoulders slump. It was over. Even if she wasn't charged as an accessory to Jack's misdemeanours, she'd never get to stay in the force. And policing was all she'd ever wanted to do. But she wasn't angry with Jack. It had been her decision.

'You're to relinquish command of the NCD forthwith and take immediate leave pending further enquiries. Is that clear?'

'Yes, sir,' she said in a resigned tone. 'You know about the thumb, then?'

'Thumb?' echoed Briggs. 'What are you blathering on about? But before you go I want to know one thing. Who's he?'

And he threw that morning's copy of *The Toad* on to the garden roller. Mary frowned and looked at the black-and-white photograph on the cover. It was of a translucent globe hovering in space with two passengers – a woman and an alien. The woman was baring her breasts and the alien, of course, was covering his eyes. The headline read: SAUCY READING PC FLAUNTS HER ASSETS TO OUR LADS IN ORBIT.

'Shit,' said Mary, 'I didn't know they had a camera.'

'That's the best you can do? "I didn't know they had a camera"? Now, again: who is this person? I can't recognise him with his hands over his eyes.'

Briggs pointed a finger at Ashley in the photograph.

'I . . . I don't know,' she said at last, not knowing whether to be relieved that Jack was still in the clear, or annoyed and embarrassed that she had appeared topless on the cover of *The Toad*. 'I'd only met him a few hours earlier.'

'Humph,' replied Briggs, jerking his head in the direction of the garden gate. 'Go on, get out of my sight. We'll take over this investigation from here.'

'Thank you, sir.'

And she hastily made her way into the street. She looked around desperately for Jack and eventually found him sitting in his Allegro a little way up the road.

'What news?'

'I've been suspended as well.'

Jack shook his head sadly.

'The lengths these guys will go to.'

'No,' said Mary as she blushed, 'this was unrelated to the inquiry. A small . . . *indiscretion* on my behalf.'

And she told him, very quickly, about what had transpired. Jack wasn't amused, or impressed.

'Good timing, Mary. This lowers our authority to absolute zero.'

There was silence in the Allegro for a few minutes as they watched more squad cars arrive.

'I'm sorry, Jack.'

'That's okay,' he said. 'I'm sorry I dragged you into all this. I just felt we were getting somewhere, that's all.'

'That reminds me,' said Mary, 'I had a quick look round Fuschia's house and found this.'

She handed him a photo. It was a line-up of six men, all grinning and holding a giant cucumber between them. Written below the huge vegetable was '1979 Nationals'.

'That's Fuchsia, Cripps, Prong, Katzenberg, McGuffin . . . and *Bisky-Batt*,' murmured Jack, pointing at the individuals in turn. 'All dead except Bisky-Batt and McGuffin, and he's meant to be. We need some answers out of QuangTech. But with both of us suspended . . . !'

'Bisky-Batt won't know yet.'

'Mary, assuming the authority of an officer while suspended is impersonation. Add that to stealing evidence and perverting the course of justice, and I'm going to go to prison for a very long time.'

'We're NCD,' said Mary, remembering something that Jack had told her not that long before. 'This is what we do. We get suspended, battered, beaten and almost arrested. But the bottom line is we hunt for the truth and bring justice to the nursery world. No matter what.'

'No matter what,' repeated Jack as he switched on the engine. 'Want to know what I found out on door-to-door?'

They pulled into the road and headed off towards QuangTech. 'Tell me.'

'Men in Green. Three of them. They were here an hour before we arrived moving "rolls of carpet" into a red van. They must have killed him and taken his cucumbers – all of them.'

'Why?'

'I don't know. But I think Bisky-Batt has some talking to do.'

'Yes, that was the 1979 cucumber growers' national championships,' Bisky-Batt said with a smile. 'I remember it well.'

Somehow, it wasn't the reaction they were hoping for. Evasive, difficult, unpleasant – any of those might have given some sort of hint that Bisky-Batt knew more than he was letting on but he was none of those things. As usual he was helpful, open and pleasant. They turned up unannounced and he agreed to see them without a murmur.

'And why were you there?' asked Jack.

'I was giving out the trophy on behalf of the Quangle-Wangle. The QuangTech trophy for overall winner has been a mainstay for a number of years now.'

'I didn't know that.'

'Just one of many associations and organisations that QuangTech supports, Inspector. Can I help with anything else?'

Jack and Mary looked at one another. This wasn't going at all well.

'Your Advanced Weapons Division,' said Jack, frantically clutching at straws. 'Is it possible that you were developing some sort of thermal heat bomb?'

'As I think I told you,' replied Bisky-Batt with infinite patience, 'the QuangTech weapons division has been disbanded for over a

327

decade.' He smiled. 'It sounds as though you have been talking to someone on the fringes of science over that Obscurity blast. No matter what we say, there will always be others who promote a conspiracy. I suggest that these people have a yeti-shaped hole in their lives that needs to be filled in some manner, whether sensible or not. We at QuangTech are concerned more with tangible realities.'

'Like Project Supremely Optimistic Belief?'

'Cancelled, as I told you. The Quangle-Wangle saw the light after McGuffin's unhappy tenure.'

'What about the Gingerbreadman?'

'What about him?'

'He's popping up with a regularity that I find disturbing,' said Jack. 'I wonder if he had ever contacted you or the Quangle-Wangle?'

'Absolutely not,' replied Bisky-Batt emphatically. 'If he had I would have been straight on the phone to the police. Really, Inspector, I have to say that your line of questioning seems very haphazard. Can I assist with anything else?'

'GM experiments on cucumbers,' said Jack, getting desperate. 'Unable to do your own experiments you had McGuffin clandestinely conduct them via cucumber growers here in the UK.'

'This is ridiculous,' snapped Bisky-Batt, his patience suddenly wearing out. 'If we wanted to conduct GM experiments we most certainly would, in one of the many nations where it is legal. McGuffin, quite aside from being dead, was an expert in *physics*. Genetics is an entirely different discipline. Do you have any more wild accusations or do I have to complain about your conduct to the Chief Constable?'

'That's all the wild accusations we have for *now*,' said Jack loftily, attempting to pull some remnants of dignity from the wreckage. 'Is it possible to speak to the Quangle-Wangle?'

'The answer is still no, Inspector. Good day to you.'

Jack and Mary mumbled something about 'ongoing enquiries' and were seen firmly to the door.

'He knows,' said Jack as soon as they were outside the QuangTech building.

'Knows what?'

'Knows that we've been suspended. But he's doing nothing about it. Why?'

'I don't know.'

Jack looked back at the huge industrial complex. Somewhere within, safe from prying eyes, was the Quangle-Wangle.

Mary's mobile rang.

'Yes, sir,' said Mary, flicking a glance at Jack, 'I'll be sure to find him and tell him.'

'Developments?' he asked as she snapped the mobile shut.

'You could say that. Briggs wants us both at the Bob Southey *immediately*. Bartholomew's holed up inside and the bears won't give him up.'

34

Return to the Bob Southey

———

'**Most Secret Arm of Britain's Secret Service**. It is said that NS-4 is the least transparent and accountable of all Britain's secret services, but this isn't known for sure, as there are no figures to back it up. The director-general is possibly someone high up, who may or may not run the disputed department from somewhere "in the country". Their function (if they have one) is unknown and success on past missions is open to dispute. Funding is likely to come from government but this too is not known for sure, and the scope of their work involves several things that remain conjecture at this time.'

– *The Bumper Book of Berkshire Records*, 2004 edition

It took them almost half an hour to get to the Bob Southey, and by then the building was surrounded by police officers, cars, vans and marksmen. At the head of all this razzmatazz and next to the mobile control post was Briggs. He glared at Jack and Mary as they approached.

'You're here because they asked for you. Don't ask me why, but they did – you too, Mary.'

'Who's "they"?'

'We don't know. Tip-off from someone inside the Bob Southey. They said they would surrender Bartholomew at seven o'clock, and they wanted NCD personnel to be on hand. But the Bob Southey residents' committee denied they had called us and are asking for forty kilos of porridge and a dozen jars of honey as a goodwill gesture.'

Jack looked at his watch. It was a quarter to seven.

'I have experience with bears,' said Jack. 'Do you want me to speak to them?'

'Not yet,' growled Briggs, who was clearly not too happy about Agatha's behaviour the previous night. 'But hang around – out of my sight. Mr Demetrios of NS-4 turned up and he's threatening to take the whole shebang out of our hands.'

'Is he here?' asked Jack, looking around.

'No; he and Danvers had to speak to someone at QuangTech on another matter.'

'Hmm,' said Jack, 'I'd expect them to be here.'

'I'm very glad they're not,' said Briggs grumpily, and went back into the mobile control room. Jack sighed and looked around the police cars, army personnel and onlookers. As he did so, his phone rang. He moved away to take the call. It was Vinnie Craps.

'What's happening, Spratt?' he asked.

'You tell me, Vinnie. Where are you?'

'Look up.'

Jack did as he was bid. High up on the building, looking out of a window, was a well-dressed figure in a tweed suit. He waved a paw.

'There was a fourth bear in the house the morning of Goldilocks' death,' Jack told him. 'Any ideas?'

'Nope,' came the reply after a short pause. 'There's not a single bear in Reading that would knowingly harm a hair on her head. All that work she did on the right to arm bears and the illegal bile-tappers. Goldilocks was a bear icon.'

'I see. Have you got Bartholomew with you?'

'Yes.'

'Put him on.'

'What's going on, Jack?' asked Sherman in a worried tone. 'You said twelve hours and you'd have found out who killed Goldy – I trusted you about my life being in danger and now I've made things ten times worse for myself!'

'It's taking longer than I thought,' replied Jack. 'Trust me. What's the deal over this surrender?'

Jack heard an audible sigh at the other end of the phone.

'I don't know anything about it. If there was an offer of surrender it didn't come from anyone in here. Bears are trustworthy and honest and I have "Friend to Bears" status. They'd all fight to the death to protect me. But that won't happen. I'll give myself up before a single bear is harmed.'

'Keep that to yourself for the moment, sir. Are you sure there's no one there who would give you up?'

'Positive.'

'You could be mistaken. There was a *fourth* bear at the Bruins' house that morning. A bear not like other bears. A bear who is willing to kill – his own kind, if necessary. Keep your eyes and ears open. I'll call you as soon as I have any information.'

He put the mobile back in his pocket and threaded his way towards where Mary was waiting for him. She had been joined by Ashley, who was showing her some photographs of hideously crushed vehicles.

'Jack, we've traced all the previous owners of Dorian Gray's cars—'

'Mary, I hardly think that's important right now.'

'No, but I really think you should listen – *every single one of them* has died in a horrific traffic accident.'

'What do you mean?'

'Exactly what I said.'

She showed him the pictures. Every car was a crumpled heap of scrap on the road.

'All these were sold by Gray and each was totalled shortly after the sale – and there was never any other vehicle involved.'

'What are you saying?'

'I did some research on Dorian Gray,' said Ashley, 'and I could

333

only find one person with this name, born in 1878.'

'You told me this already. It can't be the same person – it would make him one hundred and twenty-six. The Dorian I met was barely thirty.'

'I thought it couldn't be the same person either,' replied Ashley. 'There wasn't a death certificate. I did some more research and found a photograph from 1911. It's . . . well, see for yourself.'

He handed over the picture and Jack felt the hairs rise on his neck. The reason was clear: the Gray in the picture was *the same one who had sold him the car*. The smile was the same; even the mole on his left cheek.

'And from 1935,' said Ashley, passing him another, 'and here, in 1953.'

They were all of the same man. Jack handed back the pictures and stared at the Allegro suspiciously. All of a sudden it didn't seem *quite* so pristine. The rubber windscreen surround looked a bit faded and there was a small discoloration on the front bumper.

'Every recipient of a Gray "guaranteed" car died in it, you say?'

Ash nodded, and Jack looked back and forth between the two of them. If what Ashley was saying was true, this was bad – worse, it was *evil*.

'Forget face creams and all that "*laboratoire*" crap you see on the telly,' he said slowly. 'There's only one tried-and-tested way to stay young and that's a pact with the Dark One. Damn. I *knew* there was a reason he had me sign the buyer's agreement with red ink.' He shook his head sadly. 'He must have been using some kind of suspended automotive decrepitude to channel a few luckless souls to Mephistopheles – and all for a few more years of his own miserable youth. What a louse.'

'It explains the reverse-running odometer,' said Mary.

'Just goes to show that if a deal looks too good to be true, it generally is. Thanks, Ash. I think this car is going to stay right where it is . . .'

His voice had trailed off as he caught sight of someone familiar in the sea of heads.

'Isn't that Dr Parks?'

He called Parks over and the lecturer moved through the crowd that was rapidly forming for no other reason than that there was a crowd forming.

'Hello, Inspector,' said Parks, panting slightly. 'I got here as you asked.'

'I didn't ask you,' replied Jack with a frown. 'But no matter – got something for us?'

'And how!' He looked around curiously at the milling crowd. 'What's the ruckus?'

'Bartholomew's holed up in there with a sloth of bears.'

'Ah! Well, check *this* out,' Parks said excitedly, handing them several photomicrographs from the scanning electron microscope.

'We had to search around but we finally got there,' he said triumphantly, tapping the image. 'How did you know?'

'Call it a hunch. I'd like you to get this on the Conspiracy Theorist website as soon as you can; spread it around so everyone knows. Okay?'

'Sure.'

'I see it,' said Mary, still staring at the pictures, 'but what does it mean?'

'It means Bisky-Batt *lied* to us – I thought all that smarmy "In what way can I assist you, Officer?" rubbish was too good to be true.'

There was the sound of a loud siren from close by and an armoured car drove up, parked and disgorged a dozen troops, all heavily armed. It was turning into an all-out siege.

'There's something else,' said Parks.

'Yes?'

'I was thinking again about the Nullarbor blast and something

335

stirred in my memory. I had a look through some back issues of *Conspiracy Theorist* and discovered that there *is* a theory that might explain the sort of damage we saw at Obscurity and on the Nullarbor. It was first postulated in the 1950s but was so far fetched that even the hardcore pseudo-science elite dismissed it as "nonsense". It was called Cold Ignition Fusion and was a way of building a small thermonuclear device using a deuterium/tritium fuel which could be self-extracting from the heavy hydrogen found in groundwater, with a mass-induced organic trigger to set it off. It's on a par with the moon being made of green cheese and a Mayan temple under Cleethorpes, but the result would be pretty much what we saw at Obscurity and all the others. A small thermonuclear blast in the region of a half to one kiloton.'

'Cold Ignition Fusion?' queried Jack. 'Just *how* impossible is it?'

'In the current climate of scientific thought, it's in frilly bonkers la-la land, but great minds have been wrong before. In 1933 Ernest Rutherford declared that the vast energies in the atomic nucleus could never be unlocked and that anyone who said otherwise was talking utter "moonshine". An undisputed genius, Inspector, yet quite wrong on this occasion. Cold Ignition Fusion is perhaps not impossible but highly, *highly* improbable – and believe me, my mind is broad.'

'But if it *could* be done?' asked Mary.

'Hypothetically?' asked Parks.

'Hypothetically.'

'If it *could* be done,' he said with a smile, 'can you imagine the value of such a discovery? Unlimited safe and cheap power from *water*. Truly, lightning in a bottle.'

'But on the other side of the coin,' said Mary, 'bargain-basement nuclear weapons.'

A cold shiver ran down Jack's spine as events suddenly popped into sharp focus.

.

'Shit,' he said, 'I've been an idiot. Quickly: using Cold Ignition, how much mass would a device have to reach before self-ignition would begin?'

'Almost exactly fifty kilos. The theory is suspect, but quite precise.'

Jack turned to Ashley.

'Ash, I just hope your total recall is as good as you say. I need the weight of Cripps's champion cucumber the last time he reported to Fuchsia.'

'110001 point 1010111.'

'49.87 kilos – Katzenberg's?'

'110001 point 1100000.'

'49.96. What about Prong's?'

'110001 point 1011001.'

'Still mighty close – 49.89.'

'You're right,' said Ashley. 'There *is* a connection. Fuchsia's was 110001 point 1001010; there's barely one per cent difference between them all.'

Jack thumped his fist into his palm.

'All a few grams under the magic fifty kilos. I've been looking at this arse about face. People didn't blow up those cucumbers. Those cucumbers *blew up the people*. The champions reach fifty kilos, hit critical mass and – boom.'

'*What?*' exclaimed Parks, who, despite being a leading light in the pseudo-science movement, was having serious trouble over this. 'Come on; doesn't that seem a bit improbable?'

'Improbable is standard working procedure within the NCD,' replied Jack grimly. 'Cripps, Katzenberg, Prong and Fuchsia just thought they were growing heavy cucumbers, but McGuffin was flitting around with his Men in Green in the background, changing, cross-breeding, bio-engineering and reseeding until he had devised a devastatingly destructive power that could be created in a grow-bag with nothing more complex than a dibber and a watering can.'

'You mean—?'

'Right,' growled Jack, 'cuclear energy.'

They all fell silent, pondering the geopolitical ramifications of such a discovery.

'Hold on a sec,' added Jack in a worried tone. 'Fuchsia's champion was almost *at* fifty kilos and he had six others almost as large that were stolen this morning – where the hell are they now?'

'There were *seven* thermocuclear devices?' queried Parks, who had latched on to Jack's outlandish explanation without too much difficulty, as should you. 'This is very worrying. The destructive power of a group of devices wouldn't be arithmetic, but *exponential* – we're talking a total yield of perhaps fifty kilotons, enough to flatten everything for a half-mile in all directions.'

'Jack,' said Mary in a nervous whisper, 'we were all *requested* to be present at the Bob Southey for seven o'clock, but no one knows who asked us.'

The implication wasn't lost on him. He turned to look at the Bob Southey, then at the crowd milling about. Everyone was here. Himself, Ash, Mary, Parks, Briggs, Bartholomew, Vinnie – even the Bruins, who were in the Southey medical centre. Everyone except NS-4, who'd legged it off to QuangTech. It wasn't a siege. It was a *trap*.

'Mary, tell Briggs to evacuate the area *immediately*, and then look for McGuffin. This is going to be one hell of a bang and he wouldn't miss it for anything. I'd start checking out distant ridges or any other good viewing points.'

Jack didn't wait for a reply and ran towards the entrance ramp of the underground car park where he had busted Tarquin Majors – and straight into a cordon of police officers.

'You're going to have to let me through,' barked Jack to the sergeant in command. 'There's a thermocuclear device in there which could destroy half of Reading.'

'Briggs warned us about your little tricks,' retorted one of the officers, Sergeant Chapman, with a faint smile. 'No one goes in, no one comes out.'

'I'm head of the NCD, Sergeant. In matters concerning my jurisdiction I have unlimited access – you know the rules.'

'You're right about that,' returned the sergeant, 'but you're *not* head of the NCD now, are you?'

'I'm here under DS Mary's orders – she's head of the NCD in my stead.'

'Think I don't read the papers?' replied Chapman with a smirk. 'She's been suspended too.'

'I don't have time to argue!' yelled Jack, and tried to push his way through, but there were four of them and they held him tight.

'For God's sake—'

'*I'm* head of the NCD,' said a voice behind them, 'and you can release my associate and let us both pass.'

'You?' said Chapman, staring at the small alien who was glaring up at him. 'An alien constable who no one else will work with?'

'I'm NCD and have a badge to prove it. In the event of a superior officer being incapacitated or suspended, authority devolves to the next ranking officer. In this case, me.'

Chapman looked at Ashley, then at Jack, then nodded to the other officers, who released him. Ashley didn't wait a second and darted through the cordon with Jack close behind.

'Thanks,' muttered Jack as they hurried into the gloom of the underground car park.

'Never mind that,' replied Ashley. 'What are we looking for?'

'Seven cucumbers, each one the size of a small torpedo. They'll be in a red van.'

They found it on the lower level one. Jack looked in through the driver's window. There were several green boiler suits dumped on the passenger seat. The key wasn't in the ignition. He cursed, went round to the back and was just about to open the rear doors when he realised that the van was radiating heat. He touched the door handle with a saliva-tipped fingertip and it hissed malevolently at him.

'Shit,' he said, 'it's begun.'

He wrapped a handkerchief around his hand and threw open the doors, ducking to avoid the hot waft of air that rolled out. The interior of the van was filled with the giant cucumbers Jack had last seen in Hardy Fuchsia's greenhouse, with the uppermost cucumber resting on a digital scale. A tube from a bottle was leading into the giant vegetable, with a time switch metering the weight-gaining contents. The digital scale read 49.997 kilos, and already the cucumber's smooth skin was turning from green to a dark orange and giving out large quantities of heat – the paint on the van's sides was starting to blister.

They both stared at it blankly for a few seconds.

'I don't know the first thing about disarming thermocuclear devices,' admitted Jack, the fear rising in his voice. Bomb disposal was usually a case of cutting the blue wire, but there weren't any wires in sight – and the reaction had already started.

'Well, don't look at me,' retorted Ashley, going a deeper shade of blue.

'I thought you were meant to be an advanced alien race or something?'

'We are,' replied Ashley indignantly. 'I'm just not that good on low-tech stuff – how are you on steam engines and windmills?'

'Okay, okay – let's not argue about this.'

Jack moved closer and winced in the heat. The cucumber was starting to glow from within and lighter patches the size of ten-pence pieces were appearing on its skin.

'We need a moderator,' said Ashley, having just worked out the principles of nuclear fusion theory from scratch. 'The light hydrogen isotopes of deuterium and tritium are combining to form a heavy helium atom and a spare neutron. It's the spare neutron that continues the reaction – soak up that and this cucumber is just a large and very hot vegetable.'

'So what do we need?' asked Jack, having not understood a word.

'Half a ton of graphite.'

'Graphite? Where the hell are we going to get that from? A million pencils?'

'Or just plain water.'

Jack looked around desperately for a few fire buckets or some-thing and then took an involuntary step back as the reaction grew *even* hotter. The light patches on the cucumber's skin formed into dimples and then collapsed inwards into *holes*, which projected shafts of pure white light from its rapidly overheating core. The same effect was beginning in the other cucumbers. Even though they were under the necessary fifty kilos, the single critical cucumber was bringing them all up to ignition.

'I'll find some,' said Jack, and made to go. But Ashley stopped him.

'It's already *full of holes*,' he said. 'There's no time. Do you have your penknife?'

Jack rummaged in his pocket and drew it out, his hands shaking as he snapped open the large blade.

'I have a liquid core that will do just as well – only take care; as well as being an excellent moderator, it's also a powerful molec-ular acid – don't get it on yourself.'

Ashley closed his eyes and pulled open his jacket to reveal his taut transparent skin.

'I need a breach in my membrane, sir. *You've got to stab me.*'

Jack stared at him. They took another step back as the heat intensified; the paint had caught fire on the outside of the van.

'I can't, Ash.'

'Jack,' said Ashley as he placed a single sucker-digit on his forehead, 'you *must* do this.'

'Of course,' replied Jack as the power of Ashley's infinitely superior intellect pushed aside the barriers of illogical emotional reasoning. 'It's all so *very* clear.'

And he plunged the knife into the alien's abdomen without delay. Ashley had tensed himself and Jack pulled out the knife.

'Stand back, sir.'

The cucumber had started to break down further and the light and heat were now so intense that Jack had to shield his eyes. Then an arc of soft blue liquid shot from the wound on Ashley's stomach and with a rapid flickering and a tearing noise the light in the cucumber began to flash and dance as Ashley's liquid insides reacted with the subatomic tumult within the cucumber's core. The light faltered, brightened, flashed, then went out, and all the cucumbers rapidly began to melt under the destructive power of Ashley's aqueous innards. But it didn't stop there. The neutron-absorbing cascade of *Rambosia Vitae* dissolved not only the cucumbers but the chassis of the van containing them and the concrete floor beneath, making a strange hissing and bubbling noise and giving off a smell like toffee apples.

Ashley had squeezed every last drop from himself and finally fell back empty like a deflated balloon, his once snug uniform falling off him. Jack cradled his now-flattened head in his arms, but he wasn't yet dead. His eyes flickered open.

'My mind is going,' he said in a soft voice, 'I can feel it. All that I am. Tell . . . tell . . . what was her name again?'

'Mary?'

'Right. Tell Mary I . . . would pluck the stars from the sky . . . 100 . . . her . . . 10010101 . . . 10 . . . 1.'

'Tell her yourself, Ash. Ash?'

But it was no good. Ashley had gone. The liquid centre that had so successfully quenched the thermocuclear device also carried the memories and experience that made him the alien that he was. Without them, he was nothing but a deflated blue bag. In a very real sense he had forgotten himself for the benefit of others.

The van collapsed in the middle as the *Rambosia Vitae* ate through the chassis. There was now a smoking hole in the concrete floor revealing the next level down, and a car that had the misfortune to be directly below was also being dissolved, albeit a bit more slowly as Ash's *vitae* ran out of power.

'Ash,' said Jack to the light blue membrane that was draped across his hands like a silk scarf, 'I'll get them, don't you worry.'

The small alien had travelled eighteen light years to find out more about our sitcoms, and ended up saving half of Reading. It was an odd state of affairs, even by Ashley's standards, but Jack had no time to dwell upon such matters – the inquiry had not yet run its course. NS-4 and QuangTech still had a lot to answer for, and the fourth bear was still out there somewhere. Jack looked up as he heard the sound of feet running down the entrance ramp.

The first on the scene was Briggs with Copperfield and several other officers close behind. They stopped dead in their tracks when they saw Jack and the empty blue transparent bag that had once been Ashley.

'Where's this "thermonuclear device", then?' asked Briggs.

'In the van,' replied Jack as the back axle finally dissolved to nothing and the Ford Transit split apart like a chocolate orange. They looked inside. It was empty, of course. The *vitae* had eaten through everything.

'It *was* there,' said Jack. 'Seven giant cucumbers about to achieve critical "cuclear" ignition – but rendered safe by Ashley's memories.'

'I was right,' said Briggs, 'you're stark staring mad.'

'I can explain. NS-4 and the Quangle-Wangle—'

'Drop the knife, Jack.'

Jack looked down. He was still holding the penknife.

'You killed the alien!' said someone at the back.

'No, no – I can explain.'

'I think you'd better come with us,' said Briggs. 'You're under arrest.'

'On what charge?'

'Almost everything I can think of – but we'll just have "murder of a serving police officer" to begin with.'

Before he could protest two officers had disarmed him, pushed him face down on the floor and begun to caution him.

'Briggs,' yelled Jack in desperation, 'it's not over—!'

'For you, it most certainly is,' Briggs replied, kneeling down to speak to Jack, who had his head pressed against the concrete. 'A plea of insanity is about the best defence you have – and from what I've seen and heard over the past few days, it will be enthusiastically and gratefully accepted.'

'Give your brain a chance, Briggs,' growled Jack. 'Ash just stopped an explosion from devastating most of Reading. We need to arrest Bisky-Batt, the Quangle-Wangle and the fourth bear.'

'And let me guess,' said Briggs. 'The Easter Bunny as well?'

'No,' replied Jack with a grunt as someone grabbed his wrist and pulled it up behind him, 'she had nothing to do with it.'

'I hope you've got a good lawy . . .'

Briggs stopped as a group of large bears walked into the underground car park from the stairwell. Jack, who was facing the other way, couldn't see who it was at first.

'Relinquish Spratt to my custody,' came a deep voice.

'Don't push it, Craps,' replied Briggs. 'Threatening a police officer and obstruction are serious offences, ursidae immunity or not.'

Jack rolled over so that he could see what was going on. The small party of human officers was being faced down by an even larger contingent of bears, Vinnie Craps at their head. They didn't look too happy, either, and they were all males. *Large* males.

'I'm not going to argue, Briggs,' said Vinnie. 'Spratt is a Friend to Bears, and bears look after their friends.'

'Like you look after Bartholomew? Harbouring murderers isn't being friendly and will land you in the clink, Boo-boo.'

Craps walked up to Briggs, towered over him and placed a single pointed claw on the knot of his tie.

'If you call me Boo-boo again,' he said in a low threatening growl, 'it'll be the last thing you do.' He raised a lip to reveal a shiny white canine. 'Last chance: leave the Bob Southey right now.'

'No way,' replied Briggs, who was showing a degree of courage that he'd forgotten he possessed, 'and if you don't surrender Barth—'

Suddenly the underground car park was full of noise. Directionless and powerful, it seemed to well up from the earth and reverberate right inside one's skull. Jack wasn't quite sure where it was coming from until he saw Vinnie with his mouth wide open. The roar was a deafening bellow that seemed to surge up from within and expel itself at furious speed; it was a deep guttural cry that spoke volumes about territory, outrage, anger and domin-ance. Everyone jumped about a foot in the air, Briggs was almost knocked off his feet and the sound set the car alarms going. The noise was brutal and, in a sort of primordial way, the kind of noise that makes anyone who hears it just leg it for the nearest cave or high tree. It also spoke of unpredictable danger. Even Jack, who was now a Friend to Bears, had an awful feeling that even *he* wasn't completely safe – that at any moment the six hundred pounds of angry bear might vent his anger on him. Abruptly, the roar stopped. Vinnie coughed slightly, cleared his throat and walked through the crowd of dazed officers, pulled Jack to his feet and escorted him to the stairwell.

'Hey!' said Briggs, suddenly regaining his composure.

Vinnie stopped and turned towards them. They all took a hasty step back.

'Leave now,' repeated Vinnie, and they did.

35
Ursula

'**Highest Ursine Decoration**. Anthropomorphised bears have a peculiar and byzantine system of merits, honours and awards that number almost three hundred. Only two of these, however, are conferred upon non-bears. Most common is the "Ursine Badge of Merit" (2,568 recipients), which is more of a measure of thanks. The second is the "Ursidae Order of Friendship", which is closer to a status than medal, and confers upon the holder unswerving protection from any bear, to death, without question. There are only five living recipients, all of whom live in Reading, Berkshire.'

— The Bumper Book of Berkshire Records, 2004 edition

They rose through the Bob Southey in one of the many luxurious oak-panelled lifts. Jack found to his surprise that he was still holding Ashley's thin but immensely strong outer membrane. It had dried out by now and resembled blue cellophane. So he rolled it up, folded it twice and placed it in his breast pocket for safe-keeping.

'Thanks for rescuing me,' said Jack, finally breaking the thoughtful silence. 'I owe you.'

'You don't owe me shit, Inspector,' replied Vinnie in his usual short manner. 'The Ursa Majors voted you "Friend to Bears" an hour ago and it's totally out of my hands. It's not a good situation. I've got a bit of clout with the authorities, but it's only a matter of time before they decide to use force to get you and Bartholomew out of here.'

'I'll surrender before that happens, Vinnie. I won't have senseless loss just to postpone the inevitable.'

Vinnie gave an imperceptible nod to show that he approved of Jack's attitude.

The lift doors opened and they walked out into a plush corridor that had thick carpet on the floor and original Lichtenstein prints decorating the walls. Vinnie walked up to a door and entered. It wasn't locked, but this wasn't unusual – bears didn't have any need for locks. In the entire Bob Southey, the only locks were those that connected the bears' world to that of the outside. The apartment was light, airy and modern, but retained the simplistic utopian ethos evident in the three bears' cottage in the forest: hard-wearing, functional wooden furniture and a minimalistic low-tech feel with simple floral designs on the drapes and small furnishings.

Standing at the window was Sherman Bartholomew. He looked tired and gaunt.

'Good evening, Inspector,' he said, rubbing his temples nervously. 'I know I'm going to regret asking this but . . . *what the blazes is going on?*'

'I'm not one hundred per cent sure yet, sir. A missing nuclear physicist, a discovery of unthinkable and devastating potential, and Goldilocks caught up in the middle. NS-4 and QuangTech are implicated and the Gingerbreadman is involved – I just don't know where. And then there's the fourth bear.'

Jack went on for some minutes, attempting to explain the complexities of the case. When he'd finished Bartholomew stared at him for a long time and then said:

'I knew I'd regret it.'

Vinnie, however, had understood it all a little better.

'So are you saying that *all* the nuclear strain of cucumbers have been destroyed?'

'No – Fuchsia told me that his "Alpha-Gherkin" was snipped off the main stalk last night. *That's* the sole remaining cucumber.

Whoever possesses that has almost unthinkable riches and power within their grasp.'

'And who do you suppose this fourth bear is?' asked Vinnie.

'I was hoping you'd be able to tell me. He's a dominant male, likes porridge, has no compunction in killing other bears – and was having an affair with Ursula Bruin.'

Vinnie pricked up his ears when he heard this.

'You've an idea?' asked Jack.

'Not me – but Ursula might.'

They took the elevator to the large vaulted atrium on the ground floor and made their way across to the Bob Southey Medical Centre.

'She regained consciousness an hour ago,' explained Vinnie, his claws clicking percussively on the smooth marble flooring. 'She can't speak but she might be able to help in some other way.'

The medical centre was one of the most modern Jack had ever seen, a reflection of the colossal wealth the bear fraternity had amassed over the years with wise long-term investments, well-planned trust funds and share portfolios. Ed Bruin was in his own room, where a small army of medical staff were giving him minute-by-minute care. He seemed to have more tubes going into him than Charing Cross station, and a vast array of high-tech equipment played an almost symphonic melody of bleeps, pings, chirrups and whistles, while several monitors spewed out long strips of paper full of meaningful ink traces.

'He's a long way from being out of danger,' said a small bear with a stethoscope draped around his neck, 'but he's getting the best care we can give him.'

Ursula was in a separate room, and had only a plasma drip and a heart monitor. She was lying on her back in a sturdy wooden bed with a crochet bedspread, and a large flower arrangement in a vase was sitting atop a table near by. The setting sun was streaming through the open window, and sitting opposite her with his chair against a bookshelf was Baby Bear. It was the first time Jack had seen him, and he was baby only in name. Medium-sized and wearing baggy trousers and a hoodie emblazoned with a flaming skull, he looked like any other teenager you might find in Reading – only with a lot more hair.

'She's very weak,' said the bear with the stethoscope, 'try not to tire her too much.'

'Mrs Bruin?' enquired Vinnie softly.

Her eyes flickered open and she stared weakly in their direction.

'This is Inspector Spratt,' continued Vinnie. 'He's friendly to bears and he needs to ask you a few questions.'

She blinked twice and gave an almost imperceptible nod.

'I know about the fourth bear,' began Jack. 'I know that he was there in the cottage the morning Goldilocks came round, and whatever you think about him, you must know that he killed Goldilocks and attempted to have you and your husband murdered to keep you quiet. You don't owe him a thing and I need to know who he is and where I can find him.'

Ursula closed her small brown eyes for a moment as two tears welled up in them. She looked at Jack, then raised a wobbly claw and pointed it . . . at *Vinnie*.

'Oh, I get it now,' said Jack, jumping to his feet. 'All the time you pretend to be on our side but actually, while using the League of Ursidae as cover, you . . .'

He stopped because Vinnie was pointing at Ursula. Her wavering claw was no longer directed at Vinnie; she was pointing it across the room to . . . *Baby Bear*.

'Oh, I get it now,' said Jack, turning to face the youngest Bruin. 'Adopted when a cub you grew resentful of your father's authority and—'

'Jack,' said Vinnie in a kindly tone, 'calm down. I think you're suffering a temporary excess of resolutions.'

He took a deep breath to compose himself. Vinnie was right. And Ursula was pointing not at Baby Bear, but at the bookcase behind him.

'She means a *book*,' muttered Vinnie, running across to the bookshelf and gathering up an armful of volumes, which he then proceeded to show to Ursula one by one. By the time they'd got to the third shelf they'd found what she meant. It was the authorised biography of the Quangle-Wangle, and most households in Reading had a copy.

Jack opened it on the first page and sat on the bed to show Ursula the list of chapters. She indicated the appendix, and Jack rapidly flicked to the back of the book. Ursula pointed to a popular ballad that described in broadly lyrical terms the formation of the characters who came together to form the Quang's business empire.

'"The Quangle-Wangle's Hat"?' asked Jack, and Ursula nodded. She then closed her eyes and relaxed, her energy spent. Jack cleared his throat and read:

> 'On top of the Crumpetty tree, the Quangle-Wangle sat,
> But his face you could not see, on account of his eaver hat.
> For his hat was a hundred and two feet wide,
> With ribbons and bibbons on every side,
> And bells and buttons and loops and lace,
> so no one could ever see the face
> Of the Quangle-Wangle Quee.

'That doesn't make any sense at all,' he murmured.
'Maybe it picks up farther on,' suggested Vinnie.

'But there came to the Crumpetty tree,
Mr and Mrs Canary;
And they said, "Did ever you see
Any spot so charmingly airy?
May we build a nest on your lovely Hat?
Mr Quangle-Wangle, grant us that!
O please let us come and build a nest
Of whatever material suits you best,
Mr Quangle-Wangle Quee!"'

'I suppose that must refer to Mr and Mrs Canary, who now run the Quang's hotel chain in the Far East,' murmured Vinnie. 'They were the first to join the Quangle-Wangle; who arrived after them?'

'And the Golden Grouse came there,
And the Pobble who hast no toes,
And the Small Olympian Bear,
And the Dong with the luminous nose,
And the Blue Baboon who played the flute,
And the Orient Calf from the land of Tute,
And the Attery Squash and the Bisky bat,
all came and built on the lovely Hat
of the Quangle . . .'

Jack put the book down and looked up at Vinnie.

'*The Small Olympian Bear*,' he said in a quiet voice. 'The SOB we can't trust that Ed warned us about. Who is he?'

Vinnie shook his head sadly.

'I'd never thought he'd do something like that,' he said with a sadness tinged with anger, 'after he had done so much and risen so high. Killing a friendly and ordering the Bruins' death. He'll never make it to the Perpetual Forest with those on his conscience.'

'I really don't think he cares, Vinnie – who is he?'

'Nick,' he said slowly and with infinite sadness. 'Nick ... *Demetrios*.'

'Demetrios?' repeated Jack incredulously. 'The head of NS-4? Danvers' superior? A bear?'

Vinnie took the book out of Jack's hands, flicked to the picture section in the middle and showed Jack a group portrait taken at the opening of QuangTech in the sixties. Standing between Roderick Pobble and Bisky-Batt was a short bear. While everyone in the photograph was smiling, the bear just glared sullenly into the camera.

'Demetrios,' said Vinnie, tapping the picture with a claw. 'He's slippery and ambitious and for many years has been the poster bear for what ursines can achieve, even in this human-dominated world. Ever wonder why no one gets to see the boss of NS-4? Well, now you know.'

This new piece of information whirled in Jack's head. Demetrios – the fourth bear. He was in with QuangTech from the beginning and must have known all about McGuffin's work with Cold Ignition Fusion. As head of NS-4 he was best placed to guard the nascent technology – until Goldilocks got wind of it and was about to go public. Thermocuclear energy in the public domain would net Demetrios, Bisky-Batt and QuangTech the sum total of zip – the secret had to be protected *at all costs*.

Jack pulled out his mobile and called Briggs. He needed to have him arrest Demetrios and then have some officers sent over to the Quangle-Wangle's facility to do the same to Bisky-Batt, as well as seize all the QuangTech files. But unsurprisingly, Briggs didn't quite see it that way.

'You're certifiably insane,' he told Jack unkindly, 'and the only thing I want to hear from you is that you're surrendering. If you're not out of the Bob Southey in an hour we're going to storm the building.'

'Can we make a deal?' he asked, ever hopeful.

'No,' replied Briggs.

Jack hung up and then dialled Mary.

'It's Jack.'

'Is it true about Ash?' she asked. 'That's he's . . . dead?'

'*Deflated* would be a better term. He was a true hero and saved us all, and asked me to tell you that "he would pluck the stars from the sky for you".'

There was a momentary silence from Mary.

'Thanks, Jack, I appreciate it. He was a fine officer, and a good friend.'

'He was,' agreed Jack, adding in a more urgent tone: 'But it's not over yet. Mr Demetrios is the fourth bear and Briggs isn't exactly pro-Spratt at present. What's going on out there?'

'You were right,' she replied. 'McGuffin *was* watching. I'm with him now and he has the Alpha-Gherkin he cut from Fuchsia's champion. He's confirmed that it's the last vestige of the strain – without it thermocuclear power is nothing more than unverifiable pseudo-science. McGuffin says it's all got horribly out of hand and although limitless free energy is a positive step, the idea that any nation that possesses an average-sized greenhouse and a trowel can have a nuclear capability is a bit of a downer, despite the truly spectacular fireballs which he says he'll miss.'

Jack breathed a huge sigh of relief.

'That's *fantastic* news. With McGuffin in custody we can convince Briggs of my innocence – and put Demetrios in the clink.'

'Not really,' said Mary. 'You see, I found McGuffin and then NS-4 found *me*. Agent Danvers is holding us both – and she wants to speak to you.'

'Hello, Spratt?' said Agent Danvers with an unpleasant sneer as she came on the line. 'I suggest you get over to SommeWorld as soon as possible. You want answers? You'll get them there. Mary says goodbye.'

And the phone went dead.

'Bollocks!' muttered Jack.

He snapped his mobile shut and turned to Vinnie.

'Bartholomew is to give himself up in twenty minutes.'

'And you?'

'I need to get to SommeWorld. Can you get me past the three hundred or so armed officers who are surrounding the building?'

Vinnie flashed him a smile.

'Do I shit in the woods?'

36

Totally over the top at SommeWorld

'**World's Oddest Theme Park**. Contenders abound in this field, and several deserve mention. "ElephantLand" in impoverished East Splotvia is odd in that it has no elephants, nor a clear idea of what one is. "GummoWorld" in upstate New York is devoted to the Marx brother who had the distinction of never appearing in a movie, and Nevada's "ParkThemeLandWorld" is a theme park dedicated to *other* theme parks, but has no attractions of its own. "SommeWorld" in the UK invites its visitors to taste the marrow-chilling fear of being an infantryman in the Great War, and by contrast "ZenWorld" in Thailand is nothing but a very large empty space in which to relax. Our favourite, however, is La Haye's "DescartesLand", which merely furnishes ticket-holders with a paper bag to put over their heads and a note reading: "If you think it, it shall be so".'
— *The Bumper Book of Berkshire Records*, 2004 edition

'Get on,' said Vinnie, indicating the pillion of his Norton motorcycle, 'and whatever happens, stay on.'

He kicked the engine into life, clonked the bike into gear and then accelerated rapidly through the underground car park, up the ramp and into the evening light outside. Jack hung on as Vinnie expertly weaved around the cordon and straight through a small crowd of onlookers, all of whom scattered as they saw him approach. In a second they had turned left and headed towards the motorway. The police helicopter was rapidly diverted and picked them up at the junction to the M4, where the bear and his passenger were easily seen heading westbound. The helicopter stuck to them like glue, and within thirty minutes a full rolling roadblock was converging on the motorcycle. At speeds of over a hundred miles an hour, Vinnie Craps kept the police at bay until his luck and petrol ran out thirty-two minutes after leaving the Bob Southey, and the Norton coasted on to the hard shoulder. The pillion passenger, much to the officer's annoyance, wasn't Jack at all – he was a friend of Vinnie's called Lionel.

While the full force of the law was pursuing Vinnie up the motorway, Jack was walking swiftly back to the Allegro. They had made the switch soon after passing the cordon. Lionel had been waiting at the side of the road in identical clothes and the swap had worked a treat.

As Jack drove past Theale the sky clouded over and several drops of rain began to speckle the windscreen. By the time he pulled up outside the gates of the deserted and unfinished SommeWorld complex, a downpour had begun. Lightning crackled overhead as he got out of the car and ran to the visitors' centre, which looked empty, dark and abandoned. He pushed open the heavy glass door with its Lewis-gun-magazine door handles and stepped quietly in, shaking the rainwater from his jacket. The centrepiece of the large domed vestibule was a First World War tank, set in a circular diorama filled with earth especially imported from the Somme itself. The marble flooring in the main atrium was engraved with the names of all those who had lost their lives in the failed offensive. The atrium was large, but the writing was by necessity quite small.

The door swung shut behind him and locked with an audible *clunk*, followed by the sound of other locks being thrown, which echoed around the building. He was trapped. Jack looked up at a security camera as he took a few steps forward and it followed him. He was expected, and he was being watched. He moved to the ticket office and turnstiles, the chrome tubing still covered with a protective plastic coating. To his right was the shop where souvenirs of the Great War would one day be sold, and to his left was the half-completed museum and auditorium, where visitors would be able to watch a five-minute animated featurette describing the events in Europe that led up to the conflict.

He walked past the outfitters where people would one day change into uncomfortable British Army uniforms before manning the trenches outside, then he moved to the main stairway that led up to the administrative offices above. In the upstairs corridor Jack could see a light shining from a half-open door, and he moved closer.

'Why don't you come in, Inspector?' said a deep voice when he was still three paces away. 'There's no sense in skulking around.'

Jack pushed open the door of the security office and stepped in.

Bisky-Batt turned from the console of CCTV monitors he had been watching. The VP of QuangTech smiled at Jack, and offered him a seat. Jack said he'd prefer to stand and Bisky-Batt nodded agreeably, took one look through the windows at the faux battle-field that was still just visible in the dusk, and sat behind the desk.

'I want answers,' said Jack, 'and I want Demetrios. Hand him over and things might not look so bad for you.'

Bisky-Batt laughed.

'I hardly think you are in a position to ask for *anything*, Inspector.' He paused and frowned. 'Do I still call you inspector? Now that you're wanted for impersonation, stealing evidence, perverting the course of justice and murder?'

'Where's Sergeant Mary?'

'I owe you our thanks for finding the Alpha-Gherkin and McGuffin, by the way. He's brilliant, of course, but *highly* unpre-dictable. He should never have contacted Goldilocks after the Obscurity blast.'

'It was just another test like the Nullarbor, wasn't it?'

'Of course. We've been monitoring these cucumbers very closely and move in as soon as they start to approach the magic fifty-kilo mark to take samples, then observe the blast. McGuffin's work at QuangTech was never about turning grass cuttings into crude; it was always cucumbers.' He smiled. 'Cucumbers that can extract the deuterium and tritium from the groundwater, store it all up and then self-ignite. Finally, cucumbers have a reason for being.'

'If McGuffin won't help you've got nothing.'

'He might be a bit recalcitrant at present, but he'll come across. We've got as long as we want with him, after all. No one's going to miss a dead man.'

'I want to see the Quangle-Wangle.'

'No one sees the boss.'

'Why not?'

'Because he's been dead for twelve years. He had odd ideas about his will – something about dismantling the company and giving the proceeds to Foss, his cat. We thought it better for all concerned – especially us – if we just placed the Quangle-Wangle in a sort of legal suspended animation and took over the running ourselves.'

Jack said nothing. It was time to start putting his plan into action. Then he remembered: he didn't have one.

'I must say,' continued Bisky-Batt, 'when Danvers asked you to come over here we really didn't think you'd come. It shows either a considerable misunderstanding of the whole situation, or a sort of boundless optimism that, while mildly endearing, will be your undoing. There are journalists and cucumberistas now dead who knew considerably less than you. The finer points of this little adventure will die with you.'

'I've told other people about it.'

'Let me guess,' said Bisky-Batt. 'Bartholomew and that jumped-up teddy bear, Craps. They won't live to see a debrief. Believe me, Danvers is staggeringly loyal to Demetrios, and if he tells her it is in the national interest, she'll do anything he asks. Your Sergeant

Mary will enjoy a similar fate, only more imaginative – two accidents here at SommeWorld in less than a week should spell the end of the theme park, and about time. A bigger waste of money I have yet to see. And even if there *was* someone with a vague idea of what's going on, will anyone believe them when they claim that it's possible to extract sunbeams from cucumbers? No. And there is no concrete connection between anyone at QuangTech and this whole shady business – aside from you.'

'We know all about the Gingerbreadman.'

Bisky-Batt paused and stared at him.

'You might think you do.'

'No,' said Jack, 'we really do.'

He pulled the photomicrographs Parks had given him out of his pocket. The scanning electron microscope had revealed to the world that which is too small to be seen with the naked eye – nestled around a tiny speck of ginger less than the width of a human hair was a *serial number*.

'This is from the Gingerbreadman's thumb, Bisky-Batt. I'm no genius, but I'm willing to bet that the suffix "QTBioWD" on this serial number stands for QuangTech BioWeapons Division – and I think most other people will too.'

Bisky-Batt leaned back in his chair and placed his hands behind his head. Jack noticed for the first time that his shirt was damp with nervous sweat. Despite the outward calm and geniality, the VP was running scared.

'Who else knows about this?'

'Not many. Just those with an Internet connection.'

'Unwise, Jack, unwise. You would have been better keeping this to yourself. Disposing of you is rapidly beginning to look less like a chore and more like a pleasure.'

'Disposing of me won't alter the fact that you were the VP when the Gingerbreadman was engineered. You knew what he was and you did nothing. One hundred and twelve deaths, Horace – and you could have stopped them all. Now: where's Demetrios?'

'He's behind you.'

Jack smiled and wagged a finger at Bisky-Batt.

'Oh no. I don't fall for the old "he's behind you" routine.'

'That's a shame, because he really *is* behind you.'

Jack froze, and then turned slowly around. Standing at the door was a bear barely three foot high. He was nattily dressed in a sharp suit and had his fur brushed impeccably in a central parting that continued along the bridge of his nose. Over one eye was an eye patch, on his cheek was an ugly scar – and in his hand was a revolver.

'I have every reason to hate you a great deal,' he said in a faintly silly high-pitched voice, 'but in many ways I hold you in high esteem. Still, I suppose none of that really matters any more.'

'They know the truth about the Gingerbreadman,' said Bisky-Batt with a tremor in his voice. 'We're finished.'

'No,' said Demetrios, '*we're* not finished . . . *you* are.'

There was a sharp crack and a dull orange flash. Bisky-Batt gave a look of utter confusion and shock, then keeled forward and hit the desk before slumping to the floor.

'Well now,' said the Small Olympian Bear, lowering his smoking gun, 'with an outlay of less than a pound I have just doubled my net worth. Now *that* was an investment worth making!'

Jack, who had been waiting for his chance, flew at Demetrios. He was dead if he didn't do anything, he was *probably* dead if he did. But since the latter of the two options was the only one that afforded even the slightest possibility of success, he took it. His fist almost connected, too. But as he lunged forward a brown arm shot out from the doorway behind Demetrios and grabbed Jack by the throat. He stopped in mid-air, choking, was twisted sideways and pulled backwards into a painful half-nelson. He could feel the sinews in his shoulder stretch. He yelled in pain but was held fast. The heavy aroma of ginger pervaded the room and made him cough.

'Hello, Jack,' said the Gingerbreadman with a friendly smile. 'Surprised?'

'Nothing surprises me,' grunted Jack. 'It's an NCD thing.'

'You were smart to put his thumb under the microscope, Jack,' said Demetrios as he moved closer. 'No one else would have thought of it. And you're right that he's one of ours. Mr G is the prototype of Project Ginja Assassin, a bio-culinary weapons technology that despite early promise remained – alas! – on the drawing board. Can you imagine a legion of Gingerbreadmen, all impervious to pity, guilt or scruples, as the advance guard of an army on the move? Front-line bakeries would have been able to churn him out by the thou-sand, then set him against the enemy with a hardwired knowledge of every method of death imaginable. He is agile, adaptable, tire-less and highly motivated – the perfect Ginja – and he can *never* be caught.'

'You're wrong. *I* caught him. Twenty years ago.'

'Sorry to disappoint,' said the Gingerbreadman with a smile, 'but I *allowed* myself to be captured. Where would be the best place to lie low and await reactivation? On the run – or in a nuthouse? And when once again I need to rest between engagements, I'll just allow myself to be recaptured. But shh. Don't tell anyone – it's our secret!'

'Isn't he just the cutest thing ever?' murmured Demetrios in admiration. 'I just brought him out of retirement as a bit of mis-direction when Goldilocks' "silencing" didn't go to plan. Who would want to look for a missing journalist when there's a psychopath on the loose?'

'I would.'

Demetrios' face fell and he stuck his snout close to Jack's. His breath smelled terrible and his teeth were in a bad state. 'Yes; I should have known better. If those dratted bears hadn't come back from their walk in the forest early, they would never have even *seen* Goldilocks, and all this would have been a lot easier.'

'And Ursula?'

'Ah, yes,' he said with a smile, 'dear Ursula. Best porridge chef there was. As for her and me, what's the point of being the supreme dominant male bear if you can't abuse it a bit? Ed was going to blow the whistle on me, and Ursula, well, she might have blabbed, so I had to order her death too. But none of that matters now.'

'What about me?' asked Jack.

'You? No one ever found out what became of you. That should sell at least twenty more copies of *Conspiracy Theorist*, wouldn't you say?'

Jack stared at him vacantly. There didn't seem a lot to add. He couldn't budge an inch in the iron grip of the Gingerbreadman, who he could feel breathing hot sugary ginger-breath down his neck.

'Justice will prevail, Demetrios.'

Mr Demetrios chuckled and shook his head sadly.

'*Justice will prevail*. Where do you policemen get your clichés? I am the director-general of the country's national security service. Justice is a purely relative term in the boardroom where I work. Bisky will take the rap for the Ginja and you'll take the rap for Bisky. Without you around I have complete deniability – and I have the Alpha-Gherkin and McGuffin. As soon as the dust has settled QuangTech will begin experiments on thermocuclear power. I may use it for domestic energy purposes or as a weapons system. I haven't yet decided. Maybe both. The sunbeams locked inside cucumbers will lead Britain's economy into the third millennium and beyond, and at the head of the power revolution will be . . . myself. This isn't just a technology, Jack, it's the saviour of the planet. They will raise statues to me in years to come as "The Bear Who

Changed the World". The name Demetrios will forever be associated with clean air and an optimistic future. And one thing is for certain – I will make an obscenely large pile of cash. They'll have to invent a new word for it – "rich" just won't do it justice.'

'The technology belongs to all mankind,' replied Jack, wincing in pain from the Gingerbreadman's over-zealous grip, 'not to QuangTech and certainly not to – ah! – you.'

'Do you know,' said Mr Demetrios slowly, 'that's *exactly* what Goldilocks and McGuffin said. Personally, I don't see it that way. But don't worry, I'll use the cash to help bears. Or at least, one bear in particular – me. The rest can go screw themselves.'

'Can I kill him now?' asked the Gingerbreadman, who was getting bored and fast becoming a cake of action rather than words.

'Why not?' replied the small bear.

'Do you think he'll just let you go?' said Jack to the Gingerbreadman, hoping to drive a wedge between them. 'You'll be disposed of just like all the others.'

'A Ginja fears nothing except failing to do his duty,' said the assassin simply. 'Demetrios is my master; I do his bidding. All other factors are secondary.'

'Didn't I tell you he was the best thing ever?' repeated Demetrios. 'He's the cub I never had.'

He clapped his paws together.

'Well, that's us done here, Spratt. I've got some unfinished business with a colleague of yours. Without anyone left in the NCD to explain the complexities of this case first hand, I rather think my future is assured – wouldn't you agree?'

'You won't get away with this.'

'There you go with your clichés again. And you're wrong – I rather think I just have.'

Demetrios looked at his watch and patted the Gingerbreadman on the arm.

'I'm off now, my faithful Ginja. Make sure no one discovers so much as an atom of his body. Are you going to kill him now or are you going to play with him for a while?'

The Gingerbreadman raised an eyebrow and looked at Jack thoughtfully.

'Since he has survived an unprecedented three encounters with me,' began the assassin thoughtfully, 'I should like to test him "to destruction", so to speak.'

'Of course,' replied the small bear gleefully, 'and to make the fiction complete, be sure he leaves some prints on this, would you?'

He handed his revolver to the Gingerbreadman and without another word departed.

Jack's thoughts turned to escape, but on reflection things didn't look terrific. The facility was locked down tight and even if he *did* get away, he wasn't sure where he could go with a killer who could run four times faster than he, and was eight times as strong, on the loose. It was a bit like being handcuffed to a hungry and demented Rottweiler, smeared with a steak and then locked in a wardrobe.

The Gingerbreadman released Jack, who took a welcome step back, rubbing his arm. The Ginja smiled again and showed Jack the place where his thumb had been.

'This was the closest I've ever been to death, and you know what?'

'What?'

'I felt so *liberated*. As if I had finally met my match. You and the delightful Sergeant Mary were a formidable team.'

'I'm glad you think so.'

The smile dropped from the Gingerbreadman's liquorice lips. 'Sarcasm doesn't suit you, Jack. You and I are going to play a little game. Ever seen a cat playing with a mouse?'

'Ye–es.'

'Ever wanted to know what the mouse felt like?'

'No, never – not at all. Not *once*. Nope.'

'Too bad. Here's what we'll do. To tip the scales a few milli-grams in your favour we'll do this as gentlemen. Back to back, ten paces, turn and fire. Any questions?'

'Yes,' replied Jack, 'are you a cake or a biscuit?'

The Gingerbreadman glared at him.

'Don't make this any worse for yourself, Spratt. Insult me again and I'll ensure that the agony of your demise is stretched out so long that you will beg me for death.'

He smiled a disquieting smile, the edges of his liquorice mouth almost reaching his large glacé-cherry eyes.

'Right, here we go, then,' he said cheerfully, handing over Demetrios' revolver. Jack's prints were now on the weapon that had killed Bisky-Batt but armed was better than not armed – he hoped.

'Five shots left. Make them count.' The Gingerbreadman drew his sawn-off shotgun and flicked off the safety catch. 'And since you've been such a tremendous sport over the past few days, I'm willing to give you the first shot. Am I not the most magnanimous of murderers?'

'To a fault.'

'There's that sarcasm again! Jack, you *disappoint* me sometimes. We'll do this out in the corridor where there's more room. You stand there. Ready?'

Jack nodded and they stood back to back. Jack thought of turning and plugging him there and then, but he had seen the speed at which the Ginja assassin could move.

'Eight paces, then,' said the Gingerbreadman, enjoying himself tremendously.

'You said ten earlier.'

'I did?'

'Yes.'

'Well, let's not be small about it. Ten it is.'

They both started to walk, the Gingerbreadman glancing over his shoulder now and again to make sure Jack was playing by the rules. Jack was walking back towards the stairs and the rest of the visitors' centre. He looked at the revolver. He'd used one only three times before; he didn't like them, and NCD work generally called for brains, not firepower. He completed his tenth pace, stopped and turned. The Gingerbreadman's paces were longer than his and he was a lot farther down the corridor than he'd anticipated, while Jack was only about two strides from the top of the stairs. He had planned to aim for the Ginja's head, but given the distance a chest shot seemed like a better option.

'Your go, then, Jack!' called out the Gingerbreadman cheerfully. 'Take careful aim, now.'

Jack lifted the gun, aimed and fired. The shot struck the Gingerbreadman in the area where his heart might have been if he'd had one, but to no effect – the slug went straight through and embedded itself in a door frame at the other end of the corridor with a resounding *thunk*. The Gingerbreadman smiled at him and said:

'Oh, I'm sorry, I should have said: bullets have no real effect on me. My turn.'

He raised the shotgun and fired in a single swift motion. Jack dived to one side as the blast struck the wall behind where he had been standing. Without pausing for a second he dashed down the stairs four at a time, and ran back into the darkened atrium to take refuge behind the tank.

'Cheat!' he heard the Gingerbreadman yell. 'I stayed still for you!'

Jack looked around desperately as he heard the assassin walk noisily down the staircase. The tank was a battle-scarred example and was peppered with shell-holes. He peered through one hole and saw the Ginja padding noiselessly across the area outside the entrance to what would one day become *The Phosgene Experience*.

Jack waited until he was opposite the turnstiles, then jumped out and fired. The shot blew a small patch of ginger off the assassin's shoulder and the Gingerbreadman bounded with surprising dexterity into the entrance to the *Scents of the Battle* Odourama™ exhibit. Jack took the opportunity to make a move and dashed across the atrium to the *Virtual Trenchfoot* attraction, shut the door behind him and then swiftly jammed a chair under the door handle.

'Come out, come out, wherever you are!' sang the Gingerbreadman as he walked across the atrium. Jack looked around desperately for a possible escape route. The room was full of desks with Quang-6000 computers hooked up to virtual-reality headsets, gloves and boots. There were no windows, so Jack headed as fast as he could for an emergency exit at the far end of the room. He pushed the bar to open it, but it was locked. He threw his full weight against the door but it wouldn't budge, so he picked up the heaviest object he could find – a computer – and hurled it at the recalcitrant door with all his strength. It did nothing except scratch the surface. He might as well have tried to throw a tomato through a piano.

He had just raised his revolver to try to blow the lock off as he'd seen in the movies when the other door was kicked off its hinges by a well-placed gingerbread foot and the Ginja assassin strode into the room. Before Jack could even react the Gingerbreadman had loosed off a single shot that destroyed the EXIT sign above Jack's head. He turned to look at the figure at the door, who was still smiling.

'Not like you to miss.'

'I didn't miss,' he said, tossing the shotgun aside and removing the belt of cartridges from his waist. 'It's just that I do so enjoy a certain "hands-on" feel to my work. Using a gun does so *distance* one from one's victims. Why, you cannot hope to smell the fear from farther than a couple of feet away. What enjoyment snipers get from their sport, I have *no* idea.'

369

Jack stared, his mind racing, but his fear under control. The abomination at the door had killed – as far as he knew – one hundred and twelve times. One more was nothing to him. The Ginja rubbed his powerful spongy hands together.

'What shall I pull off first, Jack? An arm? A leg? I could twist your head a full three hundred and sixty degrees. Okay, fun's over. I'd expected a better fight than this, but perhaps you aren't the man I thought you were.'

Jack fired the revolver again but the slug flew through the cakey body, this time hardly making a mark.

'Two left, Jack.'

He fired again and blew an icing button off the Ginja's chest.

'That leaves one. I'll think I'll do your legs first but from the knee down – a leg torn from the hip always results in rapid death through bleeding, and I want this to last. Unless you have any objections, of course?'

He smiled again, the murderous sub-routines in his gingery body running through to their inevitable end. He was built for one purpose, and existed for only one reason. Despite the ideological wasteland that governed his psychotic thought processes, he was a creature at peace with himself. His life, such as it was, had meaning.

Jack, despite having a 280-pound monstrosity lumbering towards him, was oddly calm. He found himself thinking about Madeleine and the kids. He wouldn't see them graduate, or even grow up. And then there was the wedding.

'Pandora.'

'Sorry?' said the Gingerbreadman, who was wondering whether to postpone the leg-tearing in favour of something unbelievably unpleasant he'd seen happen to Mel Gibson at the end of *Braveheart*.

'My daughter. I'll miss her wedding. It's in a month.'

'Well,' said the Gingerbreadman reflectively, 'I could just let you go – as long as you promise to come back *straight* afterwards. No, just kidding. You'll have to miss her wedding – and the birth of your first grandchild. You'll miss your own memorial, too – but only by a couple of days.'

Jack wasn't listening. He was thinking. There had to be a very good reason why Project Ginja Assassin had been cancelled. He was such a perfect warrior. Intelligent, resourceful, amoral and indestructible. Cake or biscuit? Did it matter? Jack had a sudden thought. Yes, it probably *did* matter. A cake went hard when it went stale, and a biscuit went soft. It was a long shot but he had nothing to lose. He aimed his gun at the Gingerbreadman. He had one shot remaining.

'You're a biscuit.'

'So?' asked the Gingerbreadman, intrigued by Jack's sudden confidence. 'What are you up to, Spratt?'

'This.'

He shifted his aim towards the fire-control system on the ceiling above them. The well-placed shot blew off the sprinkler head and a stream of water descended on to them both. The Gingerbreadman frowned and looked at the water streaming off himself, tiny particles of gingerbread already being washed off and falling to the floor at his feet. Biscuits soften because . . . *they absorb water.* He made for the door. The other sprinklers in the room, sensing the drop in pressure, fired simultaneously, spraying the room with even more water. The Gingerbreadman tripped over a table in his haste to escape and another stream of water caught him on the legs. They softened and buckled under him. He got to his feet and reached the door just as the sprinklers fired in the atrium; there was no escape from the deluge.

'Quick thinking, Spratt!' he shouted, turning back as the water continued to pour over both of them, larger pieces of gingerbread now falling from his body as the moisture started to soften up his biscuity tissues. He studied one of his hands with interest as a chunk of gingerbread dropped off.

371

'They designed me as the perfect warrior,' he announced with a wry smile, 'only with one fatal flaw . . . I can't get wet. I'm dying, Jack.'

'I'm counting on it.'

'Now that's not nice,' replied the Gingerbreadman reproachfully as an icing button dropped to the floor with a *plop*. He looked around and tried to pick up the shotgun but his hands collapsed into mush around the weapon.

'Rats,' he muttered. 'Well, no matter.'

He walked slowly towards Jack, who scrambled backwards and threw his gun at the brown figure.

'Congratulations,' said the Gingerbreadman slowly, as larger chunks of gingerbread started to slough off his body in the never-ending stream of water. 'I underestimated you.'

'I get that a lot.'

'Really? D'you know, in a way, I'm almost glad it was you. I'd have liked to have been your friend. Perhaps that's why I could never kill you – until now.'

The Gingerbreadman lunged at Jack, slipped on the wet floor and collapsed into a puddle of water. Jack ran quickly round to the other side of the room as the Ginja tried to get up and fell over again when his foot fell off. But he wasn't giving up, and he tried desperately to crawl in Jack's direction using arms that disintegrated into pulp as he grappled with the slippery floor. He stared at Jack, his crumpled features registering annoyance that he'd failed rather than any sort of fear over his demise. An arm gave way and he collapsed face down in the pool of water. When he raised himself up again he was without a face. His cherry eyes, red-icing nose and liquorice mouth had fallen into the large brown mass of sodden gingerbread that had gathered beneath him. He flailed around wildly as Jack looked on, the water running off his hair and down his neck, causing him nothing worse than mild discomfort. The

Gingerbreadman, now blind and mute and without any limbs, thrashed uselessly about in the centre of the room.

Within minutes it was all over. The most notorious and violent multiple murderer the nation had seen was nothing more than a soggy mass on the floor. Jack walked over and cautiously kicked one of the grapefruit-sized glacé-cherry eyes that only ten minutes before had flashed such evil confidence. Abruptly, the downpour stopped. The water ran off the tables, swirling around the brown stain in the centre of the floor. Jack paused for a moment to collect his thoughts, then splashed through the puddle and out of the door, making his way back to the tank in the centre of the atrium. Mary was still very much in danger, and if he could rescue her and secure McGuffin and the Alpha-Gherkin, all might still be well. His mobile rang and he dug it out of his pocket. It was Briggs.

'You can arrest me later,' Jack snapped, 'I'm kind of busy right now.'

'I may not arrest you at all,' replied Briggs. 'I've just been talking to Vinnie Craps, Bartholomew and Ursula Bruin.'

'She can talk?'

'She can *write*. And she's indicated a few very interesting facts about Demetrios that need closer scrutiny – and Mr Fuchsia's neighbours have positively identified Agent Danvers as one of the "Men in Green" who were there this morning.'

Jack suddenly felt a huge weight begin to lift from his shoulders. For the first time that day he had the feeling that everything might just possibly come out all right. As he began to breathe more easily, there was a thud of mortar fire, and he turned. Several parachute flares arced gracefully into the night sky and ignited above the theme park, illuminating the pockmarked landscape in a harsh white light. He turned back to his mobile.

'The Gingerbreadman and Bisky-Batt are dead, sir, the biscuit killed by me, and Horace by Demetrios. I'm at SommeWorld. The fourth bear, McGuffin and Danvers are here, and I believe that Mary is in very grave danger. If you want to arrest me you can – but please, *after* Mary is safe.'

There was a pause.

'Hold fast, Jack, I'm sending everything I have.'

Jack paused for a moment in thought then ran to the costume store. He returned to the turnstiles, used a fire axe on a large glass door and stepped into the cool night air, and the jagged unnatural landscape of the park. The star-shells drifted down, the bright white light trailing a long stream of smoke in the clear air. Then, a single faint *whompa* pierced the quiet. A barrage was about to begin and Mary was probably right in the centre of it.

Jack ran down one of the supply roads as the steady *crump, crump, crump* of the barrage began to fill the air. The parachute flares faded and died and the park was plunged into inky blackness. Jack stopped. He could hear the barrage building up, but the sky had cleared and the night was pitch black – he couldn't even see his hand in front of his face. There was another thud of mortars as more star-shells flew into the air, and with a crackle the parachute flares once more illuminated the landscape. Jack jumped out of his skin. Danvers was not more than six feet from him, and she looked as startled as he was. He didn't pause for a second, planting a fist on her chin. She went down with a thump, and he relieved her of her pistol as she lay dazed on the ground. She had a pair of cuffs, so he dragged her to a nearby Model T and clipped her to a wheel spoke.

'I'm National Security!' she yelled as she regained what little sense she possessed. 'I'll have your head on a platter for this!'

'You'll have to join the queue.'

'YOU WON'T MAKE IT TO COURT, SPRATT!' yelled Danvers as Jack ran off into the park, the recent rain making the ground slippery. Ahead of him a support trench zigzagged down the hill, the detritus of war all around him. The propane burners had just been ignited, and the park was now aglow with flames that eerily illuminated the plumes of earth that were blown skyward by the air mortars as the barrage increased in intensity. The Somme offensive had begun – but with only a couple of participants and this time, hoped Jack, without any loss of life. He took a left turn towards a forward observation post as several machine guns started to rattle somewhere ahead of him. He popped his head up in the OP and borrowed a pair of field binoculars that were lying on the firestep. He trained the glasses on the lines opposite and could see the plumes of soil lift large sections of the barbed-wire emplacements into the air. He stopped. In the middle of no man's land was an abandoned artillery piece and cuffed to it, being plastered by soil and debris as air mortars detonated near by, was Mary.

Jack ran as he had never run before. He slid into craters, pulled himself over barbed wire and climbed past piles of rubble towards the artillery barrage, the buried air mortars blasting and churning the ground, each *whompa* unleashing up to a half-ton of earth and throwing it fifty feet into the air. Jack didn't stop when he reached the wall of destruction; he just carried straight on into it.

Mary was not in what you might call 'a calm frame of mind'. The barrage had started a full thousand yards away and had slowly moved towards her, gaining in strength as it moved. She had attempted to beat the handcuffs off her with a shell casing, but without luck. The barrage moved closer and intensified around her, the harsh pressure waves making her feel nauseous, and disoriented. A small charge went off six feet away and blew her jacket and shoes clean off. Then, as the barrage seemed to reach a point at which every different explosion merged into one huge directionless noise that reverberated around her, a corridor seemed to open up in the curtain of flying soil, and a man, dressed in torn clothes and covered in mud, ran into the maelstrom and fell to the ground near her. Almost instantly the bombardment pulled back from where they were and within a radius of fifteen feet all was calm. Jack produced a set of clippers he had taken from a raider's party kit and snipped the chains on her handcuffs.

'Can you walk?'

She nodded, and Jack led her into the bombardment, which seemed to part as they moved through it. By the light of the star-shells and the flames Mary could see the artillery piece that she had been handcuffed to only a moment earlier being tossed skyward as an almighty concussion lifted it clear off the ground.

'What the hell . . . ?' she screamed, but Jack didn't answer. Wherever they walked the bombardment subsided. It was like moving through a crowd that respectfully parted to let you go in any direction. Jack led her back across no man's land and after a few minutes they were safely back on the support road. Danvers glared sullenly at them as they walked past.

'How the hell did we manage that?' asked Mary, panting with exertion and fear. 'Not to be killed by the barrage, I mean.'

Jack pulled out of his pocket one of the safety proximity alerts that Haig had shown them the first time they had visited. They could have stood in the barrage all night and not one mortar would have hit them.

'Where's Demetrios?'

'What?' asked Mary, temporarily deafened by the barrage.

'WHERE'S DEMETRIOS?'

Mary pointed to the control centre, and they both ran back towards the building, just in time to see a figure dash into the visitors' centre clutching a black leather briefcase. The profile was unmistakable.

'DEMETRIOS!!!' yelled Jack.

The bear couldn't hear him; Jack couldn't even hear himself. He yelled at Mary to try to find McGuffin and stop the bombardment, then ran in the direction the head of NS-4 had taken. The bear was not out of shape and made far better speed on all fours than Jack could manage on two. Jack caught up with him only at the car park, and then only because Mr Demetrios had stopped. It was not difficult to see why. In the car park, and facing the Small Olympian Bear, was perhaps the biggest armada of police cars that Jack had ever seen. Briggs had outdone himself. There was *everything*. It looked like a field full of twinkling blue lights. Two police helicopters hovered overhead, their powerful searchbeams centred on the small bear. Abruptly, the barrage stopped. A silence descended on the scene. Jack's ears were ringing and he continued to shout, even though it was hardly necessary.

'Demetrios!!'

The small bear turned.

'You're under arrest, bear – for murder.'

'I don't think so.'

'I do. On the ground.'

'You can't arrest me.'

'I can.'

'*You can't!*'

'He's right, Jack.'

It was Briggs, and he approached the two of them cautiously.

'He's NS-4, Jack, and outside our jurisdiction. We have to get a warrant from the Home Secretary. The Chief Constable is on the phone to her at the moment but the case is taking some explaining. Don't worry, though, we'll still have him. Once you write your report he'll be inside quicker than you can say "corrupt civil servant".'

The bear looked at Jack. He had been surprised himself at the turn of events.

'Let him go now and you'll not see him again,' Jack shouted to Briggs. 'Contained in that briefcase are the details of a technology that will grant him asylum in any nation he chooses!'

'The law is the law, Jack,' insisted Briggs. 'We can't touch him.'

Jack's shoulders slumped, and Demetrios grinned.

'Like he said, Jack, you can't arrest me. I'll be on my way with my property.' He patted the briefcase and adjusted his tie. 'Bad luck, Inspector. I guess I'll see you about.'

He looked around for transport.

'And do you know,' he added, 'I think I'll even borrow your car.'

'Be my guest.'

Demetrios smiled again, but it was a smile of *relief*. The probable chain of events that Jack had outlined was pretty near the truth. He would be out of England in less than an hour and he could then pick a country at leisure in which to instigate phase two of his plan. He jumped into Jack's Allegro and threw the briefcase on to the passenger seat. He started the car and drove slowly towards the gates of the theme park, the assembled officers moving aside to let him past.

'I'm sorry,' said Briggs. 'We couldn't hold him. Politics.'

'Don't be,' replied Jack quietly. 'He won't get far.'

As they watched, one side of the car collapsed, a suspension arm giving way. The rear screen shattered. This was followed by a clattering noise from the engine and a few puffs of blue smoke from the exhaust. With a grinding of metal the front of the car started to pull itself in, releasing a trail of brown radiator water. Rust popped out along the bottom of each door and all the lights went out. The car juddered to a halt as another suspension arm gave way and all four tyres burst in quick succession. A dent appeared in the roof, and the damage that Jack had inflicted on the car against the tree started to make itself known again, the rear buckling up as the car squirmed and shook, gently imploding with a shudder. There was an agonised cry from within as the Small Olympian Bear tried to escape, then, with a juddering and grinding of metal, the car rapidly collapsed in on itself, crushing Mr Demetrios painfully to death and leaving the car as nothing more than a piece of gnarled scrap sitting in a lake of black sump oil and rusty water.

'Gosh,' murmured Briggs, 'was that an NCD thing?'

'Not really,' replied Jack, 'but the theory's similar.'

He stared at the crushed car and thought that if it hadn't been for Mary and Ash, that might have been him winging his way to eternal damnation. As it was, it occurred to him that perhaps the Dark One had got a bum deal – Demetrios would have made his own way to hell in the fullness of time, without an Allegro Equipe to take him there.

'Jack,' said Briggs, laying a hand on his shoulder, 'you've got a serious amount of explaining to do.'

'Of course,' replied Jack. 'There were these three bears, see, and one morning they made some porridge and went into the forest while it cooled—'

'Not *now*. Get a decent night's sleep and I'll see you in the morning. You did well. Congratulations.'

'Thank you, sir.'

'Jack,' said Mary, who had just arrived at his side, 'I want you to meet Professor McGuffin. I found him in the . . .' She looked around in confusion. 'That's funny,' she murmured, 'he was here a second ago.'

Jack smiled, opened his mobile and dialled home. Madeleine would want to know he was all right, but more importantly he just wanted to hear her voice.

DCI Jack Spratt was unanimously declared 'more or less sane' by a medical review board and was reinstated as head of the Nursery Crime Division. He received a Distinguished Conduct Award for his expert tackling of the Gingerbreadman. He continues to live and work in Reading.

PC Ashley was taken home, patched, refilled with *Rambosia Vitae* and had his memories uploaded from his memory jar. Owing to the infrequency with which he had conducted back-ups, the last two weeks of his life were irretrievably lost. He still works at the NCD, has no idea why he was awarded the Ursidae Order of Friendship and hopes one day to pluck up enough courage to ask Mary out for a date.

DS Mary Mary was not charged or reprimanded over her 'lewd behaviour'. It was decided that jurisdiction could not be firmly established since the offence occurred 220 miles above the Atlantic Ocean in an advanced form of alien technology at twelve times the speed of sound. She continues to work at the Nursery Crime Division, and hopes that Ashley might once again ask her out on a date.

Nick Demetrios died from multiple crush injuries. The recovered briefcase contained notes relating to the highly improbable idea of using auto-deuterium-extracting cucumbers as fuel for a Cold Ignition Fusion reaction. Such an idea is quite impossible and belongs in the realms of loony pseudo-science. The briefcase also included a gherkin, presumably his lunch. It was consigned to the waste bin.

Professor McGuffin, despite being hazily identified by DS Mary, remains officially dead. Two years after Nick Demetrios's death, a garden near Madrid erupted into a fireball that fused soil and melted iron. No suitable explanation has yet been forthcoming, but Dr Parks is investigating.

Punch and Judy sold their house next to Jack and Madeleine, explaining that they wanted to go and make some noise next to some *real* neighbours. They were last heard of making an appalling nuisance of themselves in Slough, and continue to be the finest marriage counsellors in the South-East.

Sherman Bartholomew retired from politics and returned to his legal practice in Reading. He now specialises wholly in nursery law, and does *pro bono* work for bears. He is currently defending Tarquin Majors on charges of smuggling forty thousand gallons of surplus Euro-porridge to needy bears in eastern Splotvia.

SommeWorld is still behind schedule but problems should be ironed out 'by Christmas'. Despite this, Mr Haig insists that 'the situation is favourable'.

Josh Hatchett remains a staunch supporter of the NCD, and backs it fully in all its undertakings. The job of uninformed criticism of the NCD has been taken over by Hector Sleaze, of *The Mole*.

The Great Red-Legg'd Scissor-man was sentenced to eight years for GBH but was released over a technicality. His whereabouts are unknown. The NCD have issued a bulletin exhorting children *not* to suck their thumbs, just in case.

The Gingerbreadman's hospital uniform, fountain pen, thumb, elephant gun and a single glacé-cherry eye can now be viewed in a special exhibition at Reading Museum, along with his original seven-foot-high cutter, and declassified Project Ginja Assassin material, kindly loaned by the QuangTech Trust (Foss) PLC.

Mr and Mrs Bruin survived the attack on their lives and have returned to their cottage. They received counselling from Punch™ marriage counsellors, and are delighted to report that there are now only *two* beds in the house. They continue to eat porridge and take long walks in the forest.

Thursday Next returns in
The War of the Words
July 2007

Ashley, Jack and Mary will return in
The Last Great Tortoise Race

My thanks to:

John Wooten of Oak Ridge, Tennessee, for his assistance in matters regarding physics and atoms and fusion and suchlike;

Elmarie Stodart, of Cape Town, who coined the 'right to arm bears' phrase which lent itself well to the novel;

Bill Mudron and **Dylan Meconis** of Portland, Oregon, for their excellent frontispiece and work on my postcards and merchandising. Further examples of their artwork can be found at: <www.thequirkybird.com> (Dylan) <www.excelsiorstudios.net> (Bill)

also to:

Mari Roberts, who once again puts up with a partner who is in residential absentia for five months of the year;

Carolyn Mays and **Molly Stern**, two editors cut from the finest cloth and who never push me *that* hard, even when the manuscript is the teeniest-weeniest bit late;

Gretchen Koss and **Emma Longhurst**, the best publicity gurus in the known galaxy and whom I am lucky to have;

The unsung multitudes at **Hodder** and **Penguin (US)** who have been so utterly supportive of my efforts;

Tif Loehnis, **Eric Simonoff** and all the hardworking associates at **Janklow and Nesbit**, without whom I would as likely as not still be making Sniketty-Dicketty breakfast cereal commercials, and hating it.

and

To the master himself, **Jonathan Swift**, for the initial inspiration for this novel:

'. . . He had been eight years upon a project for extracting sunbeams out of cucumbers, which were to be put into phials, hermetically sealed and let out to warm the air in raw inclement summers . . . '

Gullliver's Travels – The Voyage to Laputa

Porridge Problems?

Too much? Too little? Too hot? Too cold?

If you are a bear with restricted quota foodstuff issues, you are not alone.
Call us toll-free for FREE, discreet advice on any illegal substance problems.

ILU

0800 3298
Or drop in and see us at the Bob Southey

This advertisement sponsored by the International League of Ursidae

10010011
10001101

101011010111000101001001datsun120a0011

1011010110 1011011110

110101

10010100100101111

1111010100111100

10100100101001001001111110010010011001001001000indexing0100111111000101
10010011010reggieperrin0111001001001110100010000001001010011001001001001
010010100100111000100100111111columbo0100100100100stylophone111001110011001
00100111100tremolos0010010100100100100100100doriangray000001110001010
100101001010010011101010001000000000001111001001002hark001001011101010111

101101101001111101100

23-24 September 2004

Tortoise
v
Hare

The mean streets of Reading once again play host to the annual Tortoise v Hare race - this year on a purpose-built 1.2-mile track around the streets of Berkshire's capital. Can the Tortoise defend his title for the 18th time, or will the long-legged lagomorph finally find it in himself to turn the tables on this most race-worthy of reptiles? View the spectacle from our new grandstands, and make the 18th TvH a race to remember!

Tortoise:

Form: 17 starts; 17 wins
Top Speed: 0.0002 mph
Fuel: Chopped carrots
Trainer: Miss E Bunny
Sponsor: HSBD Bank
Odds: 78,392/1 against

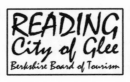

READING
City of Glee
Berkshire Board of Tourism

Hare:

Form: 17 starts; 17 losses
Top Speed: 34.9545 mph
Fuel: Lettuce / grass hybrid
Trainer: J Gammon
Sponsor: QuangTech
Odds: 7/2 favourite